THE HIGH
and
THE MIGHTY

"Storytelling of a very special kind, wonderfully done"
—*San Francisco Chronicle*

"Tight, taut, suspenseful . . . don't miss it"
—*Saturday Review*

"Gann keeps right on tightening the suspense to the last page."
—*Newsweek*

"Thoroughly fascinating"
—*Springfield Republican*

"A very readable story"
—*The New York Times*

THE HIGH
AND
THE MIGHTY

ERNEST K. GANN

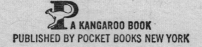
A KANGAROO BOOK
PUBLISHED BY POCKET BOOKS NEW YORK

THE HIGH AND THE MIGHTY

Morrow edition published 1953

POCKET BOOK edition published September, 1977

This POCKET BOOK edition includes every word contained
in the original edition. It is printed from brand-new plates.
POCKET BOOK editions are published by
POCKET BOOKS,
a Simon & Schuster Division of
GULF & WESTERN CORPORATION
1230 Avenue of the Americas,
New York, N.Y. 10020.
Trademarks registered in the United States
and other countries.

ISBN: 0-671-81196-7.

Printed in the U.S.A.

to . . . . "Cactus"

*"A man keeps, like his love,
his courage dark."*

QUINTON

*"The fear of death is indeed the pretense
of wisdom, and not real wisdom, being a
pretense of knowing the unknown . . . and no
one knows whether death which men in their
fear apprehend to be the greatest evil,
may not be the greatest good. . . ."*

SOCRATES

The High
and the Mighty

1

THE FORECASTER CARESSED HIS BALD HEAD AND THEN swept his bony fingers across the course from Honolulu to San Francisco. His contemptuous gesture embraced over two thousand miles of water and sky. On the paper beneath his hands, delicate lines had been drawn connecting the areas of equal atmospheric pressure. They fell into a strangely rhythmic design, swirling together across the paper as if the Pacific winds had blown them into shape. The forecaster rubbed his long nose while he regarded the lines suspiciously.

"You will find a low deck of stratus east of the Hawaiian Islands for a while, and a bare suggestion of this front north of the course. It shouldn't bother you in the least . . . perhaps light rain from aloft . . . nothing more."

He cleared his throat importantly and waited to see if the young man who stood on the opposite side of the counter was listening to him. It was not always easy for him to command a pilot's full attention. Too many of them had a way of discounting the value of a forecast no matter how carefully it had been prepared. Pilots were universally ungrateful, the forecaster reminded himself. He could not recall a single experience when a pilot had complimented him on a correct weather analysis, although there had been plenty of times when he had been chided unmercifully for being wrong. Pilots, of

3

course, were never wrong in their own opinion—except those times when they were stupid enough to get themselves killed, and then it was always too late to return their scorn.

The forecaster allowed himself a moment to hate the arrogance of all pilots. It was an indulgence he found himself enjoying more and more as the years went on. They were men, he thought, who eased through an overpaid life which was entirely undeserved. An ancient legend had somehow set pilots apart from other working airmen and somehow they had been able to maintain their status, though every thinking person knew they were nothing more than button pushers. Everyone, that is, except the pilots themselves and those mentally retarded females who still thought a pair of wings on a man's chest marked him as some kind of superman and therefore a desirable bed companion.

This last thought alone, which came to the forecaster's mind very suddenly, annoyed him almost beyond endurance. How many times had he, a Bachelor of Science, lost out to a grinning idiot who either through the machinations of a desperate government, or sheer chance, had learned to fly an airplane? Rubbing his nose and adjusting his glasses, the forecaster could not remember how many times. And since the thought of a woman, any woman who might be willing to share the nights when he was not engrossed in pressure patterns and the adiabatic lapse rates in the sky above the Pacific, caused his pencil to quiver in embarrassing synchronization with his lower lip, he forced his mind back to the weather chart. He pointed to a series of concentric circles drawn about the territory of Alaska.

"This low off Southeastern Alaska is slipping down the coast pretty fast. You'll start picking up headwinds about halfway across . . . forty miles an hour on the nose . . . maybe more."

"I haven't been living right," said the pilot. His voice was barely audible above the clicking of the teletype machines.

"As for your destination, San Francisco will be so-so . . . with a tendency to deteriorate." The forecaster cut off his last word as if its significance gave him boundless pleasure. He caressed the length of his pencil with his thin pale lips and again looked to see if the pilot was paying attention. And looking at him he knew once more the special twisting pain of anger which visited him whenever he was required to talk with pilots. He had assigned this pain, as a person might assign a peculiar greeting; he enjoyed it, and saved it only for pilots.

This man Sullivan, who stood now before him complete with wings and four stripes on his uniform sleeve, was, he thought, a prime example of the species. God had robbed others of perfect health and directed it to this nerveless chunk of flesh whose skin glowed with solid proof of the ghastly injustice. His eyes were clear, and why should they not be when they had never known the strain of prolonged study? His firm lips were compressed slightly as if disapproving, and at the end of his jawbones, just beneath his ears, there were two prominent knobs which moved almost imperceptibly as he examined the weather chart. His shoulders were broad and his hands were large and strong. He was just the type, the forecaster thought, to have gone for a touchdown during the last minute of play at his college—if, indeed, he had ever gone so far as college. He stood very firmly on his feet, leaning back a little as if he were holding the world on a leash. The forecaster was sure that he was listening with only half an ear. The rest of his attention was obviously preoccupied with the sound of engines outside the open windows—magnificent engines designed to carry him over the oceans. Against their full-throated sound, this Sullivan could preen his ego, although he would never have the intelligence to invent such machinery. He would never admit that the engines were his only salvation, or that they alone enabled him to continue his heroic masquerade—the while collecting better than one thousand dollars per month.

Matching one thousand dollars against his own salary suddenly caused the forecaster's hands to become uncomfortably damp. He rolled the pencil rapidly back and forth between his palms as if to absorb the moisture.

"How *much* are the terminals going to deteriorate? I never did like the sound of that word," Sullivan said with a slight smile.

The forecaster took a moment to compose himself. He wanted his answer to be exactly right, ambiguous technically, yet sufficiently cutting so that Sullivan would know he was not dealing with a gypsy fortuneteller.

"The prognostic chart indicates—"

"Why do you characters always use such big words? Just tell me in plain English if the coast weather is going to be good or lousy."

"Captain Sullivan," said the forecaster after thoroughly wetting his lips. "It is for you to decide if the weather is good or lousy. We simply report the facts, as they are . . . and will be."

"Let's hear some facts then and skip the theories."

"San Francisco may hold to three hundred feet and a mile . . . perhaps a mile and a half. Oakland, the same. Fairfield will be fogged in."

"That's not good. But five gets you ten San Francisco will be broken clouds."

"You, of course—*know* this?"

"Hell, no. I'm only hoping. What's for an alternate?"

"Reno. It should be wide open."

"Reno is over the mountains."

"I am well aware of such elementary American geography, Captain."

"Anything else?"

"Not unless you want to go to Palmdale."

"How about Sacramento?"

"Undependable. Fog will sock it in."

"You're probably right."

"Thank you," the forecaster said crisply. "We are not forecasting anything so exact as an eclipse of the sun, but our information is the finest available."

That, the forecaster decided, was telling him. The meek shall inherit the sky as well as the earth if they will just come out of their cocoons. He stepped back from the counter, spread his feet in imitation of Sullivan's stance, and jammed his fists down in his pockets.

"Any ships near the course?" Sullivan asked.

Without moving his body the forecaster turned his head so that he could see the main weather chart of the Pacific.

"Besides 'Uncle' and 'Nan,' there's the *President Cleve-*

land about one thirty-one west longitude and the *Hawaiian Traveler* around one forty-one west. That's all we know about. Planning a holiday cruise on the ocean waves, Captain? A whimsey, perhaps?"

"No. I just like to know about them—in case." Sullivan noted the locations on his weather chart. "Thanks . . . and so long."

"Have a good trip, Captain."

Turning for the door, Sullivan missed the quick gleam of triumph in the forecaster's eyes. He had now other things to occupy his thoughts besides the peculiar behavior of weathermen. They were all a little whacky anyway. If they would just get their noses out of their instruments once in a while and look out the window, they'd hit the weather more accurately.

On the other side of the airport, beyond the sound of the easy Hawaiian music, yet exposed to the sun and the soft easterly wind, Dan Roman moved deliberately through the ritual of preflight inspection. He was a lean, rock-faced man whose erect carriage made him seem taller than he actually was. As the copilot it was his duty to make certain the plane was ready for the flight. The mechanics had fueled the plane and run the four engines; now Dan Roman had over fifty items he must personally observe. He was well aware that many of them, though insignificant when considered against the big ship as a whole, were potential murderers. They could kill Dan Roman and they could kill many other people with him. Therefore he regarded each item with suspicion, as a skilled detective might contemplate known prisoners in a morning line-up. The years had taught Dan Roman the criminal histories of the various mechanical contrivances; he knew only too well how the most innocent of them might combine with circumstance to kill. He could seldom remember the dates, or even the time of year, but it took only a moment's reflection to recall a specific accident in which he had lost a friend or a friend of a friend—"accidents" which were mysteries only to the newspapers. Usually the murderer, and accomplices if any, had been identified, though the search

7

for them might require months. When they were known, word of them was passed quickly through the tight society of flying.

And so Dan Roman was wary, not only of the more obvious wings, landing gear, and tail assembly, but of the small brass wires safetying the fuel strainers, the oil drains, valves and spigots, the inspection doors, rivets, oil and gas caps, fuses, hydraulic leaks, oleos, feathering pumps, the fire and emergency ditching equipment. Many of Dan Roman's contemporaries were no longer around because they had forgotten how the success of any complication depends on small things. Those friends were represented by a vacant chair at the Quiet Birdman meetings which Dan attended once a month. Since 1917 Dan had been a candidate for that same chair too many times. Now he was determined to die in bed.

Looking up at the big ship, admiring its contours glistening in the sunlight, Dan stood with his feet wide apart and his arms folded across his chest. He whistled softly without trying to follow a tune. Like a beached mariner watching the sea, his only thoughts for the moment were of the ship before him. It was really far more than a machine. It was a whole era which he had helped to create. He began with it, 'way back, when a man's life was all bamboo and wire. Now once more, he was a part of it—and in a way that was laughable. Dan Roman, still leaving the earth and returning to it in one piece after thirty-five years of flying. He rubbed his chin thoughtfully and it occurred to him that there were very few men who could say the same thing.

And how much remained of the old Dan Roman besides the inevitable suspended look—the appearance of not really belonging anywhere, a vague, unsettled look, acquired in time by all professional pilots? A fair portion remained, although something, of course, had to pay for thirty-five years of use. The slight limp came from the accident, and so that could not be considered pure deterioration. Glasses were easier for reading, but the depth perception, tempered by so much practice, was just as good as ever. Heart, according to the last physical, remarkably sound. Blood pressure right where it should be. Most of the withering had been external, it seemed.

Passing a hand along his face, Dan felt the lines around his mouth and eyes . . . Oh God, the lines were as deep as knife cuts! But anyway they matched the skin, which in turn almost matched the crinkled leather of the old tan briefcase now waiting beneath the wing. The briefcase had two million miles on it or better. It sagged a little here and there. It was covered with scars and weather wounds, but it still had value and durability. It was not to be thrown away any more than Dan Roman—not quite yet a relic.

Spalding, the stewardess, pretended to disbelieve those fifty-three years, which was polite nonsense, of course. Spalding, though, didn't know what it was like to return to a love—because she had yet to lose one. Nor would she understand how a man might return from the exile of inactivity and find a reason for living again.

A heavy voice behind Dan Roman broke his thoughts. "Hey, fella . . . ain't you Dan Roman?" He turned to see a square-set, concrete block of a man who wore white coveralls. He was chewing uncertainly on the dead stump of a cigar and his pale blue eyes were half-closed as if he was trying to revive a long forgotten vision. His thick black eyebrows arched upward as he waited almost defiantly for a reply. The man poked a finger at Dan's chest.

"I heard you whistlin' and I said to myself only one guy does that just so. I'd know that ugly face of yours anywhere . . . but you don't remember me, I betcha."

Dan held his breath because he did remember the man, but more so because he saw a mouse in a whirling green cage, once again. The cage was hanging from the ceiling of an operations office in South America—could it have been a hundred years ago? There was real laughter then and a crazy, lazy way of life that could never be forgotten. It was a long way from Bogota and the green mouse cage to Honolulu, but at last it had happened. Alice and Tony were back . . . and now the haunting would begin again. Dan smiled and put out his hand although he wanted to turn away.

"Sure . . . you're Ben Sneed." Ben had been a chief mechanic with Aero Colombia when it happened—when the reason for living then was destroyed in the space of a few minutes.

9

"I thought you'd be milking cows somewheres . . . on your own farm by now," Ben said uneasily. He looked at the airplane as if he had suddenly discovered it. And Dan knew he was sorry he had ever started the conversation. "Can't you stay away from these things? They're only a hunk of metal and they don't go no place in particular." It was an old joke but now it fell very flat as their eyes met again.

"I guess I haven't much will power, Ben. What are you up to?"

"I'm chief mech with Far East. It's a good job. . . ."

"I'm glad, Ben. . . ." They looked at the sky together because it was the easiest thing to do.

"Well, I have to go, Dan. I just thought I'd say hello."

"Sure . . . good luck."

"Be seein' you around. . . ."

"For a while, anyway. We'll have a talk one of these days. Take it easy, Ben."

"Yea, sure—no strain."

Two mechanics came out of the maintenance hangar when Dan Roman climbed the ladder to the ship. They stood by as fire guard while the inboard motors were started, then they waved him away. Ben Sneed watched the plane until it was halfway across the field. He retraced his steps and spoke to the mechanics. He wanted them to know about Dan Roman.

"Either one of you know that man?" he asked.

"He's sure old for a copilot. I didn't know we were so hard up."

"I remember his name from somewheres."

"Well, remember it forever," Ben said quietly. He took the stub of cigar from his lips and examined it thoughtfully. "Because there goes one of the finest men you'll ever know . . . and the most miserable. We used to call him Sad Dan, or the Whistler. I'd thought he'd blown his brains out by now, but he's got too much nerve for that. He was flying for Aero Colombia same time I was line chief down there right after the war. One day he takes off from Cali with a full load and one of them South American line squalls decides to hit the field at the same time. The wind shifts too late for him to stop and he don't make it over the little hump of ground about half a mile from the field. He hits flat, but the ship breaks in half and there's nothing but fire in ten seconds. Dan gets tossed out through the cockpit window and only gets a few scratches which leaves him alive to blame himself. The copilot is killed . . . everybody but Dan . . . and a fat German who beats everybody else to the exits. . . ."

"Sounds to me like he's pretty lucky."

"No . . . it don't work out quite that way. I knew two of the passengers. They were going down to the Coast for a holiday . . . a blond girl named Alice, and a boy named Tony. I thought they were wonderful people and so did everybody else, including Dan Roman. . . ." Ben stopped looking at his cigar and carefully replaced it between his teeth. "Alice was Dan's wife and Tony his only kid."

One of the mechanics made a small hissing sound and began to rub a spot of grease from his hand.

"So the next time Dan Roman passes through here . . . just remember he weren't always a copilot."

2

WHEN HE LEFT THE WEATHER ROOM, SULLIVAN DE-
scended a long flight of stairs. At the bottom he almost
collided with Leonard Wilby, his navigator.

"Sorry I was late, Skipper. I got hung up buying a present for Susie."

Of course, Leonard would be buying a present for Susie. He always did. It wasn't necessary to fly very long
with Leonard Wilby before Susie became a sort of extra
crew member, invisible but always threatening. She had
run through three husbands before she finally settled on
Leonard, who was twice her age, yet still as innocent as a
Benedictine monk. Sullivan had met Leonard's Susie
several times when she had driven him to the San Francisco airport. He didn't like to think what she did as soon
as her meal-ticket disappeared over the horizon. Ignoring
Sullivan's presence, she had once called Leonard Wilby a
miserable bowl of prune whip, surrounded by grey hairs.
She was full of martinis at the time and later she
called him an impotent bastard. And so Sullivan hated
her, along with everyone else who had ever flown with
Leonard Wilby and knew him as one of the nicest
guys in the business. Too nice a guy for Susie.

"It's all right, Lennie. I have the weather, such as it is."
He handed the paper folder to Wilby and they turned
down the long corridor together.

"What altitude you want to fly?"

"Let's try nine thousand for a change. They're reporting a few cumulo-nimbus but I think we can work around them without shaking anything to pieces."

"I bought Susie one of those hardwood trays."

"Fine. She'll like that." Sullivan could imagine how she would like it. Susie would chuck it in a cupboard and preserve it against the time when she might break it over Leonard's head. Poor Leonard. Twenty years of the Navy and then ten more as a mate on steamers hadn't taught him a thing—except how to navigate with uncanny accuracy. Across two thousand miles of ocean he was seldom off more than a few minutes on his estimated time of arrival. Sullivan never worried about the position of his ship in space when Leonard Wilby was along. He might be an amateur husband, but as a navigator, he was all professional.

They passed the operations offices of several lines flying the Pacific and finally turned into their own. Sullivan thought again how much it looked like all other operations offices no matter where in the world they might be. There was an uncomfortable bench which no one ever sat upon, but which served as a receptacle for coats, metal log books, octants, and the battered briefcases that were as necessary to modern airmen as their shoes. Sullivan's own was there, bedraggled testimony of the damage a million air miles can do to expensive leather. It held his operations manual, a thick book which set forth the flight policies of the company in such dull prose Sullivan had never been able to read it thoroughly.

In the book it said that "the point-of-no-return means the point beyond which the aircraft no longer has sufficient fuel, under existing conditions, to return to the point of departure or any alternate for that point." Leonard Wilby, already engaged with the tools of his trade, would be calculating the point-of-no-return and would define it far more exactly than the book. It was that point beyond which you were in a hell of a lot of trouble if anything went wrong.

The operations book covered every conceivable eventuality from how to start an engine to pertinent advice on aircraft fires, such as "land as soon as possible." In this recommendation Sullivan was willing to agree the

13

book was absolutely right, if a trifle obvious. He carried the book only because the law required it.

Beyond the counter, which now served as a desk for Leonard Wilby's calculations, there was a large blackboard listing the whereabouts, arrivals, and departures of the airline's ships. Sullivan saw his own name chalked after the figures 420, the number of the airplane he was to take across the water. Then the letters HNL-SFO . . . Honolulu to San Francisco . . . ETD—estimated time of departure—22:00Z. That would be twelve o'clock Honolulu time—an hour from now.

Beneath the blackboard two teletype machines erupted spasmodically. As if carrying on a conversation, one would chatter and then fall silent while the other spoke its piece. No one paid the slightest attention to them.

Beyond the machines a red-faced young man was working out the weight and balance figures for the flight. He referred frequently to an oversized slide rule and neatly recorded his observations on a large white form. Looking up from his work, he caught Sullivan's eye.

"Three thousand and fifty be all right for take-off, Cap?"

Sullivan considered the amount. Three thousand and fifty gallons of gasoline at a normal consumption of two hundred gallons per hour would postpone the normal relationship between men and gravity for approximately fifteen hours. That should be ample, but if the coast weather really turned foul and he was forced to continue to Reno the extra distance would add at least an hour to the flight time. There could be ice over the mountains and there also might be some delay while holding for traffic, or perhaps an unsuccessful stab at an instrument approach—another two hundred gallons gone.

The law required fuel enough to reach the intended destination plus distance to the alternate airport, plus one hour and a half reserve. Sullivan wanted all the fuel he could carry, yet the matter of economics must also be considered. For every extra gallon, six pounds of pay load must be left behind. A hundred gallons extra, known as "gas for Mama," would be aboard, anyway, under a sort of tacit understanding whereby everyone knew it was there, but no one concerned with official figures admitted

14

it was there. There had been times when that little extra had saved a ship, and its presence in defiance of the books rested upon the same practicality as listing every passenger at one hundred and sixty pounds regardless of his true weight. It averaged out.

"How about it, Cap?"

"Sounds all right, but let's see what Leonard says." Sullivan leaned over Leonard Wilby's shoulder and watched him as he rapidly added up the figures on his flight plan. The winds, whether favorable or unfavorable, would, of course, determine the exact amount of gas required, but then no forecaster had ever been exactly right about the winds.

"It looks like about twelve hours and sixteen minutes," Leonard said, still writing. "If these winds are anywhere near right."

Sullivan called across the counter to the red-faced young man. "Okay. Thirty-fifty take-off."

The young man pressed the lever on a squawk box just above his head and yelled at it. "Hangar!"

After a moment, the box replied in a tired dry voice. "Go ahead! It's your nickel!"

"Thirty-fifty take-off for Four-two-zero."

"Roger!"

Sullivan interrupted. "Ask him if Roman is down there."

"Is Roman down there, Hangar?!"

"Who's he?"

"Roman! The copilot!"

The only answer from the box was a series of clicks like the snapping of dry twigs. Then the tired voice came through again. "Yeah! He's here!"

"Tell him to bring the ship to the ramp," Sullivan said. "We won't go over for it."

"Tell him to taxi the ship to the ramp!"

"Roger!" The box subsided as if it had been insulted.

There was a bulletin board opposite the cluttered bench. Strolling toward it, Sullivan thought about Dan Roman. Why in the name of God had he been stuck with a has-been? Good copilots with sufficient education and enough flying time to qualify for the job were hard to find these days, but why not let old fire-horses graze

15

in their pastures? Especially those who whistled until it was enough to drive anyone crazy.

Again, as he had done on the westbound flight, Sullivan tried to calculate Dan Roman's age. He had to be at *least* fifty. This was a guy who had survived history. His name was famous in aviation before Sullivan had ever thought of leaving the ground. There were endurance flights, a wild try over the North Pole that ended in disaster and still caused Dan Roman to limp slightly . . . that would have been about 1926 . . . and there were half-a-dozen air races at Cleveland where the name of Dan Roman and his perilously hot little ship, the *Meteor,* were always in the money. Dan Roman had designed and built the ship himself. Pilots did such things in those days. Then the air mail in the open cockpit days, when the rival lines would try to chase each other out of the sky for the sheer hell of it. And finally there must have been at least ten or fifteen years with Trans-World, followed by the war in which Roman used his multitude of flying friends already in the Air Force to wangle a major's commission, although he had never had an hour's military training in his life. He didn't join to fly a desk, either. He flew a bomber on the Ploesti oil field raid . . . took his cracks at Germany in B-17's and finally wound up with a B-29 squadron on Okinawa. After his discharge rumor placed him as operations manager of a nonscheduled line flying out of Miami, and then he had suddenly disappeared. He said he'd been running a fruit farm—very unsuccessfully.

It was less than a month ago that Dan Roman had walked into the office of Sullivan's line. Garfield, the operations manager who had known Roman when balloonists were still wearing red tights, gave him a job as copilot! Garfield must have been right out of his head. If he had taken Roman on as an executive assistant or somehow in a supervisory capacity, that might be understandable. But a copilot's job was for kids—twenty-three, maybe twenty-four years old, kids like Hobie Wheeler. They usually had two or three thousand hours, sometimes a little more, sometimes less. They were paid five or six hundred a month according to the kind of flying they did, and were content to wait and learn for a few years until the chance came to qualify as captain. Ideally, this put them in charge of an airplane when they were about thirty.

Now here was Dan Roman, a man known to have more than twenty thousand flying hours, almost twice the time Sullivan could record in his log book—and flying as copilot. The difference made Sullivan uncomfortable. What about his seniority? Though it was an insult to the intelligence of all but the weakest pilots, it still governed their lives and, unfortunately, had been allowed to grow until it dictated the very bread they put on the table. Promotion to captain depended on this ridiculous selective system and so Roman's chances of ever getting a command before he was too old to fly were simply nonexistent. It was sad and it was embarrassing, Sullivan thought. A choir boy didn't tell a high priest how to run the mass. Garfield should have known better.

Sullivan scanned the bulletin board for something he hadn't read before. He found nothing except the usual cautions against low flying over the city of Honolulu, the stale notices to airmen setting forth the areas in which antiaircraft firing would take place, and a letter from the Department of Agriculture threatening crew members with severe fines if they failed to keep the cockpit windows closed after landing.

There was a photograph from a magazine pinned to the board. It depicted an astonished monkey sitting forlornly in a pond. The water was almost up to his shoulders and the expression in his eyes was one of utter dejection. Someone had scrawled in pencil just beneath the monkey "Copilot who forgot to check the gas tanks."

A wistful smile played across Sullivan's lips. In his mind he wrote a memorandum to Garfield. ". . . suggest the monkey photo on bulletin board at HNL be copied, framed, and placed in the cockpit of all our aircraft. . . ." But he knew he would never write the memorandum. For reasons no one had ever been able to explain satisfactorily, pilots seldom wrote anything down unless it was actually required—it had something to to with the trancelike separation of a man when he left the earth as a means of making a living.

Hobie Wheeler, the third pilot, came into the operations

17

office. He was a dark-skinned, wiry young man with eyes that slanted in such a way he might have passed for an Oriental. He licked thoughtfully at an ice cream cone and joined Sullivan before the bulletin board.

"Did you get the frequencies?" Sullivan asked.

"Um-huh." He seemed completely absorbed in licking at the cone, so that not a drop would escape him.

"How's your ATR coming?" Sullivan asked the question because he made it a point to take an interest in the personal lives of his crew members. It was part of being a good captain, and being a good captain was Sullivan's life. He must be as much on guard to appreciate the problems of his crew members, however private they might be, as to dip his transport's wings exactly on a cross-wing landing. He had been trained in a rigid school, and could think of several superb examples of the perfect air captain. His one desire was to equal them. Good captains bred loyalty as they had done at sea for thousands of years—now in the air, that loyalty was tighter, more confined perhaps, but in many ways it was more necessary for survival than ever. In Wheeler's case, the matter of his Airline Transport Rating was a pressing one, for it would be a major step toward a command of his own. In addition to practical experience and a rigid flight test, Hobie Wheeler faced a long written examination covering every phase of his profession. Without a thorough review Sullivan would have hesitated to take the written test himself.

"I flunked meteorology," Hobie Wheeler said. He licked at his cone and his brooding eyes continued to examine the bulletin board as if he had no other concern in the world.

"That's too bad."

"I go up for it again next month," Hobie said with easy confidence. "Most of it is malarkey, anyway. I'll pass next time."

Studying his perfectly relaxed face, Sullivan suddenly felt old for the first time in his thirty-five years. How could Hobie seem to care so little? No, that was really easy to explain, and behind the explanation lay the reason commercial pilots were not allowed to fly more than eighty-five hours a month. Years before, someone had been smart and discovered that a flying command could consume a man, burn.him inside though his exterior remained undamaged. Whatever it was that used the man, responsibility for many lives, or an invisible nervousness because he was out of his element, was definitely present; and after a time it aged the youngest of men. After a very long time it made a Dan Roman. Though he could manipulate the controls with assurance and ease, Hobie Wheeler had still to learn what it was like to fly.

"You want to sign this, Skipper?" asked Leonard Wilby. He held out the completed flight plan. Sullivan glanced quickly down the lines of figures and scribbled his name. Before he left the ground he would sign his name at least ten more times.

"Me too!" said the red-faced young man. He slammed the weight and balance form on top of the counter. Sullivan examined it more closely. Twenty S.O.B.—souls on board—the rest cargo and fuel, all neatly represented in columns of figures with the center of gravity given at twenty-six point eight per cent. Here it was written that with a hardly perceptible flexing of Sullivan's arms he could lift seventy-three thousand pounds from the surface of the earth and transport it at high speed for better than two thousand miles.

The red-faced young man spoke as if reciting a litany. "I said it to Orville, I said it to Wilbur, and I say it to you . . . the thing will never leave the ground."

Sullivan smiled automatically because he had heard the phrase a hundred times before. He signed the form.

The passengers were beginning to gather before the ticket counter. Alsop, the ticket agent, who had once been a night clerk in a Nevada hotel and so considered himself a shrewd judge of his fellowman, checked them in one by one. He was surgically neat about his work, entering each name precisely on his form and blowing away the leavings of erasure when a change in baggage weight was necessary. He pronounced the name of each passenger with meticulous care, passing his hand ceremoniously across his high forehead as he did so.

"Donald Flaherty?"

A neatly dressed man with a grey bristle of mustache mopped the perspiration from the bags beneath his eyes. "Yes?"

The one word reeked with the smell of whisky. Good whisky, Alsop noted in his file-book mind.

"Nice to have you with us, Mr. Flaherty. Please check with immigration. You will board in about thirty minutes." Alsop inclined his head toward the blond girl who stood beside him. "This is Miss Spalding, your stewardess."

Flaherty examined the whole of the girl in a single glance. Approval crossed his watery eyes and then subsided, as if he had been caught peeking in a window.

"Where's the bar?"

"Just across the lobby, Mr. Flaherty. Your flight will be announced."

"Thanks."

"Mr. and Mrs. Joseph?"

"Righto. The Waikiki kids!" Edwin Joseph seemed to force his way toward the counter although there was nothing to hinder him.

Alsop's eyebrows arched slightly as he examined the man and woman who faced him with almost pathetic eagerness. They tumbled into his mental card file as two very small people almost entirely obscured by flower leis. Only their painfully sunburned faces emerged from the floral display.

"Just put us down as a float for the Rose Bowl parade," said Edwin Joseph. Mrs. Joseph giggled and made a motion with her trim small body which Alsop recognized as an attempt at the hula. He glanced quickly at Miss Spalding, then looked down at his immigration sheet.

"Your age, Mr. Joseph?"

"Today?"

Mrs. Joseph giggled again and Alsop smiled wanly. ". . . if you please, Mr. Joseph."

"Thirty-eight as I live and breathe."

Alsop thought that if Mrs. Joseph responded with a giggle he would throw off his years of training and reach across the counter to slap her.

"Birthplace, please?"

"Passaic, New Jersey."

"And Mrs. Joseph?"

"Shall I tell him, honey?" Alsop heard Mrs. Joseph giggle and cringed in spite of his discipline.

"I'm—a . . . twenty seven . . . and—a I was born in Ogden, Utah."

"Many thanks." Alsop looked through and beyond the Josephs as if they had been suddenly lifted to the ceiling by invisible wires. He nodded to a blond woman who was curiously attractive in spite of a figure that was apparently held in place by the strongest of whalebones.

"My name is Sally McKee." As she stepped closer Alsop noticed that her eyebrows consisted entirely of paint and the line of her face make-up matched imperfectly her strawlike hair. The total effect was of a mask, worn slightly askew. It is Halloween, Alsop thought.

"Your age and birthplace, Miss McKee?"

She hesitated. When she spoke Alsop was surprised at the beauty of her low voice.

"Thirty. I was born in Riverside, California and then I moved to—"

Alsop smiled. "It's unnecessary to tell me any more, Miss McKee. We are simply obliged to make this check before you pass through immigration. You're still a United States citizen?"

"Oh, yes. Of course."

"Thank you, Miss McKee. Your flight will be announced." As she turned away Alsop wondered at her attractiveness.

"Spalding," he said softly, "though she may be put together with paste and flour, that woman has something. What would you say it was?"

Spalding's cool blue eyes warmed a little.

"Practice . . . plenty of practice."

Alsop threw her an appreciative salute and returned to his papers.

"Mr. Gustave Pardee and wife Lillian?"

"Right here!" The voice came from an enormous, sloppily dressed man. His eyes bulged and his small mouth gasped heavily for air as he rearranged the

21

elaborate photographic equipment hanging from his shoulders and sought uncertainly for his tickets.

"Aren't you—?"

"Yes. I'm Gustave Pardee."

"I've enjoyed your shows very much."

"Good. Delighted. Here are our tickets. I'm forty-seven and I was born in New York City." He looks like a tired walrus on a rock, Alsop thought as he placed checks by his name. He should groom himself only half as well as he does his New York shows.

"And Mrs. Pardee?"

"I'm thirty-one and was born in Owosso, Michigan." And a lovelier thirty-one I never laid eyes on, Alsop said to himself. If indeed she was his wife, then Gustave Pardee had once more shown his sense of the exquisite. She reminded Alsop of a porcelain vase he had once seen in Tokyo, smooth and polished with delicate touches of color here and there—harmonious color that set off the luster of Mrs. Pardee, as it had the vase. Alsop wanted to tell her that she had done all right for a slim brunette from Owosso, but instead he took the time to introduce her to Spalding.

"How will the weather be?" Gustave Pardee asked anxiously.

Looking into his sad, unnaturally bulging eyes, Alsop knew that he was afraid of flying. "Fine, Mr. Pardee. You should have a very pleasant trip."

A deeply tanned man with his grey hair brushed in a tight pompadour pushed his tickets toward Alsop. His face was lined and beefy, and again the odor of whisky drifted across Alsop's papers.

"Ken Childs . . . fifty-three . . . born Philadelphia." Every word was a brusque command.

"Oh yes, Mr. Childs." Alsop straightened a little. Kenneth Childs, "Ken," as he was better known to the world of aviation, was a very important person. He owned stock in many airlines and knew the presidents of all of them. He was one of the few men in the world who had made any money out of aviation, and he commanded a great deal of respect for having done so.

"I don't know where the hell my baggage is. The Royal was supposed to send it down."

"We'll keep an eye out for it, sir. May I introduce Miss Spalding, your stewardess on the flight."

"Hello, sister." Ken Childs made no attempt to hide his examination of Spalding, from her eyes to her nylons. "You're new, aren't you?"

"Four months now with the Company, Mr. Childs."

"Good . . . good. I don't understand where they get some of the girls. Things are improving." Suddenly he reached for the lei around his neck and handed it to Spalding. "Here. This damn silly thing will look better on you than it does on me." He turned quickly and walked away before Spalding had time to thank him.

Alsop consulted his list again. He went through the motions of checking the names as if it were impossible to guess the name of the girl who had moved so quietly to the counter. He had noticed her standing almost immovable behind the others, looking strangely out of place in her black silk dress and white gloves. Alsop found her patience and dignity a matter of such rare pleasure he let her wait before him a moment longer, reluctant to disturb the tranquility of her face.

"If you please," she said, placing her ticket envelope on the counter, and Alsop discovered her voice held a plaintive quality. He took up the tickets without looking at them.

"Dorothy Chen . . . ?"

"Yes. . . ." A suggestion of a smile played about her delicate lips.

Alsop's mind conjured a moon and a willow tree before he could direct it back to his papers. "Born in Antung, Manchuria?"

"Yes . . . but I am Korean."

"You have your passport handy, of course?"

"Oh yes."

"Please take it to immigration across the lobby. It's a pleasure to have you with us, Miss Chen." Her head tipped in the slightest acknowledgment and then she moved away. Alsop looked after her, surprised at the pleasure he found in watching her graceful walk. He was glad that for the moment, at least, there were no more passengers to be checked.

23

In the beginning, the Pacific skies were nearly empty. Only a few birds flew at the lower levels.

Now, those who are bound to seek favor from the skies, those who must be beloved of its wilderness, have a way of thinking on the matter of their environment. The sky above the Pacific becomes feminine while the Atlantic sky is masculine. The reason for this division of genders is unknown. It happened that way.

The difference in oceanic temperament may have caused airmen to feel as they do. The Atlantic's moods and behavior are without subtlety. Its harshness is direct and predictable. The Atlantic sky shouts and blusters, yet in its brief seasons of peace, it embraces the airman handsomely—making of him a valued fellow warrior to be loved. There is nothing lush about the Atlantic sky.

As if part of another planet, the Pacific sky is different in all things. The Pacific sky can cause a man to lose his head, arouse in the most phlegmatic of airmen both love and deep hatred. The Pacific sky is passionate. It can enchant his senses, bore him, make him feel great or insignificant. Or it can, with the most feminine witchery, lull him into a sense of security. The Pacific sky can never be laughed with, or at—any more than it is possible to find mirth in the constellations.

And yet there is nothing cold about the beauty of the Pacific sky. Airmen find in it great warmth and engagement. The Pacific sky can fascinate and hold a man perfectly quiet while he contemplates its immensity.

Airmen like Sullivan easily recognized the differences between the two areas of sky. Though the benign weather over the Pacific caused the flight through it to become known internationally as a "gravy run," there was one thing Sullivan and all the others bore constantly in mind.

The Pacific sky was not to be trusted.

24

3

THE LAST OF THE PASSENGERS SURROUNDED ALSOP LIKE grapes on a stem. Because they were a trifle late they were more eager than the others, as if they feared the plane might leave without them. They were hot and tense, fanning themselves periodically and trying to push a little ahead of each other. Alsop had left his counter momentarily to process a sick man named Frank Briscoe who now sat waiting patiently by the souvenir stand and would require help to board the plane. He had also sent the Bucks, Milo and Nell, on their way—the newlyweds who had come before him in a haze of endearing whispers and floated away from the counter still speaking as softly to each other as the eastern wind.

Spalding watched them out the door, envying the new Mrs. Buck. She built a whole future for them in her mind, exactly as she would want it herself. She was sorry when they became lost in the crowd.

Alsop was talking to a woman named May Holst. She gave her age as fifty and her birthplace as Rockland, Ohio. Spalding thought she was a very well-preserved fifty except for her eyes, which were pouched until they were only slits in her face. But what could be seen of her eyes spoke merrily and her voice was the kind that should only be heard through a bedroom door—

sensual and chuckling, knowing, and to Spalding a secret delight.

"Will I be glad to get on that airplane!"

"We're happy to have you aboard, Miss Holst," Alsop said mechanically.

Winking at Spalding, she leaned far across the counter so that only Alsop could hear her. "You can take all of the Hawaiian Islands and you know what you can do with . . ."

"You haven't enjoyed yourself, Miss Holst?"

"I always enjoy myself, honey, but cocoanuts and beach boys will never replace Toledo." She turned away still chuckling, and Spalding resolved to spend extra time with her on the plane. There was always something to learn from a woman like May Holst.

Howard and Lydia Rice moved to the counter. He was tall and very pale of face. Spalding wondered if it was his tie or the way he wore his narrow-brimmed hat that made him look like a curiously aged undergraduate. There was a flash of jeweled cuff links at his thin wrists as he reached for his tickets. Little Lydia Rice, her doll-like head barely level with his waist, moved in almost exact unison with her husband. They could have been dancing, Spalding thought—to the tinkle of her bracelets.

"We're connecting with the New York plane," Howard Rice said to Alsop. "We've only an hour between . . . going to make it all right, aren't you?"

"Of course, Mr. Rice."

"Where can I send a cable?"

"Just across the lobby opposite the souvenir stand."

When they went away Alsop and Spalding took a moment to look at each other.

"She smells like a perfume barge," Spalding said slowly, ". . . and sounds like a hardware store."

"You are becoming bitter too early in your career, Spalding. That little lady can afford it. Kindly note her middle initial—S. You should appreciate such things as long as you are going to be in this racket. S, in her case, stands for Stanley. Mrs. Rice had a grandfather of that name who left her both riches and brains. She bought her husband an advertising agency not long ago, because he wanted a new toy and because it has become fashionable for even Harvard men to work. The firm is known as Rice and Larrabee."

"How do you know all these things?"

"It is my business to know . . . and, Spalding, it should be yours."

Now a small dark man was standing patiently at the counter. There was a look of abject apology in his large brown eyes. He was wearing a cap and a cheap green suit, and though his shirt was freshly laundered, the points of his collar curled upward as if they were designed to repeat the line of his eyebrows. When he laid his ticket carefully on the counter, Spalding saw that two fingers were missing from his right hand. He stood so quietly, seeming to beg Alsop's pardon for intruding, that Spalding found herself feeling very sorry for him.

"You are Mr. Locota?"

"Yes, yes . . . José Locota . . . that is right . . . that is me. I go back to San Francisco now."

"Your age, Mr. Locota?"

"I dunno. Fifty-one . . . fifty-two, maybe three . . . I dunno, see?"

"On the immigration paper you gave your age as fifty-one, Mr. Locota—"

"Sure, sure! I tell 'em anything they want to hear so long as they stop askin' questions. What difference so long as I'm an American citizen? Full naturalized . . . all the way around."

"In the future, Mr. Locota, might I suggest you stick to one age? It makes things so much easier for people who have to write things down."

"Sure . . . sure! I don't want to make no trouble for nobody."

"Thank you, Mr. Locota. Your plane will be announced in a few minutes."

"Thank you . . . yes, thank you very much!" Mr. Locota stooped, and so disappeared momentarily beneath the counter. When he turned away Alsop saw that he was carrying a large package.

"Mr. Locota! Your package. Wouldn't you like to have us check it through for you?"

"Check through?"

"Yes. It will be returned to you with your bag in San Francisco. Our regulations limit the size of cabin packages—"

"But—" Mr. Locota looked down at the package he held beneath his arm. Finally his brown eyes sought Spalding's and she saw they were full of bewilderment. "But—"

"Your package will be safe with us, Mr. Locota," Spalding said quickly.

"Oh yeah, sure . . . but . . . ?" He moved uncertainly back toward the counter. His eyes still appealed to Spalding. "Only I have here . . . my things to eat . . . for the trip!"

Spalding almost laughed and was instantly ashamed. "You've hurt my feelings, Mr. Locota. To think you wouldn't eat my lunch or the steak we're going to have for dinner. Wine, too, if you care for it."

Mr. Locota placed the hand with the missing fingers to his forehead. "Ma'am . . . miss? I don't know about these things, see? I never flew before and don't want make trouble for nobody."

"Serving you will be a pleasure, Mr. Locota. Please let me."

"Of course, ma'am! Absolutely, of course! I didn't know, understand? Excuse me, please."

"I'll take care of your package," Alsop said. "Just give them this check when you arrive in San Francisco."

José Locota backed away from the counter. He bumped into two soldiers before he could take his eyes from Spalding and look where he was going.

"And I suppose you know all about that little man, too," Spalding finally said to Alsop.

"No . . . the ticketing sheet hasn't a thing on him except statistics. I'm afraid he falls into the nobody category."

"He's going to be more than a statistic to me. I like him."

Alsop clipped the copies of the passenger manifest together and told Spalding she was lucky because it was a Tuesday and consequently there were few passengers for her to look after. Most people went to the mainland either just before or after a week end.

"You can catch up on your reading and your sleep."

He took a moment to reappraise the almost mathematical perfection of her appearance. Just off the top of a cake, he thought. Not a strand of her short blond hair was out of place and her complexion could never have come from a make-up kit. Soap and water—lots of it—plus an appetite that was not ashamed of itself. A sort of serene challenge to feminine complication.

"I'd like to ask you a personal question," Alsop said.

"Why not?" Indeed why not—when God was in His castle and there was nothing for a girl like Spalding to hide.

"What do you normally eat for breakfast?"

"That's a funny question."

"I have a funny mind . . . and I'd like to prove something to myself."

"All right. An orange, or bananas . . . and a couple of eggs with ham if I can get it, toast—"

"How many slices?"

"Two or three . . . it depends."

"Don't you ever worry about—"

"Getting fat?" She laughed softly. "What's wrong with being comfortable?"

Alsop shook his head admiringly. "Nothing . . . absolutely nothing, Spalding. I should have known you wouldn't settle for a cup of tea."

His eyes passed down the line of her immaculate white blouse, pausing only a moment to sense again the full breasts beneath it. Though he could not see the backs of her strong legs, Alsop was certain her stocking seams would be perfectly straight. He thought he would like to buy her breakfast—several of them in sequence, and it wouldn't make too much difference if that was all there was to it. Because if there had been anything the night before, Spalding would have given without motive, as a young healthy animal, and the man who received her would know great peace. There would have been no danger, no by-play of intellects, no hurts or small angers, or complications—just Spalding. And any man of wisdom would have sense enough to be content with her.

29

Alsop's secret pleasure in his thoughts was broken by a man who came toward the counter at almost a full run. An old-fashioned black valise bounced crazily against his legs. He slid to a stop before the counter and began a frantic search of his pockets.

"Can I help you, sir?" Alsop asked. He was still thinking of Spalding, and his voice was indifferent.

"San Francisco! I got to go to San Francisco. Your plane hasn't left yet?"

"We're departing in five minutes . . . but our manifest doesn't show—"

"Mr. Kenneth Childs is on your flight, isn't he?"

"Why, yes. Mr. Childs—"

"You must have room. I must get on that plane!"

"Very well, sir. Fortunately we have space today. If you are an American citizen we have just time."

"I am . . . oh, I am! . . . for sure!" He mopped frantically at rivulets of perspiration streaming down his face. His long nose drooped over his wisp of a mustache as if exertion and the heat had melted it. His eyes bulged and the whites were flecked with yellow. Only his large ears seemed to be holding his sagging cheeks from complete collapse. He looked like a sick gargoyle, Alsop thought, and without reason he found himself disliking the man.

"What is your name, sir?"

"Humphrey Agnew."

"Place of birth and age?"

"Morristown, Pennsylvania. I'm forty-five."

"Do you have a travel card, Mr. Agnew?"

"No. I'll pay cash." His tobacco-stained fingers plucked two hundred-dollar bills from his wallet and his hand shook as he laid the money on the counter.

"If you'll just step across the lobby and check with immigration, then come right back here, I'll have your ticket ready."

There was so little time remaining Alsop had to concentrate almost entirely on his paper work. Yet Spalding was still beside him and he hated to think of her leaving. And so, still writing, he said, "Sometimes I feel like Charon, Spalding. It's writing down people's names with all their statistics makes me feel that way. I find myself looking into their mouths to see if someone has placed a coin on their tongue for me."

Her lips parted in doubt, Spalding looked at him uncertainly. "What in the whole wide world are you talking about?"

"Fellow with a boat . . . traditionally a rowboat, I think." Of course, Spalding would not know about Charon. Stay on the top of your cake, Spalding, and do not bother your tranquil soul about such things. "He rows back and forth across the river Styx," he added lamely.

"Is that in Germany?"

"I'm not quite sure just where it is. Forget I mentioned it, will you?"

"Sure thing." Spalding eased herself from the table to the floor. She made a minute adjustment to her skirt and checked her wrist watch against the wall clock.

"So long, Alsop. Have fun."

"You don't have to leave quite yet."

"It's that time. Aloha."

Alsop glanced up momentarily from his work. He met Spalding's friendly eyes and wondered again at her ability to be both sensual and prim. His hand made a small gesture of farewell.

"I'll weep at your wedding, Spalding."

Dan Roman set the parking brakes and cut off the two inboard engines he had used to taxi the plane across the field. He removed his headphones and yanked open the window at his side. For a moment he sat completely still. He was suddenly tired, already tired, and the realization that his weariness was more mental than physical disturbed him.

How many thousands of times had he done this? From the beginning of his memory it seemed he had been bringing planes into places and waiting for them to be filled with people who wanted to go to another place. In the old days there were never more than a few people and the place of waiting was seldom more elaborate than a shack erected beside an open field.

He smiled at the memory and then sobered almost

instantly because he had caught himself doing it again—enjoying memories more than the present. It was a trick of age, and a habit, especially now, to be avoided for as long as possible. Yet staring out the cockpit window at the great field with its long, smooth concrete runways stretching almost to the vanishing point, it was impossible not to think of Chicago in the twenties. Then, it was only a vacant lot. And there was a strip of flat gravel beside a New York amusement park which was now called LaGuardia Field. And there was Newark —just a few tin buildings surrounding a black patch of cinders. Syracuse was a lovely little meadow of bright green grass. You could side slip down over the trees at Syracuse then, and set a ship so lightly upon the grass the floating sensation of real flight lingered pleasantly, only easing itself away when the engine was still. And if all of this had been transformed in less than one lifetime, then no wonder there was weariness inside, deep—for all of those things were gone.

Airports were safer now, he thought, but they all looked too much alike. They had sacrificed character for vastness. It was like falling in love with the most simple of country girls, and awakening one day to discover she had become a vain-glorious woman who had forgotten how to laugh. He remained motionless, looking into the distance and fondling the idea. Fancy thinking for Dan Roman—Sad Dan, who didn't know when to quit.

Smiling thoughtfully he reached down for the lever which controlled the fore and aft position of his seat and slid the seat back as far as it would go. He twisted around the control pedestal, avoiding its bristling knobs and levers with difficulty. Then he took the one step down from the forward flight deck and walked back past the navigator's position and the radios, to the crew cabin.

The room was small and entirely functional. There was an electric galley along one side, with a porthole above it. The door to the crew toilet was forward and two Pullman-style bunks were opposite the galley. On the after side of the room a door led to the passenger cabin and beside it was a washbasin and mirror.

This room served the crew as a refuge during the long

overocean flights. Here the pilots could rest so they would be fresh when they approached their destination—the time when the demands on their alertness would normally be the heaviest. Leonard Wilby could leave his charts between hourly navigational fixes, and flip through a magazine. Spalding could escape the demands of her passengers long enough to smoke a cigarette or heat coffee for the crew.

Dan heard their voices as they came forward in the ship through the passenger cabin. He could hear Sullivan's above the rest, the firm, almost arrogant voice of a vigorous young man who had complete confidence in himself. Dan remembered when his own voice had sounded the same way—not really too long ago. It was before Alice and Tony, before he had begun to dream of flying and the dreams had sometimes become nightmares. Sullivan wouldn't understand; not yet, if he ever would. Like most professional pilots he would sleep like a child, never tormented by visions so sharp and tangible it was like living the holocaust all over again. He would probably never wake up screaming, and see the bundles that were people only a few moments before, smoking bundles, kicking in a final spasm before they were entirely still— pieces of them scattered over the ground, crazy, quivering pieces that could never be put back together. And then to wander dazedly among them, hoping, looking for something that could resemble your own, and knowing— that was the worst—*knowing* they had all trusted in you. If such a thing should ever happen to Sullivan, then his voice, too, would diminish until it became a little, thinking voice, hesitant and always slightly afraid, as if humility alone might wipe out his sin. Sullivan would sound like Dan Roman then, and the sound of his own voice would frequently appall him.

Sullivan came through the door first.

"Everything okay, Dan?" He tossed his briefcase onto the lower bunk, took off his coat, and loosened his tie. Leonard Wilby and Hobie Wheeler repeated his movements almost exactly.

"Three thousand and fifty aboard. There's a crack in the number-one exhaust stack, but it's not too bad."

"They'll get around to fixing it when we're old and

grey," Sullivan said, and then looked suddenly at the ceiling because any reference to age or greyness was obviously out of place when Dan Roman stood before him.

"How long does it look like?" Dan asked.

"Lennie says twelve hours and fifteen minutes . . . about."

Leonard Wilby laughed and moved forward to his station. He held up a cautioning finger and said, "Twelve hours and sixteen minutes . . . exactly."

As they moved forward to the flight deck almost together, Hobie Wheeler held back a little. Unlike the others he still wore his uniform cap. He took a quick side step so he could see himself in the mirror and after a moment's study made a delicate adjustment to his cap. He tried a slightly different angle, then removed the cap and tossed it onto the bunk beside the others. He ran a comb through his thick hair and, with a last smile at the mirror, turned forward to the flight deck.

They moved into their positions like musicians seating themselves before a concert. Sullivan sat down in the left seat and fastened his safety belt. He put on his earphones and began a slow survey of the instruments and controls which almost completely surrounded him. Dan sat down in the right seat and took off his tie. Just behind him Leonard pulled a chart out of his briefcase and carefully taped it to his navigation table. He laid out other papers in neat formation along the top of his table—the wind forecast, weather analysis, howgozit curve, log, and loran chart. He arranged his several pencils, his dividers and computers in a precise line, then put his briefcase beneath the table and sat down on his stool. Self-consciously at ease, Hobie leaned against the metal stanchion which ran vertically to the ceiling just behind Dan's seat. At the moment there was nothing for him to do. Later, when the flight was well under way and Sullivan was satisfied all was well, he would sit at the controls for a few hours at a time, alternating with the others.

"Let's get going on the check list," Sullivan said. Dan leaned forward and began to turn a small illuminated scroll. As he read off the items printed on it, Sullivan touched each one.

"Battery cart?"

"On."

"Seat belt, no smoking?"

"On."

"Hydraulic hand pump?"

"Closed."

"Cowl flaps?"

"Open."

"Mixtures?"

"Idle cutoff."

"Gear handle down and flaps up?"

"Check."

"Superchargers low? Autopilot off?"

"Check."

"Trim tabs set? Parking brakes on? Hydraulic pressure?"

"One thousand pounds."

"Props high rpm? And cross feed valves off?"

"Check."

"Carburetor heat?"

"Cold."

"Main tanks on? I checked the fuel quantity. Airspeed static selectors safetied?"

"Check."

"Pilot heaters? Anti-icer fluid?"

"Thirty-five gallons."

"Generators?"

"Off."

"Fire warning . . . test?"

Sullivan pressed a button beneath the crash pad. An alarm bell clanged behind his head and four red lights glowed along the instrument panel. After a moment the clanging ceased and the lights winked off.

"That about does it," Sullivan said. "Did you check the radios, Dan?"

"Yes."

"Hobie. Let me have the log book a minute." Hobie moved quickly to hand him a large metal-bound book. Opening it on his lap, Sullivan noted the time on each engine and then entered his name as captain. Without turning, he handed the book back over his shoulder to

Hobie. And now a peculiar, almost visible excitement passed among them; as if the crew themselves were eager passengers embarking on a long anticipated flight.

"Get your hardwood tray aboard, Lennie?"

"Yes, sir! Let's deliver it!"

Sullivan looked at the black-faced clock on the instrument panel. It was exactly twenty-two hundred Greenwich Time.

"Anybody out there, Dan?" Dan looked out of his window. A mechanic stood waiting with a fire bottle. The mechanic held up three fingers.

"Clear on number three!" Sullivan closed the master magneto switch while Dan reached for a switch on the ceiling to energize the starter and prime the number-three engine. He waited twenty seconds, then pushed the mesh switch. Sullivan advanced the number-three throttle slightly and watched the fuel-pressure gauges.

"Switch and boost!"

Their hands worked in perfect unison and suddenly the whole ship came to life. The number-three engine backfired once and settled to an even rumble. The hydraulic system whined and a pleasant vibration flowed through their legs. Strangely, it seemed to increase their own animation and they worked more quickly through the other three engines. As all four subsided into an even rhythm, Spalding came forward at a brisk walk.

"Pins aboard and sixteen passengers, Captain."

Sullivan turned to smile at her. "Only sixteen. You're on a vacation!"

"Nice people, too—" She was gone again before Hobie could be sure she heard him say that with so few passengers, she should have plenty of spare time for the crew.

"Meaning myself—" he murmured just loud enough to hope she alone would hear.

Dan Roman held a microphone to his thin lips.

"Honolulu tower from Four-two-zero. Ready to taxi."

His headphones, pushed well up on his temples, rattled the reply. "Roger, Four-two-zero. Cleared to runway four. Wind east at twelve miles. Altimeter . . . thirty-zero-one."

A tremor ran through the ship as Sullivan released the

brakes and gradually advanced the throttles. At the passenger gate, Alsop automatically waved his hand in farewell although no one was looking back at him. Then he turned his back to avoid the propeller blast.

4

THOUGH IT WAS TWO MINUTES PAST NOON AND SO TWO minutes past his lunch time, the thin man who was called "Breezy" by the other controllers could not leave his post in the airy room atop the administration building until his relief arrived. Before him, on a vertical board, were bits of paper representing the positions and altitudes of all the airplanes in the Honolulu control area. Philippine Airlines was at fourteen thousand feet on the way in from Wake Island—estimating Honolulu at twelve-fifty-six. British Commonwealth Pacific had already passed beneath them at twelve thousand, westbound. A flight of six Navy Panthers was coming in from bombing practice in area "B"; Pan American and United were ten minutes apart at nine thousand, just east of Maui intersection. Breezy had the contents of the atmosphere at his fingertips but the sweep of mileage, the millions of square acres it was his duty to police, could not be considered as nourishment. If I'm not relieved in five minutes, Breezy thought, I will start chewing on this telephone. He reached out with his lips and took an experimental nibble at the chest phone which curved toward his mouth. How could a man keep airplanes from running into each other when he was starving to death? Concentration on altitudes and positions was impossible on a rumbling stomach. But United wanted to let down, Pan American was yelling for further clearance, and Four-two-zero wouldn't sit on the end of the runway waiting forever. Breezy pressed the switch on the desk before him.

"Tower?"

"Roger."

"Clearance for Sullivan—Four-two-zero."

"Shoot."

"Via green airways North Dog line to San Francisco airport . . . to maintain seven thousand . . . climb visual flight rules to Mokopu point maintaining well to right of course until past North Maui."

"He wants nine thousand."

"Well, he can't have it. Pan Am is coming down through. He can stand by for further clearance at fourteen hundred hours if he wants."

"Roger. Will advise. Why so grumpy?"

"I'm hungry. My sonofabitching relief must be taking a siesta."

Spalding moved slowly down the aisle checking on her passengers' safety belts. For once there had been no quick maneuvering for seats. Everyone who cared about it had a window to himself and her passengers were distributed all over the cabin. Too far, Spalding thought, for their own enjoyment. A few games of bridge later would bring them together. The newlywed Bucks were away up forward, huddled together in silent pleasure. That Mr. Flaherty, still distinguished-looking in spite of his obvious hangover, had also gone forward, picking his way carefully along the seats like a blind man. He sat down opposite the Bucks and closed his eyes. Sleep would do him good. Then, Kenneth Childs, already surrounded by a fence of newspapers. He looked much older with his glasses.

"Our forecast flight time is twelve hours and sixteen minutes, Mr. Childs."

"Thank you." He looked up, smiled mechanically, and went back to his newspaper.

Remember, special attention for Mr. Childs. Then Miss Holst opposite him looking out the window. If she couldn't sit right next to Ken Childs, she had made a good beginning, anyway. Only two empty seats separated them. As Spalding passed down the aisle, she held up her hand.

"Miss? What time would that make us arrive in San Francisco?"

"About two-thirty in the morning. They're two hours ahead of us, you know."

"What a hell of an hour to arrive anywhere!" She looked across the aisle to see if Ken Childs had heard her, but if he did, his attention remained with his paper.

The Pardees sat behind May Holst. Gustave Pardee of Broadway, Spalding remembered. He already looked like he had flown all night.

"May I take your coat, Mrs. Pardee?"

"Yes, please."

Spalding took a deep breath as her fingers touched the lush mink. A coat like this could cover a multitude of faults—in the woman, and more so in the man who bought it. Even the rumpled, sad-eyed Gustave Pardee.

Miss McKee was next—opposite and one row behind the Pardees. Was it Miss or Mrs? Well, it never hurt to call a Mrs. Miss. The plane turned and the hot sun moved the shape of the window across her face. If she so much as squints, Spalding thought, her make-up will break off in a million pieces. Her hands were folded across her lap.

"Seat belt fastened, Miss McKee?" Spalding bent over her and was surprised at the honest warmth behind her smile.

"Oh yes."

"Let me know if you need anything. My name is Miss Spalding."

"Thank you."

The man with the missing fingers sat directly behind her. Locota? Lokata? Sweet little man, with an astonished friz of hair standing up along the rim of his bald head. Alsop said he was a nobody. With those deep, kind brown eyes?

"Everything all right, Mr. Locota?"

"Oh yes, yes!" He nodded and his whole face lit up. His grin revealed two missing front teeth. There might be several things missing about the physical Mr. Locota

40

—check on that name spelling—but inside he was all man. "Will we fly very high?" he asked apologetically, as if he had no right to ask such a question.

"Seven or nine thousand feet, sir. It depends on our clearance." The "sir" surprised him even more than Spalding thought it would. She left him puzzled and still grinning.

Mr. Briscoe was directly across the aisle. He was sitting away from the window though the seat by it was empty. Mr. Briscoe looked very sick. He was staring at his carefully polished high-top shoes when Spalding moved to his side.

"Don't you want to sit by the window, Mr. Briscoe? There's plenty of room today." He looked up at once. The despair—Spalding wondered if she hadn't been mistaken about that—vanished from his eyes. She found them full of quiet humor.

"You know somp'n, young lady? This was as far as the old carcass would go. I'd rather look at you than what's outside anyhow." He said it without the slightest suggestion of a leer and Spalding knew she was going to like Mr. Briscoe.

"Your seat belt isn't fastened. Shame on you." He squirmed in his seat and attempted to reach the belt, but a grimace of pain flashed over his face. He fell back against the seat, smiling—and Spalding was certain the smile was not easy. She reached across his lap to bring the belt together.

"My arm," he said, still holding the smile, "it just won't bend around like it should. Holes in my bones or so they tell me."

"I can't see any holes, Mr. Briscoe."

He laughed and the strength returned to his voice. "You know somp'n, miss? Neither can I."

The man behind Mr. Briscoe was crouched far down in his seat. He was staring at something away forward and Spalding found herself following the line of his stare. She found nothing to deserve such intense concentration. This was the man who had come running up last . . . Andrews? . . . no, Agnew. Humphrey Agnew, with the shaking, tobacco-stained fingers. Now she saw that he wore a small pearl stickpin in his tie and his eyes seemed

41

to bulge even more than when he came to the counter. There was something about Mr. Agnew that frightened Spalding. He looked as though he were about to spring out of his seat. Passengers on their first flight were sometimes that way just before take-off, but there was something else bothering Mr. Agnew. Spalding broke a rule of her own and passed him by without greeting.

The Rices and the Josephs sat in a line of four seats across the plane. Mr. Joseph, his head sticking incongruously out of the concentric rings of flower leis, was waving his hands importantly as he talked across the aisle to Howard Rice. Mr. Joseph, Spalding thought, had already won her vote as the man she would least like to be marooned with on a raft. Starvation would not be the problem since boredom would take over first. His mouth had been going ever since she first laid eyes on him and now he had cornered Mr. Rice, who apparently wasn't quick-witted enough to seat himself further away.

"May I take your coat, Mrs. Rice?" The diminutive woman handed it to her as if she was throwing it away. Another mink, as good if not better than Mrs. Pardee's. Spalding pressed them together across her arm, but this time there was no pleasure in it. She wondered if her sudden hatred of mink were merely envy.

"Would you like to have me take your leis, Mr. Joseph? I'll put them in a cool place and they'll keep better."

"Now, that's just about the smartest idea anybody ever had," Ed Joseph said expansively. "Gotta make 'em last as long as we can, you know . . . gotta get back to the old salt mines tomorrow!" He began to lift the leis from his neck and his wife obediently followed his motions. She handed hers to Spalding and giggled.

"Mahalo nui . . . that's thank you in Hawaiian."

"This one was given to me compliments of the management," Ed Joseph said, holding up a pikaki lei. Then he raised his voice so it almost reached the length of the cabin. "We stayed at the Royal Hawaiian."

"I'm so glad you enjoyed yourself," Spalding said.

"Yup, yup. Say . . . come here a minute." He reached for Spalding's wrist and pulled her down until her face was close to his own. He spoke as a conspirator, keeping his voice just loud enough for his wife and Howard Rice to hear.

"Say, let me tell you something. If we get into any trouble . . . you know, serious trouble the pilot can't handle . . . you just have him send for Ed Joseph. I'd be glad to go up there and help him out if he really needs me. Got it?"

As he released Spalding's hand with a confidential pat, Clara Joseph giggled until Spalding thought she might choke. Howard Rice smiled wanly.

"I got it, Mr. Joseph. I'll let you know if you're needed." She stepped away with a sigh of relief. At least with his wife so close to him Mr. Joseph would have a hard time being much of a wolf.

Spalding hung the coats carefully in the rear of the ship and then placed the leis in a special compartment in the women's lounge. She returned to the cabin just as the plane came to a stop and sat down next to Miss Chen.

"Do you mind if I sit beside you during take-off?"

"Oh, no. I would be so pleased."

They studied each other openly for a moment. We are the same age, Spalding thought, and yet she is so much older than I am, so much more beautiful.

"I am happy you wish to sit next to me," Miss Chen said solemnly, "because I have been watching you walk down the aisle and have the desire to say a thing to you."

"I forgot to take your coat. Oh, I am sorry—let me—"

"No. It is quite all right beside me now. I only wish to ask the information if all American girls are like you. Because I must say you are the first real alive one I have ever greeted in person." It wasn't so much the very faint accent, Spalding thought, as the melody and rhythm of speech that made her voice so enchanting. She smiled, not knowing what to answer.

"You are so very beautiful," Miss Chen said as if the discovery pleased her immensely, "I fear I shall feel terribly the ugly one if all the girls in America are so beautiful and kind."

Spalding swallowed and sensed that she was blushing outrageously. What kind of girl talk was this?

"I don't think you're going to have to worry about a thing." She was grateful when she heard the engine run-up begin outside the windows because Miss Chen's obvious sincerity had left her completely disarmed.

Dan Roman checked the free movement of the flaps and the fuel cross feed system as they taxied to the end of the runway. Now stationary again, he worked with Sullivan and their hands moved with the deftness of surgeons as they checked the magnetos on all four engines and then the propeller feathering mechanisms. When they were satisfied each engine would deliver its rated power, when they had set their gyros and altimeters and uncaged their artificial horizons, when they knew as certainly as they could ever know that all of the temperatures and pressures were exactly as they should be, then once more they went through the printed check list. For no matter how many times they had repeated this exact routine, a chant that through years of repetition was engraved on their memories—they knew better than to trust their memories. This was not an adventure and it was not a time for lightness. It was the opening of a business in which the penalties for failure could be more final than bankruptcy. As professionals they recognized that, regardless of near mechanical perfection, there were and always would be certain penalties for movement. Their training and experience had all been aimed toward eliminating these hazards, or to overcome them quickly if they should occur. The plane in which they sat had been conceived by men whose passion was the conquest of gravity; clever, brilliant men who hammered their dreams into realistic machines of marvelous efficiency. And yet when their work was completed they were nearly helpless to insure the final result, for even their genius could not control the design of a pilot's mind. The burden in the end, fell upon men like Sullivan with his big sure hands, and Dan Roman with his always deeply troubled eyes. Their pride in their part of the endeavor, their total absorption in this little time before the take-off, was an unlikely mixture of emotion and cold concern with numerical facts. Hobie

Wheeler could not as yet fully appreciate either the pleasure or the seriousness of their mood. He thought their reactions slow and overcautious. This was, after all, just another flying machine. Given the chance of command, he would have been off the ground two minutes before. Now waiting, unable in his innocence to pace his thinking with the others, he looked up through the astrodome and yawned at the sun.

"Tower from Four-two-zero. Ready to go."

"Roger, Four-two-zero. Clear for take-off."

Sullivan advanced the throttles slowly, keeping the power equal to the four engines with a slight twisting motion of his wrist. The instrument panel came alive as the needles recording oil pressure, fuel flow, rpm, and manifold pressure began to swing around their dials.

Sullivan watched the instruments, hardly bothering to glance at the runway ahead, and Dan also watched them carefully. For there was still time to yank the throttles back and slam on the brakes if a single indication of trouble occurred. But the needles were steady and when Sullivan was entirely satisfied, he left the throttles to Dan. His own hands sought the control wheel. When the air-speed read eighty miles an hour he pulled back slightly on the control yoke—just enough to raise the nose wheel off the ground. The runway slipped rapidly back beneath the windows, its great length consumed as if it were wound upon a swiftly turning roller.

The air-speed climbed rapidly. At a hundred and twenty miles an hour Sullivan pulled back still further on the column and suddenly there was flight. The runway sank and Sullivan extended the palm of his hand. He raised it upward in a concise gesture of command.

"Gear up!"

Hobie, standing just beside him, reached forward to pull up the landing gear lever. Three green lights on the instrument panel blinked out. The hydraulic system sucked up the heavy wheels and struts as the air speed increased rapidly. Sullivan held the nose down, for speed was safety. Now with a hundred and thirty miles an hour one engine could fail and the loss could be handled with relative ease—with a hundred and forty-five miles an hour, two engines could fail and still they could make it back to earth in safety. Neither Sullivan nor Dan expected either one of these difficulties to occur, but they were ready and wary if they did.

"Thirty-five inches and twenty-two fifty rpm." Sullivan spoke clearly and distinctly so there could be no mistake, not because he had the slightest fear Dan might misunderstand him, but because it was good doctrine to give commands in a manner no one could misinterpret. The air-speed climbed to one hundred and fifty miles an hour—the altimeter wound smoothly around to five hundred feet.

"Flaps up! . . . five degrees at a time." Sullivan pitched his voice just above the sound of the engines and the gradually increasing woosh of air through the flight-deck ventilators.

"Climb power!"

Dan pulled the throttles back still further and then the propeller controls, adjusting them with his sensitive fingers until the three synchroscopes, which so resembled swimming golliwoggs, settled and the four engines beat as one.

"Off the ground at twelve!" Leonard called from his station, noting the exact minute of take-off.

Now the professionals were open for business. As the Aloha Tower slipped beneath the left wing and Sullivan made a turn away from the beaches toward Diamond Head, Dan picked up his microphone.

"Honolulu tower from Four-two-zero, we'll be off and clear."

"Roger, Four-two-zero. Good trip and so long."

Dan leaned toward the radio panel and switched to the frequency they would guard for the next twelve hours.

"This is Four-two-zero calling Honolulu Overseas Radio. How do you read?"

A voice stronger and clearer than the tower returned to him. "Roger, Four-two-zero. Read you loud and clear. Your reporting time twenty minutes past the hour."

"We were off Honolulu at twelve. Climbing to seven thousand."

Somewhere in the sunlight below a man Dan Roman had never seen, a man whose stomach grumbled with hunger, made an angry notation on a slip of paper and slipped it into place. There was a single word of acknowledgment and then only silence.

"Honolulu. . . ."

The moment the no smoking sign went out Humphrey Agnew stopped caressing his stickpin and reached into his pocket for a cigarette. His yellow fingers trembled as he put it between his lips. He flicked his lighter a number of times before it ignited—all the strength seemed to have left his fingers, until the mere twisting of the miniature wheel became an effort. He sucked heavily on the cigarette and then exhaled the smoke in an audible sigh. He was replacing the lighter in his pocket when his hand reversed its motion and came back to his lap. His thumb traveled slowly over the engraving on the lighter, feeling the words he knew so well. *For My Darling Husband—Martha.* And then half an inch below those words, the date—*1950.* A gift from Mrs. Agnew to Mr. Agnew on their first anniversary. A gift from a woman of thirty who professed to be pure, to a man of forty-five who had spent all of his waking moments building security, scheming and ignoring the insults of other men so that one day he might be able to spit on them.

He squeezed the lighter tightly until his knuckles were white, then he suddenly threw it on the floor. If there were some who had called Humphrey Agnew cunning, the now Mrs. Agnew would see how really clever her husband could be. The whore would twist in her misery—knowing for the rest of her life, without being able to tell anyone, how Kenneth Childs came to die. It made a pretty picture. The dead lover and the living slut. Martha would be the lover's last conquest. She could weep while Humphrey Agnew laughed. Laughed and *kept* her, forever. No lawyer in the world could take her away. No judge would refuse the money Humphrey Agnew was willing to pay to keep Martha Agnew, Mrs. Agnew. Wife-in-hatred, to a man whose genius had made them rich. Everyone would know about *that.* . . . Oh yes! And they would know by inference, by words

47

dropped in just the right way, that Martha Agnew had been faithless, and probably would be again. Men would look at her and think, and Humphrey Agnew would help them with their thinking.

Cigarette hanging from his mouth, he gripped the arms of his chair and closed his eyes a moment that he might see the vision better. The steps of his office building, for example; headquarters of fast-growing Agnew's Aids to Better Life—from which all monetary blessings flowed. Arthritis?—Ague?—Asthma?—Bladder Trouble?—Biliousness?—Cancer?—Colonic Disorder?—Diabetes?—Agnew's Aids had a curing pill for all of them, at only one dollar the bottle. Your money back if not satisfied, and Humphrey Agnew had always been careful to soothe those few who asked for their money back. Why not? There were always new thousands to believe the radio and the generous advertisements in the Islands' newspapers. Ignorance, mass ignorance waiting for exploitation, was the one and only thing a man could depend upon.

Let's see now . . . you would be standing there on the steps and another couple, the Listers maybe, would chance by . . . about noon, say. And because Amos Lister made bottles and would like to have the Agnew account, he would invite the Agnews to lunch with them. And Martha would be about to say, "How nice," when you could break in with something like, ". . . it's a fine idea but I'm afraid Martha has made another engagement . . . she's a very popular girl, you know." Martha would look at you bewildered because this might be the first time you had been in Honolulu. after it was all over.

She might say later, after the Listers had walked away, "Humphrey . . . I haven't any engagement." And you could answer, "Really? I thought you always had lunch with Ken Childs, or is he losing out?"

Then would come the joker, the real twist that would go on until she admitted everything. Martha could come right out and say, "Ken Childs is dead," or she might try to cover with a half-truth. "If it makes you so unhappy, I'll never see Ken Childs again." Indeed she would not. For there the man sat, just a few seats away. And here Humphrey Agnew sat—waiting.

It was wonderful how the resolve to do a certain thing could wipe away the nausea. It was probably a very good thing so few people knew how exhilarating the idea of killing a man could be. You were suddenly lighter than one of those clouds out the window, floating in the same way after so many days of heaviness. The joker would be when you said, "Yes, Martha. For once you've told the truth. Ken Childs is dead. I killed him and you know why." Oh, her face then! Ah . . . her eyes! "I killed him in San Francisco and if you wish to be the cause of two deaths, why don't you call the police?"

His fingers traveled back to his stickpin, then he leaned to the window and looked down at the water. It would only be a few hours, hardly more than a day and a night before he would be back in Honolulu. He would not be missed at the office—a phone call explaining a touch of fever had taken care of that. Only Martha would know he had ever left the Island. And Martha, beautiful, faithless Martha, would know at last that she was married to a man instead of an easy cuckold. She would keep still.

There was time to relax and complete every detail now, because Ken Childs could never slip away. He was locked in a floating room with Martha's husband, living out his last hours without knowing it for the deliciously simple reason that Martha had never felt it necessary to bother with an introduction. She was obviously ashamed of her husband. The gun would be your introduction, the gun in your coat pocket . . . resting there so quietly, pressing against your chest, hard and almost alive.

Spalding's voice broke his reverie.

"You dropped your lighter, Mr. Agnew." She was holding it toward him in her hand.

Startled, he answered her curtly. "It's . . . it's not mine. I'm not married."

"Oh. . . ."

"Bring me some matches."

"Of course, Mr. Agnew."

Before she went to the rear of the ship for the matches Spalding bent over Frank Briscoe, who sat just one seat ahead.

"Did you drop this lighter, Mr. Briscoe?"

"Not me, honey. I don't smoke."

"Oh, I'm sorry. I thought it might have slipped to the floor behind your seat."

"Anyway, my wife's name was Helen."

When Spalding brought the matches, Agnew took them with a broad smile. He called himself a fool. How many Marthas were there in the world? If this girl read about the death of Ken Childs tomorrow in the newspapers, even this stupid girl might begin to wonder. She might remember the name on the lighter. Watch these little things, Humphrey Agnew. You wouldn't allow a mistake like this in your business. Such tiny mistakes, made because there hadn't been time for the most careful thinking, might start a whole chain of investigation. It could conceivably make things difficult. It was wrong to deny the lighter simply because you hated it. From now on, for the next few hours do absolutely nothing, except sit and think. Hold every detail as if it were made of tissue paper and examine it most carefully. There is plenty of time.

"Here are your matches, Mr. Agnew."

"Oh, thank you very much."

"If you want anything else, just ring the button over your head."

"Tell me . . . what happens when you find an expensive lighter . . . like that one must have been?"

"What happens?"

"Yes. It doesn't seem to belong to anyone aboard now."

"I turn it in to the lost and found. Usually the owner will inquire about it."

"Yes. . . ." He gave Spalding the same smile that adorned his advertisements. "Yes . . . I suppose the owner would."

From her seat directly opposite him, May Holst could easily observe every move Kenneth Childs made. It was not the first time she had watched him; they had stayed at the same hotel and she had seen him on the beach during the day and in the bar at night. She liked his face even more now than the first time she had seen him. Good whisky had smoothed the bone structure here and there and a few more years would probably find him too heavy around the jowls, but there was still great strength in that mouth and jaw. His eyebrows were grey, undisciplined fuzzes protruding defiantly from his forehead, and below them the crinkles around his eyes spoked outward as if waiting for a good belly laugh to set them in action. Everything about him, May decided, from his blue eyes to the way his strong knobby hands moved his newspaper, spoke of virility, an increasingly rare quality in men these days, she decided. And the guy was loaded with the long green, obviously. A man who was not loaded would never dare cock his cigarette holder in the air the way Ken Childs did, or bang through the newspaper, slapping it into place contemptuously, as if he already knew what it had to say. But when he reached the stock market page, he would slow down to check up on how his long green was doing. Just as Sterling had once done.

For a moment she looked away from Ken Childs, forgetting him entirely while she remembered Sterling. She was walking in the early morning rain with him again, hand in hand, as they had done almost every morning for fifteen wonderful years.

"I guess you're just about the most wonderful mistress a man ever found. . . ." She could almost hear his strong, clear voice.

"You didn't find me. I found you . . . a little drunk, but there you were."

"I was plastered."

"You had reason to be." It was possible to say things like that to Sterling later on, but during the first few years he was touchy about his reasons for drinking. Touchy and belligerent like he was the first night he reeled into the joint and yelled for a girl. The one he got was May Ladzeny—just a kid trying to get the hell away from the poorest Polish family in Toledo. When Sam, who ran the joint, introduced you as May, a new hostess, Sterling thought he said Holst—or so it sounded through the ringing of champagne in his ears. So May Holst it was, from that first night when you half-dragged him back to your little flat and put him to bed. And

May Holst it still was, legal now, and forever. It was also the last night you worked at Sam's joint. Sterling took over in his own fashion. It wasn't love until much later. He set up the apartment and bought the clothes, the best of everything, and gradually you became the kind of a woman he didn't have to be ashamed of on the street or anywhere else. You found out about his wife, one of those broads who spent her life in bed, for everything but the right reason.

"She's a professional invalid," Sterling said, and that was all he ever said about her. It was all you wanted to hear. Surprising how it lasted, and how quickly those fifteen years flew by. Never a trip together, never really a whole night together except the first one, but he dropped by the apartment, or at least called, every day. And there were always those early-morning walks. It was worth rousing out at seven, no matter what had gone on the night before, just to see the pleasure on his face when he met you at the special corner. It was a two-mile walk to his plant, sometimes clumping through snow, sometimes laughing along easily in the sunshine. But mostly it seemed to be raining and the walk back to the apartment alone became a good time for thinking how much you loved the man.

Then that morning when there wasn't any Sterling waiting on the corner. And the paper said there never would be again, because a heart as big as the man had stopped, in the middle of the night. Sterling paid for this trip, as he had paid for the rest of May Holst's life.

"I want you to be comfortable," he said. "It makes me happy."

All right, Sterling . . . your gal is comfortable. The Polish is beginning to show around the hips and there's the beginning of another chin you wouldn't care for . . . but you left me without a thing to worry about, so I'm as comfortable as I ever could be, without you.

The plane turned and the sunlight blazing on the wing almost blinded her. She turned quickly away from the window and knew almost at once that Ken Childs had been watching her.

5

As the ship turned on course, Mokopu Point, the last land they would see for more than two thousand miles, slipped away beneath the left wing. Consuming three hundred and fifty gallons per hour in the climb, the engines snored evenly. The altimeter unwound past three thousand feet as Leonard Wilby apologized to Hobie and, pushing past him, taped a small piece of paper on the instrument panel just beside Sullivan's gyro compass. On the paper he had written the figure 51—the initial compass course toward San Francisco.

"Let's try that for size," he said.

Sullivan looked over his shoulder and smiled. "Are you sure it's not just plain fifty, Lennie? Do we have to make it exactly fifty-one?"

Leonard was willing to go along because the one degree in question would not make the slightest difference in the flight as a whole. He had deliberately chosen the odd figure to start comment.

"As you know, Skipper, navigation is an exact science. When Wilby says the course should be fifty-one, it means that if you desire to carry out a perfect flight, you should have no truck with a loose fifty."

Dan glanced out of his window and, after studying the

ocean below for a moment, turned back into the cockpit and shook his head solemnly.

"I dunno, Lennie . . . the surface wind is from the north. Don't you consider a course of, say, forty-nine would be better? After all, it's so soon . . . what have you really got to go on?"

Leonard looked at the floor and then at the elaborate instrument panel as if he might discover his answer there. These were the moments of flying he would like to capture and take home to his wife Susie, telling her about them, so she might have some remote idea why he had no ambition to become anything other than a navigator. In many ways they were the best part of every flight, no matter where in the world it was bound. For it seemed that during the climb the crew became strangely exhilarated, their voices were a little higher than normal, their movements quick. Everyone was fresh and rested. If there had been any ill humor it usually slipped away during this time. It could be the sensation of rising, so pronounced here on the flight deck, had a way of severing the crew from anything on earth not only physically but spiritually. Leonard had tried to analyze this behavior many times. He knew it occurred within himself and he could always see it in others— but he had never had much success with his analysis. He rubbed his big nose thoughtfully, as if giving Dan's question the most serious consideration.

"Well, I tell you, Dan. Us amateurs don't really know the way to San Francisco. Now some experts might go so far as to pick forty-nine degrees for a course and get there eventually. But it just so happens I'm fifty-one years of age this month and I can't seem to think of any other number."

"Fifty-one it is then," Sullivan said. "Seems like a very sound reason to me."

At five thousand feet they brushed through a layer of broken clouds. The ship heaved a few times and a droplet army of moisture squirmed across the windshields. Then suddenly they broke out on top and the air was perfectly smooth. The ship swam upward without apparent guidance or effort, like a great silver whale rising from the depths. Sunlight filled the flight deck, the glare causing the ship's marks of utility and age to stand out garishly. The feet of countless pilots had worn the paint from her rudder pedals and the screw drivers of innumerable mechanics had scarred the areas around the fastenings which held the instrument panel in place. The leather on the crash pad took on a withered look and the placards above Sullivan's head which diagrammed the ship's intricate fuel system and maximum take-off performance, looked faded. The sun, streaming down through the astrodome in the top of the flight deck, revealed a few scratches on the curved plexiglass. Hitting the red linoleum floor, the glare exaggerated the hundreds of dents and scufflings where the flight crews, mechanics, cleaners, and baggage handlers had left their marks. And above Leonard's table the paint around the porthole was beginning to peel.

"This bucket is about due for an eight-thousand-hour overhaul," Hobie said. He had the metal log book open on his knee and was writing down the instrument readings during the climb in a long column of printed boxes.

"How many hours does she have now?" Dan asked.

Hobie studied the log book. "Seven thousand four hundred and twenty."

"She's practically a virgin. This ship will be flying long after you and I are gone."

"Maybe you . . . but not me." Hobie said it laughing, but Dan knew that he was right. There were a lot of scratches and dents on Dan Roman, too.

Sullivan reset his altimeter to standard pressure so that it would match all the other ships over the Pacific. When they reached seven thousand three hundred feet, he rolled the stabilizer forward slightly and began a gradual descent back to exactly seven thousand. By exceeding his assigned altitude slightly and then sliding back down to it, he put the ship "on the step." During the first hours of any long flight when most of the fuel weight had yet to be consumed, this was a delicate and sometimes frustrating maneuver. It required him to combine the intelligence he received from the instruments and from the seat of his pants to sense that fine point at which the ship flew with maximum efficiency, instead of merely wallowing through the sky. The ship was poised on an invisible fulcrum; the most minute adjustment of the controls could make as much as ten miles an hour difference in air speed. To gain the precise balance required under varied conditions of load and atmosphere, was a matter of considerable pride among many pilots. For in this single instance humans were more sensitive than instruments and so the pilots left science almost entirely and returned with considerable satisfaction to art.

Now the tempo of operation became easy and deliberate. It required only a nod of Sullivan's head for Dan to know he was ready to reduce power. The altitude and the temperature of the outside air both governed the setting Dan would give the propellers and the throttles. Although he could have guessed almost the exact setting required, he consulted both the carburetor air temperature gauges and the graph above his head before he slowly pulled back on the levers. At two thousand rpm the engines settled to a low rumble. He closed the cowl flaps, for now the ship's increased speed would cool the engines sufficiently. Then he bent across the control pedestal to move the mixture levers down into the cruising slot. The fuel flow meters swung down to two hundred gallons per hour.

Dan toyed with the propeller controls; though the synchroscopes were reasonably steady, there was still a beat among the four engines which annoyed him. There were those pilots who would not have cared about the beat; the extra concentration and care required to eliminate it would hardly have been worth the trouble. But Dan was not that kind of a pilot and he knew Sullivan was not. It would be a mark of censure if Sullivan had to reach over later and make an adjustment in the propellers. He would not say anything, but he would think Dan Roman was inclined to be sloppy about details. And sloppy pilots were the hyenas of the profession. They had been known to kill themselves and their passengers.

After a few minutes Sullivan was satisfied that he had the ship on the step. The air-speed registered one hundred and seventy-eight miles per hour which pleased him. Still holding the control wheel tenderly, he pulled a small circular slide rule from his shirt pocket and, fingering the discs to correspond with the ship's altitude and the outside air temperature, he found the true speed to be one hundred and ninety-five miles an hour. No longer preoccupied with the ship's performance, he reached forward and adjusted the knobs on the automatic pilot. He engaged it and then sat back to light a cigarette.

"Anyone up here like a cup of coffee?" Spalding was suddenly standing just behind Sullivan and Dan. Her appearance was so without warning, it was a moment before any of them could break their concentration on flying. There was something unnatural about a girl standing on the flight deck—a hard place, composed of metal and instruments and controls which tolerated only the most logical thinking. A girl in these surroundings could only seem more feminine than she might upon the ground; her softness became obvious almost to the point of embarrassment. In Spalding's case, the faint scent of her perfume took over entirely where there had been only the odor of leather and hydraulic oil. Her presence on the flight deck had a remarkable effect upon the crew. On the ground they had almost ignored Spalding, but now their gestures became exaggerated and their voices more animated. The shaft of sunlight that came down from the astrodome formed a golden band around her head and shoulders and even Sullivan unbent long enough to sigh audibly. Hobie, in a moment of youthful exuberance, turned his head and pretended to gnaw on the metal stanchion.

"Spalding," Dan Roman said solemnly, "you're the best-looking thing these tired eyes have seen since the Civil War."

"I know . . . you were flying a Confederate balloon then," she laughed.

"Not quite. The Spanish Civil War, honey. Just bring old Dan a straight black coffee."

"Cream and sugar in mine," Sullivan said.

"I'll help you make it," Hobie offered eagerly. He left his stanchion and started for the crew cabin.

"How's everybody getting along back in your department?" Sullivan asked.

"They're all happy . . . but I have one weirdie."

"Come again?"

"Weirdie. I always draw at least one. Look at this." She handed Sullivan the gold-plated lighter.

He examined it curiously and then passed it across to Dan. "Expensive. Where did you get it?"

"I found it on the floor next to a funny little man who claims it isn't his."

"Seems like a person would be glad to get something like that back if he lost it."

"That's what I think. He was smoking a cigarette when I came up to him, yet the first thing he asked me for was matches."

"Maybe he made fire by friction," Hobie said. He was disappointed when no one laughed.

"He said it couldn't be his because anyway he wasn't married."

"He could have been."

"I checked on the immigration form and he told them he was married."

Sullivan made a brief and thoughtful examination of the instrument panel. He leaned forward and turned the rudder knob on the automatic pilot until the magnetic compass read exactly fifty-one degrees.

"Sounds to me like you've got a wolf instead of a weirdie. He's after something. Probably you."

"Not this one. I've had plenty of wolves in my short time . . . experts. I've seen approaches they never taught us in stewardess training class . . . but this fellow has something else on his mind."

"Call on me if you need your honor defended," Hobie said.

Spalding raised an eyebrow. "And jump from the frying pan into the fire?" She turned back to Sullivan.

"When you have a little time, I wish you'd come back and talk to one of my passengers."

"Sure. After a while."

"He's Mr. Pardee . . . the big rumpled-looking man sitting halfway back on the right. Alsop said he had something to do with the theater."

"What's his problem? Don't tell me he wants to put you on the stage?"

"Nothing could be further from his mind right now.

58

He's just the original frightened Freddie. Everytime you change propeller pitch or bank a wing he goes all white and grabs his seat like it was an electric chair."

"All right." Conversation with groundlings was always difficult, but the company held that it was part of a captain's duty. Sullivan sighed and worked the knobs at the end of his jaw unhappily.

"Okay . . . okay."

"You can't miss him. He looks like a great Saint Bernard who can't find his way down a mountain. While you're at it, have a word with the Korean girl in the last seat. She's nice."

Spalding stood on her toes for a moment looking over their shoulders at the blue sea below, then she turned back to the crew compartment, pausing just long enough to whisper in Hobie's ear. "Come see me when you grow up, junior."

After she served the coffee, Spalding smoked half of a cigarette and then crushed it in the paper cup which served Leonard as an ashtray. Smoking was a recently acquired habit and she was already sorry she had ever begun. It was messy and unclean, she thought—it stained the teeth and it was boring. She deliberately left her package of cigarettes on the flight deck and resolved to forget them for the rest of the trip.

Before she returned to her passengers, she paused by the mirror in the crew cabin for a quick check on her appearance. She touched a strand of hair into place and then opened her lips to examine her teeth. Yes, smoking was beginning to stain them. It was disgusting. She would be strong and never touch another cigarette.

She was just closing her lips when the mirror shivered. Her face was thrown completely out of focus, as if she had been bending over a clear pool and someone had thrown a pebble into her image. It was a sharp jolt, different from the ship's normal vibration, yet it was over so quickly she was not sure it had really happened. "Even the mirror protests," she murmured. She spoke so softly the actual sound of her voice was lost against the steady rumble of the engines.

She turned to the main cabin door, still thinking of the mirror. It was a silly idea. She had looked in the mir-

59

ror a hundred times before . . . and it had never objected. And hadn't there been a definite shock against the soles of her feet, as if something had slapped at them from below? If there really had been, should she tell Sullivan about it? But how could it have anything to do with the ship? Sullivan would only laugh at her reason for standing in front of the mirror.

Spalding shrugged her shoulders and entered the main cabin. It meant nothing to her that the mirror was in an exact line with the ship's propellers.

"What in the world are you crying about, Nell?" Milo Buck asked his bride. "Golly . . . there's nothing to turn on the waterworks about that I can see." They were in the first seats in the cabin and so were almost isolated except for the man with the bristly grey mustache who sat alone on the opposite side of the plane. "Golly, Nell . . . have I said something or done something to bring on the waterworks?" His only answer was a delicate sniffle, followed by a quick little catching of her breath. He thought she sounded like one of his old hot rods trying to get started when the points weren't adjusted just right, but he decided not to mention it. You never knew how Nell was going to take things since she was so entirely different from any other woman in the world. *Entirely* different. She could ski and swim like a man, and cook like her mother, on top of which she was strictly a good head. Then her hair was blond with only a little help from the hairdresser, and except for the freckles which just happened to be extremely attractive on Nell, her face was just about all any man could ask for. She had a terrible temper and flew off in a rage in all directions sometimes, yes—but the thing to do then, was just tackle her around the hips and sling her to the floor for a good wrestling match. It was strenuous sometimes because she was far from an easy match with those shoulders of hers, but the results were always remarkable. After a few minutes of to and fro she always started laughing and finally gave out with little yelps for mercy. Then you were both panting and excited and if there was no one around the finale was always the same. Nell

60

was a long ways from being cold and when she had a good hold on you she didn't like to let go. But now she was weeping like someone had turned on the Shasta Dam floodgates.

Milo reviewed the events of the past two weeks as well as he could remember them. There was the marriage in San Francisco, which was already a little vague in his mind. The Honolulu trip for a wedding present was a last-minute surprise gift from the familes and it had required so much scurrying around to get Nell the right clothes, the ceremony just had to sort of fit in between things. But it didn't matter too much to anyone except Nell's mother because if Nell *hadn't* finally become Mrs. Buck everyone would just have wondered, that's all. Now it was done and Nell was crying for the first time since you had known her and it was confusing in the extreme. Fights, yes—there had been some whistlers, but this left a man with the damnedest helpless feeling because there just wasn't any reason for it.

"Now listen, Nell . . . be reasonable. We promised each other we'd never hold back no matter what we had to say, remember? If I did something wrong, tell me about it and I'll try to explain—" This was very embarrassing. Suppose the guy across the aisle woke up and saw Nell crying like this, or the stewardess, or the pilot came along—they'd think you were abusing your wife. *Wife!* That word was going to take some getting used to! "Aw cut it out, Nell."

"I'm . . . I'm trying to. I just can't . . . that's all." Her breath caught again and Milo pressed his handkerchief into her hand. She blew her nose very delicately and tried to wipe her eyes.

"You want some water, Nell?"

"No . . . no thank you. It's . . . it's just that it's *over* . . . that's all."

"What's over?"

"Our honeymoon . . . doesn't that mean anything to you?"

"Of course, it means something to me . . . but it isn't really over for another twelve hours or so . . . and it doesn't ever have to be as far as I'm concerned."

"Oh, Milo—"

He decided he should have kept silent. Now he had said something nice and it started her all over again. All right, Nell—the silent treatment it is.

"Milo . . . I'm scared. Just plain scared, that's all. This is the first time I've stopped long enough to think thoughts about it."

He decided to abandon the silent treatment. "Well, stop thinking thoughts. What in the world are you scared of? Golly . . . the whole world's in front of us!"

"That's just it—" She was having trouble taking a full breath again.

"*What's* just it? You can talk in more circles than any woman I ever knew." In trying to think of how other women had talked, Milo was astonished to find he could remember only two, and these had made far less sense than Nell. There was Nancy when he was seventeen and Ginger when he was eighteen—the rest of the time, the whole last four and a half years, there had been no one but Nell. "Golly . . . part of the best part of our getting married was we didn't have to get acquainted with each other! Knowing everything about each other just made things sensible, that's all . . . at least that's what we decided, wasn't it?"

"Oh, Milo . . . it's just that we're so young and . . . like you say there's the whole world . . . and it scares me because now we've got to face it."

"Well, for the love of Mike! Is that all you're bawling about?"

"It's enough. . . ."

"I'm twenty-two! We've got an apartment and fifty dollars left in the bank. Good gravy . . . what have we got to cry about?"

"You haven't even got a job . . . !"

Milo threw up his hands in mock despair. "A job! What's a job? Why, there's a million jobs I can get!"

"How . . . ?"

"Just go ask for them, that's all. Just get up real early some morning and go see some joker and say look here you need Milo Buck in your organization, that's all."

"Oh, sure. . . ."

"What's the matter? Haven't you got confidence in me? I thought we went all over this a million times."

"Of course, I've got confidence in you. I'm just worried about the people outside, that's all."

"What people outside? There you go in a circle again."

"The people in the world. They don't know you like I do. Suppose I was pregnant and you didn't have a job?"

"You're not supposed to get pregnant." A touch of anxiety colored Milo's voice.

"But suppose I *was*—"

"All *right!* All *right!* You're pregnant and there isn't any food in the apartment . . . and I haven't got a job . . . and it's snowing outside . . . and the sheriff is knocking on the door. . . ."

"Oh, Milo . . . I didn't mean it that way." She took his hand between her own and pressed it against her breasts as if she would draw the strength from it. She bent her head quickly and kissed his hand. They moved their bodies even closer together and pretended to look out the window. She had stopped crying and her eyes were dry when Milo finally spoke in a voice that was almost a whisper.

"Are you . . . ?"

"Am I what?"

"Pregnant?"

"Me . . . ? Ha-a!" She chuckled as if the secret of her amusement could never be explained. "No-o-o-! Whatever gave you *that* idea?"

A groan escaped Milo Buck. He looked over his shoulder and, seeing the man across the aisle was still asleep, he quickly covered his bride's mouth with his own.

Ten feet six inches forward of the mirror at which Spalding had chastised herself for smoking, Dan Roman felt a sudden thud against the seat of his pants. Through the years, this portion of his anatomy had become acutely sensitive to the slightest variation in any airplane's performance. Instinctively his head snapped toward the window at his side and for several seconds his entire body remained cocked—completely motionless, like a highly trained hunting dog uncertain of a scent. But there had been only one thud—or had there really been any at all? Bowing to his social obligations, Sullivan had reluctantly gone back to the passenger cabin. Hobie now sat in his seat and if he had felt any thud he gave no indication of it. He sat there very confidently, a young man entirely absorbed in his flying. Dan turned to look behind him at Leonard. He had not even looked up from his computations.

I am getting old and I am getting jumpy, Dan thought. Garfield was right when he said—well, go ahead, Dan, and try a few trips just to convince yourself, if nothing else. It can't do you or us any harm and it may do you a lot of good . . . but I'll bet a bottle of Old Grand-Dad you won't really like it . . . down inside. No, you won't, pal, because as much as I hate to point this out, you're getting ancient and you'll find there's a lot that's passed you by. And I'll bet a second bottle of whisky you'll come to me in two months and say well, thanks, I've had it . . . and the hell with it.

Yeah. Your confidence was beginning to get mildewed around the edges. Dan Roman was no longer like Sullivan or Hobie Wheeler, or any of the others. For just one reason. Fifty-three years was fifty-three years. And so there wasn't any thump. It was just aging imagination. Timidity, they called it. Start looking for a pasture, you beat-up old fire-horse.

Slowly, the tension that had come to his body subsided. He began to whistle, thoughtfully.

6

DONALD FLAHERTY WAS RELIEVED WHEN, THROUGH THE lattice of his fingers, he saw the Bucks' heads together. It would no longer be necessary to pretend he was asleep. Sleep? What was that? He hadn't really known it since the explosion at Anaka. He would never know real sleep again. Not after watching the secret. Secret, secret . . . everything was so secret. The secret would soon be to live, in spite of the secret. Goddam every man and goddam his twisted soul. And goddam most of all, the brilliant ones who had contrived the secret. Roast them, sear them in their own hell. Defense! Balls to defense. The miracle would be to find some way to defend man against himself. And you could only stay drunk so long —if you knew about the secret. God, toying with the universe, had let the stars burn economically and so they lasted billions of years. But man was not content with such puny furnaces. He had to tinker with fission, and stumble on a way to reverse the process. Helium could now be converted into hydrogen, goddammit, and science gone berserk, was actually rejoicing. And Donald Flaherty, who came out of a womb like anyone else, was as guilty as the rest of them. Jesus Christ in agony! Science had earned a new coat of arms and Donald Flaherty would design it. How about a gibbering water-head rampant on a field of bleeding fiends? No . . . forget you ever heard of a guided missile and go back to painting mountains in the mist, peasants walking in the evening, meadows in the forest. Swear you'll do it as you swore at them— and forget about the missile.

A man worked the better part of a lifetime, broke his brain on the phenomena of physics and electronics, wrote papers and was honored with recognition. Men with a lot of letters after their names listened respectfully when you had something to say on the subject of electronics. Only a few years ago, par for the course with this equipment used to be a seat on a good campus, genteel poverty on five thousand a year, tweeds and final senility. It was a pretty, comfortable picture but it was not so easy to attain any more.

The commission invited you to lunch and casually mentioned a salary that would make any professor gasp. And travel? Oh, travel with expenses, of course, all first class just as long as you did a little coordinating. There was finally in this world such a queer and improbable animal as a solvent professor—many of them—and a pity taxes took the most of it. Of course, technically the sky was the limit—indeed the limit. The object was to blow up the sky, or parts thereof. And secrets! Sh-sh-sh-sh. No one, not a single pitiful, beautiful human being must know about the secret. Take a special secret badge and proceed furtively to the secret toilet, where some said the feces of the unfortunate learned were sifted for signs of an improper attitude. Well, now they knew your attitude.

"We realize you've been under considerable strain, Professor Flaherty, and deeply regret that a man of your caliber apparently finds it quite impossible to sympathize with our efforts . . . blah . . . blah . . . blah . . . blah . . . and so under the circumstances it would seem advisable for you to return to the States, blah . . . blah . . . and we need hardly caution you . . . blah . . . blah . . . blah." So spoke those antiseptic minds while they sat on a lovely atoll in the middle of the Pacific Ocean. They never looked at the cobalt lagoon with an eye to its color, never heard the soft melody of the Marshall Islanders' gossip as they sat on their haunches in the evening breeze, never listened to the lament of a trade bird calling for direction in the night. They were too busy scheming to blow it all up. Not with guns, not even with airplanes about which there might still remain a vestige of romance, or a quality known as human courage. Now it was guided missiles, the most impersonal, inhuman weapon of destruction ever conceived by humans. And they were accurate, very, *very* accurate— thanks to Donald Flaherty, Yale Sheffield, class of twenty-two.

Well, they had picked the wrong man. It was going to be paint box and easel from now on. . . .

As he walked down the long aisle, Sullivan was uncomfortably aware that most of the passengers were watching him. It was always so, but why passengers should invariably display such intense curiosity about their pilot, staring at him as if he were a performing bear, defied analysis. They would look up from their reading or stop right in the middle of a conversation until he had passed; not even veteran air travelers seemed capable of ignoring the man who flew them. A very few pilots, he knew, enjoyed the little act. Sullivan believed they mistook curiosity for admiration and in time came to fancy themselves as social personalities—a sort of winged branch of the sales department. Some of them would spend considerable time in the cabin explaining the most intricate details of an airliner's flight. The role was not for Sullivan nor for most of the pilots he knew. He subjected himself to a cabin tour because the company had requested it, in a most reasonable way. If they had commanded the expedition he would have told them to go to hell. That was one of the better things about a flying career. Unless he was derelict in his actual flying duties, or failed to pass a physical every six months, it would be very difficult for the company to fire him. There was an old saying—"God is your only real boss." Unfortunately, there were times when it was only too true, and, of course, that was one of the drawbacks to flying for a living—or was it living to fly?

Sullivan had never been quite sure how to regard his

chosen work. He was vaguely conscious that he might be very unhappy working in an office, as his brother had done for almost the same numbers of years he had been flying, but those few people who had told Sullivan he was in love with flight, or that he was an extremely restless person in spite of his solid manner, were usually rebuked by one of his favorite remarks. "I don't care if I ever leave the ground again."

There were times when he liked to think of flying as simply one way to provide a reasonable living for his wife Wendy and his daughter. Now there was another baby on the way and, with some care, flying could take good care of it, too. Yet here again, there were certain penalties. Like so many flying families, the Sullivans were insurance poor. To meet the payments on their policies, the Sullivans found it impossible to live as their income might otherwise allow; the insurance companies were perfectly willing to insure passengers at a reasonable rate, but the piloting profession was considered by the actuarial departments as somewhat more hazardous than coal mining. The comparison, made by an agent who had recently tried to sell Sullivan a new policy, made him furious. And yet he had almost stretched his slim bank account once more and bought it. It *could* happen.

Twice in his career Sullivan had been the "friend" who was sent to be with a wife when the airport called to tell her she was a widow . . . "We have some very bad news for you, Mrs.—" The vision of Wendy receiving one of those calls, and the inevitable race between the airline authorities and the newspaper people, was always deep in Sullivan's thoughts. At home, the subject was always carefully avoided, but he knew that every time he left on a trip Wendy held the same quiet fears.

He stopped beside the Pardees. There was no mistaking Gustave Pardee's houndlike face after Spalding's description. He sat on the chair arm just in front of them and shoved his uniform cap slightly back on his head. He crossed his legs and said, "Hi. . . ."

"Hello," said Lillian Pardee while her husband smiled unhappily and twisted in his seat. Sullivan wondered how he would be received if he walked into Gustave Pardee's New York office. He had read about the man and his lavish productions for years. If the reports were anywhere near accurate he was an extraordinarily shrewd producer and probably made more money in one week than Sullivan made in a year; but now his eyes were confused. Here was a man who was really out of his element, Sullivan thought, reminding himself that he would undoubtedly feel the same way if he were set down in the middle of Times Square.

"How are you getting along?"

Gustave Pardee swallowed with difficulty. It took him a moment to find his voice and, when he did, Sullivan was surprised at the contrast between it and his flabby appearance. The voice was strong and heavy. His words came in a sharp, half-jumbled staccato, as if it was impossible for the muscular equipment of his jaw and mouth to keep pace with the rapid fire of his brain.

"Thank you, Captain . . . we're getting along all right, but frankly I wish to God we'd taken the boat. I once flew from Paris to Madrid and swore then I'd never do it again. Now I wish I'd remembered my vow, but I suppose it's too late to turn back?"

"Sorry you feel that way, Mr. Pardee. What seems to be the trouble?"

"Altitude is for mountain goats."

"I'm sure my husband means nothing personal by that, Captain," Lillian Pardee said with a little laugh. Sullivan supposed that Pardee's wife must be considered very beautiful, even in the world of the theater, but her exotic brunette coloring only impressed him as rather unclean-looking. He preferred the kind of woman who looked her best in sunlight.

"Let me ask you something, Captain," Gustave said, and now there was an obvious desire on his part to make the conversation as friendly as possible. "I make it my business to be interested in the emotional reactions of other human beings. I assume you have made this trip before. Aren't you sometimes a little afraid?"

Sullivan hesitated as Gustave's pale eyes searched his own. This was a very clever man; smarter than Sullivan had expected. He would not be fooled or comforted by a lie.

"I've made almost two hundred trips across here and

69

I feel a lot safer than driving my car. The most dangerous part of any flight is the trip to and from the airport."

"You hedged, Captain. You did not answer my question." Gustave cocked up one eyebrow and pattered the tips of his fingers together as if in his mental exploration of Sullivan he was at last enjoying himself. "Would you tell me that you have never really been afraid up here?"

". . . no. Perhaps I have . . . once or twice."

"What of? Come now . . . be a good honest fellow and tell me exactly what frightened you."

Sullivan looked out the window and twisted around on the arm of the seat. He pushed his cap further back and wished he had remained on the flight deck. This was worse than listening to Dan Roman's whistling. He was certainly not going to tell Gustave Pardee about the time he had the hydraulic fire and the whole ship became so filled with smoke they could hardly see across the flight deck; that was not exactly what the company had in mind when they requested that the captains establish good passenger relations. Nor was he going to tell him about the freak thunderstorm last year which tossed a plane exactly like this one so violently it cracked a main spar. But Pardee was still pattering his fingers, waiting expectantly for an answer.

"They were technical incidents . . . I don't think you would quite understand if I did explain—"

"I understand perfectly, Captain. You were afraid, and the exact reasons for it are really unimportant . . . you were afraid you would not reach your Biblical span of life, which is precisely what is bothering me at the moment. I am convinced I could not swim from here to the nearest shore."

"You won't have to swim, Mr. Pardee."

"How can I be sure of that? Suppose one of your motors ceases to function?"

"If that happened in the next few hours we would simply turn around and go back to Honolulu. These airplanes fly beautifully on three engines. I doubt if you'd even know we'd shut one down. If it happened beyond our point-of-no-return, we would simply continue on to San Francisco. Our arrival might be an hour or so later due to our decreased speed."

"Suppose *two* of your motors became uninterested in further toil?"

This was more familiar ground to Sullivan and he had his answers ready. "Each engine is independent of the other, Mr. Pardee. The chances of two quitting during the same flight are so remote we hardly consider it. But even if it should happen, that million to one chance, we could still fly . . . lower and much slower, but we'd get there."

"You are very reassuring, Captain . . . but why is it then that I read about so many air crashes?"

"The newspapers figure it makes good reading, I guess. They always exaggerate the importance of an air accident."

"It would be very important to me if I were in one."

"You won't be, Mr. Pardee. Relax and enjoy your flight." Sullivan stood up. The blond woman sitting alone across the aisle had beckoned to him with her eyes and, though he had no desire for further passenger talk, she would at least be easier to handle than Gustave Pardee.

"Just one thing more before you leave, Captain," Pardee said quickly. "How far are we from shore now?"

"About three hundred miles."

"So we have another two thousand miles of water to go?"

"If it will make you feel any better"—Sullivan answered more sharply than he intended, and was instantly sorry—"if it will make you feel any better, there are two Coast Guard cutters along our route. As we pass over them they give us the latest weather reports and a check on our position."

"Are they always there?"

"Twenty-four hours a day . . . every day of the year."

"Could we land beside them if we had to?"

"Yes." Again the annoyance crept into Sullivan's voice. To hell with Pardee and his gloomy questions. He was going to wish the ship into the drink yet. Spalding should give him a sleeping pill or a knock on his head. "Yes, we could land beside either one of them . . . but I'm not about to try it. I prefer airports, Mr. Pardee."

Sullivan regretted his manner the moment he turned

away from the Pardees. He had been needled into a position in which he had almost told a passenger the complete truth about a flight. It was a near loss of self-control and would have accomplished nothing. Sure, the ship would fly with one engine out, but if there were only two working it wouldn't fly worth a damn. He would have to dump gas to lighten the load and she would finally settle to within a few hundred feet of the ocean, and the two remaining engines would be beating their brains out trying to stay even that high. The extra strain on them, running very near maximum power, would probably get them to shore if nothing gave way—but there would be a lot of perspiration off Sullivan's brow before they made it. Or the extra strain could knock off a third engine and then Pardee would certainly get his swim. Anyone could give themselves the willies if they sat still long enough and thought of all the things that could happen to an airplane, no matter how remote the chances might be.

Ordinarily Sullivan would not have accepted an invitation to sit beside a woman passenger who was obviously traveling alone. It was asking for trouble in many ways and it was always more difficult to break off a conversation if you actually sat down. But there was a different ring to this woman's appeal, a plaintive quality in her voice when she said, "Please, Captain . . . I want to talk to you just for a few minutes," that made him violate his own rule.

"It can only be a few minutes . . . then I'll have to go back to work," he said uneasily. He tried to look into her eyes and then looked away. There was something wrong with this blond woman, something hidden behind her heavy make-up that depressed him almost immediately. He studied his hands, not wanting to look at her again. She was probably not more than thirty-five years old—Sullivan knew he was no judge of such things—yet her face sagged in the manner of a much older woman. She was extremely nervous and he hoped he would not have to deliver another lecture on the safety of flight.

"I'm afraid I'm going to embarrass you, Captain," she said.

"It's my day for it . . . I guess."

"My name is Sally McKee. I used to work in reservations for Pan American."

"Fine. I'm glad you decided to try a trip with us." At least the aviation lecture was out. If she worked for Pan American she should know her way around.

"Aren't there two exits to this plane . . . one up forward where you and the rest of the crew leave?"

"Yes . . . we usually go out that way when we get to San Francisco. It's a little easier with our luggage."

"Could I leave the plane that way . . . with you and the crew?"

"Well . . . now why would you want to do that?"

"Please . . . it's very important to me. . . ."

Sullivan groped for a definite answer. He had listened to a great many strange requests, but this was a new one. He could no longer pretend to be interested in the lines of his hands and so he was forced to meet her eyes. To his astonishment they were filling with tears.

"I . . . I don't think it would be practical for you. The ladder they put up for us is not like the passenger ramp . . . it's very steep. You might hurt yourself, and the company—"

"I know what you're thinking, and you're only partly right. Yes . . . I'm going to be met in San Francisco, and I do want to avoid it . . . but it's not the police . . . or anyone else who would get you into trouble." She wiped her eyes with a piece of face tissue and Sullivan was thankful that the tears seemed to have ended as suddenly as they had come.

"It . . . just wouldn't work. . . ." He should never have visited the cabin on this trip. A man couldn't fly an airplane and play nursemaid to a bunch of passengers. That was Spalding's job.

"Look, Captain. . . ." She dug quickly into her crowded purse and after a moment's search brought out a page that had been torn from a magazine. It was so well-worn where it had been creased, it almost came apart in Sullivan's hands. He recognized it as a page from the house publication of Pan American Airways. There were several photographs of girls, all young and rather attractive. At the top was a stunning blond girl. The caption beneath her picture labeled her as Sally McKee—winner

73

of Pacific Division Round Trip Award for 1948. Sullivan could find very little resemblance between the photo and the woman who sat beside him.

"Confused, Captain . . . ?"

"Well . . . no, that's you."

"Thank you for being so perceptive. It *was* me . . . twelve years ago."

"Um-hum . . . very nice." Sullivan could feel the back of his neck reddening. He tried to return the page without seeming to push it away.

"I've lost my nerve, Captain." Her voice was suddenly very low and soft. "Two years ago a man in the States saw that picture. He wrote to me in care of the company, and because it was a very nice letter and because I was terribly lonely, I answered. That was the beginning. We corresponded for two years . . . and last month I agreed to marry him. I never quite got around to telling him the picture was eight years old when it was published. I just couldn't. I've been kidding myself it would all work out, right up to the time we left Honolulu. Now I know it won't. Please understand, Captain . . . I don't want to bore you with my troubles, but this dream has kept me sane for over two years. I know I'm a mess, and I'm so much older than he thinks I am—"

"So you want to leave without ever meeting him . . . ?"

"Yes . . . please. I would only destroy our dream." She put her hand on Sullivan's. "*Please* understand. . . ."

"Do you have a photo of him?"

She brought a snapshot from her purse of a young man wearing a lumberjack shirt, boots, and breeches. Though he wore glasses and his hair appeared quite thin, Sullivan was certain he could not be more than thirty.

"His name is Larsin and he's a forest line patrolman for Pacific Gas and Electric," she said. "I guess he just had a lot of time to write . . . because his letters were always so beautiful."

Sullivan returned the photo and eased out of his seat. "What you're asking is not exactly in my line, Miss McKee. Let me think it over a while. I'll let you know." He touched his cap and turned quickly up the aisle toward the flight deck.

Sullivan thought he had safely made the door to the flight deck when he heard a man's voice call to him. He turned around and walked back to Ken Childs.

"Hello, Mr. Childs. Sorry I didn't see you before. Nice to have you on board again."

"Thanks." He carefully inserted a cigarette in his long holder. "Something has caught my eye and I won't be satisfied until I find out about it . . . the crew list on the door there . . . is your first officer old Dan Roman's son, by any chance? Dan was a little before your time, but you might remember hearing of him."

"No, sir. That Dan Roman is the original article."

"He's still at it?" Ken Childs was mildly incredulous.

"Very much so."

"Well, I'll be damned."

"He's forgotten more about flying than most men will ever learn." Sullivan was surprised at the unmistakable pride in his voice. "Do you know him, Mr. Childs?"

"Know him . . . ?" Ken Childs looked out the window. He took a long draw on his cigarette, then almost closed his eyes as the exhaled smoke gathered in a cloud around his head. "Yeah . . . we knew each other pretty well. If he has time later on, maybe you'd ask him to come back and say hello."

"Sure. I'll tell him."

"By the way . . . how are we doing?"

"I was just going to check. We should be around four hundred miles out."

"Good enough. How's the Coast weather?"

"Frankly, not so hot." It was a pleasure to give information to passengers like Ken Childs. You could tell the truth.

"I'll keep my fingers crossed for you."

They winked at each other and Sullivan went on to the door.

Ken Childs did not stir in his seat until the ash from his neglected cigarette dribbled onto his trousers. He swept the ashes away and went back to staring at the banks of cumulus clouds beyond the window. He was thinking of a failure and how a minor defeat could sometimes seal a man's happiness—while the man was busy looking the other way.

It wasn't really a failure. The Childs Hawk was really a good airplane for its time . . . for 1934. It would have made a good Navy fighter except that 1934 was not the time to succeed with anything unless you had a safe full of hard cash. Childs Aircraft, an Ohio Corporation with principal offices and factory in Cleveland . . . that was a laugh . . . there was only one office and it was a twenty-foot-square room behind a former saloon . . . and the factory was another laugh because it consisted of rented hangar space . . . Childs Aircraft was never a very healthy enterprise. It was long on youth and hope—very short on money. The two engineers, four mechanics, and one secretary were lucky when they collected half their salary. The president of Childs Aircraft lived in a furnished room and did his own laundry in the washbasin . . . with help and advice from Martha. Martha was everything in those days—*almost* everything; secretary, confidante, inspector of her young boss's apparel, spark plug when the Childs machine tended to run down with discouragement. She was only nineteen years old then, and she had more sense than anyone connected with Childs Aircraft. When her meager pay was short she just came right out and said she was in love with the president and that was enough—only the president didn't have sense enough to be in love with her. No, Ken Childs had to be the big shot. Little Marthas weren't good enough then, although now they were too good for you. So look how it finally worked out. Within a very few weeks Ken Childs went from disaster to ease—or was it the other way around? Things happened so fast . . . and they still did, when Winona was around. Winona would have to be told about flying on the same airplane with Dan Roman. If she would stand still long enough to listen.

Winona Milhausen, who had a father in the cement business; asphalt, concrete, tile, and a lot of other things. All heavy stuff, much heavier than airplanes and much much better rated in Dun and Bradstreet. Winona was taking flying lessons, mainly to get rid of excess energy. She saw the Childs Hawk in the hangar one day and said it was cute. She met the president of Childs Aircraft and thought he was cute. The word was a little sicken-

ing now. She had never looked at an airplane since—
dog shows, the Red Cross, and Symphony subscriptions
took most of her time now, but in those Cleveland days,
she suddenly became fascinated with flying machines—
especially the Childs Hawk. Even Martha couldn't
get through the concrete wall she erected around you
in less than a week.

The Hawk was ready for testing, the last and most
important phase of development before the Navy had a
look. You just didn't send up a company's entire assets
and hopes with any old pilot. You hired a man who
knew his business thoroughly, and whose approval meant
something in the industry because of his reputation. Such
men didn't start a test program for peanuts. They didn't
have to work for the kind of money Childs Aircraft could
pay. So it was easy to listen to Winona.

"Ken . . . you've got to hire the best. Send him to
me on pay day and we'll settle when you get the Navy
contract." It was shoot the works or possibly blow the
whole dream. There wasn't any better man than Dan
Roman. His price was four thousand a month . . . in
advance. Winona paid him and the testing began.

Dan was quite a handful in those days. Dan, the whistler. He had a way about him that made a name for
him on the ground as well as in the air. He posed for
publicity pictures as easily as he did an Immelmann
and his lean, weathered face seemed to have been ex-
pressly sculptured for wearing helmet and goggles. He
threw money around like a maharaja and he was extremely partial to redheads. There were a few girls
who were said to have dyed their hair just to qualify
for Dan's league. He also drank fine whisky in quantities
that would have stunned a lesser man. Yet no one
had ever seen Dan Roman drunk. He simply became
more animated and mischievous. Like the night he insisted the redhead's watch was wrong—what was her
name now? Tracey! . . . yeah Tracey . . . a good three
inches taller than Dan, and built like a Rubens nude.

Tracey's watch was a gift from Dan—she managed to
stay in favor much longer than any of his other redheads.
But according to Dan it was wrong by more than half an
hour. Tracey claimed it was right, and the more whisky

she drank the more positive she became. It turned into one of those Bourbon-inspired little quarrels no one could stop. Finally Dan thought he had to show Tracey who wore the pants.

"Listen, Chum," he said solemnly. After twenty years you could hear him as if it was only last night. And remember how everyone, male or female, was 'chum' to Dan Roman then? "Listen, Chum . . . the goddamned watch is wrong and I'll prove it to you!"

"You're full of manure," Tracey said. Considering her earthy nature, Tracey was being very delicate that night.

"I'll bet you a week's pay against your saying 'Yes, Master, I await your orders,' every time I see you for the next month."

"You're on," Tracey said.

The party was in a little restaurant across the road from the airport. Before Tracey knew what she was getting into, Dan hauled her over to one of the hangars and bundled her into an open cockpit airplane—not the Hawk, thank God. It was a cold, black, rainy night, but Dan took off and flew right down Euclid Avenue just above the building tops until he came to the illuminated clock on the Terminal tower. He zoomed at the clock several times, almost knocking the hands off it. When she sobered up later Tracey said she was sure he was trying to scoop it into the cockpit.

"Now, tell me, woman!" Dan yelled. "What time is it?"

"Yes, master! I'm a half-hour slow!" This much could always be said for Tracey, who finally wound up marrying a mild little florist in Erie, she stuck by the bargain. It was a kick to watch Dan Roman wiggle his finger and see Tracey come running with a "Yes, master."

During the day, Dan was strictly business. He flew the Hawk exhaustively and he did everything he could to make his skill and knowledge pay off for Childs Aircraft. Then there was that awful afternoon he came down out of clouds, just like those out the window now. He walked slowly into the office and sat on the edge of Martha's desk and began to whistle. And all the time he was looking across the room at you.

78

"Look, Chum," he began in a voice that told you he was hating what he had to say. "The Hawk is a good airplane . . . or, rather, the beginning of a good one. How much money have you got in the till?"

You told him the truth because Martha was also looking at you.

"Then let me give you a piece of advice because that's what you paid me for. Forget the whole thing. The Hawk has a bad tail flutter in a dive, a yearning to Dutch roll when there's no reason for it, and beyond ten thousand feet she climbs like my great-grandmother. My guess would be at least fifty thousand dollars for redesign. As she stands, the Navy, even the Bohemian Navy, wouldn't take a second look at her."

You didn't say a thing for a long time partly because you were thinking of Winona Milhausen. There was something nice and solid about the cement business.

"I wish I could help you more, Chum. To show my heart's in the right place, I'll give you back half what you paid me."

You told Dan to forget it, but that was the end of Childs Aircraft.

In less than two weeks the little company was dissolved and Winona Milhausen became Winona Childs. Dan Roman disappeared over the horizon and so did Martha. It was almost ten years before you got back into the aviation business. A little note, written in Martha's neat hand, found its way to your office a few months ago—just a nice card with inquiries after your health and saying that she was now a Mrs. Agnew and living in Honolulu. So you tucked the card away, half-forgetting it, and by sheer luck came across it again just before you left on this trip. Seeing her again was one of the nicest things that had happened in years. She was no longer a girl, of course, but if the years had done anything, they had only improved her. Balanced against the rest of the trip those two lunches you had with Martha now seemed to be the high points. You had a lot of solid laughs together talking about the old Cleveland days. It was also obvious Martha still thought a great deal of you, but both of you had the good sense not to discuss what might have happened if Winona had never come into the picture. Those were nice lunches and in some ways you hated to see her drive away as soon as they were over. That Agnew was a lucky guy—a lot luckier than Ken Childs.

He looked out the window again, finding it easier to lose himself in the past against the towering backdrop of clouds. A part of his vision was obscured by the length of the wing and the engines, and for a time he admired their fixed design moving smoothly along the endless variety of cumulus. He was suddenly conscious of an irregular movement about the number-one engine. There was a line of division behind the cowl flaps, where the engine itself was joined to the sweeping nacelle. The line gave him a point of reference and he was almost certain he had seen it change position very quickly a number of times.

He watched the number-two engine, trying to compare it with number one. The corresponding line on number two remained perfectly fixed. Again he studied the number-one engine. Now it was also smooth—No! There . . . it did give a jerk, a very small one which you would never have seen if you hadn't been looking right at it . . . but there it was again. No question about it that time. Someone on the flight deck was probably checking the magnetos, or perhaps there were a few fouled plugs. Anyway they would know about the engine, too. That's what engine instruments were for. They had probably checked it long before and decided it was nothing worth bothering about. You might mention it to Dan if he came back, just in passing, but it was certainly nothing to call the stewardess or get alarmed about. Flying airplanes from the passenger cabin was a universal hobby you had carefully avoided so far in your travels. Why take it up now?

There . . . the number one engine was perfectly smooth again. Up forward they had probably richened the mixture a trifle.

He went back to the clouds again and once more there was the picture of Dan and his recalcitrant redheads. He began to chuckle, very quietly at first, and then more audibly as details of each escapade returned to him.

"If it's so funny, the least you could do is share it

with a fellow passenger. . . ." He turned to see the woman across the aisle leaning toward him. "I'm bored stiff," she said. He liked her eyes. They were full of fun.

"Well. . . ." He spread his hands helplessly. "It's kind of a hard thing to share. I was just thinking about a time when laughs came very easily."

"Don't they now?"

". . . not quite in the same way."

As if drawn to each other by mutual agreement, they moved across their seats until only the aisle was separating them.

"My name is May Holst. I hope you don't think I was prying, but the sight of a man laughing to himself is bound to arouse any woman's curiosity."

"I'm Ken Childs and I don't mind at all."

Spalding saw their heads leaning across the aisle and she was glad when after a few moments she saw Ken Childs rise and seat himself beside May Holst. It made her job much easier when the passengers found their own amusement.

Just ahead of Spalding, Humphrey Agnew also observed the change of position. He was not surprised. So now Ken Childs thought he would seduce some other man's wife. Tonight perhaps, in San Francisco? Only this time he would not be successful. He would be slightly incapacitated for conquest of any kind. Humphrey Agnew, who was no man's fool, would see to that.

7

LEONARD WILBY'S CHOICE OF COURSE BETWEEN THE
Hawaiian Islands and San Francisco would have confused an experienced albatross. He had drawn an intended path across the Pacific vastness represented on
his chart, well to the north of a straight line between
the point of his departure and destination. An old-time
square-rigger captain would have approved, however,
since Leonard's course was designed to accomplish the
journey in the shortest possible time. By flying the "North
Dog," as the course was known, he hoped to take advantage of the northwesterly winds which had been forecast as prevalent during the last half of the flight. There
were no tangible signposts along either the "North Dog"
or the straight rhumb line course; any more than there
were signs elsewhere in the oceanic spaces which stretched
for thousands of miles beneath Leonard's well-polished
black shoes.

Except to rest his mind and eyes in appreciation of
the gigantic cloud structures, the airscape to be seen from
the flight-deck windows held little interest for him.
Navigationally, the sea could have been the North Sea, or
the Tasman Sea, and the clouds might be over Green-
land or the Gold Coast of Africa, according to the mood
of the seasons. And so he confined himself almost entirely to intelligence received from long beyond the hori-

zons. Leonard's subsequent discovereies enabled him to mark the ship's hourly position on the chart in a series of minute triangles which appeared like stepping stones along the line of the "North Dog." Large as the ship was, its proportions in relation to the element embracing it were less than those of a single molecule to all the iron in a skyscraper; yet Leonard sat quietly at his table recording with perfect confidence the facts and figures upon which his life depended.

The information which allowed Leonard to relax and caress thoughtfully the hardwood tray he had placed against the bulkhead, came to him in various ways. He had the sun, which was already yellowing and slipping down behind the ship's tail. Climbing on his stool, Leonard had elevated himself until his head projected into the plexiglass dome in the ceiling of the flight deck. There he observed the exact position of the sun through his octant and compared his observations with those already calculated in the books on his table. So he obtained a "sun line," which in this instance enabled him to make a mark across the "North Dog" and compute the actual speed of the ship toward its destination. Later there would be the stars and he would use these in much the same way. These were celestial observations and the methods of using them were as old as the first navigators. Though Leonard's procedures were considerably quicker of solution than those employed by square-rigger captains, they would have understood them easily.

He supplemented his celestial observations with occasional sights through his drift meter—more to satisfy his curiosity about the present effect of the unseen winds aloft than anything else. This was a squat black instrument placed just behind Dan Roman's seat. Bending over it, Leonard watched the white caps on the ocean surface as they passed along a series of illuminated hairlines. By twisting a knob he could adjust the lines so that the waves moved parallel to them, and then read the amount of drift in degrees to one side or the other of the ship's course. Combined with a stop watch, his electric altimeter, and the regular altimeter, Leonard could also compute the velocity and direction of the wind. Radioed to the shore stations, these reports were helpful to the meteorologists who were even now drawing new weather maps of the Pacific area. But the drift sight was a hangover from the very earliest days of flying and was entirely useless when clouds obscured the surface of the sea. Leonard would have been unhappy if he had to depend upon it entirely.

His most valuable ally was an instrument of relatively recent invention—the loran. It was a black box hung just over Leonard's head. There was a small round screen on the face of the box and, by turning the knobs surrounding it, Leonard could cause a series of eerie green lines to dance across the screen. These were the signals transmitted by the master and slave stations located along the coast lines of the world. When they were translated into numerals and time, he could construct a triangle on the chart and so locate the ship within a very few miles. There were few places about the earth where the loran was inefficient, and best of all it could be used in almost any kind of weather.

Leonard was not surprised when he took a loran fix at zero three hundred hours Greenwich and found that they were fourteen minutes behind time. He had been keeping careful track of the wind for the last two hours and at one observation found it to be blowing at forty knots directly on the ship's nose. This gave the wind considerably more strength than the forecast had predicted, but a more recent observation proved it had diminished to a mere eighteen knots. Now, he was sure, the wind would gradually swing around to the north, and in time become favorable. He finished his report for the ground stations two minutes before it was due. He handed it to Hobie who studied it intently.

"Jesus, Lennie . . . how did we get so far behind time?"

"I'm lost . . . completely and absolutely lost."

"Fourteen minutes . . . and we're really just getting started!"

"Patience, son. Just think of the flying time you're building up."

Leonard winked at Dan and turned back to his navigation table. Hobie picked up his microphone and called Honolulu.

"Four-two-zero from Honolulu. Go ahead." The voice was far away and distorted now, like a man calling through the end of a long tube.

"Position report . . . zero three hundred . . . twenty-eight degrees thirty minutes north . . . one four eight degrees west. . . ." Hobie continued to read off the series of numbers from the paper. They covered many things besides the ship's position—the wind, intended track, drift, gallons of fuel remaining, air speed, ground speed, the weather and cloud conditions to be observed from the flight-deck windows. When Hobie reached the end of the column of figures he pressed the headset against his ears and listened while Honolulu repeated his message.

"All correct. Four-two-zero."

"Roger. Honolulu." Once again, there was only the crashing of static in Hobie's headphones. The sound was nerve-wracking. Although he was anxious to rest his ears, he was careful not to muss his hair when he pushed the headphones to a more comfortable position.

There would be at least forty minutes before Leonard would have to start work on the next position report. He left his table and walked back to the crew compartment. He took a paper cup from a box beneath the mirror and turned the spigot on the electric urn. He searched further in the box that held the paper cups and found a ham sandwich—it was always ham, dammit—was there really ever any other kind of a sandwich on an airplane? He removed the wax paper covering and after examining the sandwich with disapproval, he took a bite out of it. Then he stood for a considerable time, munching on the peculiarly tasteless bread and washing it down with the coffee, which was also nearly flavorless. He stared at the porthole. The sun had now gone behind it, leaving only a circle of blue-grey sky. He wondered disconsolately if altitude could somehow destroy the taste of any food. Then suddenly, just as a portion of the sandwich formed a small round ball inside his cheek, he laughed softly to himself. Why, you old shellback! What in God's name you got to complain about? You haven't had it so good in fifty years. You not only have a job which is no strain, but a fine wife . . . there just isn't any finer girl than Susie. What if she does have an extra Martini once in a while? That is just youth . . . after all she is only thirty-two. As for a little tantrum now and then, that's not temper . . . it's spirit. And who would want a girl who doesn't have spirit? You can't expect to marry a girl considerably younger than yourself and not have some friction. Natural as pie. Supposing some people did think it was funny you did most of the cooking and the dishes, too. What was wrong with that? Nobody kept a more spotless apartment than Susie Wilby, and she never looked like somebody's maid either. Watch what she does with that hardwood tray. She'll set it out somewheres in the apartment, maybe beside the little bar she bought to keep herself company while you were away on trips . . . and she'd keep the tray polished and show it to all her friends . . . the fellows and the girls who always dropped in when you were away.

"Look at this sensational tray Leonard brought me," she would say, and hold it up for all of them to admire. Susie did the same with everything you bought her and that was one reason it was such a pleasure to get anything for her. Like the car—she spent most of her time riding around in it, keeping herself busy like she said, so she wouldn't get too lonesome. And again it was only spirit that made her drive so fast . . . just little-girl mischief. She wouldn't get so many tickets if the car wasn't yellow. Cops were always on the lookout for yellow cars . . . they looked like they were going faster than they really were. And Susie was *not* drunk last December when she spent the night in the San Mateo jail. She might have been a little tipsy a few other nights, and she might have had a drink or two on her breath that night, but she was definitely not drunk. Not according to the barman where she said she had been just waiting for the movie to start. She drank maybe two Martinis or so. And the barman also said, "You sure got a fine wife there, Mr. Wilby. Full of fun." He had the right idea but the wrong word. It was spirit. A real thoroughbred.

Now about the tray. The thing to do was not to just give it to her the minute you stepped off the ship in

86

San Francisco. It would be about two-thirty or three local time, or later, then . . . depending on how that damn northwest wind swung around in the next few hours. It would be too late to take Susie anywhere even if you weren't dog-tired, so why not go straight to the apartment and cook her up some scrambled eggs with sausage. Susie would be hungry and maybe you could have a cold beer together while you were waiting for the eggs . . . have a beer and tell her about the trip. Then, just before you went to bed, you could bring out the tray and surprise her. Yeah. That was the way to do it . . . only why don't you quit kidding yourself, Leonard Wilby? Why don't you admit things never work out that way?

It will be after two-thirty, all right . . . much later if the winds don't start to cooperate pretty soon. Susie may or may not be at the airport depending on what else is going on. If she is there, she will be drunk, because she is always a little drunk even when some miracle gets her up in the mornings. When you arrive she will be good and plastered, her hair all mussed, and her lips smeared with pink beyond the line of make-up. She will complain about waiting, as if you can control the winds . . . or there may just be a scribbled note like there was the last time you had a late arrival. "Welcome home, Fatso. Sorry I got sleepy and couldn't wait so you better take a taxi. Don't make too much racket when you come in. Love. Susie."

But these aren't good thoughts . . . not about Susie. No matter what she does it has to be all right . . . you don't forgive something that is all right anyway . . . it *has* to be . . . because you are in love with her. And that, my potbellied friend, is the greatest thing in the world.

When he turned away from the porthole, Leonard was surprised to see Sullivan lying in the lower bunk. His arms were folded across his chest and his body was completely relaxed although his eyes were open. Leonard wondered how long he had been watching him.

"Hello, Skipper. Have some coffee?"

"No thanks. How are we doing?"

"Fourteen minutes behind on the last fix."

"So?"

"We should make it up, though, if the forecast is any-where near right. The wind seems to be swinging around now."

"Good. How's our fuel?"

Leonard formed a mental picture of the graph he had plotted along with his position reports. This was the howgozit curve with which he kept constant track of the distance covered against fuel remaining and consumed. If the consumption line went beyond the danger curve and continued so, then they would have to turn back to Honolulu. It seldom happened.

"We're doing all right. Still on the safe side." Leon-ard crossed the compartment and sat down on the edge of the bunk. He sipped at the last of his coffee, enjoying this moment of relaxation with a man he admired so much. He would have liked to talk about ground affairs with Sullivan, about Sullivan's wife perhaps, and then maybe about Susie, because it was always a pleasure to discuss such things in an offhand way with a man who shared your working life—but he could think of no easy beginning. Sullivan, like many other captains, kept to himself and whether he had any children or was content with his home affairs, Leonard did not know.

"It's kind of nice having a fellow like Dan Roman around," he said. "For a change I don't feel like grand-father up here."

"Yeah. He certainly makes things easy for me. I can lie here and take it easy."

"I sort of hate to see a man like Dan have to fly copilot. Did he get in trouble somewheres?"

"No. I don't think so. He's just one of those guys who can't stay away from airplanes and I guess that's his real trouble. It's like a disease . . . the incurable kind."

"Haven't you ever caught it?"

"Not me. In five years I'll be forty. In five years I won't even look up when one of these things goes over my head."

"What will you do, Skipper . . . if you don't mind my asking?"

"I've got two parking lots now and they're beginning to show a fair little profit. I'm after a garage and even-

He hitched up his pants and without haste walked forward to the flight deck.

The pain began at the base of Frank Briscoe's skull, then daggered down his spine until it passed through his arms and flowed out of his fingertips like rivulets of molten metal. Yet he held perfectly still in his seat, gripping the chair arms with all the strength remaining in him, hoping no one would notice the heavy beads of perspiration on his forehead. His face was grey and his lips trembled as he sought desperately to ignore his agony. No one must know about Frank Briscoe, because if they did find out, then there would be the obligation of sympathy, and that emotion in itself could hasten the destruction of Frank Briscoe. Not that cancer of the bones, multiple myeloma, as the doctors called it, needed any hastening. The bones were already only fragile casings with no more resistance to a shock or an overquick twisting, than an egg shell. Frank Briscoe, who only five years ago could bend a silver dollar with his bare fingers.

Oh God, please give me a minute's peace . . . just one. Or take me now and let's have it over with.

A moment's peace? There would soon be an eternity of it. Another month, another two, even six months perhaps, and you would discover what it was like to be without life. It was a damn funny thing how people in good health always envisioned themselves as living to be at least eighty years old and so planned their lives on a distant dream. The insurance companies were past masters at selling this hokum.

Yet in some ways the old Frank Briscoe would live in another man. That was all arranged—all signed away, along with everything else transferable. These eyes would go to the Stanford Hospital. A few hours later some stranger could emerge from his terrible darkness and see. It helped the pain to think of the stranger. Would it be simply an optical transfer permitting the stranger to see light and shade, or could there possibly be some retention of the beautiful things you had seen? Maybe the stranger could look at people who were anatomically almost the ugliest of living creatures, and discover, with the combination of his own mind and your eyes, how the most forlorn of them could become quite beautiful. As children did before speech poisoned their sight. Maybe he could see beyond the dangling arms, misshapen legs, and frequently horrible projections called noses, upon which some humans dared to base their judgments of other humans; maybe the stranger would see beyond their foolish adornment, which was also used as a criterion of judgment, and maybe he would be able to strip away the idiotic trappings of legend and prejudice until he could regard other humans with the same love he bore for himself. That would *be* something.

"Are you all right, Mr. Briscoe?" Spalding was standing beside him. She placed her hand gently on his arm and he looked away from her just long enough to slip a mask of ease over his face.

"All *right*? Little girl, I'm getting along like ten million dollars!"

She returned his smile, but the slight increase in pressure of her hand told him she knew he was lying.

"Can I get you anything, Mr. Briscoe? I'll be serving your dinner in an hour or so, but perhaps a cup of tea or coffee would taste good to you now."

Looking into her eyes, he saw not sympathy but understanding, and he thought it remarkable that so young a person could appreciate the difference. She knows I am going to die, she knows it as well as I do, yet this kid doesn't try to cover her natural fear of sensing death by performing the rituals set down for those who expect to continue living. She might be one of those rare persons who could understand that it was entirely possible a man might be congratulated on his approaching demise.

"How about it, Mr. Briscoe?"

If I am slow in answering, he thought, it is only because I want to prolong this moment in all of its warmth. She is offering me far more than tea or coffee—behind those clear blue eyes there is a whole ocean of warmth, an open desire to give of herself, and so she is beautiful.

Before Frank Briscoe could answer, there was a faint chiming in his vest pocket. So delicate was the sound that

Spalding leaned forward and cocked her head to one side unbelievingly. "What . . . was that?"

A bewildered smile crept across her lips as he reached into his vest pocket and slowly withdrew a small gold watch. He held it in his open palm for her to see and forgot the pain in his enjoyment of her childlike surprise.

"It's five o'clock," he said.

"You mean . . . it *chimes!*"

"You heard it. I picked it up several years ago in Switzerland. Funny thing . . . it happens to be the last possession I haven't signed over to someone else."

Spalding knelt in the aisle beside his seat. "Oh! It's the most entrancing thing I have ever seen! Please, Mr. Briscoe. May I touch it? Oh, I wish it would chime again!" He unfastened it from the gold chain that crossed his stomach and placed it in her hands. Then he watched her for a moment as she caressed the watch, turning it carefully over and over in honest wonderment. "What a wonderful way to keep track of the time," she whispered. "How you must enjoy it! If I had a watch like this I couldn't wait until the next hour came . . . and the next one."

"You know somp'n, miss? I used to feel the same way, but right now I'm in no hurry for the hours to pass." Spalding moved to return the watch to him, but he pushed her hand very gently away. "No . . . the watch is yours. I want you to have it."

"Oh, Mr. Briscoe, you. . . ." She laughed uncomfortably and her cheeks filled with color. "Really . . . you couldn't." She returned the watch to his hand and closed his fingers firmly around it. "I couldn't think of accepting it."

"Please. I assure you the last thing I'm going to need is a watch. You know somp'n? I would like to think of it marking the kind of hours only a young girl can have. Exciting hours. You will make me very happy if you accept it."

Now Spalding's eyes filled with tears. She shook her head mechanically, unable to believe her fortune. She took the watch from his hand and pressed it against her cheek.

"All right, Mr. Briscoe. If you put it that way. I can't thank you . . . I've never met anyone like you, but I will remember you for the rest of my life."

"I'd rather you remember it's only a possession, miss . . . and so not worth very much."

"I will . . . *always,* Mr. Briscoe." She brightened suddenly and a little nervous laugh escaped her. Wiping her eyes, she said, "We can hear it chime together because it need setting, you know!"

"How come?"

"It's seven o'clock in San Francisco. We might as well set it ahead."

"Sure, I forgot." She chuckled with pleasure when he reached for the watch and turned the hand around to six. They waited, smiling together, while it chimed six times. "Now you turn it," he said. And they both laughed when it chimed seven times.

"Is it really seven o'clock, little girl?"

"As far as this airplane is concerned."

"You know somp'n? I don't want tea or coffee."

"A glass of ice water?"

"Water is for bathing, but if you can put some Scotch in it I'll feel cleaner. It's 'way past my cocktail time."

Spalding stood up quickly. "Yessir. Right now!"

Looking beyond her he saw that José Locota had been watching them from across the aisle. A friendly smile sliced dimples into his weathered cheeks and revealed the gap left by his missing front teeth.

"How about my friend over there? Will you join me for a drink, mister?"

"Ah. . . ." José Locota nodded his head up and down very quickly. "Yeah . . . yeah . . . thank you very much." His smile broadened as Spalding introduced them. He shyly extended his three-fingered hand.

"Will you have soda or water, Mr. Locota?" Spalding asked.

"Oh anything, miss . . . anything you got."

"I'll make yours the same as Mr. Briscoe's then."

Spalding walked briskly to the buffet. She could not remember when she had known such pleasure in serving passengers. It was not until she had mixed the two

94

drinks and was bending down to pull a serving tray from the buffet compartment that she noticed how the glasses seemed to take on movement of their own. They stood on the Monel metal counter and so were exactly level with her line of sight. The ice in the glasses appeared to shiver as if stirred by an unseen hand.

Spalding held herself rigid, waiting to see if it would happen again, but the ice remained still. She pulled out a tray and was reaching for the glasses when they danced away from her hand. The movement was very quick, covering hardly more than inch of the metal counter, yet she knew for certain that they had moved. Now that was a funny thing. The next time she went to the flight deck she would ask Sullivan how glasses could move when the air was perfectly smooth. It had never happened before.

Spalding's smile was thoughtful as she started up the aisle with the tray.

8

Seven thousand feet below the aisle carpet on which Spalding walked so easily, the U. S. Coast Guard Cutter *Gresham* heaved in lonely dignity against the seas. She was currently ocean station "Uncle" and had been so designated for four of her five weeks' tour of duty. Twenty-eight days she had drifted, or maneuvered at dead slow power according to the weather, maintaining her outpost in the same small area of the Pacific. The *Gresham* reported the weather to land stations, served as a transmitting station for en route aircraft to take bearings upon, and in addition gave radar fixes to the planes as they passed overhead. It was a valuable, if unexciting assignment. Boredom and the weather were the only enemies, and, of the two, the *Gresham*'s crew found the weather by far the easier to conquer. In desperation on this evening they had run one movie backwards because they had seen it so many times, and experimented with another movie whose dialogue they knew by heart. They turned off the sound apparatus and, selecting certain crew members to provide the voices, ran the movie silently. Considerable imagination, much of it highly censurable, had spiced the dialogue and the movie had been a resounding success. Second-class Radarman Hulchinsky, whose furry voice had replaced Betty Grable's in the more pungent love scenes, enjoyed par-

96

ticular acclaim. Now, as he leaned across the long plotting table in the *Gresham's* instrument-crowded radar room and sipped at his fourth mug of coffee, he was discontented in spite of the praise lavished on him by third-class operator Finian and striker Golding, who shared the watch with him.

"I'm tellin' you for a fact," Finian said, pounding home his point for the tenth time, ". . . this goddamned Hulchinsky has got the sexiest goddamned voice in the whole goddamned Coast Guard! It's a *fact*." He smacked the table beneath the radar screen which faced him. "If you would just shave real close, Hulchinsky, and put on somethin' besides them goddamned dungarees, somethin' real filmy like in a sultan's harem, and maybe throw a little perfume around . . . so help me, I could screw you!"

"How you boys talk!" Hulchinsky said, resuming the voice he had used during the movie. "A nice person with a feeling for the finer things isn't safe on this ship."

Finian's enjoyment of the moment overwhelmed him. He bent over double and shook his head forlornly.

"See what I mean, Golding? Can you beat it? This goddamned Hulchinsky never misses. I'm goin' to ask the Chief for a different watch. I can't stand this bearded broad any longer. I'll get to be a sexual divert and if a broad don't have a beard and bow legs exactly like Hulchinsky, I'll be what they call im-*pot*ent when, as, and if I ever get ashore again!"

A strong clear voice came from the loudspeaker above the plotting table and broke his helpless laughter.

"This is Aircraft Four-two-zero calling ocean station 'Uncle.' Our position is approximately twenty-five miles north of you. Altitude seven thousand. Course four zero degrees magnetic. Would you give us a radar fix and ground speed, please? Over."

Hulchinsky moved quickly around the plotting table and took down the microphone.

"Roger, Four-two-zero. This is ocean station 'Uncle.' Stand by."

Before Hulchinsky had finished speaking, Golding's entire attention was devoted to the radar. The pale green light from the screen gave his face a sickly look, but his eyes were alert as he followed the slow movement of a small white pip near the edge of the screen.

"Coordinates. . . ." said Golding without taking his eyes from the screen.

"Aye aye," answered Hulchinsky. Poised above the illuminated plotting grid, he held a black grease pencil ready for marking.

"Twenty-seven and zero five."

"Aye aye."

"Twenty-seven and zero eight."

"Aye aye." Each time he acknowledged, Hulchinsky made a cross on the grid with his pencil.

"Twenty-seven and one one."

"Aye aye."

Golding continued calling out the coordinates until there were seven crosses on the plotting grid.

"That'll do it," said Hulchinsky and Golding sat back to light a cigarette. Hulchinsky placed his speed dividers on the first and last cross, read off the result, and reached for the microphone.

"Aircraft Four-two-zero, this is ocean station 'Uncle.' Radar plot shows you twenty-seven miles north of our position. Course four zero magnetic. Ground speed one hunert and fifty-two knots. How does that check with you? Over."

"Four-two-zero to ocean station 'Uncle.' That checks dandy. Thanks very much. Our ETA San Francisco ten one five Greenwich. Over."

"Roger, Four-two-zero. Good trip. Ocean station 'Uncle' out." Hulchinsky hung up the microphone and reached for his coffee mug. He stood beside Golding for a moment watching the small pip complete its crossing of the screen and, when it had disappeared beyond the edge, he sighed heavily.

"I sure wish to Jesus I wuz on that there airplane," he said.

"Darling . . . sweetheart!" Golding answered morosely. "You wouldn't leave *me?*"

The day had already begun to fade beyond the flight deck windows. The ship's speed toward the east hastened

98

the normal descent of the sun, and now a deep violet haze softened the horizon. The pastry-like cumulus clouds had given way to less imposing decks of broken stratus and the higher levels, perhaps fifty miles ahead, were brushed with old gold. Evening had come very swiftly to the Pacific sky.

Dan Roman and Hobie Wheeler had exchanged seats. Now Dan was on the left, leaning forward occasionally to correct the automatic pilot, while Hobie wrote in the log.

Sullivan stood between them. His hands were jammed down hard in his pockets and the knobs at the ends of his jawbones worked rhythmically. He was not looking at the expanse of sky beyond the windows. His whole attention was devoted to the array of instruments which stretched across the interior limits of the ship's nose. These instruments were the nerve ends of the ship's physique and from their staring intelligence Sullivan could ascertain not only the flight attitudes and course, but also the well-being of the four engines.

Normally. Yes, normally any impending trouble would betray itself on the instruments. The cylinder head temperature on an engine might rise or an oil pressure fall. Fuel trouble, a ruptured diaphragm in a carburetor, faulty pump, or a far less serious mechanical ailment would become instantly apparent on the fuel flow meters. The instruments were sensitive and marvelously accurate and so Sullivan, like all his kind, had come to depend on them implicitly. Yet he surveyed the instruments warily, as a clever broker might examine the opening quotations on a stock board. There were still such things as hunches —a feeling that things were not quite as they should be in spite of outward appearances, and he was a little disappointed when he could find nothing to confirm his suspicions. The propellers were in perfect synchronization. The golliwogg synchroscopes were quite still, and the even rumble in his ears was entirely satisfactory. Then why had he been so sure that at least one propeller was moving in and out of phase when he was back in the crew compartment?

Because of the speed of his ship, Sullivan was always obliged to think far ahead of its progress. It was axiomatic that he should not become too absorbed in what was happening at the moment, particularly when things were going well; rather he must project himself hours ahead, a thousand miles beyond the horizon, and conceive of the things that could happen if his thinking was careless now. Only by such seven-league anticipation could he prevent a circumstantial mixture known as "snowballing"—wherein a minor imperfection in a flight could eventually combine with those impossible to foresee, and start an avalanche of difficulty. No one had to tell Sullivan or Dan Roman, or even the comparatively innocent Hobie, that the original cause of many crashes could be traced to an insignificant mistake made early in the flight. It was a natural result of extreme complication and a captain's concern inevitably split itself over a decision of what was really important and what was not.

Sullivan's immediate thinking was further complicated by an emotion that was new to him. It was a secret which he intended to keep entirely to himself, although he knew other captains had experienced it and were sometimes quite frank in confessing their affliction. Gustave Pardee had probed this new wound and probably if he had been able to penetrate Sullivan further, he would have discovered the occupational disease which came upon some pilots more slowly than others, but which eventually came to them all. Sometimes it lasted to their retirement, or was even the cause of it—sometimes they managed to overcome it completely, and sometimes it stayed with them until their end. No flight surgeon, engaged in giving a pilot his bi-annual physical examination, could be sure when his subject would enter this phase of his career, the time when he would find that he was frequently afraid. The degree of his fear was, of course, dependent upon the pilot's basic personality and capacity for mental discipline, but it came as surely as the hours mounted in his log book. Sullivan recognized it as both a good and a bad thing, but he considered it a weakness and hated those moments when he caught himself behaving like all the others.

There were little signs to betray the feeling—the need for a cigarette when he had just finished one, asking for a cup of coffee when he really didn't want it. The emotion bred caution, which was good, but it also caused little things to assume unwarranted importance, and this, he realized, could be the beginning of the end. Little by little, exaggeration of those small things bound to occur on any flight could wash against a pilot's judgment, withering it, until his thinking became unstable. The effects were first noticeable in a reluctance to go to the airport, or refusal to talk of flying, or even feigned illness when a special flight would be assigned. Eventually, if the pilot was unable to conquer the disease, the destruction of his confidence would become more obvious—there would be abortive turn-arounds when there was no sound technical reason for returning to a point of departure, there would be missed approaches to airports during bad weather, and sometimes distress signals sent when there was actually no need for them.

Sullivan was determined to fight against this uncomfortable phase of his air maturity. It was like wetting the bed. He would cure it before his chief pilot, his wife, or anyone else might suspect it. And so he watched the instruments, regarding them in cold silence for a long time. There was nothing wrong. Every temperature, every pressure, was exactly as it should be. And Dan would certainly have said something if he sensed anything wrong. An airplane carrying mail, and passengers who had paid their fare in the expectation of being delivered to a certain city, could not be turned back because its captain was nursing a secret. There was nothing wrong.

After a time, Sullivan turned away from the instrument panel and stepped back until he could watch Leonard plot the radar position received from ocean station "Uncle." Leonard was not recording fact, but history —for even as he worked the ship moved ten miles east of the small *x* which symbolized their past position. Every sixty seconds, more than three miles of space slipped beneath the wings. In a hour or so they would pass the point-of-no-return, which Leonard had marked with another *x*.

"Looks like we picked up about four minutes," Leonard said. "The wind is finally beginning to swing around."

"Good."

"Things look better to my tired old eyes. I may pass a miracle and hit San Francisco right on time." Leonard patted the chart affectionately as if it were a living thing and Sullivan thought how wonderful it must be to feel so entirely sure of anything. "Have a lifesaver, Skipper?" Leonard held out a packet of mints.

"No thanks . . . maybe after we eat. Let me know, will you . . . when we pass the point-of-no-return?"

"Naturally. . . ."

Leonard had a perfect right to the look of mild surprise in his eyes, Sullivan thought. When the time came, it was as routine for him to announce the point-of-no-return as it was for him to wind his hack watch. It was a silly request, like asking if the evening outside the windows would soon become night. It was an admission that he was concerned about the point-of-no-return, and so an admission of nerves. Nerves that weren't held any by guys who whistled their heads off all the time.

Sullivan waited for his disgust with himself to subside before he tapped Dan on the shoulder.

"Take a breather, Dan. I'll turn the knobs for a while."

Dan stretched his arms upward as far as he could reach, wiggled his fingers, and yawned.

"Okay. I can stand a nap." He unfastened his seat belt and Sullivan was sorry for him when he saw how unnaturally he had to twist himself so that he could work his way around the control pedestal. That gimpy leg of Dan's—it must have been one hell of a crash. Sullivan had seen the leg when Dan was taking a shower in Honolulu and he had wanted to ask about it, but such questions were never asked by pilots with two good legs. Where had Dan found the nerve to come back? Did he know about the disease, too, or had he been in the game so long he just didn't care any more?

"Funny thing," Dan said smiling, and Sullivan was conscious of a new warmth in his eyes, a look of understanding that was almost embarrassing. ". . . funny thing how sound a man can sleep with four big engines hollering their heads off a few feet away from his ears. And he only wakes up in a hurry if they stop hollering. Imagine silence waking you up at home. No human being should put up with such a crazy arrangement." Then just as he turned for the crew cabin, he reached out with his fist and jabbed Sullivan gently in the ribs.

He knows, Sullivan thought . . . he knows about me.

He lit a cigarette and stared moodily at the clock on the instrument panel, watching the sweep second hand move around and around.

No matter what Howard says to me I am not going to answer him, Lydia Rice promised herself once more. There is no hope in trying to reason with a child, a stupid, incompetent child who should be selling neckties instead of trying to run an advertising concern. I hate him. If I had listened to Aunt Helen in 1944 when she said, "Look, Lydia, Howard Rice *is* a spectacularly handsome man, particularly in his uniform, and I'm quite sure he must be immensely valuable to the admiral as a sort of social aide . . . but really, my dear, couldn't you find a young man better suited to our own way of life? I've always thought Howard's brain might fit very nicely in a demitasse." Oh, Aunt Helen you were so right. Howard was still pretty, even out of uniform, and remember that husbands were hard to come by in 1944, but behind those grey eyes there was an absolute vacuum. I hate him.

She squirmed in her seat, carefully rearranging her tiny feet so that the distance between them and her husband's became the maximum possible under the circumstances. She tried looking out the window, as it seemed she had been doing for days, but now the sky had become a dull purple and the ocean below was black. Both, she thought, were as boring as her husband's face.

I did everything for this man but give him the moon. He even sold the moon for a dollar and ninety-eight cents. Anything to make himself feel important—the big operator. Operating on my money, which is now all gone. In debt to his beautiful grey eyes. Oh, what the hell am I going to do? I should have gone to bed with Howard, had a bang-up affair with him and let things go at that. Bed is the only place he will ever distinguish himself, and there, indeed, he should represent America in the Olympics. Did a man necessarily have to be stupid to be good in bed? What about the bright ones? I'll find out as soon as I'm no longer Mrs. Rice . . . maybe before, if it takes the lawyers too long to make out all the papers. Wash my mind out with soap and water, but how else can I feel when I hate the man I married?

Imagine trading stock in the agency for some Canadian mines no one with any sense of responsibility had ever seen. And not telling anyone about it until it was too late . . . all because he wanted to accomplish something on his own and live in the great big outdoors. Just get a picture of Lydia Rice in a Canadian mining camp, ten jillion miles from nowhere and twenty jillion miles from "21," the Cub Room, or even the Plaza! You should have sent Howard to a psychiatrist . . . a little couch work without benefit of perfume might have saved things. Pine trees and fish, indeed! What was Lydia going to do while her husband clumped around in his boots and lumberjack shirt? Have cocktails with the chipmunks? Play bridge with the Eskimos? I suppose there are Eskimos. There must be *somebody* . . . not the Willards perhaps, or the Depews, or the Cooleys, or the Saltons, or Marty Wren, or Jules Healy, or the Bresslers, or any of those charming important people who knew better than to stray very far from Manhattan, but there must be *somebody*. François the trapper, no doubt, who will have sixty-six children, and Ugug, the Eskimo who will have just as many wives. Scintillating company for Lydia Rice. I hate him. *I hate Howard* . . . write it one hundred times on the blackboard of your mind and don't say a single word to him between now and the time you get back to blessed, wonderful New York unless it is absolutely necessary. "Where is the baggage . . . ? Have you got enough money left for this taxi . . . ?" Survival phrases only.

She pulled her compact from her purse and examined her nose to see if it was shiny. Like everything else about her it was a very small and delicately formed nose although it did have an annoying tendency to become moist if not checked frequently. Of course such a condition would not make the slightest difference in the Canadian wilderness . . . Lydia Rice of the north! Two-gun girl of the Arctic wastes! The whole scheme was preposterous, conceived by a man who had the sensitivity of a polar bear.

"Lydia . . . if you're through pouting we might try talking things over in a reasonable fashion."

"We have nothing to talk about." She snapped her compact shut and stuffed it angrily into her bag. Then she turned her face to the window.

"I should say we have a great deal to discuss . . . providing you are willing to approach this thing sensibly."

"Sensibly? Look who's talking."

"Perhaps I did put it to you more abruptly than I should have. But I am possessed with the old-fashioned notion that a wife might be more happy if she followed her husband wholeheartedly in whatever enterprise he attempted."

"Even when he makes an ass of himself?"

"Yes . . . even then. But in our case that has not as yet happened."

"Anyone who would sell a New York advertising agency for some God-forgotten Canadian mine is well on the way to being an ass. And I'm quite certain that any or all of our friends will agree."

"I am not the least bit interested in what our so-called friends might think. In fact there are times when I wonder if they ever do think."

"They will unquestionably reach the same verdict about you."

"Let them. Lydia . . . I just can't believe you've been really happy in that atmosphere. It is the goddamnedest social whirlpool since Roman times. You see the same faces every day and the same faces every night . . . only at night the faces are a little drunker. None of them produce a damn thing except gossip and an occasional bum play. Most of them are even afraid to produce children. They live in a world of late breakfasts, long lunches at whatever place happens to be smart momentarily, and king-sized cocktails spiced with diesel bus smoke, sex, and pseudo-sophisticated yap-yap that passes for conversation. I want out of it."

"You're out of it and I hope you're satisfied."

"I'm not in the least satisfied. There are too many things I want to do. It was only because the war was just over and I was confused that I ever consented to run your advertising agency in the first place. It's not for me, Lydia, and it never will be. I want to get up in the morning with the feeling that whatever I accomplish that day is due to my own efforts . . . not because my wife happened to inherit a business—"

"The fact it was your wife's originally didn't seem to bother you when you decided to sell it . . . without even consulting me."

"There wasn't time. I've explained for two days straight. I'll pay you back as soon as the mine—"

"Haw—"

"In three years you should have every penny."

"Haw." In three years, Lydia thought, I will have missed thirty of the best parties given in America, more than thirty good shows, and heaven knows what else. In three years I am supposed to come down from the Canadian wilderness and take Manhattan by storm. In three years I would be a genuine country bumpkin with skirts around my legs when they ought to be around my knees or the other way around. The formerly chic Mrs. Howard Rice came in what might pass for a period costume, a sort of ruffled calico. . . . Poor, dear Lydia . . . *where have* you been? Nuts.

"For the last time, Lydia . . . I'm asking you to come with me."

"I'm glad it's the last time you're going to make that insane request so I won't have to say no again. I'm getting a divorce as fast as I can."

"You're out of your head."

"I've never seen things more clearly. I picked a boy to do a man's job."

"Running a New York advertising agency could hardly be classed as a man's job."

"My father thought so."

"Your father was a pioneer. There wasn't any advertising business when he started."

She turned to look squarely at him for the first time since they had boarded the plane. Her small mouth became a miniature rosette and her little fists were clenched so tightly the knuckles were pure cream.

"All right, Daniel Boone. Go off to your primeval forest. Get up with the pigeons or whatever kind of birds they have around there. Put your mind in mothballs and get calluses on your hands. Be a great, big dirt-under-the-fingernails boy. Make fire by friction and eat out of cans. Wait around for the mail to come in once a month and be so hungry for something to read, the *National Geographic* will look hotter than the last *New Yorker*. Take a bath on Saturday nights and go to an Eskimo hoedown, teach them to samba, for all I care . . . do just as you goddamned well please if it will make you feel like a man, but don't ask me to share your juvenile adventures. It's bad enough having to pay for them." She whipped her trim little body around until she faced the window. Her shoulders were set back defiantly.

Howard reached out to touch them and then slowly withdrew his hand. "Is that your last word, Lydia?"

His only answer was silence. He knew she would not be crying. Not Lydia Stanley Rice who measured every man by his clothes and his wallet. The poor, wretched little girl who was afraid to leave the prison compound known as the Upper East Fifties.

He turned away from her and began to massage his eyes very slowly, finding relief in the slow rhythmic movement of his own hands. After a moment he felt someone tugging at his elbow. It was the man across the aisle, that absurd Mr. Joseph, or whatever his name was.

"Hey, fella . . . you got nuthin' but trouble, right?" Howard could only look at him steadily and try to keep the astonishment from his face while Ed Joseph continued in an eager cracked whisper that seemed to fill the whole airplane. "Now listen, fella . . . I can see you think I got no business butting into your affairs. I can see that okay . . . but it so happens we got a club back home, about like the Kiwanis or the Optimists, see? Meets every odd Thursday for lunch, and a sweller bunch of fellas you could never want to know. It's the Good Neighbor Club and you'd be surprised at the program we got . . . summer camp for kids, hospital benefits, plugging for the Community Chest and the like. We got a motto and a song which one of our fellas wrote called 'Help Thy Neighbor' and you'd just never believe what a good all-around thing it is . . . especially thse days when nobody seems to give a whoop about the next guy—"

"I assure you, Mr.—"

"Oh, I know what you're going to say . . . with you everything is hunky-dory and you don't need help, especially from strangers. That's the first thing a fella in trouble always says. Now it so happens evrybody has troubles and the booby hatches are full of people who keep things to themselves because either they're scared to tell the truth, thinking it will make a monkey out of them, or they figure no one else could appreciate how bad their situation is, anyway. Okay? So that's human nature and you can't win, you say. The Good Neighbors believe it ain't so and we've proved it plenty of times."

Ed Joseph took a quick breath. "Now you just had a little hassle with your wife. . . . Oh, don't take offense, please . . . I wasn't eavesdropping, but from where I'm sitting anyone couldn't help but hear, and I would be a liar if I didn't admit that the missus and me have a round or two once in a while just for laughs. . . ." He paused again to catch his breath and peel a flake of skin from his sunburned nose. "You ever heard of Alcoholics Anonymous?

"Well, in a way, the Good Neighbors is like that organization. I never had to go to AA, thank God, but they tell me when a fella gets in trouble with too much booze, other fellas who have had the same problem sort of take him in hand and help him over the rough spots. Good Neighbors operates along the same lines. And sometimes our lunches are funnier than hell. When you come into the room, the B.P.O.E. let us use their downstairs hall, every fella gets issued a towel, see, and he takes it to his place with him. Then over the speaker's table is hung another great big towel with the letters 'For Crying Out Loud' embroidered on it. So every fella has his crying towel, get it? . . . Just in case he's got so many troubles he can't stand it any longer. And sometimes when a real bad case comes in, a couple of the Good Neighbors will hold the towel for the fella, just so he can concentrate on weeping and not have to use his energy for anything else. I'm telling you, when one of our fellas stands up and starts bawling out his troubles in front of the rest of the gang, it's one of the funniest things you ever heard or seen . . . it gets to be a regular old-fashioned revival meeting and the fella who hasn't got any particular troubles at the moment really feels left out of things. . . ."

Howard Rice shook his head in disbelief. He forgot the words he had chosen to stop the eager man across the aisle. He began to listen.

". . . of course, the fellas don't give with the details of their real troubles, which nobody cares about anyway . . . they just cover their headaches in a general way if it's financial, and sometimes, say, they're weeping for a friend if it's personal . . . but the effect is the same . . . always the same. If the fella doesn't wind up actually laughing at himself, at least he feels better and the main thing is, everybody else does, too, because nine times out of ten they think the other fella is worse off than they are. . . ."

"What do you sing at the end of your meeting? 'Pack up your troubles in your old kit bag?'"

"How did you know? But I forgot to tell you. When one of the fellas has real trouble . . . like maybe he can't pay his income tax, or his wife just smashed up the car, or his new house shows cracks all along the foundation, we have an organ that plays real sad music. It's a kick, believe me."

"I'm beginning to think it might be."

"Don't get the idea the fellas tell their real troubles, like some we know have a wife maybe dying, or the business is *really* going broke . . . what they confess is little troubles, like maybe they can't get somebody to mow their lawn, or they can't break a hundred on the golf

109

course . . . it's all relative, see, and if a fella gets in the habit of laughing at the little things that go wrong and finds out it just don't pay to take himself too seriously, why then it's much easier for him to keep from blowing his top over the geniune serious things he wouldn't tell anyone. Get it?"

"I'm beginning to follow you, Mr.——?"

"Ed Joseph. I sell furniture. Now in your case, fella . . . maybe you'll feel better if you hear me cry some. I want you to understand how the Good Neighbors works, so just imagine me with a towel and hear this."

Ed Joseph took a deep breath, smiled quickly at his wife, and leaned far across the aisle. "I don't know how long the missus and me have been saving up for this trip, we don't make a lot of money, understand, and we got two kids to support besides ourselves . . . anyway, we scrimped along on a lot of things for at least three or four years so someday we could take a trip to the Hawaiian Islands. You know, palm trees, sunshine, sand, and stuff like we don't have at home. Okay? We dreamed about it together all that time and never took another vacation so we would have plenty of money for this one. Once in a while we'd break down and buy a Hawaiian record just to get us in the mood, but most of the time we just pored over travel folders and counted the pennies. So what happens? Finally one day we decide there is enough in the kitty to make the trip the way we want to, and all our dreams are going to come true. So I get everything fixed to be away from the store for three weeks, and the missus persuades a woman to stay with the kids for the small sum of ten dollars a day, which is more than I made the first five years we were married. Anyway, we get to San Francisco and have ourselves all set in a nice room on the boat. Unpacked and everything, with bon voyage packages from our friends and one from the Good Neighbors, too. Only the boat doesn't sail. Just before they pull up the gang plank, the stewards call a strike and there we are.

"So we have to take an airplane which was not part of our dream. We can't take all our baggage including some of the new dresses the missus has bought just for this trip. Dresses she gave up a lot of other things for. The baggage is supposed to come along later, but it gets lost in the confusion and I don't know if we ever will see it. All right, we're lucky. We get the last two seats on the airplane and pretty soon, there we are in the land of our dreams . . . okay?

". . . so we get to the hotel, the Islander, which is small and just figures in nice with our budget . . . only there has been a mix-up in our reservations, it seems another couple named Joseph from Milwaukee have come in the day before and there's no room for us. Not unless we want to make a fuss and kick these other people out of our room, see? And after we thought about it, well, maybe they had a dream, too, so we call all over town and finally wind up at the Royal Hawaiian, which is very fancy, but which we can't afford unless we knock three days off our dream trip. That cuts out any chance of going to the other islands understand . . . ?

". . . so what happens next? The first day nothing. We're dead. We lie on the beach and look at the ocean and think this is really it. We talk about how we used to date each other and how much fun it is going to be dancing under the stars just like we used to do only never with such romantic surroundings. Okay? Comes evening. The missus gets into the one evening dress she could bring along, and I get into the tux I haven't worn for ten years . . . only I got no shirt studs or cuff links because I forgot they are in the baggage we left behind. So I have to send out for some and they don't come cheap in Honolulu. . . .

". . . but finally we're all rigged out like we're going to have dinner at the White House or something and we start down to the dining room, where I got a table all reserved, and we are going to make with a little of the light fantastic. Now get the picture of this. . . .

". . . there's a flight of marble stairs in the hotel which leads from the lobby hall to the dining room and the missus is wearing a new pair of shoes she paid twenty-five bucks for to go with her new dress. The heels are a lot higher than the kind she is used to and the first thing we know she is sailing through the air like a rag doll. Those steps are hard. She lands right on her tokus and ten minutes after we have left the room we are right back in it, with the missus flat in bed and the house doctor saying she has twisted her sacroiliac. That ends any dancing for the trip and for two days we see the Hawaiian sunshine through a window . . . at thirty bucks a day.

"Okay? Everything passes. Finally she feels well enough to hobble down to the beach again. Even the Doc says some sun will do her good. But the sun doesn't know this and it rains bullfrogs for three straight days. Remember how it poured last week? We're back in the room again and beginning to wish we'd never left home. All we've got to do is write postcards back home about what a wonderful time we're having."

For a moment Howard Rice observed a wistful look in his eyes, but it passed very quickly. A mischievous smile came to his face.

"Now, fella, part of any trip is the people you meet, right? Sort of join up with another couple and enjoy things together? So we get talking one day with this pair from Minneapolis. I won't mention their name. Anyway they're just swell and lots of fun during the day. But they're chameleons, understand? They don't live like other people, I guess. Anyway, after two drinks at night they both start in full blast. The husband he goes hammer and tongs for my missus, and his wife, she thinks I'm Clark Gable. It's a regular marathon and my missus can't run very fast on account of her sacroiliac. And, fella, you haven't lived until you've been chased around a palm tree by that guy's wife. Neither one of them care who's looking either. Real maniacs. So we spend the rest of our dream trip sort of creeping around corners and eating away from the hotel so we don't run into these people all the time and have to play post office.

"Our last two days, the sun comes out and, of course, we have to make the most of it. Whoever heard of coming home from a dream trip without a tan? We're desperate, see? So we oil up and lie on the beach, just like in the folders. The missus has a third-degree burn on her shoulders and I don't dare put any weight on my back. We're lucky if we have any skin left at all when we get home, let alone a tan. I'm going to have to borrow from the bank to pay next month's food bill if we ever do get home. . . ."

A deep sigh escaped Ed Joseph. He shook his head solemnly and then began to laugh.

"If you still think you got troubles, mister . . . I'll be glad to lend you my towel."

Howard turned away for a moment to look at his wife Lydia. She was still looking out the window although it was now so dark outside he knew she could not possibly see anything. He smiled in spite of himself and turned back to Ed Joseph.

"I wonder," he said quietly, "if you and Mrs. Joseph would care to join me in a drink? You can have your towel back now."

9

THE *Cristobal Trader,* AN ANCIENT RUSTING FREIGHTER of Panamanian registry, sploshed awkwardly through the black Pacific. She was headed toward the east, parallel to the long ominous swells which heaved down from the north. The combination of their strength against her slow ten-knot speed caused her to wallow miserably. Since the black night wiped out the horizon, the extreme limits of her rolling were impossible to estimate and there were times when Manuel Aboitiz, her second radio operator, swore she would just keep right on going and roll to hell and gone in a complete circle.

He sat in the radio shack with his feet braced against the wooden bulkhead and his fat back jammed hard against the panel of his antique transmitter. It was the only way Manuel could keep from sliding the full length of the room. He sat very quietly, listening to his belt creak and watching his loose stomach move sluggishly from side to side as his weight was redistributed with each roll.

He closed his eyes for long periods of time while he alternately cursed his fate and dreamed of those days when he was a radioman first-class in the United States Navy. And on an aircraft carrier at that. All finito now. The only thing left was knowledge and most of that was useless or forgotten, anyway. Except for one thing—

the aircraft band receiver which he had built with his own hands. No collection of surplus parts ever worked better.

Manuel's boss, the *Cristobal Trader*'s chief radioman, objected to the receiver, and once in a fit of drunken anger had almost thrown it overboard. He shouldn't have tried that. Manuel almost killed him. He loved his high-frequency receiver and said to all who would listen that it was the only thing which kept him from going crazy during the endless months it took a freighter to go anywhere. On the receiver he could hear the trans-Pacific aircraft working and he was an aircraft man, wasn't he? . . . even if it was ex . . . ? Someday he would work with aircraft again, leave the turtle-speed thinking of ships and mariners, and resharpen his mind to the quick, staccato ways of airmen who had no time to waste.

Whenever Manuel was on watch, the high-frequency receiver was turned on. Sometimes not a sound came from it, and other times it would be rich with facts and figures concerning the movements of the ships above his head. Manuel found it easy to transport himself aloft and join with the communications, although he was never more than a silent partner. The fact that he was not invited to join in on the conversations distressed him, but he refused to blame the airmen. The International Wireless rules were at fault. They dictated his social exile.

Now as his head rolled from side to side, moving smoothly on a miniature ocean of swarthy chins, Manuel suddenly opened his eyes and listened intently while voices came through his precious receiver and broke his loneliness.

"Hello, Honolulu . . . this is Four-two-zero with a position report."

There was no answer. Manuel waited impatiently. Why weren't the bums in Honolulu on their toes? He, Manuel Aboitiz, would have answered instantly. Yes, even quicker than that. Bending over his paunch, he reached out to twist the tuning dial slightly.

"How do you read us, Honolulu?"

Still no answer. Manuel ran his sausage fingers through

his thick hair and spit on the deck. The evidence would give his chief apoplexy, but Manuel didn't care. Why didn't the bums answer? There was a longer silence.

"Four-two-zero, this is San Francisco. Go ahead with your report."

"Okay, San Francisco!" the voice sang out. Manuel sighed with relief and leaned back to listen. "San Francisco from Four-two-zero . . . copy Honolulu. Position at nineteen fifty-seven . . . latitude thirty-four thirty north . . . longitude one forty west . . . seven thousand feet . . . thirteen hundred gallons remaining. . . ."

Manuel did not wait for the rest of the report. Grunting with delight, he heaved himself out of the chair and fought his way up the slanting deck until he reached the door. The aircraft was reporting a position almost identical to that of the *Cristobal Trader!*

The night wind whipped at his loose shirt as he slid down to the boat deck rail. Grasping it firmly, he braced himself while he turned his face straight up and listened. But the sky was overcast and there was no sound except the sea and the whipping of his shirt tail. Manuel beat his fist on the rail. Just now he wanted actually to see the airplane as badly as he had ever wanted anything.

He waited hopefully for several minutes until the night wind caused him to shiver and drove almost the last of his hope away. He was about to launch himself back to the radio shack when he caught the first hint of foreign sound. It was like a distant waterfall heard from the base of a mountain. Then rapidly, it became louder, less gentle, until it compounded into the easy snoring of a giant. Manuel forgot the cold wind. He frantically searched the blanket of cloud above him in every direction, trying to place the sound exactly. Then just as it began to diminish, he observed a rent in the cloud deck. It was toward the south, almost abeam of his ship, and framed a few stars which glistened wetly, as if they too had been dipped in the sea. But Manuel ignored the stars, for passing between them, almost rejoining them it seemed, were the winking lights of an airplane.

The clouds obscured the vision in a moment, but not

before Manuel had time to crook his thumb as if to beg a ride. When the very last of the sound deserted him, he waved his hand and turned from the rail. He was strangely exhilarated. He would listen very carefully now for the reports from that airplane, as long as he could hear them. It was much better having actually seen the plane. He even knew the number . . . Four-two-zero.

And so Manuel Aboitiz was no longer lonely with the night and the sea.

"From the window at my side, I can see the stars," Dorothy Chen wrote in her careful English script. She was writing to her brother, who remained in Korea, and she would tell him of all the things to be seen in this new American world.

"You will please be my eyes," he had asked quietly on the morning of her departure from the house in the hills near Seoul, "until I can make the journey myself." And now because it meant so much to him, Dorothy Chen was already writing her third letter in as many days.

Dear brother, these stars are like the many many things I must now begin to learn. What a terrible condition that it is I who make the trip and still can never speak or write this language so fine as you. But the best way to learn, yes? . . . is to write and speak always without fear of peoples laughing, and so some day we forget how strange this really is. So I speak many times with people, if you please, and the attendant on this aircraft who is a girl, is nice to say I speak very well. You would like this girl who is of blond hair and very white teeth and is like the pictures in the magazines at home. Her work is to wait on the passengers but this is not the same like the serving girls other places. No. She is of the same class as the passengers and speaks with them many times and quite as she pleases. Also she understands the Columbia University where I will study, and has tell me it will be most pleasant. Oh, happiness!

This midday we depart from Honolulu and I have

117

already a mix-up about what time it really is but wonderful to tell you that America is all around me in every way. And so soon it is night.

There are several American ladies sitting in this same aircraft with me and they smell very fine and wear clothes that make me feel like a very poor person. Yes, dear brother, they are all beautiful it seems, even the ladies with many years, but they do talk very loud like every person is deaf and this I think is not so nice. I know I must have care not to say disagreeable things about American persons who permit me to entry their country, but this I have observed.

The aircraft flies very smooth over the ocean and I have not any sickness. Yes, I am very well except for carrying the excitement in my heart about my new life, and also the sadness hurting me because I will not see you or Mother or Father for two years. Still, as you told me, it is bad to think back and I must live in the future always now in the manner of these people.

Do you understand a funny thing? In Honolulu I must be inspected by the American Customs and of course by the Immigration persons, and do you believe dear brother, there was not one soldier to guard things. I look everywhere for soldiers with guns and—

Dorothy Chen paused uncertainly. She could not think of the word she wanted to write and now there would be a space where there should not be one, and her brother would be ashamed. She closed her eyes and tried very hard to remember the English word. Then a voice startled her.

"Would you like your dinner now, Miss Chen?" It was Spalding bending across the vacant seat beside her.

"Oh yes, if you please!" Before Spalding could move away, Dorothy Chen caught her hand. "Please . . . I am so stupid. Here is a letter to my brother in English, and I cannot remember this word. It is that thing soldiers wear on the end of their gun, like a sword, you understand?"

"Bayonet?"

Dorothy Chen rocked her head and pressed her thin fingers against her smooth cheek. "Ah yes! I am so very, very stupid! Thank you. I am embarrassed."

"Anyone who can write more than one language should never be embarrassed," Spalding smiled. "Being the original dumb-bunny, I can hardly write my own."

"Dumb-bunny?"

"That's slang for mentally retarded American girls like me."

Dorothy Chen wanted to laugh, but she covered her mouth so Spalding would not think her impolite.

"Dumb-bunny? How delightful. I must tell my brother of this."

"Tell him you met the number-one stupid rabbit. If he knows any American girls, he'll understand. Now I'll get your dinner."

Spalding went back to the buffet and began to make up a dinner tray. She set out the salad, a roll with butter, and took a steak from the electric hot box. She filled a cup with soup from the big thermos and set it down on the tray. Then suddenly the whole tray came to life and skittered several inches across the Monel counter. The movement was so violent it dashed hot soup on Spalding's hand. She grimaced with pain and quickly put her tongue to the burn. The same thing again! That terrible vibration. She left the tray on the counter and, still holding her hand to her mouth, she walked rapidly up the cabin aisle toward the flight deck. The tears were hard to keep back.

She passed through the darkened flight compartment and almost collided with Dan Roman, who was climbing out of the bunk. She went straight forward to the dimly lit flight deck.

"Captain Sullivan . . . there's something very wrong back there, the trays—"

"I know. I felt it, too." He was holding a spotlight against his window, directing its beam toward the number-one engine. His voice was strained and unnaturally thin.

". . . the plates . . . the whole tray . . . jumped. It happened a while ago, too. I burned myself. It hurts . . . like hell."

Now the whole crew were huddled together on the flight deck. Dan, rubbing the sleep from his eyes, and Leonard were pressing forward on each side of Spalding. Hobie leaned anxiously across the control pedestal, waiting for Sullivan's analysis.

"Christ," Dan said, "it woke me up . . . right now."

"I could swear it's that number-one engine," Sullivan said. He peered out at the engine again and then turned back to the instruments. "But's it's running perfectly . . . they all are."

"Maybe there's something wrong with the tail," Leonard said unhappily. "If our little girl got burned maybe it was worse back there."

"Dan. Get your flashlight. Go have a look through the tail cone. It might be something back there. Report to me as soon as you can. Leonard, take a fast fix and let me know our position now, and every ten minutes from now, until you hear differently. Spalding, get back with your passengers because if this thing lets go again they're going to start wondering. Hobie, you get on the radio and tell San Francisco we're experiencing some unusual vibration. Tell them to keep the circuit open and to stand by until further advised."

"Do you want to declare an emergency?" There was fear in Hobie's voice.

Sullivan's eyes swept the instrument panel. The knobs in his jaw stood out like rocks. He pressed his lips tightly together and shook his head.

"No . . . not yet."

At the extreme rear of the ship, behind the buffet, the rest rooms, and the small space where Spalding hung the passengers' coats, there was a small door which led to the tail cone. Dan Roman opened it, squeezed through the entrance sideways, and let himself down about three feet until he stood on the frames which formed the structural strength of the ship. He switched on his flashlight, more to comfort himself than with a hope of finding anything wrong. For this compartment, almost never visited by the flight crews, was an eerie place in which the sense of true flight was far more pronounced than in any other part of the ship. Although the compartment was hardly more than ten feet long, it was shaped like the end of a funnel and had no windows, so that the sensation of confinement in a swiftly moving projectile was bound to make any airman uncomfortable. There was no solid sound of engines here, only the whirring rush of air against the thin aluminum skin. A sense of great loneliness descended almost immediately on Dan, as if he were standing in space without hope of rejoining his fellowmen. It was bitterly cold and without horizon of any kind; the slight swaying, as the tail answered the course corrections of the automatic pilot, caused Dan to feel dizzy. He found it necessary to reach for the bulkhead to steady himself.

The control wires to the elevators, trim tabs, and rudder were stretched tautly between the bulkhead behind Dan and the narrow end of the tail cone. He moved the beam of his flashlight along each one of them and the fair-leads over which they passed. There was nothing wrong and there had not been the slightest vibration since he lowered himself into the compartment.

He waited and tried to think of what could be wrong. Structural failure was a thing of the past—it just didn't happen any more; and yet, strangely enough, it was the one thing that still gnawed at most pilots' secret fears. You couldn't go out and repair a torn wing and you couldn't go back and pick up a tail that had parted from the main body of a ship. But those were the one-in-ten-million freak failures impossible to explain. Furthermore, such rare failures had always occurred under conditions of extreme stress; some unholy combination of the elements that would always remain a mystery because there was never anyone surviving who could testify about them. Transport airplanes, built exactly like Four-two-zero, had withstood fantastic physical strains and held together long enough to make their destination. They had been tossed completely on their back in waterspouts, bashed through treetops, tossed like chips in thunderstorms, and yet they suffered only minor damage. Then how could anything go wrong structurally on such a smooth trip?

The more Dan thought about it the more convinced he became that he was wasting his time in the tail cone. It had to be something else. One of the engines was about to freeze a master rod, anything—but the trouble was up forward where he had first felt that bump. He cursed himself for not saying something then, before they were in mid-ocean.

He snapped off his light and climbed back into the passenger cabin. Spalding was waiting for him as he closed the door. She was trying to smile.

"Everything okay?"

"Yes. We're still in one piece."

"There hasn't been any vibration since you came back."

"No."

"Will we be all right, Dan?"

"Sure. Just make like nothing ever happened."

"I was starting to serve the passengers. Should I go ahead?"

Dan hesitated and ran his finger down one of the deep lines beside his mouth. His mind was traveling through the whole ship, seeking through its complexity for the right answer.

"I guess you might as well carry on. Sometimes these things never do get explained." Then still rubbing the line in his cheek, he walked foward toward the flight deck. Just as he reached the door he heard his name called.

"Hey, Dan! You too high and mighty to come see an old chum?"

"Well, Ken Childs! How the hell are you!" They shook hands warmly.

"Sit down a minute, Dan, and let's catch up on a few things. Ye gods, I never thought you'd still be flying."

Dan blinked at the reading light over Ken Childs' head and smiled. His whole thinking was with the ship now. He didn't want to talk to Ken, or alarm the woman who sat beside him. They were obviously having a good time.

"Well, you know how it is, chum. Getting away from these things is like giving up opium."

"This is Dan Roman . . . Miss Holst." Dan touched his cap brim. "Come on, Dan," Ken said. "Hang up a minute and tell us what's wrong with this airplane." He laughed and nudged May Holst, who returned his laugh.

"Is there something wrong with it?"

"Cut it out, Dan. Something popped so hard a while ago it spilled my drink."

"Well, order another. We're not stingy."

"So you won't talk?"

"You bet, Ken . . . when we get to San Francisco. We'll have a lot to talk about." Dan smiled as easily as he could and turned for the door again.

"I bet we're late," Ken Childs called after him.

"It's barely possible. . . ." Dan answered, then he closed the door behind him.

He quickened his pace through the dark crew cabin, but when he reached the narrow galley leading to the flight deck, he was forced to pause because a pair of legs barred his further passage. The legs were Leonard Wilby's. He was standing on his stool taking a celestial fix through the astrodome. Beyond Leonard's legs Dan could see the dim lights on the flight deck, pink and soft yellow, like the lights of a primitive village seen from a great distance. Above them all, centered between the black windows, was the faint gleam of the magnetic compass swimming in its liquid. The course had not been changed. Sullivan had not turned back for Honolulu.

Dan tried to twist past Leonard's legs, but abandoned the attempt when he found he would surely jostle him. He didn't want to disturb Leonard just now. Let him complete his delicate observation of the stars for an exact position. It could be very important.

While he waited Dan listened to the droning of the engines. Their even rumbling passed through his feet and moved upward through his whole body, soothing him. He sensed the tremendous power on each side of the narrow passageway, and as a musician might value a perfect cadence, he found it easier to wait. He told himself that there was really nothing to get excited about.

A light flashed on in the astrodome, then Leonard climbed down from his stool. When his face came level with Dan's, he looked at him searchingly.

"Find anything?"

"Nope."

"What the hell do you suppose it could be?"

"It beats me. Where are we?"

"Wait till I figure it up. I'll let everybody know in a couple of minutes."

Leonard turned up the rheostat-controlled light over his navigation table and anxiously opened his computation books. Dan walked forward until he stood between Sullivan and Hobie. Sullivan had loosened his collar and pulled down his tie. There was a thin film of perspiration across his brow, yet when he turned his head to look at Dan, he asked only with his eyes.

He has himself under perfect control, Dan thought, and that is good, but he is afraid—I can smell it. Fear leaks out of a man's skin somehow; you have to know what controlled fear is really like yourself before you can anticipate it in others.

Sullivan's fear was not good. In an emergency it could spread to the others.

"There's nothing wrong in the tail," Dan said quietly.

Sullivan pulled a cigarette from his shirt pocket and placed it between his lips. His movements were slow and deliberate, overly so, as if he found it necessary to command every reflex separately. The flame from his lighter was explosion-bright against the black windows. His eyes became slits. His jawbone knobs were tight still.

"The number-one head temperature has gone up five degrees in the past hour," Hobie said. His voice was hushed, almost inaudible over the hissing of the ventilators, and Dan thought it held a new note of respect for whatever Sullivan might say. But Sullivan said nothing. He glanced up at the offending temperature gauge, then seemed to return to his private thinking. There was a long silence among the three of them while they listened and felt of the ship with all of their senses. Suddenly Hobie pressed his receivers against his ears and reached for his microphone.

"San Francisco wants to know what is the nature of our trouble . . . ?"

Sullivan looked at him quickly. His voice was angry. "Tell them if we knew we'd have told them in the first place!" Then instantly his manner changed. He spoke more calmly. "No . . . don't say that. Tell them . . . ? Just say we still don't know . . . and to keep standing by."

Hobie was repeating Sullivan's words into his microphone when Dan felt a hand on his shoulder. He moved slightly, allowing Leonard to come forward. Leonard turned a flashlight on the chart he held in his hand.

"I got news for you guys. My three-star fix shows we just passed the point-of-no-return."

10

DONALD FLAHERTY HAD ONE THING TO SAY TO HIMSELF.
It was no good being alone when you were bagged. No
damned good at all. And you are catty-wampus bagged,
Professor . . . whatever that means. Bagged to your sore
eyes on what the stewardess had brought and what came
from the paper bag between your feet. But nice bagged,
Professor. No poise, no skyrockets, no trouble to anyone. Yipperee!

Getting bagged and staying bagged was going to be the
only solution. The only solution in the whole wide world.
It allowed a man to forget the explosion and the bloody
missiles. Couldn't do it any other way . . . could you now?

Just temporarily, of course. Once you settled down
again, back among people who think (that was a laugh in
itself), then there wouldn't be any more getting bagged.
Just a polite cocktail before dinner. And it would be completely absorbed in the jello someone's wife called des-
sert. Oh balls, Flaherty. You can never go back to that.
If you're to live, then you've got to live in the future.
Otherwise . . . you've bought it, old boy. The future is
the only cure for the hideous visions that pad so softly
through your mind. There is no loneliness in the future.
It is always an escape.

And the future is sitting right opposite you, also looking lonely and confused in spite of their youth—still

holding the glasses the stewardess had brought them. The glasses were empty now. They could use another drink. Anyone could. Go speak with them. Give them the benefit of your undeniable charm and test yourself. See if you can suffer them and they you, while you still hold from them the secret of their inevitable disaster. If you are so certain of it, then try facing them directly, while the haunting is so persistent. Let them help you drive away the vision of their chubby baby (it would have to be chubby), an infant split apart and smashed flat by a pressure blast.

Flaherty rose unsteadily and sat on the arm of the chair opposite Milo and Nell Buck.

"Hello. Would you let an old man buy you a drink?" They looked at him in surprise as he tried to gather his dignity.

What dignity, Flaherty? You are looking into the honest eyes of youth and you have no honest answer to match them.

He spoke to Nell, who looked at him the more sympathetically, and also it was easier and more pleasant talking to a woman.

"I'll be perfectly frank. I'm bagged. . . ." Can't you think of a different word, Professor? Limited vocabulary, limited mind . . . well now, wasn't it a great big relief to have a limited mind for a change? "I'm also quite lonely. It's a chronic condition with me these days. Please don't misunderstand me. I would guess that you are recently married and I have no desire to thrust myself upon you. My eyes are watery and the muscles which normally control them somewhat better, are tired . . . but as fellow passengers, I rather hoped we might have a drink together. . . ." Quite a speech, Professor, although your voice faded away at the end. The punch evaporated somewhere—it became lost in the misery of your own despair. Oh what a fatuous, self-pitying, phrase-making snob you are, my dear Professor—manufacturing drama as if it would excuse your intrusion upon these superb young animals, who were ever so much happier before you arrived. You should have been a politician, a bagged politician, of course, going about kissing little babies who would one day be split.

Flaherty reached deeply within himself and for a few words found his voice again.

"It would be my pleasure to provide. . . ." He waved the paper bag in a helpless gesture. The Bucks looked at him curiously but they made no reply.

Oh God . . . wouldn't one of them please say something?

Once more he held out the bag, his thin hands trembling slightly.

"All right, mister," Milo Buck said. "Sounds like a good idea." He offered his glass and then reached for his bride's.

Flaherty took them eagerly. He could not recall when anything had made him so happy—he would at this moment have given them all he possessed, the few thousand he had accumulated on that hateful island, the riches of his mind, though it would be the cruelest punishment to transfer such a tarnished package; he would give them anything if he could only join them honestly for a single hour.

He poured their drinks and leaned back to watch them in anticipation. Then suddenly, studying their open faces, he knew that he had tricked himself. He should not have looked at them, for their faces were unmarked by fear of any kind. He was alone again. He wanted to hide himself from their eyes; crawl away instead of facing them. Just an old man, a bagged old man who after a while would begin to babble nonsense and expect attention, though the prophecies would be faulty and the reminiscences half-imagined.

Please! Don't stare at Donald Flaherty like that. Let me inhale of your clean breaths a little, suck of the air about you so that somehow I may begin to live again. Share your youth with this corpse, if only for a few minutes . . . and I will promise to forget the missile—which, God willing, you will never see.

When they were ready, Flaherty raised his glass.

"To your happy future!" he said in a clear strong voice.

José Locota was the first to become concerned with Humphrey Agnew's behavior. Many years before he had seen a man conduct himself in the same way, and the sharpness of the memory was now beginning to sour the rare pleasure of the last half-hour. José would have preferred wine instead of whisky, for wine was more likely to bring peace rather than excitement. But drinking with the sick man across the aisle, who was an extremely fine gentleman and would not admit that he was sick, and who also had the courtesy to appear interested in the effect of water temperature upon commercial fishing in the Hawaiian Islands, was worth the dizziness brought on by the whisky. Now the whole effect was spoiled because the thin man with the long nose and the fancy stickpin in his tie, was acting so much like Sal Vetricco.

It was on a tuna clipper, the *St. Anne*, that Sal broke loose from his moorings. The same trip you left two fingers in the well-deck winch. A Mexican Chubasco had kept the *St. Anne* hugging the harbor at La Paz for a week and that was hard for everyone to take with only half a load below decks after three months' hard fishing. Sal was a big Azorean and he hated the bait man, whose name was Nicholas. Sal hated Nicholas because he yelled at him so much when they were in the fish, and kept saying over and over again that a ten-year-old boy could pull harder and faster. It wasn't true, and Nicholas didn't really mean what he yelled so often, but every time he would pinch the eye out of some hot bait so the little fish would swim in circles, and toss it over Sal's head, he would yell, "Now see how I am so foolish to waste good bait on a half-man half-woman!" Everybody in the racks had a laugh then and said things like they would give up to a sixteenth share if the woman half of Sal would come to their bunk that night. It kept the crew in good spirits when the fish sounded for hours, and it made them pull faster and harder when they started to hit the bait. Everybody laughed except Sal, who was really a powerful man and very proud of his strength.

Then came that long wait. The sun brought the tar oozing out of the deck seams and there was nothing to do. Sal paced up and down for days, keeping more and more to himself—and he carried the same look in his eyes this man had now. It was a crazy look, like some-

129

body was yanking at his insides with a gaff hook. One day he was pacing and he came face to face with Nicholas, who hadn't said one word. "You porgy bastard," Sal said, "shooting your big mouth all over the ocean alla time. I'm gonna kill you." And he did. Before anybody could stop him he put a rusty chum knife straight into Nicholas's stomach. And so Nicholas died in the Coast Guard plane on the way up to San Diego.

Now this long-nosed man had made three trips up and down the cabin aisle, pacing just like Sal did. He was spoiling everything for José Locota, especially when he would stop and stare at the man who looked like a big shot—the guy who sat with the laughing woman three rows ahead and used his cigarette holder in a way that only real big shots did. Maybe no one else in the cabin could see what was happening. It was pretty dark in the aisle and the only light came from the little square holes above each passenger's head. It made a nice light to read by, or drink with the sick man, but it was a no-damn-good light for seeing eyes . . . unless you had known Sal Vetricco.

José transferred his drink to the hand that had five fingers and leaned far across the aisle.

"You notice anything funny goin' on, Mr. Briscoe?"

"The plane gave a hell of a bump a while ago. Maybe we ran off the pavement."

"No . . . I don't mean that. But this guy who goes up and down the aisle—"

"Yes. He's getting plenty of exercise. Maybe he thinks he's on a ship and trying to work up an appetite for dinner. Fifty times up and down is a mile or something."

"He's lookin' for trouble."

"What makes you think so?"

José rubbed the fuzz of hair on his head.

"I dunno exactly. But I seen a man act like that once. It ain't so nice."

Frank Briscoe leaned beyond the seat ahead of him to watch Agnew. The whisky had driven away some of the pain. He chuckled.

"Looks like an undertaker who's lost a client. By God, he *is* mad about somep'n."

Agnew had stopped beside Ken Childs and May Holst. He was standing with his feet placed wide apart and he was leaning forward belligerently. His fists were doubled and he was breathing heavily. His eyes seemed almost to pop from their sockets and his thin lips worked constantly.

"You're Ken Childs . . . aren't you." His voice took on a piercing timbre, almost female. "Well? Isn't that your name?"

Ken looked at him in surprise, then he turned to smile at May Holst, and finally, because something had to be said, he nodded.

"Yeah. Why? I . . . I don't think we've met before."

"No, we haven't." Agnew was beginning to shake throughout his body. A fleck of white spittle formed in the corner of his mouth. "No, we have *not* met . . . because . . . no one wanted us to."

"I'm not so sure I'm glad it happened. What can I do for you . . . Mr. . . . ?"

"Humphrey Agnew. Does that name mean anything to you?"

Ken Childs hesitated. "You couldn't be . . . Martha's husband?"

"I am."

"Well. . . ." Ken sought unhappily for his cigarette holder and finally found it in his vest pocket. "Congratulations."

"Is that all you have to say, Ken Childs? Nothing like it's nice to meet you or something like that?"

"Well . . . of course. . . ."

"Of course not!" Agnew spit out the words.

"Look, Mr. Agnew. This lady and I are having a quiet drink together. You seem to be disturbed about something. Now if I can help you in any way, perhaps a better time for us to talk would be after we've eaten. So if you'll excuse—" He turned back to May Holst, whose nervous smile matched his own.

But Agnew would not be ignored. His voice rose hysterically. "Oh no, you don't! You don't just snap your fingers and send *me* on my way! Because you owe me a great deal . . . and I can't be bought off, either. Not me!"

"Listen, Mr. Agnew . . . if that really is your name.

I don't know what's eating you and I don't care. Why don't you go back to wherever you came from and sit down." Ken's face was very red and his heavy jowls shook as he spoke. Only the restraining hand of May Holst kept him from rising from his seat.

"Tut . . . tut, now," she said good-naturedly. "At your age, bad for your heart, baby."

"This man is a nuisance—"

"So I'm a nuisance! I have no doubt of that. And I must have been a nuisance to you and Martha in Honolulu when you were scheming to avoid me so you could be alone. But you must be accustomed to nuisances like me, and you think you can dismiss me as just another man whose wife has laid down for you—"

"You're right out of your head. I took your wife to lunch twice because she's a very nice girl and a long time ago she happened to work for me. The worst crime she is guilty of is shaking my hand. Now stop insulting her and making a fool of yourself. Beat it."

"I knew you would have some fancy explanation. But I'm not such a fool as you and Martha think I am. I'm a very clever man, Mr. Childs . . . so smart I'm going to let *you* worry about what I'm going to do for a few hours . . . worry, and think and think and *think* like I've been doing. . . ." He reached out suddenly and seized Ken's coat sleeve. He twisted it between his clutching fingers. His voice rose still higher until he was almost singing.

"I've heard about you for years and I'm sick of your name! A real devil with the ladies . . . a real conqueror! You should be interested in that, lady . . . except your handsome friend made a mistake. He made a whore out of my Martha and that's—"

"I've had enough of this!" Ken set his drink deliberately on the floor and, quickly accelerating the movement, spun away from Agnew's grip. He reached his feet quickly. His fist went back and he lunged heavily at the man in the aisle. For a moment they struggled inexpertly together in the muted light, gasping for air, and grunting as they pushed each other against the seats. But in a moment they were torn apart. José Locota, who was barely half their size, moved swiftly between

132

them. His short, thick arms pinned them on opposite sides of the aisle.

"You guys crazy? Break it up!"

Now Milo Buck came to hold Agnew, and Howard Rice arrived to put his hand firmly on Ken Childs.

"He's got a gun! I felt it! He's crazy!"

Spalding came running up the aisle.

"Here, *here!* What's all this about?"

Spalding never received an answer. For even as she joined the group there was a quick surge of noise as if someone had set off a dozen pneumatic drills together. Spalding was thrown to the floor. The whole assembly around Humphrey Agnew was scattered over the seats as the cabin swung violently to the right. Instantly there was a terrible shaking. Silverware and dishes crashed in the buffet. Clara Joseph screamed.

The shaking ceased as suddenly as it had come. There was a moment of awful silence. Then Sally McKee, pressing her face against the window at her side, screamed.

"The wing . . . ! We're on fire!"

There was no warning except five seconds of intense vibration. Sullivan was crushing a cigarette in the ashtray by his side when it happened. He threw the shredded end to the floor only in time to feel the final shock through his bones. Then came the swerve toward the left wing. The automatic pilot fought crazily to correct it.

"It's number one!" Sullivan yelled. Even as he reached instinctively to retard the throttle, the bright red fire-warning light flashed on. The alarm bell clanged. There was the sickening noise, as the whole instrument panel shook on its rubber mountings. The instruments became a wild blur. An orange light blossomed outside Sullivan's window and quickly became so intense it illuminated the whole flight deck.

"Jesus Christ, we've got a fire!" Hobie groaned hopelessly.

Sullivan, his voice unbelieving, said, "Yeah . . . yeah . . . it's that number one all right. . . ." He moved by rote, pulling back the throttle, the propeller control,

133

shutting off the gas to number one, and punching the feathering button above his head.

"Pull the bottle on the bastard!" Dan said.

"Yeah . . . quick! Hobie! Pull the bottle."

Hobie reached far across the flight panel directly in front of Sullivan, and pulled the selector valve to number-one engine. He did not stop to wonder why Sullivan had not reached for it himself. Then he pulled a second valve which would release carbon dioxide to the area.

"Get on the radio! Tell San Francisco!" Sullivan ordered. His voice returned momentarily to normal, yet he seemed physically paralyzed. He forced himself to look out his window again and Dan pressed close behind him. Their faces, like two heads on a coin, were bronze in the firelight.

"The prop! The whole damn propeller is gone!" Sullivan's voice faded away once more as if the fact were beyond his comprehension.

"And that engine is hanging down at least ten degrees. She's off her mountings!"

They were hardly breathing. Their bodies were rigid, poised in fear, while they thought about one hundred octane gasoline. There would be only a few more seconds. The fire in the engine would either go out or the whole wing would explode.

"Pull the other bottle, Dan! I'm starting for the water!"

As Dan pulled a second series of valves, Sullivan seemed to rediscover his muscular control. He disengaged the automtic pilot, closed the three remaining throttles, and pushed the control yoke forward until the ship was in a steep dive. The hiss of air through the ventilators increased to a heavy thrumming. The rate of descent wound around to two thousand feet a minute. The air-speed quivered at two hundred and twenty.

It could have been the carbon dioxide discharge or it could have been the changed angle of slip stream plus the greatly increased speed which blew the fire out. They were simply aware, very suddenly, that the night outside the windows was black again and that they were still a flying unit.

"Thank you . . . sweet Lord," Leonard intoned softly.

134

Sullivan eased back gradually on the stabilizer and the control yoke. He began to breathe again.

"She's out," he said uncertainly. "I don't think she's going to burn any more."

But Dan, who had been watching all the instruments, said nothing. For he had observed one instrument which made him sick, and for the moment he wanted to believe it was wrong. He waited and watched hopefully as Sullivan leveled the ship off at five thousand feet.

"I can't raise San Francisco!" Hobie said in a voice that was almost a cry. "The static . . . skip . . . something . . . they don't come back!"

"Try the secondary frequency."

"I did. I've been trying them both."

"Try emergency. Give them a May Day call."

"All right."

"Leonard. Have you got our position?"

"Right, Captain. All ready and waiting. Are we goin' into the water?"

"No. She flies lousy with that engine hanging down, but I think we can stay in the air. How long to the coast?"

"Six hours . . . about. But that was at regular cruising speed. I haven't figured up how long now."

"Well, figure it."

"How can I when I don't know how fast we'll be flying?"

"I'm sorry. Wait a minute until she settles down. I think I can hold a hundred and thirty-five. . . ."

"Jesus! Is that all?"

"The engine drags. It slows us . . . I'll have to sink down lower."

"We'll be better off at two thousand feet anyway," Dan said evenly. Without taking his eyes from the instrument which disturbed him so, he lit a cigarette.

"Hobie! Have you contacted anybody yet?"

"No."

"Well, keep yelling."

"I am . . . wait a minute . . . I got somebody . . . a ship!"

Dan sucked hard at his cigarette and watched the needle on the instrument. It was placed in a relatively inconspicuous position on the panel, one of a series of like gauges, and ordinarily it would be checked only at regular intervals. It measured the amount of gasoline remaining in the left main tank.

11

As THE *Cristobal Trader* CONTINUED HER PONDEROUS dance, Manuel Aboitiz sat in a bath of sweat. The armpits of his shirt were large dark patches extending almost to his waist. Another splotch covered his back and globules of moisture found their way from his forehead to his heavy eyelashes, until it was sometimes difficult for him to see the dials before him. He wiped his eyes angrily as he twisted the dials, for he was desperately anxious to unite himself with the frightened voice in the sky somewhere above him.

He was invited now. The social barriers were down. The words *May Day* had been spoken and any voice that might help was welcome. Manuel wanted to be the voice, and yet he must be careful not to blank out those more directly concerned with the emergency. Such interference would only complicate matters and possibly make them worse. Poor, beautiful thing of the sky, he thought, passing so easily among the stars only a little while ago. Now she was in agony and Manuel shared her suffering as if she were a living extension of himself. She was calling and calling, crying in the immense wilderness of the night, and for some reason she could not, or would not, hear the answers.

Manuel could hear the answers clearly. San Francisco answered every one of the ship's pleading transmissions. But the aircraft was deaf, it seemed. Either her receiver was not functioning or the eccentricities of radio had temporarily found her in a spot where reception from a distant station was impossible.

Manuel decided it was time to break his silence. Yet now, with the decision made, new doubts tormented him. The transmitter which he had so lovingly built from surplus parts—would it really work? When he had first put it together, he had stolen readings on its antennae output by pressing the microphone button. But he had never dared to talk, much less hope for a reply on a frequency illegal to ships. And so he sweated even more as he reached for the microphone, for if his work was a failure at a time like this, then he knew something would fail within himself—his boasts to the Chief would be empty.

"This is the *Cristobal Trader* calling Four-two-zero. I can hear you clearly. Do you read me?" Manuel's heart pounded as he twisted the receiver dial slightly. He wiped the moisture from the palms of his fat hands on the sides of his pants. Then the answer came through the speaker in front of him.

"Roger! Roger! What ship was that?"

Manuel answered quickly. "This is the *Cristobal Trader* . . . WTYH . . . I heard your May Day . . . you passed right over me about ten minutes ago. I can also read San Francisco on eighty-two twenty. Do you want me to relay your messages?"

There was a pause, then the voice came again. "Roger . . . *Cristobal Trader.* We read you five by five but are unable San Francisco or Honolulu. Please advise San Francisco . . . wait a second . . . stand by. . . ."

Manuel pulled a message pad toward him and poised himself for writing.

". . . advise San Francisco we have lost our number-one propeller. Fire started . . . but it is now out. Engine is hanging down on mountings approximately ten degrees. Maximum indicated air speed obtainable one hundred and thirty-five. We are now at five thousand . . . but sinking. Request they clear all altitudes below us. Did you get all that?"

"Roger, Four-two-zero. Stand by." Manuel knew he should call his chief, but that could come later. If

Four-two-zero was losing altitude there wasn't time. He pressed his microphone again.

"WTYH . . . the *Cristobal Trader* calling AIRINC, San Francisco. Did you hear the report from Aircraft Four-two-zero?"

A distorted voice came back to him immediately. "Roger, WTYH. Please advise him to stand by for interception instructions. Request if he is going to ditch. Over."

"The *Cristobal Trader* to Four-two-zero. Did you hear San Francisco just now?"

"Negative, *Trader.*"

"Message advises . . . stand by for interception instructions. They want to know if you are going to ditch. Over."

"Stand by. . . ."

Manuel braced himself against a heavy roll of the ship and wondered what it would be like to land in mid-ocean at night. He was suddenly very glad of the *Cristobal Trader*'s solidity.

"Four-two-zero to the *Trader*. Negative on the ditching for now. We will attempt maintaining two thousand feet. What is the state of the sea about you . . . just in case? Over."

"Heavy northwest swells. We are rolling approximately thirty degrees. It's very rough."

"Roger."

"WTYH from San Francisco. Request Four-two-zero's present position and true course."

"Stand by. *Trader* to Four-two-zero. San Francisco wants to know your present position and course. Over."

"Magnetic or true course?"

"True."

"Wait a second . . . our position approximately one three seven west . . . thirty-five degrees north. Course fifty degrees true. Please stand by in case we want to come back and ditch beside you. Over."

"Roger, Four-two-zero. Did you get all that, San Francisco?"

"Affirmative, *Cristobal Trader*. Advise him to try working us on eighty-seven hundred. We will stand by on all frequencies. Over."

"Cristobal Trader to Four-two-zero. San Francisco wants you to try eighty-seven hundred."

"Will do."

Now Manuel thought the time had come for an expression of his personal interest. He knew enough about airplanes to hold little hope for them against a night sea. He was uncertain as to how his thoughts should be phrased, but he wanted the men in the sky to know that Manuel Aboitiz was personally affected by their misfortunes.

"Keep that ship in the air if you can, boys," he said finally. "It's wet down here."

The reply which came to him was faint, but strangely unafraid.

"Thanks, *Cristobal Trader*. We'll try. Thanks for everything."

Pickering, a sedate man who mouthed his pipe as if it were a candy stick, had been handling the overseas panel at San Francisco AirInc radio. Now as the tape recorder turned in the room behind him, his pipe was nearly cold. He had laid it aside when Hobie Wheeler's voice first came through the panel and there had been no time to reach for it since. Pickering had transferred his routine work with five other airplanes over the Pacific to his fellow operators and concentrated on trying to establish direct communication with Four-two-zero. It was inconvenient working through Manuel Aboitiz, but for the moment he was grateful to him.

Pickering was very busy. He had to tap out every word spoken by Hobie or Manuel on the teletype machine before him. The teletype automatically advised Overseas Air Traffic Control and the airline office whose name was painted the length of Four-two-zero. After the first long silence, Pickering spun around in his metal chair and quickly dialed two phone numbers. The first was the Coast Guard Air-Sea Rescue unit. Their station was only a few hundred yards away and he heard their alarm signal hooting through the open window, even before he hung up the phone.

Pickering's second call was to the Coast Guard Rescue coordination center in downtown San Francisco. When he returned the phone to its cradle a few moments later, he knew that within the next half-hour more than a thousand men would be directly involved in the fate of Four-two-zero.

The Air Traffic Control Center for the Pacific approaches and the San Francisco region was located across the Bay in Oakland. Here, Four-two-zero was represented on a metal plate which held a card. In squares following her number, the air speed, altitude, and position had been recorded and the estimated time of arrival noted each time Leonard Wilby prepared his position report.

Now all of these figures were changed and one man was delegated to observe the progress of Four-two-zero. A call was sent immediately to a westbound military aircraft flying at four thousand. He was to climb immediately to eight thousand five hundred. The change would clear all of the sky below Four-two-zero. A United Stratocruiser and a British Commonwealth Pacific DC-6, both flying less than two hundred miles from Four-two-zero's last reported position, were advised to converge on her at their captains' discretion, and to stand by for possible relay of messages.

For several hours, until Four-two-zero approached much closer to the California coast, there was very little more the men in Overseas Air Traffic Control could do to help the situation. And so they continued quietly with their exacting business of keeping arriving and departing aircraft from smashing against each other in the acres of sky above them. Before Four-two-zero could become a further complication, over twenty planes must be guided. And the weather was thickening, with San Francisco already reporting visibility less than two miles. The problems, then, were normal—yet a new tenseness filled the large neon-lit room. The men handling the routine traffic to the south, the east, and the west could not refrain from walking the full length of their long, flexible telephone wires. They peered at the designator for Four-two-zero, waiting word of her

141

progress. And when no word came as regularly as they hoped, they discussed her dubious position in quiet tones.

Lieutenant Mowbray was still talking to Pickering on the telephone when he completely destroyed the peace of the Coast Guard Air Rescue station. Holding the phone in one hand, he boosted himself up in bed and pressed the red alarm button on the wall. A klaxon instantly shook the bachelor officer quarters where he had been sleeping. He heard men running in the hall; that would be Keim, his copilot, and Pump, his navigator. As he slipped on his own pants and shoes, Lieutenant Mowbray heard men running from the enlisted men's barracks across the concrete ramp. He heard an engine start on his B-17 before he dashed cold water on his lean face, shook his head to drive the last of his sleep away, and started down the hall. He took the stairs to the lower floor two at a time. He arrived at the front door simultaneously with Keim and Pump. Their faces held the vacant look of young men who were still not awake. Keim was pulling angrily on his pants' zipper.

"I'm gonna get smart some day," he growled in frustration, "and go back to buttons on my fly."

Pump grabbed the navigation kit that had been placed on the end of the bar, and they pushed out the door together. Trotting across the concrete toward the waiting B-17, they glanced at the low overcast sky and breathed deeply of the dank night air.

"What's the poop?"

"An eastbound's lost a prop. Had a fire but that's out. Can't keep his air speed, though, and looks like he's headed for the drink."

"How far out is he?"

"Thousand miles, maybe."

"Oh, my achin' eyes!"

"They'll give us more poop in the air."

"Go-ud da-yim this zipper!"

Exactly fourteen minutes after Hobie Wheeler's voice had first troubled the night air, the Coast Guard Air Rescue B-17 left the ground at San Francisco and pushed her snout into the thick overcast.

Leonard was trying not to think about Susie and the hardwood tray which had been dashed to the flight-deck floor by the first impact. The tray had been chipped at the ends, until now it had the appearance of something he might have picked up in a second-hand store. Yet Leonard wanted to think about Susie and the tray because he believed that even the vision of Susie drunk, with her lipstick smeared and her hair a mess, was preferable to the shocking disorder of the flight deck.

The physical changes about the flight deck would have been almost imperceptible to anyone not a part of the functioning crew. One throttle was pulled back and one propeller control. A gas valve was in a different position from the other three, and a red fire shutoff valve handle projected out from beneath the windshield crash pad. These minor changes were inconspicuous against the array of instruments, or the twenty-six red, blue, black and white handles which sprouted like flowers from the control pedestal. The magnetic compass still swam in its miniature aquarium and, although the three functioning engines seemed to groan against their extra burden, their beat was strong and constant.

The ugly disorder came from an interpretation of the instruments and the appalling change their readings brought to the men who only a little time before had been entirely different men. Sullivan had been so transformed his whole body appeared to have shrunk. His normally straight back was rounded as he hunched over the control yoke, holding to it desperately as if its metallic hardness might give him strength. He lit one cigarette from the end of the other, and his orders came in a voice that had slipped away from certainty. His eyes never left the air-speed indicator. The most minute fluctuation of the needle caused the knobs in his jaws to work nervously in a manner Leonard had never seen before.

All of the youthful bounce had left Hobie. Leonard thought he seemed like a child caught in a tree and waiting for someone to tell him how to climb down. His carefully groomed hair was no longer so. It was awry with his earphones, and those he moved constantly to different positions. Somehow he had lost coordination as he worked the radios. Four times now Leonard had seen him reach for the wrong switch or knob when he wanted to change control.

Only Dan Roman, who stood between them, seemed the same, although the easy, rather sad smile, which Leonard had come to like so much, was no longer on his lips. He was bent over his stiff leg, which he had placed on the step just behind the control pedestal, and he had not moved since the fire had gone out, except to put on a pair of rimless spectacles. He was entirely calm, almost statuesque. Leonard wished that his own behavior could match Dan's, for he was ashamed. Working and thinking alone behind the others, who were preoccupied with the immediate problems of flight, he thought it unlikely they would notice his acute misery. But he could not stop the shaking, either of his hands, which clutched the octant, or of his mind, which refused to settle down and swiftly execute the most familiar chores of addition and subtraction.

Leonard was standing on his stool with his head in the astrodome. All about him was darkness. Above his head, a few stars were visible through the plexiglass, but they were already fading behind the dismal overcast which was rapidly masking the heavens. Altair and Deneb were still visible—Polaris, which might have provided a quick and entirely reliable north line, was already gone. It was difficult enough trying to shoot accurately while the ship was in a slow descent (his pleas to hold steady had not even been answered by Sullivan); it was even more difficult trying to work with stars of relatively low magnitude, stars that under the best of conditions Leonard would never have bothered to consult.

Yet the shaking was the worst. He could not only feel it, he could see it. It was like peering inside of himself. He pressed his eye hard against the sponge-rubber finder on the octant, and his trembling fingers spun the mirror control knob until Deneb swam into view. It looked sickly and inconsequential. Only by the utmost concentration of his whole body could he align it so that it showed in the center of the octant bubble. He must hold it there for two full minutes, while the mechanical averaging mechanism wound down and transposed his observations into degrees and minutes of arc. After Deneb he would shoot Altair, and then the planet Jupiter, which he would save until the last because it was the brightest and still might be visible if the overcast continued to thicken. All three of these pinpoint bodies had to be transfixed in the eye of the sensitive bubble which insisted on dancing off in all directions of the aperture, as if it were trying frantically to escape the confines of the octant. Some of the wildness could be blamed on the fact that the ship was descending, but Leonard knew most of it was due to his own trembling. It had to stop. Now the lives of everyone on board Four-two-zero could depend on his delicate adjustment of those minute light specks behind the bubble. It was not a job for a shaking man. It was like balancing a glob of mercury on the end of a pencil.

He drove Susie from his mind and concentrated grimly on Deneb. When the two minutes had passed and the recording mechanism cut off, he flashed on his little light and wrote down the angle and time of sight on a slip of paper. Then he turned cautiously on his stool and, bracing himself against the ventilator outlet at his shoulder, sought Altair in the sky, and fought the trembling for two minutes longer. He told himself that these stars were his friends, as familiar as peaks to a mountaineer —they had always been his friends—and by looking up at them to gauge their angle, he could locate himself exactly in the wilderness.

To discover and plot their angle was absolutely necessary for a variety of reasons—all interrelated, and all pointed toward the single element of survival.

Sullivan believed they would not have to ditch, and his reasoning was based on the fact that continued flight was still possible on the three good engines though their progress would be slow. There was enough reserve of gas to make the California coast and, if it seemed at all doubtful, everything movable would be thrown overboard to lighten ship and so conserve power. Making the coast, then, should be a sure thing, but it was always possible Sullivan had underestimated the effect of the dragging number-one engine, or the winds themselves could change, or another engine fail. They would have to find the *Cristobal Trader* then, or the Coast Guard's *Gresham* already far behind them. To set a proper course to either vessel, they would have to know where they were at the time such a decision might be made. Just as important was the interception ship already reported under way. To join with it successfully—two microsopic specks presuming to meet in the night's vastness when their combined speed approached three hundred miles an hour—was an undertaking requiring the most expert navigational finesse. Theoretically it was easy, a mere matter of careful computation. Actually, it was a navigational nightmare. And so Leonard's mind was full of these things as he turned on his stool once more, and sought the planet Jupiter.

When at last the final two minutes had passed and he was done with Jupiter, Leonard climbed down from his stool. He switched on the light over his table and bent eagerly over his books. Normally he could shoot and plot a three-star fix in ten minutes; now, aware of the confusion in his mind, he thought more slowly, checking and rechecking his figures against the chance of error. And gradually he settled into the familiarity of his work. The trembling subsided as he drew a small triangle on the chart. He became confident of his sights as they agreed with his dead-reckoning calculations. As soon as the triangle was completed, he would further prove it with a loran fix and know for certain that unless there was an incredible change in the winds, there was nothing more to worry about. I will be late, Susie . . . but I will be there. I will walk in a little past dawn and give you the hardwood tray.

"Skipper! I've got a position!"

"Name it!" Sullivan took his eyes off the air-speed just long enough to turn around.

"To the Coast . . . five hours and forty-seven minutes if you can hold this air speed! Wind looks about north at forty giving us twelve degrees right drift—"

"Sweet land of liberty," Hobie said.

"How's for fuel?"

Leonard consulted his graph.

"Enough. Just. We only need about a thousand gallons and we have eleven hundred fifty according to my graph. It's pinching things close, but—"

"You can throw your graph away, Leonard. . . ." Dan said very gently.

"Huh?"

"I said you can throw your graph away, chum. We haven't got eleven hundred gallons."

"How do you figure that?" Leonard was almost belligerent in his challenge.

But Dan's face remained immobile. He seemed not to care about the stunning impact of his statement or how the others received it. Straightening slightly, the first movement he had made in a long time, he pointed his finger at the lower portion of the instrument panel.

"Look at the gauge on number-one main tank," he said in a voice that was still abnormally soft. "Watch it . . . because I've been watching it long enough. When we lost the prop, the gauge read two hundred gallons. Now it reads . . . one hundred . . . and we may lose most of that—"

They stared at the gauge in silence, until Hobie said incredulously, "How the hell can it be?"

"I don't know for sure . . . I'm afraid to go back and find out. My guess is number-one prop kicked a few holes in the wing when it left us. The tank is ruptured . . . so unless we can pass some kind of a miracle . . . it looks like we've had it."

For a moment they stared in silence at the offending gauge. Hobie, hoping the needle was stuck, pushed at it gently with his foot. Then they looked at each other almost accusingly, as if the loss of fuel might be blamed on human error and so the penalty involved made somehow less compromising. Leonard shook his head, and to hide the trembling, which had returned again, he passed both hands slowly through his grey hair.

"We just can't make it this way . . . I'll figure up again, but the winds—" He paused while the invisible force of the night wind outside the flight deck became a tangible enemy and caused a bewildering jumble of figures to cascade through his mind. "The winds . . . maybe . . . maybe they'll change some."

"The gauge could be wrong," Hobie said wistfully.

No one answered him. Though fuel gauges were paradoxically the most unreliable of all the instruments, their errors were never so great, nor would a loss be shown so rapidly. Hobie was allowing himself to become the victim of convenient thinking, the kind that had killed many airmen. He was trying to persuade himself that the instruments were wrong, not the fact—because it was more comforting to believe them so. Sullivan and Dan Roman knew better.

"We're going into the drink," Sullivan said as if he felt obliged to put all of their thoughts into words. His strong hands made a caressing movement around the control wheel and he was suddenly aware that this previously ordinary machine at his command had become a precious unit which he hated to damage. If he could only get hold of himself! Already his own preservation had become secondary, and that was as it should be, but now all of the doubts and illusions that had been gnawing at his courage for months, the haunting fears of failure or of mistakes made when they should not be made, the mannerisms and thoughts he had carefully concealed from his wife, his chief pilot, and even himself were resolved. He was afraid, but he no longer cringed. He straightened in his seat. He had been waiting for this time ever since his flying maturity and he knew that he must somehow discipline himself and prepare for it.

Technically, the problems were very nearly insurmountable. They lacked fuel to make the coast. The drag of the number-one engine would have made the ship fly miserably, regardless of fuel. Radio communication was poor. The wind was screaming in the upper night, and below, the surface of the sea, which he would not be able to appraise until the very last moment, was a turmoil of stone walls, because water took on the consistency of concrete when struck at a plane's landing speed. Sullivan would be fortunate indeed if he could make the last maneuvers of his big ship quickly enough to land in a trough. Even then, the physical damage before it finally sloshed to a halt, must be very nearly disastrous. Those left alive would have the terrifying chance of sliding into the cold sea and clinging to rafts until some form of rescue reached them. Sitting so far in the nose, Sullivan knew that his own chances were hardly worth considering. All of these things came to him very suddenly and without complication, because he had been thinking about them for so long. And still, now that the time had arrived, and his responsibility pressed nearly to the breaking point, he knew something had been revived within himself. He was not alone as long as Dan Roman was beside him. He remembered signing the clearance in Honolulu—S.O.B. . .21—souls on board, twenty-one. They were all his now; and the years of training which enabled him to register as an airman first-class, must be called to accounting. Looking at Dan, he sighed heavily. For the moment he was in complete control of himself.

"Yeah . . . sooner or later . . . it's just a question of when we decide to do it. I'm wondering if we'd be better off turning around now and going back to 'Uncle,' or that *Cristobal Trader*. We could dunk beside them."

Dan cocked his head thoughtfully to one side and rubbed his leg. "We've got plenty of time. Let's not rush off in the heat of the day about this. The sea is rough all the way to the Coast, but it's rough back there, too. We *could* miss finding either one of those ships and then where would be be?"

"Better than a thousand miles from dry land," Hobie said.

"I'm for holding on awhile and see what the wind does," Dan said evenly. "The interceptor is on its way. She can follow us down and vector any ships in the vicinity toward us. There should be several around then because we won't be very far off the coast . . . maybe only a hundred miles or so."

"But the water will be colder along the coast," Sullivan said.

"Yeah, it will be. And maybe even rougher. Still . . . I think we ought to stretch things as long as we can."

"All right. I'll go along with you on that. It will give us time to get squared away. Now I'll want you up here with me when we really start down, but in the meantime get everything set in the cabin. You'll have to work alone unless you can find a passenger to help you because I'll need Hobie here for radio, and, God knows,

149

Leonard has his hands full. Start by throwing everything overboard you can move. A thousand pounds or so will make some difference in our speed. Make sure Spalding gets a Mae West on every passenger and tells them how to use it . . . and what to do after we hit."

"I'm wondering if it will pay off throwing things overboard. It's going to scare hell out of the passengers and they're going to have a long wait."

"They'll have to sweat it out."

"You want me to tell them they're going into the water?"

"No . . . wait a minute. Maybe you should. I don't know, Dan. Use your own judgment when you see how things are back there."

Dan straightened and took off his glasses. He placed them in a case and carefully buttoned them into his shirt pocket. He began to whistle automatically and then stopped after a few notes.

"I may be gone quite a while. I'll get back as soon as I can."

12

Somewhere in the confusion which followed the fire, Spalding lost her small uniform cap, which had been perched exactly on the back of her head. Her hair was mussed and there was a new flush to her ice-cream complexion. There was a bruise on her leg where she had been thrown hard against a seat. A button had been torn from her white blouse when she stepped between Agnew and Ken Childs.

Now, with things a little easier, she realized there had been no time for fright. Sally McKee's scream had reduced everything to plain work. There was no panic—only the one echoing scream from Mrs. Joseph, and then they went quickly to the windows, all of them, and watched the blazing engine as if it had nothing to do with them. Though it was hardly twenty feet away, it seemed remote—almost an innocent spectacle for their entertainment, and they said nothing to each other until the fire flickered out and the night was black again. Even then there was only silence among them. They gathered in a tight group about Sally McKee's seat and spread along the aisle, pushing as near to each other as they could. They looked at each other and then at Spalding, their strained faces asking for some explanation.

Gustave Pardee became the focus of the group, partially because of his size, Spalding thought, but more so because he seemed the most at ease with what they had seen. His great beefy, hangdog face was newly alive. His bored eyes, which Spalding had thought houndlike, sparkled with animation. The complete lack of color in his wife's face made her even more beautiful and he held her close to him, soothing her. He was the first to find his voice and, when he did so, the dilettante quality had disappeared entirely.

"I know nothing whatsoever about airplanes," he said easily, ". . . but this one acts like the Fourth of July. I told Mrs. Pardee we should take the boat." Then he smiled at the formation of frightened faces and said, "Amen."

The effect of his words was magical. Everyone began to talk at once.

"I shouldn't have screamed . . . but I was so scared. . . ."

"We seem to be all right now—"

"Think we'll go back to Honolulu?"

"I couldn't care less," Flaherty said thickly.

"Oh, my heart!" breathed Dorothy Chen, trying to smile. "Please return from the ceiling."

"Troubles? Wait till I tell the Good Neighbors about this!"

"You know somp'n? No matter how much you hurt . . . it's surprising how spry you can be when—"

"We'll be late. We'll miss our connections now—"

"Just everybody keep their fingers crossed—"

"But what happened, Milo?"

"Leave it to Lydia. I would be sound asleep when somebody pulls the champagne cork. This could become goddamned interesting."

"Things were getting pretty interesting before it happened, dearie," May Holst said. "These two apes were trying to kill each other." She poked her finger against Agnew's chest. "Now you go on and sit down like a good boy. Come on, Ken. There's no sense in running a good thing into the ground . . . Oh! What am I saying!"

"Please! *Everyone* sit down," Spalding said. "I'm sure there's nothing to worry about. They'll come back from the flight deck in a few minutes and explain everything.

152

I'll just hold up dinner for a while, but if anyone wants coffee I'll be glad to get it."

Spalding had been waiting for Dan or Hobie Wheeler. They should come back. The passengers had to be told something, but for the moment she hesitated to leave them. Reviewing her emergency duties, she wished she had taken them more seriously in stewardess school. Should she put on their Mae Wests now, or wait? What about the life raft by the door, and the ditching rope? She could telephone to the flight deck from her buffet, but was this the time to bother them? They were descending—she could feel it in her ears. Oh, why didn't someone come back?

Gradually the tight group of passengers melted, but they did not return to their original seats. Instead, they settled themselves as near as they could to Sally McKee, who had first seen the fire. Every seat in her vicinity was claimed although no one actually settled down. They sat on the arms of the seats, or stood in the aisle, or leaned across the seat ahead of them, and found comfort in their talk. They offered each other cigarettes and Donald Flaherty persuaded Spalding to get them paper cups so they could all have a drink from his bottle. And when his bottle was empty before half the cups were filled, those who had whisky shared it with the others.

Only Ken Childs and Humphrey Agnew ignored each other, looking away each time their eyes met and straightening their ties and collars when they thought no one was looking. Agnew sat in the last of the seats beside José Locota, who had taken his gun.

"I'll just keep it for you, guy . . . until we make San Francisco. I don't know yer business and I don' wanna, but you can get in plenty of trouble with them things."

Outwardly at least, there was a warm, almost party-like air about Spalding's passengers, and for this she was deeply grateful to Gustave Pardee, who had tipped them all the right way at a moment she knew could have led to hysteria. How she had underestimated that big, flabby-looking man! He, who had been the most afraid, so nervous on a simple take-off he could hardly sit in his seat, was now the center of strength. He was actually laughing as he talked with that inane Mr. Joseph. It was a combination Spalding would never have attempted to bring together, though they might be the only two passengers on an airplane.

Mr. Flaherty was drunk—what a shame for such a distinguished-looking man, and where did he get the bottle?—he was making no trouble, but he would have to be watched. Miss Chen was all right. She was sitting beside Frank Briscoe, bless his heart, and she was listening to him talk, which was a good thing for both of them. That Agnew man—uuff!—what a person! He was apparently subdued and most certainly the brown mouse, Mr. Locota, had no qualms about handling him. How strong could a little quiet man be? You just never knew about passengers when they came through the door. The Bucks were all right for the moment—bending their heads together and feeling for each other's hands as they watched the older passengers. The Holst woman was sticking close by Ken Childs. The Rices had stopped fighting long enough to talk over the back of their seats to Sally McKee—another impossible combination. If the spirit would just hold among them, and let the full realization of their danger come slowly, everything was going to be all right.

She was wondering if she should turn the lights full up according to the emergency instructions in her manual, or leave them as they were, when she saw Dan Roman standing in the doorway. She looked quickly at his eyes, trying to question them, although he was almost the full length of the cabin from her. When she was certain of the expression behind his weary smile, she found it nearly impossible to keep her nerve.

"May I have your attention for a minute?" Dan said. He walked slowly down the aisle until he reached the center of the group. As they leaned toward him anxiously, he sat down on the arm of Ken Childs' seat and carelessly pushed his cap to the back of his head. A shaft of light from the ceiling cut down across his weathered face, sharpening his features and illuminating his head and shoulders in such a way that they appeared separate from the rest of his body. He ran a finger the length of the long crease beside his mouth and lit a cigarette before he spoke again. Then finally, when they were gathered about him like children waiting breathlessly for a story, he began to speak in a casual voice that was pitched just loud enough to dominate the muffled beat of the engines.

"I guess I don't have to tell you people that we've had a little trouble . . . and maybe if I explain what has happened . . . you'll feel better all around. I won't try to minimize it, and I certainly won't make it any worse than it really is, but there are certain things you have every right to know." He took a long drag from his cigarette and thoughtfully examined the creases in his trousers. Then he looked into the white masks pressing about him and decided that whatever he might say, could be accepted without panic.

"I don't blame you if you're scared. I am, too. I've been flying since 1917 and I don't like this sort of thing any better than you do . . . however, with all that flying you'll notice I'm still very much alive . . . and Ken Childs here, who happens to be an old friend of mine, will tell you my flying was not always the easy kind. Forgive me for getting personal at a time like this, but I hope it will help to gain your confidence, and full belief, in what I have to tell you.

"Now. . . ."

He paused and ran his finger down the line in his cheek again. "We've lost our number-one propeller. None of us know why, any better than you do. It's one of those things that just never happens . . . but does . . . once in a billion miles of flying. Fortunately, it did not come through the cabin. Probably a master rod broke . . . whatever it was, the engine must have frozen and a fire started. You undoubtedly saw it. We extinguished the fire with carbon dioxide and there is no further danger from it. Our speed has been slowed considerably because the outward pull on a propeller blade is about thirty tons and when this one left us, the resulting quick change of force partially twisted the engine from its mountings. It is hanging down about ten degrees now, causing a serious drag . . . something like dragging your foot in a rowboat."

He waited and watched the masks again. They were only more solemn. Gustave Pardee held his wife more closely and Clara Joseph stifled a sob, but they were otherwise perfectly quiet.

"Now comes the hard part," Dan said uncertainly. "Can you take it?"

There was a moment's silence; then Lydia Rice placed her small jeweled hand on Dan's shoulder.

"Please tell us everything. I think we all want to know."

"Are we going to crash?" Milo Buck asked.

"Let's have it, Dan. Go on," Ken Childs insisted.

"All right. But wait a minute. There's something I want to check on first. I didn't want you to see me poking around until I had at least given you some idea what it was all about."

He took a flashlight from the pocket of his jacket and stood up. Then he crossed the aisle and, leaning over Frank Briscoe and Sally McKee, he pointed the flashlight out the window toward the top of the wing. There were four black gashes in the outer panel and two in the mid-section. A fine spray of gasoline was still siphoning from three of the holes. The fuel gauge was telling the truth. Dan clenched his teeth and switched off the flashlight. He returned to the aisle. Again he searched their faces and finally reached a decision.

"Well. . . ." he began, looking at the flashlight in his hands rather than the faces about him because it was much easier, ". . . this . . . is it. We are really very lucky . . . because that propeller could have caused a great deal more damage than it has. Anyway—" Fighting for seconds, he returned the flashlight to his pocket very deliberately and spoke more slowly.

"Anyway . . . we have suffered some damage. There is just nothing we can do about it. The propeller cut several holes in the wing when it left and that's where our fuel is stored. When it let go, we were past the point of returning to Hawaii. Now . . . with our loss of fuel, plus the drag of the engine . . . we just don't have enough fuel to quite make the California coast. Which means. . . ." He swallowed hard and tried to find a pair of sympathetic eyes. ". . . that we will probably have to ditch this airplane in the sea."

Clara Joseph could no longer hold back the sobbing. The broken sounds coming from her handkerchief tore at

Dan's composure as he forced himself to go on. "We'll be killed . . . we'll all be killed," she said again and again.

"That's a possibility we might as well face, but . . . if you will remain as calm as you are now, there is a chance you will only be in the water a few minutes." He was beginning a deception which he had never intended, but Clara Joseph's sobbing unnerved him. Alice might have wept like that, not for herself but for Tony—if there had been the time.

"You will have a least four hours, probably more . . . to wait. I realize it isn't going to be easy . . . it won't be for any of us, but if you at least try to think about something else it may help. A rescue plane is already en route to intercept us and if you look out the left side in about two hours, you'll see him. There may be several more planes before we actually go down and some of them will be the kind which can land on the sea . . ." Again a deception in part, because the sea was much too rough for any successful landing.

"These planes could land very close to us and pick you up. In addition, every surface ship in the vicinity will proceed toward us at full speed, and because we will be at least fairly close to the coast, there should be a great many of them." Would that woman please stop crying!

"There are certain things we can do to make our ditching a possible success . . . something to telephone your friends about when you reach shore tomorrow, some time. . . ." What time? Unless Sullivan was the luckiest bastard in the world against the waves, it would be a very, very long distance call—from hell.

"Airplanes have gone down into the sea before and no one received the slightest injury except a slight dampening." Dan tried to smile and was agreeably surprised when his smile was returned by Lydia Rice.

"The only casualties recorded have come from panic. You must not hurry. Miss Spalding and the third officer will be back here with you. Do exactly as they tell you to do, and remember they have been thoroughly trained in ditching procedure." In a swimming pool, yes—but an airplane didn't smack the sea first and knock their senses

157

crazy, it wasn't blowing forty or fifty miles an hour in the pool, and there wasn't five thousand miles of liquid strength behind the wavelets in the pool. Nor any screaming passengers.

"Miss Spalding will show you how to put on your Mae Wests and how to work them. They are the finest life preserver ever made. That big yellow roll back there is an inflatable life raft. It's a wonderful gadget and has everything in it but T-bone steaks. It will hold all of you very comfortably and we will put another one out from the flight deck." *If* you can get the controls and the instrument panel out of your face and stomach, and if you don't drown in the process.

"The third officer . . . you might as well know his name because he's a nice young fellow . . . is Hobie Wheeler. Anyway, the third officer will come back about ten minutes before we actually land. Take your shoes off then, because we don't want you cutting holes in the raft when you jump into it. The door back there has an emergency release." If it doesn't jam because the whole ship might be out of line from the second impact.

"Hobie Wheeler will open that door by pulling the release . . . then he will shove out the raft and lower the ditching rope you see hanging just above the door. Do not leave your seats until he calls for you. There will be plenty of time so you might as well take it. These airplanes have been known to float so long they become a menace to navigation and have to be sunk by gunfire." They have also been known to sink in a few minutes.

"Do you want them to put on Mae Wests now, Dan?" Spalding asked.

"I don't see why you should, until at least three hours from now. There's no sense in being uncomfortable any longer than you can help. But when you do—everyone put on all the clothes you can find to wear . . . overcoats . . . everything. It may be a little chilly." It's going to be freezing and unless those surface ships are damned quick about it, exposure will account for most of the casualties.

"After you are in the raft, remain in a seated position, or even lie down if you want to. Wheeler will show you where the emergency rations are if you get hungry—"

"How can we get hungry if we're only going to be in the raft a few minutes?" May Holst asked. "You're giving us a lot of malarkey about being picked up." There was no malice in her good-humored face; it was only an honest statement.

Dan turned to her quickly. He had slipped and he cursed himself for doing so. And the other woman was sobbing louder now. She was saying something about her babies.

"Malarkey? Maybe . . . a little. But we just don't want any bad things said about the service or cuisine on this airline—"

"No doubt, there'll be caviar," Gustave Pardee said quickly. "It would be most arduous if there were no caviar."

Dan looked at him gratefully. Wasn't this the big man Spalding said was scared to death?

"I'll speak to our emergency chef about it, sir."

"I don't think this is anything to joke about," Humphrey Agnew said sourly.

"You're wrong. When you get in the raft, the more jokes the better. Sing if you feel like it. In fact, it might help to pass the time if you dug up a few old songs and started practicing now."

"I was once a middling fair bass," Howard Rice said.

"I can't carry a tune in a basket," Frank Briscoe said, "but I'm sure loud."

And looking at them all, studying their eyes, Dan thought suddenly that if he had ever wanted to see a group of passengers survive, these he would pray for. They were strangers and yet they were not; they had somehow drawn great strength together and they were using it. Their behavior could no longer be credited to innocence. It was exactly the opposite of what he had expected—and dreaded.

"Now this is very important, and then I'm about through with speechmaking. When we actually ditch, there will be two shocks. You won't be frightened if you know about them. The first will be hardly noticeable, about the same as a normal landing. The second may be quite severe." How severe, Sullivan, depended on you and your luck with the waves . . . "It may throw you against

159

your seat belts quite hard." It may rip your seats from the floor and tumble you in a hopeless, smashed confusion of broken bodies and seats against the forward bulkhead.

"Expect that second impact and be ready for it, by bracing yourselves. The lights will probably go out very soon afterward, but both Wheeler and Miss Spalding will have flashlights. Unfasten your seat belts, wait for Wheeler's call, and *keep calm*. Shortly after you are in your raft, the captain, the navigator, and myself will come around from the front in our raft and join you." Providing we have strength enough remaining to lift our raft straight up through the astrodome when we're standing waist-deep in water and providing the wind doesn't blow us to hell and gone the minute we cut the mooring rope.

"Now is there anything you don't understand, or that you think I should explain more fully?"

"Could we send a radio message to our families?" Nell Buck asked. "I think they'd like to know . . . they were going to meet us at the airport . . . and they'll be standing there. . . ." Her voice faded. "It will be terrible for them . . . the waiting. . . ."

Her own waiting would be so much easier, Dan thought bitterly. And yet she had obviously not even considered it. The pleading in her eyes was hard to discourage.

"I'm sorry. Our radio is extremely busy giving our position and contacting the rescue planes. It just can't be done, young lady."

"I have some rather important papers in my brief case," said Flaherty. He was swaying rhythmically as he leaned against his seat, and he seemed to find it easier to see clearly if he bent his head and peered at Dan from beneath his lowered eyebrows. "The papers represent almost a year's work. Can I take them with me?"

"Not unless you can stuff them in your pockets. No baggage of any kind. None."

Flaherty smiled weakly and then rubbed the back of his hand across his mouth.

"Come to think about it . . . they're not so important, after all. Won't help the human race one bit. Bottom of the sea's the besh place for 'em."

"Now, there's one more thing," Dan said, "and you have as much right to know about it as you have the rest. I must caution you not to raise your hopes, but there *is* one chance in a thousand . . . and it's just about that percentage, that we *can* make the Coast. Let me emphasize that this is *not* possible unless there is a marked change in the wind conditions and, according to our forecast, it just isn't going to happen. However, it *could* happen and we're going to do everything possible, including praying, to help matters." Are you kidding them, or yourself?

"One of the things we can do right now is to lighten ship. We will use a little less fuel that way because we'll go slightly faster and every gallon counts. If any of you have ever had the urge to throw things out of windows, here's the chance of a lifetime. I'll need two men to take that buffet apart and two more to help me up forward."

"How about us girls?" May Holst said. "I love to throw things."

"Good. Then you help Miss Spalding move every dish and tray to the foot of the door. I'll even let you kick them overboard."

"I think I'd better stay with my wife," Ed Joseph said apologetically. "She's so worried about our kids."

"Please let me help," Dorothy Chen said.

"I'll sue the airline for this. It's not the kind of passage I paid for," grumbled Agnew. "But I suppose I must volunteer even though my doctor says I should avoid any exertion. My heart—"

"You know somp'n, mister?" Frank Briscoe said, shaking his head back and forth in spite of his pain. "Your heart . . . is breaking my heart."

Dan had more than enough volunteers. He appointed José Locota and Howard Rice to the job of dismantling the buffet. "It weighs plenty. You'll need a screw driver for some of it, but start kicking the rest to pieces." He chose Milo Buck and Ken Childs to go forward to the crew compartment with him. He stationed Flaherty, whose stance was obviously unreliable, near the bulkhead door. He could at least pass things back. The work of lightening ship began in desperate silence.

There was a small hatch in the floor of the crew compartment barely large enough to admit a man. Dan lowered himself into it and began handing up baggage and boxes of cargo to Milo Buck and Ken Childs. There were other baggage holds in the belly of the ship but entrance to them in flight was impossible. The suitcases and containers were passed from Buck to Ken Childs and then through the bulkhead door to Flaherty. Behind him, the women had formed a line, Nell Buck first, then Lydia Rice, Sally McKee, Lillian Pardee and Dorothy Chen. Gustave Pardee stood puffing at the end of the line and stacked the bags by the rear door. A beautifully appointed bag she recognized as her own passed Lillian. It contained certain jewels she treasured and a Mainbocher frock. She groaned in anguish and then quickly said, "The hell with it!" She passed it on.

They worked diligently for several minutes, too busy to realize fully what they were doing, and finally Dan announced that the hold was empty. He led them back to the rear door.

The results of their efforts, Dan thought, were really pitiful. There could not have been more than seven or eight hundred pounds stacked by the door. But with the dishes and trays which Spalding and May Holst had piled on the other side, and the pieces of the buffet which were accumulating in the rear aisle, there might be almost fifteen hundred pounds. One mile, perhaps two miles, more per hour in air speed. It was almost meaningless.

"Now hold on to me," he told Pardee. While the big man held him about the waist, Dan pressed down on the heavy door handle. He pushed cautiously against it, gauging its movement against the slip stream. As it opened very slowly the night came into them with a roar. Exposed to it for the first time, the protection of the cabin broken, they lost their will. They drew back, wanting to return to their seats, hating the sensation of standing on the edge of the thundering abyss.

"Start kicking things out!" Dan yelled above the booming of the night. "And careful! Always keep behind me. This first step is a son-of-a-bitch."

As Dan held the door, they began to regain their

nerve. At first they pushed things timidly toward the forbidding ledge, yet near the end of the pile they became more daring and in a very few minutes there was nothing more to go. Dan allowed the door to slam shut and locked it. The contrasting silence was like a warm soft blanket.

"That does it," Dan said, wondering why he bothered to wipe his hands. "Now all we have to do is . . . wait."

13

CERTAIN SKY LAWS NOW BECAME EVEN MORE POWERFUL and greatly limited Sullivan's field of decision. And the nearly hopeless feeling which he had successfully conquered for a time, returned as soon as Dan left him to enter the passenger cabin. Four-two-zero was no longer an efficient flying mechanism, nor could Sullivan's knowing hands make her so. The crippling effect of the number-one engine was multiplying in various ways, each one of which twisted itself tightly around the fuel shortage.

The laws were viciously dogmatic. In addition to the drag of the number-one engine, Four-two-zero had lost twenty-five per cent of her available power. To compensate for this infirmity, Sullivan had to call upon the three remaining engines for additional power, and though this was not in itself a serious matter, he had to make further compromises to ease their increased burden. From the feel of the controls alone, Sullivan was constantly reminded that the loss of a second engine through overstrain might render prolonged flight impossible at any altitude.

"Hobie! Give me twenty-two fifty rpm!" It was a command Sullivan hated to give because of the laws.

As Hobie pushed the three good propeller controls

forward, the corresponding surge of power and noise became the signal for more compromises. Heat became the brother of power and the laboring engines must be additionally cooled, or they would soon fail themselves.

"Crack the cowl flaps, Hobie!" These were metal fins surrounding each engine. By adjusting them from the flight deck, the amount of cooling air to the cylinders could be regulated. In normal cruising flight they were closed, and therefore aerodynamically clean. Even slightly opened they increased the drag of Four-two-zero enough to slow the reading on Sullivan's air-speed two miles per hour. Yet it had to be done.

"Watch the head temperatures, Hobie. Don't open those cowl flaps an inch more than you have to!"

At two thousand five hundred feet there was more body to the air and the ship flew less eccentrically. Sullivan was relieved to escape from the sensation of walking a loose tightrope stretched between a point of flying and an incipient stall. Yet the laws were still unrelenting and continued to plague him in many subtle ways.

The original cruising altitude allowed Four-two-zero to slide along in the clear, comfortably, beneath the stars, where she should be. The higher air was smooth and the delicate balance of her most efficient flying altitude could be maintained with a minimum of effort. There, above, was speed and grace; full utilization of her remarkable ability. But now she could not fly so high without the push of great power, and since power was fuel as well as heat, Sullivan had been forced to descend. He was trading ease for maximum range.

The lower altitudes did not welcome Sullivan. He slipped into a thick overcast at four thousand feet and instantly the stars were gone. Rain spewed at the windshields with firehose intensity for several minutes; then it would subside briefly, and then come on again. The noise of it was like exploding steam from a sheet metal boiler and, although Sullivan knew it was harmless, the sound did nothing to ease his tension.

The turbulence he encountered at this lower altitude was more serious than the rain squalls. It was not violent, not the kind to be found in a newly formed cold front or a thunderstorm, not really enough to turn on the seat belt sign—but it was sufficient to cause undesirable changes in the flight attitude of the ship. These changes inevitably resulted in small subtractions from her speed, no matter how assiduously Sullivan applied himself to the flight instruments. As a consequence, he was able to maintain only one hundred and thirty miles per hour.

The straining engines seemed to growl a heavy melody over and over again. Speed was time. Time was distance. Distance was fuel—and the last was a commodity which all of Sullivan's desires could never manufacture over the Pacific.

And the laws bore down very hard on Leonard Wilby. He was deprived, now, of the stars to fix their position. He must rely entirely on his loran equipment. Matching the new fuel consumption against the air-speed and plotting the result on his corrected graph, Leonard became more doubtful of their ability to reach the Coast. He encouraged himself with one hope. At this lower altitude, the opposing winds might be weaker.

Yet even in this hope there was a compromise. Both Leonard and Sullivan were confident of a successful union with the rescue ship; at least they should be able to make contact within a relatively small sky-space through comparison of their own known position and mutually exchanged radio bearings. The radar equipment on the interception ship, however, was notably inadequate, and the chances for a successful meeting of the two ships would be greatly increased if the crews could visually observe each other's lights or pyrotechnics. There was probably sufficient space beneath the overcast to complete such a contact, but Sullivan could not be sure of it, any more than he could afford to expend the last precious altitude they would need if they ever did make the Coast. And so a rider to the laws specified the overcast must break or clear away altogether if the interception ship was to observe their place of ditching exactly and direct the surface ships to them. All of these factors became tighter, and the compromises more difficult to assume, as the sweep second hand on the instrument panel wound around unforgivingly before Sullivan's tiring eyes.

Sullivan found that the sweep second hand was beginning to fascinate him. Its circular motion became so hypnotic he had the greatest difficulty concentrating on his flight instruments, though they were more directly aligned with his vision. Where the hell was Dan Roman? Minutes and minutes were going by, each one strangely more precious than the last, and still Dan had not returned.

Suddenly two impulses almost overwhelmed Sullivan. He wanted to smash the clock on the instrument panel, and he wanted to cry out for Dan. He wanted him by his side—near to him. He wanted him to take over the physical work of flying, a responsibility he could not trust to Hobie because it must be exactly right; he wanted to hear Dan's calm and careless voice in the midst of this pandemonium, and he wanted to know that Dan appreciated his nearly hopeless position. Hurry, Dan. Quick . . . before I break, or that sweep second hand runs out of time altogether! Hurry, before I start thinking about Wendy or the kid, or the new kid who's coming—and what happens if we really have to go in the water. Let's not be all night about it, Dan—come on!

Then as quickly as the need for Dan struck him, Sullivan righted his mind. Now listen, he told himself, Dan Roman is a broken has-been—a good man, perhaps, for what he is doing, handling the passengers and seeing to their needs, but his flying judgment is rusty with time, and he has less than a hundredth of your overocean experience. He is only a much used man. He cannot fix the number-one engine or defy the laws any more than you can. This is your ship. Fly it as custom and prudence have always declared—alone.

"Hobie! Give me another inch or so of boost!"

"But the fuel, Skipper. Look at the meters! We're pouring it in!"

"I can't help it. We're slowing down."

Hobie reluctantly inched the throttles forward. The fuel flow meters moved upward another fifteen gallons per hour for each engine. Sullivan read two miles faster on his air-speed. The rain hissed at the windows and a rivulet of water found its way down over the crash pad to his pants. Leonard Wilby clung desperately to his loran set, fondling it as if its flickering green screen could prophesy everything. In spite of his unwilling preoccupation with the sweep second hand, Sullivan lost track of the actual time. He could not be sure how long he had fought his lonely battle when he knew without turning to look that Dan stood beside him again.

"I see we're still in the air," Dan said.

Sullivan did not answer because he would not permit himself to say what was uppermost in his mind. He wanted to tell Dan how much more capable he felt now that he had returned.

"Have some coffee," Dan said. He held two paper cups in his hand. He handed one to Hobie. "It will warm you up."

Sullivan wiped the perspiration from his face.

"I'm plenty hot enough now."

"Then it will cool you off."

After a moment, Sullivan took his eyes from the instruments. He reached for the remaining cup in Dan's extended hand. The beginning of a smile relaxed his face.

"Thanks—Dan."

The beautiful complacency which Lillian Pardee had developed during the ten years of her marriage was almost entirely destroyed. Her loss, she knew, was not an immediate result of this airplane's startling behavior; she had actually experienced a feeling of exhilaration when she first realized there was trouble, and Dan Roman's talk had only served to sharpen certain emotions which she had believed were permanently dormant. Nor did the possibility of struggling in the night sea oppress her. Instead, she found it a time to search within herself and, with this newly arrived perception, to question her most secret thoughts. Why, in the passage of a very few minutes, had her whole feeling for Gustave, who wore the mantle of a husband so carelessly—why had it changed so completely?

Gustave had bought her on the market as shrewdly and as cold-bloodedly as he might option a play which he knew contained the ingredients for a success. He

168

had seen her modeling at a fashion show, speedily arranged an introduction, showered her with attention and gifts, one of which consisted of a trip to Bermuda. He made a notable holiday of it, and denied himself even the suggestion of an advance, although he was already quite as famous a libertine as a producer. There were flowers and bicycle rides and cocktails in the evening with a middle-aged press agent and his wife whom he had brought along in the role of escorts. There was considerable purchasing of cashmere and tweed, which Gustave pronounced agreeable to her figure— and nothing more. They returned to New York and the surprisingly platonic association continued throughout the production of a new play which proved to be one of his rare failures. That was the first act.

Whether the diversion of Gustave's attention had anything to do with the play's early demise was questionable, but certainly the second act began on the day they lunched long at Sardi's and he proposed marriage as only Gustave Pardee would do. She could see him now, sitting regally beneath the caricature of himself on the brown oak wall, nodding at other patrons from his mountain of power over many of their careers, ignoring them when he pleased, and sometimes raising his glass of ice water in greeting to those he considered his equals or nearly so. Deliberately setting the scene in this, his very special world, Gustave effortlessly raised the curtain on matrimony.

"Now, dear Lillian," he began in a manner that was an incongruous mixture of his almost mystic charm and pure business. "I suppose you have been wondering from time to time about the rather unorthodox course of our relationship. It would be perfectly natural for you to do so."

Gustave frequently asked a question and provided the answer himself—both question and answer being always of the kind that left little room for argument. His understanding and immediate appreciation of others' emotions, no matter how cleverly concealed, was a source of great pride to him and he was justified in believing that he could frequently foretell a companion's reactions long before they had a chance to surprise him.

"Now," he went on, easily, "I have a proposal, which I hope will interest you. I find that I am in need of a wife. Ordinarily this would not be a difficult problem to solve since, heaven knows, I am constantly involved with females who would like nothing better than to produce progeny under my banner while at the same time furthering the careers they passionately cherish. It is my deep-seated mistrust of all actresses that has led me to seek elsewhere."

Gustave had paused then. His eyes swept the room quickly, and in a voice that suggested the matter was already settled, he returned to his subject.

"You . . . have not once shown those unmistakable signs which betray the secret yearning to expose yourself publicly, present in so many women. For this alone, I cherish you. You are also a lady, know how to wear clothes and handle people without making a clumsy spectacle of yourself. I cannot envision you as the kind of hostess who would get swacked at the wrong time or, worse yet, insist on proving your charm by talking instead of listening. It is even conceivable that were we ever to wish a divorce, you might leave me with enough money to produce a recovering show . . . or am I deluding myself?"

"You pass very quickly through the subject of marriage to divorce, Gustave."

His eyes swept the tables in the room again as if he had completely forgotten the conversation, then he hunched his big shoulders and very carefully unfolded his napkin.

"My dear girl . . . recognizing possible pitfalls is not necessarily an invitation to them. I merely mention divorce because I would like you to understand that my whole proposal is not an inspiration of the moment. I've given it considerable thought in the last two months."

"Have you given it any heart?"

"If you are speaking of love, and I believe you are, may I say that the very fact you mentioned it proves you are sufficiently unsophisticated to stay out of mischief . . . and my guess is that you will probably remain so."

"But what about love? Won't you even admit its existence?" It was not a question of being serious with Gustave that day, it was just a discussion with a strange man who had a curiously aloof mind. The idea of marrying Gustave Pardee then, or later, was fantastic.

"Certainly I admit its existence . . . as a word only. You will find it in Webster and in more nonsensical volumes. It is a word behind which are hidden the innumerable frustrations and juvenile desires of our miserable human race. I, fortunately, have passed the age of mental puberty and have emerged without frustrations of any kind. I am wealthy. My digestion is excellent unless some oaf has used too much paprika, and I sleep like a baby. I enjoy my work. Therefore I have no need to anoint any worldly wounds with whatever word mixture currently identifies the illusion of love. Though I am professionally compelled to foster the masquerade of love in my plays to the point where I could frequently throw up . . . what I personally need is a wife."

"You will never get a wife unless you hire a writer to provide you with more romantic dialogue."

"On the contrary, I believe that I will. Specifically you. You are a remarkably intelligent girl, Lillian, and I would like to point out a few things which should vitally concern you. For one thing you are already accustomed to wearing fine clothes and enjoying the company of stimulating people. While the actual money may be small, your work as a model has brought you into contact with a world you would now find extremely difficult to forsake. After some reflection, I am sure you will look with distaste on the doom of marriage to an up-and-coming young man whose limitations would force you to gamble away your most enchanting years in a suburb . . . ironing his shirts. Nor would you be satisfied having a few beers with the neighbors on Saturday nights, no matter how ardent or frequent his protestations of love. You are, in a sense . . . trapped, dear Lillian."

"Which play did you steal that approach from?"

"If it wasn't Ibsen it should have been. But I ask you to consider that you may either marry such a young man, or continue as you are for perhaps ten more years . . . after which the frequency of your engagements will diminish with alarming rapidity. It will then be too late to make any choice whatsoever. A barricade will exist which a great many once attractive American women are appalled to discover they have erected about themselves. I believe that you are too intelligent to allow any such thing to happen. I believe that in return for certain obligations, mainly social, you will eventually reach the conclusion that I am offering a great deal."

"What about your girls, Gustave? What in the world would any wife do about your girls?"

"An intelligent wife would do nothing about them."

That was the beginning of the second act and it had lasted for ten years. Gustave remained the intellectual, scorning any suggestion of love. Although he continued his extracurricular activities quite openly, he was otherwise a perfect husband. The whole second act had not been scarred by a single argument.

And now, apparently, the curtain was up for the third time. Gustave was, as usual, providing a surprise for his audience. In a very few minutes he had changed his character completely. What had happened to the biggest baby in the world? What had happened to the child-man who was actually so afraid of the dark he slept with a light burning? Where was the flabby sensualist who had always arranged his life to resemble a Roman emperor's—as nearly as modern times would permit? The infant, the great mass of self-indulgent flesh surmounted by a brain, was gone. It was impossible to believe that this was the same spoiled Gustave who had been known to burst into tears if the laundry put starch in his shirts, or the truffles were underdone. He couldn't be this good an actor, and besides he would have normally considered his audience woefully lacking in distinction.

First, he had single-handedly prevented panic among his fellow passengers—and on reflection it was all too obvious that the chance for panic was there. Later he had appointed himself a model of behavior, and even now was kneeling in his seat so that he could lean over the back of it and comfort the woman who could not stop crying.

". . . of course you're worried, Mrs. Joseph," he was saying gently. "But I'm quite certain we'll come out of this quite all right. By tomorrow we can look on it as an interesting experience. By the by . . . how old are your children, Mrs. Joseph?"

Imagine Gustave Pardee inquiring about *anyone's* children! He had always hated them—possibly because watching them must have been like looking in a mirror.

Mrs. Joseph was responding by blowing her nose and trying bravely to stop her tears.

"Jennifer is six and Edward is four. Oh——!" The crying would have conquered her again if Gustave had not pressed his interest.

"Jennifer is such a delightful name, Mrs. Joseph. How fortunate you are. The name Jennifer has always brought to me a suggestion of the Scottish moors, heather . . . great peace . . . and the vision of little villages nestled against the hills . . . that sort of thing. Is your Jennifer anything like that, Mrs. Joseph?"

"I . . . I don't know exactly what you mean. She's always been a quiet child. Easy to get along with."

"Exactly. Somehow I knew that would be so . . . in Jennifer's case. And Edward, I've no doubt, is growing so fast you won't recognize him when you get home."

Mentioning home was almost a mistake. Only the absolute assurance in Gustave's manner kept her from breaking down again. Yet gradually she began to talk of her children, which was what Gustave intended she should do.

Watching his face in disbelief, Lillian decided her husband was either the greatest combination director and actor of all time—or she had sorely misjudged his parental urges.

He was occupied with Mrs. Joseph for some time and only when she appeared safely over her hysteria did he say he would like to hear a great deal more about her children at some future meeting. Only then did he turn in his seat and slump down beside his wife. Watching him as he calmly lit a cigarette, Lillian knew that she was in danger; for the emotion she had deliberately starved for so long, the word Gustave so despised, was almost on her lips. He was magnificent. She wanted to tell him so, and she wanted to say it would be very easy to fall in love with a husband who had somehow transformed himself into a man—yet how could she dare challenge ten years of training?

"You seem to have developed a surprising interest in small fry," she said, hesitating even to use the word *children.*

"That poor woman. She was terrified, but I think she will be all right now."

"Thanks to you. Her husband couldn't make any progress with her. Gustave . . . let me ask you something. You told her we would get out of this all right. Do you really believe that?"

He hesitated. A little pile of cigarette ash fell to his lap which he thoughtfully brushed away.

"No. In spite of what that pilot said, I think we're batting at a very sticky wicket."

"And yet you're not afraid?"

"Yes . . . and no. I'm not sure just how I feel . . . but I know that fear at this time would be extremely inconvenient. It's too real. If I were openly afraid now, the others might become so. I was guilty of the cheapest theatrics a while ago . . . and now it seems, I'm stuck with it."

She looked into his eyes and saw there the same absolute self-honesty she had always seen, but the cynicism, the reproach with which he denuded every sentiment, was gone.

"Gustave. There is something I would like to tell you. And if we don't get out of this I'd like you to know it even more. I've never said it before and probably you'll never want me to say it again."

"What is on your twisted little mind?"

"I'm in love with you, Gustave. I guess I always have been."

There was no surprise in his face when he turned to look at her—nor ridicule. He simply reached for her hand and, much to Lillian's surprise, held it very tightly.

Spalding came to the seats where Flaherty sat beside Sally McKee. She had already shown Ken Childs, May Holst, and the Bucks how to use their life vests, and thought they had accepted her instructions with admirable calm, she was not so sure about Sally McKee, who had been the first to scream. And she was wondering if Flaherty, whose head was nodding sleepily, could understand anything. She held out the yellow vests to them and smiled.

"Remember," she said, "these are only a precaution and you don't have to put them on now . . . but this is the time to learn how." She opened the flap on each side of a vest revealing a small metal capsule.

"These preservers are not inflated now. If you jerk this cord on either side, carbon dioxide will be released from the capsules and the vest will inflate immediately." She put her head through the opening and tied the ribbons together in front of her. "Pull these straps around your legs and buckle them here. That's all there is to it."

"So tha's all?" Flaherty said. "Wha' the well-dressed man will wear in the middle of the Pacific Ocean."

"It's impossible to drown if you're wearing a vest," Spalding said. She was not at all sure the statement was true, but she hoped it sounded encouraging.

"Anybody ever try it? I ask you . . . would Lloyd's insure me if they knew my only ship of Fate was one of these things?"

Spalding ignored him. She was watching Sally McKee's face, which had become white beneath her heavy make-up. Her eyes were half-closed as if she were about to faint.

"Are you all right, Miss McKee?"

"Yes . . . I'll be all right. I . . . it's strange . . . I don't really seem to care what happens."

Spalding wondered if the next thing she must say would cause Sally to lose control of herself entirely. Trying to look away from her, she began the most difficult part of her instructions.

"If we should happen to go down, I will give you plenty of warning. Cross your arms like this . . . right in front of your face, and brace your hands on the seat just ahead. Bend your head down between your arms and keep it there until we have stopped completely. Remember to remove your shoes . . . and, Mr. Flaherty, it will be better if you loosen your collar and tie."

"Why?"

Spalding only suspected the real reason. In school someone had said something about the impact force choking a person or breaking his neck . . . it wasn't clear now, just what they said. She decided very suddenly that the less the subject was explored, the better.

"The small packets here in front contain sea marker," she went on hurriedly. "It's a green dye that will stain the water about you and make it easier to spot you from the air."

"How can anyone see it at night?"

"Well . . . it's really for daytime."

"But the pilot who talked to us said we might be in the water only a few minutes," Sally McKee said in a dull voice. "He was lying to us."

"I'm sure he wasn't, Miss McKee. I just thought you'd like to know about the dye. . . ." She hesitated, wanting to leave them and go on to Frank Briscoe, who sat further down the aisle with Dorothy Chen. She resolved not to mention the dye again. "It's just there," she finished lamely. ". . . and I thought you'd like to know. Now if you want anything at all, just call for me."

Leaving them, she heard Flaherty mumble something about how he could use another half-dozen drinks. She went quickly to Frank Briscoe and knelt beside him.

"Hello, Mr. Briscoe. Everything all right?"

He smiled and reached for her hand.

"Little lady, I dunno when I've felt better in the last five years." He tipped his head slightly toward Dorothy Chen. "You know somp'n? It's a false theory that old men don't like excitement. They love it. If I could just be sure the company would be as nice as Miss Chen here, I'd spend the rest of my days riding around on one of these things. First girl I ever met from Korea, and also the first girl I ever met who would let Frank Briscoe rattle on . . . just as if she was really interested in what I had to say."

"I'm jealous," Spalding said. At this moment she wanted to put her head in his lap and cry out the fear which was becoming more and more difficult to conceal. Being close to Frank Briscoe was like standing beneath a strong tree in a storm. She looked upward to his face and could not detect the slightest hint of concern, although

176

the marks of his pain were everywhere about his mouth and eyes.

"I've just elected Miss Chen as the girl I would most like to be on a life raft with," he said. "Of course now . . . she might prefer a younger man—"

"There is in my family, a very, very old saying," Dorothy Chen said in her soft, smooth voice, and watching her Spalding knew that she too was determined to hide her fear. "I will try to translate it for you." She hesitated and then spoke more slowly, feeling for the words. "The youth of man will never die . . . unless he murders it."

Frank Briscoe laughed aloud.

"I plead not guilty!" he said. Then looking down at Spalding, his face became more serious. "What's all that paraphernalia you've got there?"

"Your life vest, Mr. Briscoe. I want to show you and Miss Chen how to use it." She reached to place the vest over his head. He pushed it away, gently but firmly.

"Nothing doing. If you put anything around *my* neck that weighs more than an ounce, my head's liable to roll off. My bones are only held together by my imagination. If we actually go down and hit, I'll come to pieces like the one-horse shay. The doctors call me Humpty Dumpty."

"But you must, Mr. Briscoe. You might have to use it."

"A burial at sea would save my heirs a lot of money. You know somp'n? I've been scheming around for the past few years trying to figure out a way to beat the high cost of savage funerals. Want to keep my family and relatives from being nicked outrageously for a six-foot chunk of real estate . . . that if they had any sense they would never take time from their own full lives to visit. Now, maybe that one little problem will be solved for me."

"I'm ashamed of you for talking like that, Mr. Briscoe. If it has to be, young man, I'll put it on you by force." She held out the vest again.

"Tell you what. We'll compromise if it'll make you happy. You just stand there and put the thing on your-

177

self and show me the gadgets while I watch. I'll bet we won't have to use them, anyway."

Spalding sighed, but she stood in the aisle, and showed them how to don the life vest. When she had finished, she reached down and loosened his tie.

"Why do that?"

"You just look more comfortable that way, Mr. Briscoe. You sort of impress me as the open-collar type . . . rugged, you know?"

"Outdoorsie, you mean?"

"Yes. Now you behave yourself. I'll be coming back to make sure you're being nice to Miss Chen."

"It's a rough assignment for an outdoor man without his horse, but I'll do my best."

Envying them being so close together, she went on to Humphrey Agnew. He was sitting in the last row of occupied seats, next to José Locota. As she approached him, he looked up defiantly. His thin lips were pressed together so tightly they were almost invisible. His mouth was like a small, newly made cut. And his inflamed eyes, protruding grotesquely from his drawn face, frightened Spalding. She was very glad that José sat beside him.

"Miss," he said thickly, before she had a chance to hand him a life vest. "I demand to know what is being done about this airplane and our safety. I have been thinking about it and am convinced we are in the hands of incompetents. What is being—"

"You are quite wrong, Mr. Agnew." Spalding cut him off quickly while she could still keep the anger from her voice. "Mr. Roman explained everything to you and the rest of the passengers are very satisfied. As for Captain Sullivan and his crew, their experience—"

"Nonsense. This sort of thing doesn't happen on other lines. An investigation will undoubtedly prove this airplane was ready for the junk heap when we bought our tickets. I demand a refund and I demand—"

"Why don't you shut up?" José said.

"I have a perfect right—"

"You ain't got no rights at all for some time to come, and if you don't keep your mouth shut no life vest is going to keep you from drownin' because I'll hold your goin' to say, miss?"

"I just wanted to show you how to operate your vests, and how to brace yourself if we have to ditch."

"I know about them vests, miss. We got the same gimmicks on our boats. But show our friend here, if you still think he's worth it."

Agnew pressed himself tightly against the back of his seat. His whole body was suddenly rigid and he stared fixedly at Spalding as if he was looking directly through her. After a moment he moved his tobacco-stained fingers to his chest and speculatively massaged the region around his heart.

"My heart . . ." he breathed heavily. "Everybody . . . everything . . . is against me. You've started an attack. You hate me. You all hate me because I tried to do what was right. My wife hates me—"

"Who could blame her?" José said. "Now, will you listen to this nice miss?"

"Don't touch me! I cannot stand the slightest exertion or annoyance when I'm like this!"

"You're a faker, Agnew. Do what she says. Go ahead, miss . . . and don't pay no attention to him."

"I could give you a Seconal, Mr. Agnew. It would calm you."

"Keep your hands away from me. I demand that you leave me alone!"

"You're giving me a very bad time, Mr. Agnew. I'm only trying to help you."

"Go right ahead, miss. If he moves a muscle, I'll take care of him."

Dreading to touch him, Spalding bent down and cautiously slipped the vest over his head. As she explained the capsule lanyards and the strap buckles, his body remained stiff and he avoided looking at her. When she had finished at last, he relaxed slightly and passed his hand slowly across the wound that was his mouth.

"I will see this airline is put out of business. You may be quite sure of that!" He spoke the words so angrily several particles of moisture flew from his mouth to Spalding's face. She straightened quickly and wiped them away in disgust. She wanted to slap him.

179

"Remember your heart, Mr. Agnew. Lawsuits might be bad for it."

She smiled gratefully at José and then walked away while she still had control of herself. She went directly to the last seat in the plane, an area that was now deserted, and sat down. She wanted a few minutes alone. It would help to smoke a cigarette, but she dismissed the idea when she remembered why she had left her pack on the flight deck. The mirror . . . she should have told Sullivan about the shivering mirror and perhaps this whole thing would never have happened.

She looked around her, at the back of the cabin which she knew so well. Now it was only empty and forbidding. There were marks on the wall where the buffet had been, and bits of wreckage projected from the carpetless floor. The coats she had hung up carefully in Honolulu swayed rhythmically with the new movement of the ship. She saw the two minks and thought how useless it had been to envy their owners. She wondered how the coats would look, soaked with salt water, and saw in her mind a quick, terrible vision of a mink-clad woman floating lifeless on the sea.

Forward, the view was more reassuring. She could see the elbows and hands of the passengers who remained in their seats and some of them, Ken Childs, the Bucks, and Mr. Joseph had left their seats to move about again. Only the yellow splash of color from the life vests here and there suggested that this was anything but a normal flight. The rising smoke from several cigarettes made narrow opaque bars of the small reading lights—it was only the sound of the engines that was wrong. There was an urgent tone to them now, a desperate, uneven pounding Spalding had never heard before. Combined with the increasingly erratic movement of the ship, the noise made her feel sick.

She leaned toward the window, wanting to look at the stars, and found them gone. Instead, the trailing edge of the wing was only dimly visible, slicing through the heavy murk. The green navigation light on the end of the wing exploded with constant regularity, each time forming a ghastly, comfortless blossom against the cloud.

Spalding shivered and thought of praying, a thing she had never done before in the air.

Her soft lips were forming the first words when she became aware of a faint sound which instantly changed her thinking. She sought quickly in the pocket of her blouse and brought out Frank Briscoe's watch. It was chiming the last of the hour—ten o'clock Coast time. She held the watch in her hand, caressing it gently with her fingers. This watch belonged to a man who refused to surrender ungracefully. Frank Briscoe was dying, and he had known of it for a long time. Yet he still intended to live as long as he was able, no matter how painful the living might be.

She brought the watch slowly to her lips and kissed it. Then she replaced it in her pocket. She changed her prayer to one of Thanksgiving.

When the red needle on the direction finder swung completely around to indicate they had passed over the Farallon Islands, Lieutenant Mowbray set the Coast Guard B-17 on a course of two hundred and thirty degrees and pressed the button on his interphone.

"Pilot to lookouts. You men can stand down for about two hours. It will be at least that long before we reach the intercept area . . . maybe longer. When I give you the word, stand to sharp again, and give your observation sector strict attention. With this wind, this is going to be a tough baby to pin down. Sparks? Anything more from Sea Frontier?"

The radioman came back to him at once. "Only the winds I gave you, sir."

"Anything from Four-two-zero?"

"Not a sound out of them, sir."

"Let me know the minute you hear anything."

"Aye aye, sir."

Lieutenant Mowbray released the button and looked at Keim, who sat in the copilot's seat on his right. He was working on his pants with a pair of pliers now, trying to release the zipper. He shook his head unhappily and his voice was barely audible over the hissing of the rain against the windshields. For one moment Keim broke his melancholy concentration on the zipper and assessed the night with a bitter look.

"Those people. If they have to ditch . . . tonight they don't stand a chance, I'm thinking. Not much more than we do of finding them if this stuff doesn't clear."

14

THE HEADQUARTERS OF COMMANDER WESTERN SEA
Frontier were in San Francisco. There in a single room,
not much larger than a fair-sized office, the movements
and whereabouts of every Coast Guard, Navy and
Merchant vessel on the Pacific, and the airplanes en
route over its expanse, were represented on a large
map which covered a wall. When Four-two-zero first departed Honolulu a yeoman tacked a small airplane to
the chart and moved it eastward each hour according
to advices received from Overseas Traffic Control.

There were several men in the room, and most of
them had been drinking coffee and complaining about
the high cost of a complete uniform—until the first
distress message came through. The coffee cups were now
cold. Every man was talking on a phone, alerting those
vessels at sea and those moored in San Francisco Bay.
Three Navy destroyers en route from San Diego to Seattle
were commanded to alter course and proceed at full
speed toward a point two hundred miles off the Farallons. The Coast Guard picket boats at Monterey, San
Francisco, and Eureka were dispatched to the same area.
The Army air-sea rescue unit at Hamilton Field was
advised, in a condescending manner, that they might as
well contribute a few additional seach planes if they were
so minded. A Greek freighter and a Danish freighter
shown on the wall chart as being near the area, were

contacted after much confusion through Nan Mike Charlie, the Coast Guard radio station, and commanded to stand by for instructions. A general call went out from the same station to all fishing vessels in the vicinity to watch for an airplane in distress and report any findings to Nan Mike Charlie. The call brought no acknowledgment and it was assumed the high winds and heavy seas had driven all fishermen to port. The cutter *Chatauqua,* which had been docked at San Francisco for minor repairs, was ordered to proceed through the Golden Gate immediately. A Japanese tanker inbound from Yokohama and a heavy tug southbound from Astoria were advised that Four-two-zero might pass over their position. They were to render such aid as they could.

In the space of an hour, twenty-one surface vessels were alerted and were either standing by or already proceeding toward the course line flown by Four-two-zero. Even the cutter *Gresham,* far to the west, was commanded to abandon ocean station "Uncle" and proceed at full speed in the direction of San Francisco.

"This is going to cost the taxpayers a lot of dough," a yeoman said when the pressure eased and the alert board was in order once more.

His grey-haired chief, who had just ordered two Martin Mariner seaplanes and a helicopter to stand by on a three-minute alert, and had finally received acknowledgments from the FCC direction-finding stations on his priority messages, was in no mood for levity.

"What would you do?" he growled. "Have 'em swim home?"

On the *Cristobal Trader,* Manuel Aboitiz thoughtfully considered the case of a matador he had once seen in Guadalajara. He recalled how for a few glorious moments, the matador stood on the brink of immortality as he made pass after pass at a particularly audacious bull. And suddenly, in the midst of a mortal combat, the bull had sighted a bouquet of flowers thrown into the ring. Oblivious to his wounds, the bull lost immediate interest in the matador and no effort could persuade him from nibbling contentedly at the flowers. The bull, thought

Manuel, and the matador, too, were probably still living—but both had been led from the ring like sheep. They had worked up to a climax, tasted the wine of fateful action, and at the last moment—been found wanting.

Manuel believed that he knew how the matador felt when he trudged back to obscurity. For now his own interplay with the shore stations and an aircraft in distress was ended. Four-two-zero had established direct communications with San Francisco and Manuel had been summarily pushed aside—to stand forgotten behind the barrera, he thought, and watch in silence while the show proceeded. He could still hear them although he found the role of a spectator insipid, and the focus of affairs was now far to the east.

"Four-two-zero to San Francisco. Position report."

"Go ahead . . . Four-two-zero."

"At twenty-two thirty-seven we were at one three three degrees west . . . thirty-five degrees fifty minutes north . . . course four seven degrees magnetic. Our altitude two thousand five hundred feet . . . indicated air speed one hundred and thirty-four miles per hour. Our calculated ground speed only one hundred and thirteen knots. Request latest winds aloft forecast one three three degrees to San Francisco. Also state of sea and progress of interception ship."

"Roger. Stand by, Four-two-zero."

Manuel scratched the hair on his chest and thought more about the matador as he listened to the faint crackling in the loudspeaker. It was a pity, he considered, that he could not at least bow, or doff the montera which he could almost feel on his head. Adios, friends. One day Manuel Aboitiz will walk off this accursed rust bucket and rejoin you in the sky.

"Four-two-zero from San Francisco. Ready to copy winds."

"Roger."

"One three three to one three zero west . . . north at thirty knots. One three zero to one two six west . . . northwest thirty-four knots. One two six west to San Francisco . . . west northwest forty-eight knots. Following is a sea condition report . . . moderate to heavy northwest swells with moderate to heavy chop on top . . . Spume. . . ."

"Repeat last word?"

"Spume . . . Sugar-peter-uncle-mabel-easy. Water temperature estimated forty-two degrees. Coast Guard advises B-17 will intercept you approximately zero zero four zero. They request you display all lights and fire pyrotechnics every ninety seconds from that time on. Did you read all that?"

"Affirmative, San Francisco. You're coming through loud and clear. Request latest San Francisco weather."

"San Francisco two two zero zero observation . . . ceiling measured six hundred feet, visibility one and one half miles. Light fog. Wind west southwest twenty with moderate gusts. Temperature forty-five, dewpoint forty-four. Altimeter two nine eight two."

"Roger, San Francisco. Thanks."

"Commander Western Sea Frontier requests if you intend ditching and if so approximate position you intend to execute same."

"Stand by, San Francisco."

Manuel Aboitiz rubbed the stubble on his chin for a time and then went back to scratching his chest. Now this was a time when the *Cristobal Trader* should be able to lift herself from the sea. She should roar like a speedboat over the crests and arrive at the location just in time to pluck the survivors from the waves. Manuel Aboitiz could then read about himself in the newspapers.

"Four-two-zero to San Francisco."

"Go ahead."

"Advise Sea Frontier new winds may permit us land San Francisco. Decision will be made at zero one thirty. If winds incorrect we will ditch approximately two hundred miles off shore. Over."

"Roger, Four-two-zero."

There was silence. Manuel's fingers became still as his eyes moved upward to observe the clock on the bulkhead. Zero one thirty. . . . That would be only two hours away. . . . In those two hours a great many things could happen. Yet the voice from the ship had new vigor when the winds were received. Those would be tail winds, wouldn't they? Four-two-zero was eastbound and the winds were blowing from the west? Some hope there—a break. The bull would not stop chewing on flowers, it was too late for that, but at least a ray of sunlight had penetrated the arena. I am happy, Manuel thought. I am very happy for them. And this is a far more stimulating feeling than if I actually stood in the ring. For these people I will pray and ask that my mother and my father reach down to hold them. From where they live, beyond the stars.

Manuel pried himself out of the chair and, gauging the potential roll of the *Cristobal Trader,* waddled downhill to the door. On deck he waited until the ship reached a moment of comparative equilibrium and then went quickly to the boat-deck rail. He did not hear the staccato reports of his shirttails flapping in the wind. There was too much else to think about as he crossed himself and concentrated on the forbidding world above him.

There was a sense of moving through subterranean depths rather than the heights. No single thing was responsible for this reverse impression which came to the men on the flight deck almost simultaneously. The rain, yes—Four-two-zero was moving fast enough to make almost a solid of its density, and now the electrical potentials in the cloud layer combined to produce St. Elmo's fire. Enormous balloons of green light, ever changing in shape and size, enveloped the entire ship. Halos of green light spun pinwheel-like around the propellers, and on the windshields the rivulets and single globules of water, that were always in quick motion, became phosphorescent. Bland, ghostlike explosions of green vapor occurred frequently just ahead of the nose, and sometimes the intensity of the ghostly fire was enough to illuminate the faces of the men who secretly told themselves three things. St. Elmo's fire was beautiful, it was harmless, and they didn't like it.

They did not have to observe the altimeter to confirm their sense of moving through the depths. The habitual dryness of the upper altitudes, to which they were long accustomed, was gone. Cigarettes again tasted like cigarettes instead of poorly wrapped autumn leaves. The partial lethargy always evident above seven thousand feet because of oxygen lack, was replaced by an unnatural desire for movement about the flight deck. They could hear each other's voices somewhat better at this level, but they had lost the familiar and comfortable feeling of high suspension, and they sensed throughout their bodies that the customary position of their private selves and their ship in the scheme of the night atmosphere, had been grievously infringed upon. They could not, for any reward, even a guarantee of their safety, have explained this feeling to each other. It was an entirely solitary perception and, strangely enough, served to separate them when they most wanted to be together. Though they could look at each other and easily reach out to touch each other, they were alone. They were like members of a family sorely embarrassed by an unmentionable scandal. Each held his private opinion of the number-one engine and the effect it would have on their future, yet they refused to speak of it, now that its betrayal was obvious. They spoke with abnormal seriousness, carefully selecting their words so that they would never reveal their despair.

There were outward changes in their manner and appearances—by-products of the low altitude, their newly guarded anxieties, and time.

Leonard had become an old man whose indefinite movements would have been better suited to pottering around a garden on a Sunday afternoon. It was warmer at this altitude, there was a closeness that approached suffocation, and he could hear his own heavy breathing even above the sound of the engines. A shallow pool of moisture showed in the hollow of his throat, and the points of his shirt collar turned upward like a pair of ill-balanced horns. His belt had slipped below his potbelly and his wrinkled shirt hung over it until it was invisible. The pure white stubble of his beard was rapidly softening the planes of his face and a nervous development in his stomach, which he blamed on the sandwich he had eaten so long ago, caused him to belch frequently.

Hobie was the least affected of the men on the flight deck, although the sheen had gone from his hair and the tie which he had carefully turned into a large knot was now a loose black yoke separated an untidy distance from his neck. Preoccupied with the radio and the correct repetition of Sullivan's messages, Hobie at least maintained contact with those in a safer world and, through the voices in his earphones, found some measure of security.

Sullivan was the most alone, although since he had turned over the actual flying of the ship to Dan he had managed to assume an air of detachment which he hoped would conceal the violent changes in his resolution. He rubbed his bloodshot eyes frequently, because they were very tired. The back of his neck was painfully stiff and he rolled his head from time to time trying to relieve it. He knew that the pressure had only begun; he must soon make many quick decisions, any one of which could mean the difference between living and dying, and yet in spite of this certain knowledge he could not entirely clear the chaos in his mind. He wanted to think clearly, he knew he *must* think clearly—and still the stubborn snake in his brain would not be killed. It was fear squeezing his thoughts, the same fear he had successfully held in check for so long. If it was victorious now, bled him until it captured his strength, then it would be all over. There were many things he had to place in a hairline balance, weigh them, and be sure that his final estimation was exactly right. Again he must think many miles ahead of his ship.

The newer winds received from San Francisco had given them all a few moments of hopeful speculation. Beside himself with joy, Leonard had matched the winds against his new fuel consumption graph, quickly found their future speed over the surface of the earth if the winds proved correct—and declared that it was possible to make San Francisco.

"It will be damn near dry tanks, Skipper!" he yelled, "maybe twenty—thirty gallons left . . . less, but if those winds are right we can make it!"

Marvelous . . . if true. But what if the winds failed to come up to the forecast, which had been made in a warm, steady office by a group of men who would go home to their women this night after presuming to say what the disposition of nature might be. The difference between making safety at San Francisco airport and not making San Francisco, even by their calculations, was perhaps five minutes. That wasn't very much. The opportunity to risk a long low-powered glide during the last fifteen or twenty minutes, with the engines consuming a minimum of fuel, was long gone. Twenty-five hundred feet would barely clear the hills around San Francisco—it was in fact technically illegal; but this was not a time to be concerned with legality if the hills could actually be missed. Approaching from the sea, it would just be possible, provided the utmost care was taken in flying the beams during the final minutes.

And those final minutes would be another thing. The weather at San Francisco airport was anything but favorable. A routine chore of work to land safely under normal conditions—a real nightmare with one engine out, poor air speed, and the pumps sucking the tanks dry during the last few minutes of descent. And if the tanks actually went dry, the penalty for waiting and hoping that they would not, would follow immediately. Completely starved for power, the heavy ship would assume the flying characteristics of an express train. He would have to shove it almost straight down, yielding everything to the laws of flight; and the landing field would be the hills, the streets of the city, or, at best, a bay criss-crossed with bridges and islands. With a low ceiling and limited visibility the chances of avoiding a disaster, Sullivan reckoned, would be about one in five hundred.

The alternative was not inviting and, because many of its hazards were unknown to airmen, it seemed a miserable choice. No one could even guess how Four-two-zero might finally hit the water. A wing tip could catch the crest of a wave and cartwheel her in two seconds. She might bounce off the top of a swell and porpoise straight down into the next swell. Once the decision to ditch was made, there would be no retreat from it. Still there would be one invaluable advantage over a last-minute attempt to land in San Francisco. The ditching could be carefully prepared for in every respect. There would be time for that, and the water could be approached cautiously with the ship under full control since there would still remain enough fuel to give the three engines power. Sullivan could hold the ship in a power stall and, with the engines aiding him, might hit as slow as a hundred miles per hour. If it was a half-decent landing and if the surface ships were quick about it, at least a few people would stand a chance. There were less than two hours left.

"Leonard. What's with the wind?" Sullivan said it as casually as he could, not wanting to press his navigator.

"It's good, Skipper. We'll make it. I know we'll make it."

Sullivan bent over him, trying to forget the snake which clutched at his vitals and concentrate on Leonard's figures.

"How do you know?"

"This loran fix I just made. See . . . ?" He parted his steel dividers and stretched them between a red cross and the San Francisco airport. "We've picked up four minutes in the last hour, Skipper. The tanks will be dry, when we get there, but I'll be full of beer soon after. Tonight I might even lace it with a few whiskys."

Four minutes. Four pitiful minutes. That much could be lost in a single circle of the airport. Leonard could easily be that far wrong on his position. The slightest change in the wind, an increase in the turbulence, even very heavy rain could hold them back four minutes.

"We've got to do better."

"If we pick up another four in the next hour . . . that'll be eight altogether."

"Are you wishing or calculating?"

Leonard flexed the fingers of his hands and looked at them. "I . . . I guess I'm wishing."

"Stop it. We can't afford the luxury."

"What are you going to do, Skipper?"

"I don't know yet."

"Do you want me to break out our life raft and get the other stuff ready?"

"No. Stick with your navigating. We'll take care of that when the time comes. Get your flares ready, though.

We'll need them for the interception ship in about an hour."

"You want some smoke flares, too? They might help you judge the wind if we have to ditch."

"Drop some if you want to." Sullivan shrugged his shoulders. "I never saw one that worked yet."

The continued turbulence was getting on Dan's nerves. Although he understood the cause of it and believed that it would gradually increase as they approached the California coast, he was unable to command his reflexes so that the ship flew in a manner which pleased him. It had been a long, long time since he had flown on instruments—was it three or four years?—ever since South America. What had once been a skill in the smaller ships was now an art complicated by the sluggish responses of great weight.

And the weight was full of meaning, Dan thought, for it was composed of more than fashioned metal and liquid fuel. There was treasure behind him; to someone unknown waiting on the shore, those faces were as dear as Alice's and Tony's had once been. Standing firmly on the earth and talking idly with comrade airmen, it was all very well to fall back on the old pilot's saying—I'm in the front of the ship and if my ass gets there, they'll get there, so why give the passengers a second thought—but the pilots who relied on that phrase to mitigate their responsibility were not those who had lost an Alice or a Tony, nor had they ever looked into faces like those waiting hopefully in the cabin. The faces returned to Dan now singly and sometimes in groups, and they seemed to stare beseechingly at him from the depths of the instruments. There was the young blond girl and her husband, the white-faced brunette and the big man who had apparently discovered himself in danger; there was the sick-looking fellow with the sprightly eyes and the woman who could not stop crying. There was the sedate Oriental girl, the drunk who was too confused to care, and even an old familiar face to prod the memory of times when there was an Alice and a Tony.

After a half-hour's intense application to his flying, Dan found that his skill with an airplane was not lost

192

forever. Gradually his instrument work smoothed, his corrections became smaller—the altimeter and the gyro-compass behaved themselves. He knew he was getting the most out of the ship in spite of the turbulence and he was able to think of other things. He came reluctantly to the conclusion that the faces in the cabin had been unfairly set up for punishment. Their only sin was buying a ticket, yet in doing so they had unquestioningly placed their lives in the hands of a man they had never seen. How could they have known that Sullivan was a good man, a highly skilled and desperately sincere man just now, but how could they know he had been caught at the wrong time, when his natural resistance to insecurity was at the lowest point it would ever be? Sullivan was like a steeplechase rider who had thoughtlessly sailed over the most difficult jumps without injury for a long time and then come one day to look at the course in a different way—and see all at once, that he might be hurt. It would pass. The confidence of any man who really knew what he was doing returned eventually. And he was a better man for the period of doubt because he would have conquered his instability with reason instead of bravado.

But now there was no time for Sullivan to turn over his nerves and examine the other side of them. His nerves should be his shield; instead they were already raw and exposed to every new assailant.

It was doubtful if the other crew members had observed the disintegration of their captain. Hobie was too busy and too much in awe of him. Leonard was himself besieged with fright. They had not noticed the change in Sullivan's voice, how it seemed to crawl exhausted from the depths of his chest, nor had they noticed his eyes, which darted furtively from instrument to instrument, absorbing little from any of them. Before he had turned over his seat to Dan, his flying had deteriorated into a miserable exhibition. He lost and gained two hundred feet of altitude either way and his course sometimes varied as much as ten degrees. These were time-consuming errors. Fully in possession of himself, Sullivan would never have made them.

There were even more disturbing evidences of Sullivan's inability to concentrate relentlessly on the salvation of his ship. His wait-and-see attitude was sound enough—it was still too early to make any final decisions—but the foundations for both choices should be firmly laid now, whether they were actually used or not. If Sullivan was going to try for a landing at San Francisco he should have the range book out, refreshing himself on every detail of the approach, instead of pacing up and down in a cloud of cigarette smoke. Time, every moment, would be priceless over San Francisco. And radio bearings should be requested constantly from the shore to confirm Leonard's observations. San Francisco should be advised that a landing was contemplated and the control tower should be instructed to turn every light to full intensity and to stand by for immediate clearing of the entire area. Information on possible breaks in the overcast along the coastline should be obtained; the abandoned airport at Half Moon Bay was a few miles closer and would at least be adequate for an emergency landing. It could be wide open with the stars shining down upon it for all Sullivan knew. What was the weather at Drake's Bay? With a northwest wind the water would be smooth there and a ditching, if it had to be, far less dangerous. Even the Farallon Islands, rugged and inhospitable as they were, promised dry land. They were twenty-eight miles off shore, only pinnacles of rock, perhaps, but a small boat was stationed there. Sullivan was just not thinking of everything.

His every expression of thought indicated that he was already resigned to a ditching in the open ocean, a terrifying prospect in view of the wind and the seas. Even so—Sullivan had yet to make any attempt to contact the interception ship.

"Say, Skipper?"

"Yes, Dan?"

"How about shooting a call to the interceptor? See how he's doing. . . ."

"All right." He seemed to twist away from a firm answer. "I guess it's about time. Try to raise him, Hobie."

Hobie called the B-17 on very high frequency. His face lit up when he received a reply almost immediately.

"Roger, Four-two-zero. We've been waiting for your call. We read you loud and clear. Advise if you are on instruments. Over."

"Affirmative . . . B-17."

"Any breaks in the overcast?"

"Negative. Solid with moderate rain."

"Okay. We are also on instruments. This will complicate our intercepting you, but don't worry about it. We'll catch you. We estimate our position at one hundred and forty-five miles east of you. Expect interception in approximately twenty minutes. Turn on your direction finder now and tune to five hundred kilocycles. We will transmit on that frequency every three minutes. It will not be necessary for you to fly the course you read on your own direction finder. Continue on your planned course and merely transmit your readings immediately. Your bearings will be supplementary to our own, but very helpful. When your needle point begins to fluctuate rapidly, advise us immediately, regardless of the time space. We will then be approaching very close to you. Do you understand all that?"

"Roger . . . B-17."

"Okay . . . for your information there are several surface vessels en route to your course line. Give us at least thirty minutes' notice before you ditch, so we can direct them to your exact position. If you do go down you will be under observation constantly. We have enough gas to stay above you until morning if necessary, and two seaplanes are standing by to take over when we have to leave. This transmission is being broadcast simultaneously on five hundred kilocycles so you should have the first bearing by now. How about it? Over."

Their heads close together, Dan, Sullivan and Hobie watched breathlessly as the red needle swung around and halted on the direction finder dial. When it stopped on forty degrees they looked at each other and very suddenly their relief burst through the tension which had kept them apart. They were like men who had come upon a cache of long-sought diamonds. They shouted words which had no meaning or connection with the moment. They pounded each other on the arms and the back. They called to Leonard so that he, too, might be encouraged.

At last they were no longer alone in the night. There was company—other men of like inheritance were speeding toward them, and for the moment it meant nothing that they would be helpless to extend any direct aid. And the voice of the man who spoke from the B-17 was exactly right—easy, sympathetic, and reassuring; the voice of a man who somehow, over the miles, understood their wretchedness.

Sullivan took the microphone from Hobie's hand and pressed it to his lips.

"Four-two-zero to the B-17. Our bearing shows you forty degrees magnetic. That would put you five degrees to the north of our course . . . but we're damn glad to know you're around, anyway."

"Roger, Four-two-zero. We know what you mean. Your bearing agrees with ours so we'll ease over a few degrees. What is your present exact altitude?"

"Twenty-five hundred and sixty feet."

"Can you climb any higher? This stuff is not supposed to be very high and if we could get on top, interception would be much easier."

"Negative. We can climb, but don't want to use the fuel to do it. Every gallon is a mile nearer shore for us."

"Okay . . . forget it. Our radar is not all it might be, but we'll pick you up on it sooner or later if we keep these bearings going. What is the total number of people you have on board?"

"Twenty-one."

"What is your exact indicated air speed, outside temperature, magnetic course, and calculated ground speed?"

Leonard fed the information to Sullivan on small slips of paper. The knowledge that another navigator would soon be near to confirm his position had accomplished a magical change in him. He had straightened perceptibly and the shaking was gone. He worked quickly and his figures were marked down almost defiantly on the paper. Leonard was the first to notice that Spalding had joined them. She was leaning weakly against the bulkhead which supported the mass of radio equipment, and she was trying to smile. Leonard put his arm around her and for a moment she allowed her head to rest against his shoulder.

196

"I had to come," she said. "I needed to . . . just for a minute. I just couldn't stand it alone back there any longer."

"Sure," Leonard said and from him flowed both tenderness and his new-found strength. "We kind of forgot about you."

"The passengers are all right. They're wonderful."

"You can tell them to cheer up. We just contacted the interception ship. They'll be alongside in about twenty minutes."

"Are we going to ditch?"

Leonard nodded toward Sullivan, who was still bent over the radio panel watching the direction finder.

"He ain't saying . . . but all things in time, honey. Just take it from your old Uncle Leonard, you'll sleep in your own warm little bed tonight."

"Do you want anything . . . coffee or something? I saved one thermos and there's still a few sandwiches left in the crew compartment."

"No thanks. Dan brought some coffee a while ago. How about yourself?"

"I couldn't. My stomach is doing flip-ups. I guess I'm scared."

"Why don't you lie down in the bunk for a few minutes?"

"No . . . I'll be all right in a minute. Really. You're all busy. I'll go back now."

"You're a brave kid, honey. Just hang on to yourself a little longer. Everything is going to work out fine."

She thanked Leonard with her eyes and watched him a moment while he turned to his loran set and began twisting the knobs. She wanted to stay on the flight deck although it was far from the well-ordered place she was accustomed to see. It smelled strongly of leather and metal, and from above her head the radios poured down the acrid odor of overheated wires. The smell of the men was different, too, and she wondered if tobacco and perspiration could alone account for it. Sullivan turned backward for one moment to glance at the astrodome. He looked through and beyond Spalding; his harassed eyes gave no hint of recognition. Then there were only backs again, Leonard's, and Sullivan's, and Hobie's and Dan

197

Roman's. They were busy. They were lucky, Spalding thought. They had something to do with their hands and their minds to help them through the waiting. So do you, girl—even if the things to do are not so clearly defined.

Feeling more apart from them than she ever had before, Spalding took a last look at their backs and went slowly through the crew compartment toward the passenger cabin.

15

OCCUPYING THE FIRST ROW OF SEATS, MILO AND NELL Buck were physically isolated from the other passengers. The only people who might observe them were Howard and Lydia Rice, who were just behind them and who, Milo said, would need a periscope to do so. Ken Childs and May Holst were diagonally across the aisle. Milo said they would need a series of mirrors to see anything and besides they were absorbed in each other. To complete their seclusion, Milo had turned out the small lights above their heads and removed the tubular seat-arm between himself and his bride. For some time they sat quietly together in the darkness. The muted red light on the left wing occasionally defined the window and touched their young faces with faint color when it flashed against a heavier area of the overcast. They were otherwise nearly invisible and as time drew them closer they lost all awareness. As naturally as if they were alone beneath a tree in a forest glade, they came together. Their voices fell to a whisper and soon they found ways to fit their bodies as they desired them, in spite of the seats' limitations. There was great warmth where their bodies met and Milo could feel the moist softness of her lips pressing against his cheek. He passed his hand slowly from her throat to her breasts. pausing to trace the contours of them. She quivered slightly as he touched them, like a pool signaling the approach of a storm wind. Milo heard her breath catch as her lips sought the lobe of his ear.

"Milo . . . please. . . ."

"Are you still afraid?" he whispered.

"No . . . no, my darling . . . no. Everything is all right now."

"I don't mean the airplane. I mean . . . us . . . our future."

"No . . . I'm not afraid of anything, Milo."

"I can't hear you."

"When you hold me like this . . . I could never be afraid of anything. I love you, Milo."

"Good. Wonderful. Let's get married."

"We are, you silly."

His hand moved downward, following the flow of her hip. "Milo . . . no. . . ."

But now the excitement had passed very quickly from his fingers to his loins. The soft pulsating of the blood in his ears was enough to deafen him. He covered her lips with his own and for a moment subsided in the warmth of her mouth.

"Milo . . . you must stop."

"Why, little one?"

"Because . . . think where we are."

"I'm thinking how awful it would be if this was the last time I could ever hold you like this."

"We'll have years . . . all our lives. . . ."

"If this airplane makes it."

"Careful, Milo. . . . I'd be so . . . embarrassed if anyone saw us."

"No one can see us. Be quiet, little one."

A soft chuckle escaped her. She turned partly away from him, saw only darkness and then returned almost at once, more willingly. She waited, tingling with anticipation.

"Milo . . . please . . . you're insane—"

"Quiet. . . ."

Their first movements were separated and cautious, and if there had been any variation of sound to disturb them, they might have broken away. But the droning of the engines lulled them into a sensuous trance. "Oh,

Milo. . . ." Her words were lost in his mouth. She groaned softly, and then they were silent for a long time.

Directly behind the Bucks, Lydia Rice slipped off her shoes and thoughtfully rubbed the soles of her tiny feet. She was amused and secretly envious. God bless their hearts, she thought—I hope they're enjoying themselves. There might be a time and a place for everything but those kids just didn't care—or they were so inexperienced they forgot to remove the yearning from their eyes before they turned out the lights. And they shouldn't jiggle the seat back even so slightly if they really wanted people to believe they were asleep. But have fun, kids. No one minds, least of all me. Your friend Lydia is too busy hating Howard, who was also once an ardent lover until —wait a minute, when did it really happen—until he got mixed up in the advertising business, if the truth were told.

Ye-yes! How was that? What was it you thought, Lydia? Whoa! Back up and run over that lightly once again. You said, or thought you said while you were thinking thoughts, that Howard was not the same. No, that wasn't it exactly, he was not the same ardent *lover* he was before he went into the advertising business. *You* said that—to yourself. Now jolt the memory a bit and make sure you aren't talking yourself into something just because a bouquet of passion has drifted over those front seats.

Lydia stole a look at her husband. His eyes were closed, but she knew that he was not sleeping, or even trying to sleep. He would be thinking, probably about his goddamned mine in Canada. He was thinking as only Howard could prosecute a subject—lobbing it dreamily back and forth in the vast open spaces of his mind like a hydrogen balloon. Howard masticated any subject, chewing on it with the dolorous concentration of a milch cow browsing a hillside. It took him forever to reach a conclusion and, when he eventually did, he had blocked off every entrance for agument and so it was completely impossible to change his mind.

But he was so beautiful! Forty-three years old and he looked thirty-three. There was not even the beginning hint of excess flesh beneath his square jaw. His nose was perfectly proportioned and joined his brow decisively as a man's nose should. He had every bit of his hair and the touch of grey at his temples, which he had only recently acquired, made him look more than ever like one of those hero-doctors in Cosmopolitan Magazine. The kind who was very rich and, of course, a famous brain surgeon, and whose wife had just died leaving him with three of the world's most charming children, who tricked him into providing a new mother in the form of a tawny blond nurse who played Chopin on the piano and who dismissed all the servants one night so she could surprise the doctor with a goulash recipe inherited from her grandmother, who was a Hungarian noblewoman.

Come to think of it, just how long would Howard last on the open market these days—even with his silly ideas about going to the goddamned North woods? The life vest at your feet, dear Lydia, is not a souvenir from the airline. It has a very business-like look about it, and the pilot who came back was obviously not just making conversation.

All right, suppose the life vest has a hole in it, or because you are so small you just can't climb on the raft. Suppose you drown in the Pacific Ocean tonight and never see New York again—or the North woods even. Wouldn't Howard cut a fine figure with a black arm band sewed on his coat?

Brother! It would be all he needed with that solemn look he wore all the time anyway. He wouldn't last two days. Some blonde would spot him the first time he went to lunch, make a few inquiries, and that would be it. And what would she have to say about the North woods? Why, I think it's just the divinest idea I ever did hear . . . really! I haven't had time to tell you, Howard, but I just happen to come from a long line of Girl Scouts and it's always been my dream to go back to fundamental living. Wowie! Then the blonde would really get down to fundamentals and whilst Howard was lapping up her sympathy and understanding she would steer him to the nearest justice of the peace. Howard would find himself with permanent ballast for his North woods canoe if he ever got that far.

And it wouldn't have to be some unknown wench who

would soothe Howard Rice's grief over the sensational loss of his utterly charming wife! How about your own dear, dear friends, Lydia? They, of course, would be the first on the field, and for a while they would appear to be pretty goddamned prostrated themselves over your unfortunate end. One of them, say Grace Depew, would hold a discreet wake for poor, dear Lydia who was floating around all by herself in the middle of the ocean, and, of course, there would be a few discreet cocktails at the discreet wake—just to keep those present from bawling their goddamned heads off when anybody thought to remember that there ever was a Lydia. And Grace Depew, who was fed up with her husband anyway, would buckle on her sexual skis and go schussing down the davenport right into Howard's lap. With those long legs of hers and that health-farm look, which Howard would never guess came right out the back door of Elizabeth Arden, Grace was tough enough to handle even when you were around—live and kicking.

Elvira Cooley might have a go at Howard, too. She had changed husbands three times, and there was no reason to believe she was going to spend the rest of her life with the one she had.

Elvira would be more subtle than Grace. She would "worry" about Howard. He must be *so* lonely without Lydia, the poor, dear thing, she would say to that knucklehead who happened to be her present meal ticket, and the first thing anybody knew they would all be making a little trip together—down hunting on their farm in Maryland, probably. Howard would like that and Elvira would be clever enough to give herself plenty of target practice before she ever let him see her handle a gun. Bang bang! On their honeymoon it wouldn't be beyond Elvira to suggest they drop a wreath on the ocean . . . in memory of poor, dear Lydia.

Maybe Howard had something when he said your friends were a bunch of bums. And it was hard to keep hating a man when you could just *see* a lot of people trying to take him away from you.

And suppose it wasn't you, but Howard who drowned? How would that be. Fast-like, you can say no good at all. You would miss Howard and there wouldn't be anything phoney about it. There weren't any other Howards, bumbling idiot though he might be. Where else would you find a man who was liked by everyone who ever met him? Where else was there a man who was certain to be patient and understanding no matter what emotional gymnastics you indulged yourself with at the moment? And how many men could you be proud of at a time like this? Howard had not lost his composure for one moment, from the time the dreadful little man pulled out his gun through the aftermath of the fire. Maybe he wasn't a business genius, maybe he was right and the advertising business really wasn't for him. So he did belong in the North woods? Did that make him any less a great guy? Great? In your whole marriage, the word, as it might be applied to Howard, had never occurred to you.

Howard Rice was a great guy. Looking at him now, it wasn't too hard to believe.

The seat ahead of her stirred again. She closed her eyes and put her head back trying to ignore it. And the constant thrumming of the engines soothed her until she was once more walking with Howard along a cobblestone street in Nantucket.

The cobbles caught at her spiked heels and she cursed them silently, because, then in the first week of their marriage, Howard would have been deeply shocked to hear his innocent bride describe Nantucket as the goddamnedest collection of moth-eaten antiques she had ever been mixed up with and why the hell couldn't they take a honeymoon right in the Waldorf Towers or at least some place civilized where there were shows to see at night. Howard in his uniform, striding along beneath the elms and looking like he actually belonged in one of the old white-pillared houses complete with a maiden aunt to bring him sherry and read the Bible with him on Sundays. He breathed of the salt wind as if it was some kind of elixir; it almost made him sparkle, and his idea of a perfect day was to walk along the harbor and watch the damn little sailboats or talk to their owners, who were all disgustingly healthy-looking yokels who never got out of dungarees and smelled always of wet salt. There was nobody around who was anybody—not a living soul to appreciate Lydia Stanley's new husband, and the goddamned wind just kept blowing a symphony of boredom.

Except for the nights.

There was certainly a lot of animal in Howard. His mind might work with the deliberate slowness of a water clock, but when he was physically aroused all hell broke loose.

She slumped down further in her seat and instinctively folded her arms around her small waist, hugging herself tightly.

Those nights! Howard was two men, one during the day and another man in the enormous bed which had certainly never held anything like Howard before. How lusty could a man get? Oh Howard . . . could you ever be like that again? Even exile in the North woods would be worth it.

She stirred, far gone in her memories, and recrossed her legs several times before she realized what she was doing. Let the damn airplane go down into the ocean, let it catch on fire and explode if, for a trade, those nights could be relived.

"Howard?" She spoke without opening her eyes or moving her head.

"I thought you weren't speaking to me."

"I've been thinking . . . about Nantucket."

"Oh . . . ?"

"It was pretty sensational, wasn't it?"

"I didn't think you cared much for it."

"I was thinking of the nights. They make delicious thinking."

"Seems like a long time ago."

"It wasn't so very long ago, really." She opened her eyes and rolled her head against the seat until her face was toward him. For a fleeting moment she hoped that her nose was not shiny and then she didn't care. "Howard . . . are you absolutely through with the advertising business? You could never be happy in it?"

"I guess happiness is relative. I've been thinking I might give it another try."

"Why?"

"I'm not sure exactly. Maybe it's this airplane ride.

Nothing seems very important except getting out of it in one piece. Kind of puts a person back to thinking of basic things, if you know what I mean."

"I was thinking of basics, too, Howard. Are you scared?"

"Stiff. This waiting isn't the easiest thing I've ever done. In some ways I wish they'd get it over with."

"Would you be sorry if I drowned?"

"Don't be ridiculous. That imagination of yours is running wild again."

"I mean it. Would you be sorry? I have to know."

"I would be more than sorry."

"You could go off to your North woods without a qualm."

"Oh, stop it. It's occurred to me that maybe I've just talked myself into something. The business with the mine could easily turn out to be a pretty bad dream."

"But it *is* a dream, Howard . . . and your whole heart is in it?"

"It was. Common sense tells me to stay with advertising. It's secure. I can switch things back, at least I'm fairly sure I can. I suppose that would please you?"

"No, Howard. I don't think it would."

For the first time he looked directly at her. He raised one eybrow in disbelief.

"Is the altitude of this airplane affecting you, Lydia?"

"No. But what might happen to this airplane could make quite a difference. I . . . wouldn't want to lose you, Howard."

"It was only a few hours ago you insisted on getting rid of me."

"There are times when I'm a very foolish and selfish woman. You'll just have to put up with it. No . . . you don't *have* to actually, but I wish you would."

"Exactly what do you mean by that?"

"I think you should go up to your mine. That's you. And I think you should take me along for laughs."

"I'm hearing things. You'd be miserable."

"I know it. But it would be a great deal worse without you."

"What about New York? How about your friends?"

"The hell with them . . . and New York, too. I want

you . . . the really great guy I had sense enough to marry. I almost destroyed him and I'm sorry. You'll just have to be patient with me if I choke on the breakfast hotcakes. If you catch me putting evening gowns on the natives and having cocktails with the sled dogs, you'll just have to understand. Love me more or less regularly and I'll get over it. We Stanley girls are pioneers at heart. Mush! That's what you say to a sled dog, isn't it? I want to start practicing."

He looked into her serious brown eyes and shook his head wonderingly. Then a smile crept very slowly across his firm lips. She saw that he was beginning to sparkle in a way that he had not done for a long time, and again she thought happily of Nantucket.

"EE-yeh! . . . makes the dogs turn left," he said, "if you yell it loud enough."

"E-e-e-e . . . yeh!"

"Very good!"

The offices and hangars of the airline in San Francisco were new structures, and they smelled of fresh cement. The buildings formed a small colony and they were surrounded by vast concrete aprons which led to the runways of the airport. In the middle of the night the hangars and repair shops were mostly deserted. The low building which housed the administration offices was also dark except for one end where the lights in flight operations slanted cheerily through the mist.

The only other light of consequence burned in the watchman's shack at the gate. An elderly man, normally at peace with the nights, he had been forced several times to leave his all-night radio program and admit various individuals through the gates. They were all known to him as important officials of the company and he told himself that something had certainly gone haywire.

The officials drove through the gates impatiently and parked their cars as they pleased just in front of the entrance to the administration building, which was unusual. They disappeared at once up the stairs, presumably hell-bent for flight operations.

This was a brilliantly illuminated room, considerably

larger but otherwise almost identical to the operations office in Honolulu. There were teletype machines chattering ceaselessly, maps on the walls, a facsimile machine, and at the moment, too many ringing telephones. The dispatcher on duty and his assistant were inclined to let the phones ring. Malcolm Boyd, a tall, reedy man who was in charge of public relations for the airline and who still smelled strongly of whisky from his evening's drinking, could not afford to be so indifferent. He squinted miserably at the brilliant lights as he tried desperately to avoid a journalistic ambuscade. This was difficult to do on such short notice, since the newspapers appeared to know more about the fate of Four-two-zero than he did. Furthermore, Garfield, the operations manager, and Lyle Meeker, a vice president, both of whom held a violent antipathy for newspapers, were very much on hand.

"No, Tommy," Boyd was saying into a phone. *"No, we have not lost a ship!* No, dammit . . . it did *not* go down in the ocean and Jane Russell isn't on it. I didn't know she was in Honolulu and I couldn't care less. I'm sitting right here in operations and our airplane is still in the air. Absolutely. It's still in the air and you're going to hang yourself way out on a limb if you make anything of it. There's been a little trouble, sure . . . and I'll get the complete story to you as soon as I know what it is myself. *No*, goddammit! I don't care what the Navy says! They're just looking for glory. I don't yet know *who* the passengers are, Tommy. I just *got* here! Sullivan? Wait a second. Yeah, he's the captain . . . what about it? How the hell do I know where he lives? Tommy . . . listen to me a second and then go back to bed. If you send a photographer and a snoop out to Sullivan's house at this time of night, like you did on that last plane crash, so help me God, I'll haul every ad out of your lousy sheet for the next five years! And it won't be just a friend of Sullivan's family who kicks hell out of your people because they barge in and ransack the man's bureau drawers for a picture of the guy . . . it will be me who gets thrown in jail for assault and battery and damned glad of it! You leave his wife alone. Try being decent for once in your life and wait till I call you back with the facts!"

Boyd slammed down the phone, took a long gulp at a paper coffee cup, and reached for another phone. He watched the ominous tilt of Garfield's cigar because he found it easier to decipher than the pile of teletyped messages the dispatcher had placed before him.

"Hello, Wayne . . . yeah, I *know* what time it is. Jesus, man, you can't print that! Because it just ain't so, that's why? How can you have the greatest search ever organized on the Pacific if there's nothing to search for? Someday I'm going to get with that Navy Public Relations character and examine his head. He beats P. T. Barnum, only more imagination. Hollywood could use that boy. Sullivan's the captain. That's right. Dan Roman, Leonard Wilby . . . W-I-L-B-Y, and Spalding . . . yeah. Only would you mind telling me where you got that information?"

Boyd quickly covered the mouthpiece and stared with hatred at the dispatcher.

"Jesus, man! When something like this happens will you *please* dummy up and don't know from nothin'?" He turned quickly back to the phone.

"Roman . . . ? I dunno. I just got here. Wait a minute. . . ."

Boyd looked across the counter to Garfield.

"Mr. Garfield? Was this fellow Roman ever a racing pilot? Bendix trophy or something like that?"

Garfield, brooding over a sheaf of reports, hardly raised his eyes.

"Yeah. Some time ago."

"Yeah . . . Wayne. But what's that got to do with reader interest? This airline has operated over thirty million passenger miles without scratching a passenger. We got the safety award three years straight and we're going to get it this year, too. Go ahead and call up the Air Transport Association . . . throw your dough away on a long-distance call to Washington, for all I care. Call up the CAA *and* the CAB. They don't know anything. Sure we want to cooperate. You'll have all the dope straight from here if you'll just relax and give me time to get it organized. I just *got* here. G'by!"

Boyd snorted angrily as he slammed down the phone.

"Mr. Garfield . . . can I have a minute?"

"Just about. What's your trouble?" Garfield was a heavily built rock of a man. His deep-set grey eyes were grave now and his voice was deliberately patient. Too many years of worrying about the lives of others, and outwitting the elements from behind a desk, had aged him prematurely. He was a tired man. Long before this night he had spent his love for flying.

"The papers are on my neck. What shall I tell them?"

"How about go to hell for an opener."

"You know I can't do that."

Garfield sighed. "I know. How long can you stall them?"

"Maybe another hour. They're crying about morning editions."

"An hour might be enough. We've got real trouble."

"Does it look that bad?"

"It don't look good." Garfield seemed to forget Malcolm Boyd. He turned to Lyle Meeker, who stood beside him. "We might as well face it now, Lyle. If these fuel and wind figures are correct, Sullivan doesn't stand a chance of making it."

"This is going to be a long night."

"Not so long for us as for Sullivan. But we might as well get things ready to roll. How about you calling Honolulu for an up-to-date passenger list and start getting a line on who to notify, because there will be lots of it. I'll handle the crew families when the time comes. I don't know why, but you might get the company doctor to stand by, too—just in case a miracle happens. And let's see. . . ." Garfield passed his stumpy fingers across his eyes. ". . . that's about all for now, I guess. You might start insurance cranking . . . they'll want a man out here, and call the propeller people, who damn well should have somebody around to defend themselves. If you don't mind handling those things, I'll have more time to stick with actual operations and I want to try getting a message through to Sullivan. Okay?"

"Sure. I'll be in my office."

"Oh, the post office. Ask Honolulu for the mail load and if there's any registered. They'll want to know about it. The cargo shippers can wait till tomorrow."

Garfield clamped his cigar more firmly between his

teeth and reached along the counter for a radio message pad. He wrote methodically in heavy block letters.

SULLIVAN—420
SUGGEST TRYING LOWEST POSSIBLE RPM AND USING MAXIMUM BOOST PERMISSIBLE. MIGHT SAVE YOU A FEW GALLONS. GOOD LUCK AND KEEP COMING.
                                        GARFIELD.

After he had signed his name with a flourish, Garfield was of two minds about actually sending it. Sullivan, he knew, would be involved with Air-Sea Rescue and it was unlikely that he would appreciate any desk-side quarterbacking when his peril was all too imminent. Even so, it was Garfield's duty to make certain Sullivan was extended every aid, no matter how feeble. The idea of increasing the propeller pitch by lowering the actual revolutions per minute was an old fuel-saving trick, and Sullivan probably knew about it—but then he might not, or perhaps under pressure, the idea hadn't occurred to him. Or under the special circumstances it might be entirely the wrong thing to try—if the airplane itself was already flying inefficiently. It was just something Sullivan would have to decide for himself. He pushed the pencilled message toward the dispatcher.

"Can you get this through to Sullivan?"

"I can try, Mr. Garfield."

"Do so, then. Everything else buttoned up?"

"Yessir."

"Any improvement in the local weather?"

"I'm afraid not." The dispatcher exchanged a slip of yellow paper for the radio message. "There will be another weather sequence in ten minutes."

"We'll want a special about an hour from now."

"I'll request it, sir."

As the dispatcher moved away to file the radio message, Garfield studied the weather report for the San Francisco airport.

He had concerned himself with the weather ever since the times when the chief source of information was a quick glance out the window. Now examining the hieroglyphics on the yellow paper, he moved mentally aloft

211

and found little to encourage him. A searchlight had been shone on the base of the overcast, and by triangulation, the ceiling measured at five hundred feet. That was a loss of a hundred feet, for an hour earlier the measurement had been six hundred. Visibility was on the downgrade also. From a mile and a half in one hour, to a mile. Light fog. And the dew point and temperature were uncomfortably close—a separation of merely one degree; sure sign that as the earth gave up the last of its heat toward morning, the fog would thicken. Only the wind offered hope. It should now be helping Sullivan over the sea, and enough of it was still pouring over the coastal hills to keep the fog from settling with tragic finality on the one airport Sullivan could possibly make.

Garfield looked up at the large wall clock. In two hours it would all be over. It was going to be a long two hours.

16

In the cockpit of the Coast Guard B-17, Lieutenant Mowbray kept the lights turned up brightly because there was nothing to see, anyway. The rain had ceased very suddenly, but it would certainly come on again and the heavy overcast still obliterated everything outside the windows.

It was now certain that Lieutenant Mowbray would be forced to rely entirely on mechanical contrivances to complete his interception of Four-two-zero. While his own ship transmitted the letters *M* and *O* in alternate groups so that Sullivan could maintain a series of bearings, Mowbray switched on a high-frequency homing adapter and for a time isolated himself from all other signals. He could not hear Hobie Wheeler's voice when he transmitted at three-minute intervals; Keim could repeat anything important Hobie might have to say. Instead Mowbray heard only a steady hum in his earphones when the nose of his ship was pointed directly at Four-two-zero. If he veered off the tight course to the left he heard the letter *D* transmitted, and if he went off to the right the letter *U* was repeated. Thus he flew a nearly exact course toward Four-two-zero, feeling his way as a blind man might touch the walls of a narrow corridor.

The radarman first-class, just behind Mowbray, was already intent on his screen. It was empty.

"Radar? Anything yet?"

"No target, sir."

"Roger."

They flew on in silence for several minutes. It became more difficult for Mowbray to straddle the narrowing flight path. He called to Ensign Pump.

"Navigator? How's our position relative to interception?"

"Right on. I just got a loran fix. We should be right with them if their navigator was anywhere near right."

"Radar?"

"No target yet, sir."

"Navigator? You're sure?"

"Positive." A few minutes passed. They twisted in their seats—waiting.

"Radar?"

"No target."

"Dammit . . . somebody's wrong!"

Keim leaned across to Lieutenant Mowbray. He was all business now and his eyes were worried.

"Four-two-zero says their needle is fluctuating rapidly."

"What's their altitude?"

"Still twenty-five hundred."

"Radar?"

"No target, sir."

"There's *got* to be. We're right on top of him."

"The screen is blank, sir."

"Keim. Ask Four-two-zero to transmit at thirty-second intervals. We can easily miss this guy."

"Roger."

Keim spoke into his microphone and the minutes passed. They were invaluable minutes, for if they failed to ascertain Four-two-zero's exact position in time to turn with them, the two ships would sweep past each other bound in opposite directions, and their combined speed would separate them a considerable distance in a very few minutes. To turn then, and attempt to overtake them, would add immeasurably to the difficulties of interception.

"Radar?"

"No target."

"I think that navigator was a lot farther west than he thought he was. We're seven minutes overdue."

"Radar?"

"No target." To rest his straining eyes the radarman looked down at his bare arm. He was fond of looking at his arm for it was muscular and well molded. Two years before he had submitted to a tattooing—the only one he would tolerate on such a fine arm. It was, he thought, a unique design—a curvacious blonde wearing pink diapers. Below the blonde was the name "Booboo."

"Radar?"

His attention returned quickly to the screen.

"Roger, Skipper! Target! Strong blip four degrees left. Eight miles! Looks like he's about five hundred feet below us!"

A slow smile crept across Lieutenant Mowbray's lean face.

"Sparks! Get on the horn! Advise Sea Frontier . . . interception Four-two-zero completed at fifty-six!"

The B-17 banked through the murk, and soon the two ships flew as partners within a half-mile of each other—invisible yet together.

Leonard Wilby had begun to shake again and he found himself staring at the glistening surface of the hardwood tray for long moments, as if it might provide some measure of calm. Yet the tray was unrewarding. There was no answer written on it, no set of figures neatly spaced to rebuke him and show where he had made any mistake.

He went back over his flight log once more, searching for a lost eleven minutes. He tugged at his second chin and tried to concentrate on the simple arithmetic involved in his last two wind computations. The difference between his own recorded position in the sky and the position established by the navigator of the Coast Guard plane was preposterous. Eleven minutes to the west . . . eleven minutes farther from the Coast, eleven minutes which could mean the difference between crawling gratefully into bed beside Susie, or perhaps never seeing Susie again. She would smell of liquor, probably, she always did, and she might refuse to wake up, but she would be there, warm and smooth and so like a little girl napping after the exhaustion of play. But those eleven minutes? Sullivan was calling for them —insistently, as he had every right to do. He must know whether the Coast Guard navigator was right, or if Leonard Wilby, in whom he had placed so much trust, was right.

"Leonard! Come on, fellow! What about it? Time's wasting!"

"In a minute, Skipper. I'm still checking."

Time was wasting? Time was running out altogether. The cushion of eleven whole minutes was gone somewhere, evaporated into the atmosphere while the man who must find them and fit them carefully back into the thin fabric of the next little time space, shook like an epileptic. If you can find those minutes, the shaking will cease. Your confidence will return, old boy, so discover them quickly. Stop the shaking with the minutes. Find the minutes and find Susie. Minutes, minutes . . . who's got the minutes? Susie has the minutes and she has them speared on the end of a toothpick in her Martini glass. Susie, gave me the minutes . . . I need them instantly.

"Come on, Lennie! What's holding things up?"

"I'll be right with you."

"Hurry."

Hurry thoughts that were already speeding through the brain so fast it was almost impossible to do anything but sit back and watch them go by? You are going mad, Captain. The pressure is too much for you. Navigation is a precise and methodical business and it cannot be hurried. You must remember that I have found my way unerringly over the seas and among the stars for many years and therefore I could not be mistaken—not now, when the matter of eleven minutes means so much to all of us. It is the Coast Guard navigator who is mistaken. He is probably a very young man of little experience. He has probably been careless in his computations, because what is it to him if a mere eleven minutes vanish? He would just be eleven minutes older without suffering the passage of time. Eleven minutes to him would not seem like eleven years. He would not care about them in the slightest, because for one thing he would not have Susie to return to.

"Oh God! Sweet, merciful God!"

Leonard closed his eyes and pushed the words through his tight lips in a groaning whisper. For he had found his mistake and the enormity of it stunned him. He had done something which was past explanation—incredible. The shaking was to blame for it. It must have severed the audible senses of his brain, disconnecting them so completely they had failed to translate a most elementary message. It was easy now to read back and see exactly how and when the folly had been committed. Only a terrified man could be guilty of such absolute rejection of habit. Only a man who was frightened to his bones and blindly clinging to another man for his salvation, could make such a mistake.

The sight of the fire, the engine burning against the night, must have started the fear and it had leaped upon his brain. And watching the pilots, listening to them worry about the way the ship was flying, had completed the debacle. Leonard Wilby, experienced navigator, designated by the government and the airline as capable of finding himself without the aid of a crystal ball, had made a most rudimentary error in neglecting to transpose miles-per-hour into knots!

For years he had obtained the ship's speed from the indicator above his work table. It recorded in nautical miles, or knots, to correspond with all the world's charts. But a pilot's air-speed recorded in miles per hour, as it should, since a pilot's chief concern was with approaches and stalling speeds, and miles per hour was the traditional way of marking them, as dollars and cents represented profit and loss to a business man. Pilots thought in miles-per-hour, navigators in knots. There was an important difference. A knot was approximately one and one-fifth miles. In this case the difference had become eleven priceless minutes. Leonard could remember it very clearly now. He had verbally asked Sullivan for their speed instead of taking it from his own instrument. Sullivan, watching the flight panel, had simply called off numbers—one thirty-two, and one thirty-six. He was speaking in miles per hour and Leonard was listening in knots. And without thinking he had written the figures down as knots on his log. Later, matched against his last position fix, the projected combination gave promise that they would reach the Coast more quickly—eleven minutes sooner than they actually would.

"Skipper?" The shaking had stopped very suddenly and now Leonard was perfectly calm. His mind was clear and he was surprised to discover that he was no longer afraid. He stood up and hitched his pants over his pot-belly. "Skipper, can you come here a minute?" He knew what he had to say and somehow it would be a relief to confess his felony.

Sullivan came quickly to bend over his navigation table. "Well?"

"I got bad news." Leonard swallowed and watched the concern set more firmly into Sullivan's eyes. "The Coast Guard is right. I made a dumb kid's mistake. You can add eleven minutes on to our coast estimate."

"Eleven minutes . . . ?" Sullivan shook his head unbelievingly. "You sure?"

"I am now. I must have been out of my head. I'm sorry, Skipper. I guess I was just scared. . . ."

Sullivan did not look up from the chart. The knobs on his jawbones moved slowly back and forth, and for a moment Leonard wondered if he understood what he had said. He appeared to shrink in physical stature as Leonard had seen him do earlier. He became a bent man, more aged suddenly than Dan or Leonard himself, and it was easy to pity him. As Leonard stood waiting, the idea of pitying Sullivan fascinated him until he could think of nothing else. Sullivan, too, would be thinking of the Coast, of the lights there, and of dear people waiting. Then gradually Sullivan's face became firm again and the knobs were still. Leonard knew instinctively that he had reached the only decision left to him, really the one he had favored all along. He lit a cigarette and it must have been his last because he crumpled the package slowly and tossed it onto the chart. He reached across the table and took up the hardwood tray. He examined it thoughtfully for a moment and passed his strong fingers across its polished surface. Then he handed the tray to Leonard and looked at him not accusingly, but rather as a man determined to blame himself.

"I hope this will float," he said quietly.

At last the man who said he was a professor and who talked in such a peculiarly wild way seemed to be dozing, so Sally McKee took up her purse from the floor and sought among the many things it contained for the letter. Roy Larsin's last letter—the only one she had not read at least twenty times, because to analyze the words rather than to act on them would have ended everything. She unfolded the paper carefully, as if she were revealing a secret and brought it close to her face so that even if the professor opened his eyes he could not see the writing. Here were Roy's words again, his invitation written in large bold strokes of a pencil on cheap ruled paper. An unknown man was opening his arms to her, so obviously a simple man, who even at this moment must be waiting at San Francisco airport. He would be waiting for a woman he thought was a girl—a woman who had already deceived him.

Dearest Sally,

This will be my last letter to you and I guess that is a good thing because I am so excited about your arrival I don't think I could hold a pencil steady even if there was time for another letter to reach you.

Tomorrow I will leave these mountains and pines which will be your home too, and go down to the city for my first visit in over a year. I want to get there a few days before you come because there are some things the cabin needs to make it more comfortable for a girl. Also I have to buy a suit which will seem very funny to wear again after such a long time. Golly! You wouldn't want your groom to look like a hayseed would you?

I am still scared you won't like it up here, but that is just a chance I'll have to take. Sometimes I sit by the window and look at the glacier and wonder what in the world a young girl like my Sally will do with herself all day unless she is just nuts about the sound of a mountain stream or likes to watch the sun seem to turn a mountain peak around very slow. I warn you again that there won't be anything very exciting for you up here and our nearest neighbors are eight miles down the worst road you have ever seen. But I guess I've harped on that enough and if you just can't stand it after a while, I'll put in for a transfer to some place that has fewer animals and more humans.

We will have to spend about two days in San Francisco to fix you up with an outfit for up here. When I passed through Honolulu during the war I didn't see the girls wearing anything that would be suitable for this country. I am trying to arrange for my sister to come up from where she lives in Long Beach and have a chance to meet you, but I really don't think she can get away. Her kids keep her pretty busy. So don't count on it.

I was just thinking how lucky I am. I happen to pick up an old torn magazine I never knew existed and there is your picture smacking me right between the eyes. And only a few months later that very wonderful looking little girl is coming to share my life. Golly! You might have been married already or you might just not have been interested in a poor guy like me, but it didn't work out that way. Now I'm convinced that some great power had things all fixed up because he knew we were meant for each other. There is not the slightest doubt in my mind that this is true. (A little fawn with big brown eyes just came along the stream outside the window. He looked all around him like he was saying "Where is Sally? When is Sally going to get here? Tell Sally to hurry up!") That fawn is not half so anxious as your Roy.

So much for now. Golly, I don't know how I'm going to sleep these next few nights! Hurry! Hurry, girl! Or should I say—hurry, Mrs. Larsin!

Your,

ROY

P.S. In case the pictures I have sent have left any doubt in your mind about recognizing me at the airport, I'll be wearing a bright green tie. I'll also be the most nervous guy you ever saw.

She refolded the letter and placed it back in the envelope. Now what had made the difference? A little while ago you had dreaded meeting this man, knowing that it would be impossible for him to hide his disappointment. That's all it would take—just a glance at his eyes and the shock would be there. He would look down at you, still puzzled perhaps, and say "Golly," a word he used so much in his letters. "Golly . . . you must have had a pretty tiring trip." Or maybe he would just turn and walk away without saying anything. In some ways that would be an easier thing to take. If he didn't pretend. If he didn't try to go through with his bargain. If he just said right out "Golly, if you're really Sally McKee, there must have been some mistake. The girl I sent for was . . . well, you aren't by any chance her older sister, are you?"

And now, with the hope of meeting him almost taken away, you *wanted* to see him. It was the most important thing in your life . . . and ah! . . . there was a way! If only the pilot had been right and you would not be drowned in the sea. After the meeting, after the chance to be with him just a few moments, to touch him perhaps, then it wouldn't make any difference.

Yes, it could be done. A little acting and a careful guard on every word. Like so. "Are you Mr. Larsin? Of course, I would have known you from Sally's description. You didn't receive her cable? Oh, I'm so terribly sorry! She should have known a cable would never reach you in the mountains. I am Sally's sister, you see, her older sister as you can also see"—a little laugh then—"I was coming to the mainland anyway and she thought it best for both of you if I. . . ."

Get him alone then. If only for a few minutes, time to sense the real man behind the letters. "I don't know quite how to tell you this, Roy . . . but Sally thought it would be less cruel if I told you rather than write a letter you might not receive for several days. I'm afraid you've lost her, Roy. She's a very impetuous girl, as you may have guessed. Four days ago she met a man and, well . . . it just happened very fast. They were married yesterday morning, Roy. I'm sorry . . . very sorry."

It would work. It would have to work. And it would

put an easy end to things. Oh Roy, I want to dream just a little longer, if only for a few stolen moments!

She opened her purse, replaced the letter, and brought out her compact. Furtively, hardly daring to look, she held it before her face.

"Remarkable!" Flaherty said watching her. "A lesson to me in humanity. All human beings are wonderful and certainly female human beings are most astounding."

Sally looked at him questioningly. She snapped her compact shut and put it quickly away. She had not welcomed him into the seat beside her. He was so drunk he was likely to say anything, and she had not wanted any intrusion on her thoughts of Roy. But now he was smiling, foolishly perhaps, yet behind his grey eyes there was the dead look of great loneliness. Recognizing the look as almost an exact reflection of her own, she found it impossible to ignore him.

"What's so astounding?"

"I'm not sure whether it's faith or just habit . . . or do you always put on fresh make-up before you board a life-raft?" His short nap, Sally thought, must have done the professor a great deal of good. His mind was still whacky, but at least he spoke like a sober man.

"Do you always board a life raft before it actually has to be done?"

"You, of course, are sure that we won't have to?"

"I'm not sure of very many things."

"You're being a fatalist about this business then?"

"I'm not even sure what a fatalist is."

"Come to think about it, I'm not sure, either . . . although before this night I had always classified such a person as one who shrugged his shoulders no matter what was about to happen. Now I'm inclined to believe that a fatalist is most likely an innocent person with an abundance of self-confidence. Like yourself, for example. . . ."

"Me? You have the wrong woman. You are looking at the least confident woman you are likely to meet for a very long time."

"How can you sit there so calmly then—when a little while ago you were terrified—or so I thought? I sat down with you because I thought I might be able to help

222

you. But I'm not needed. What happened? Would you mind very much telling me what happened?"

"That would be impossible," Sally McKee said slowly. How badly she had misjudged him. He might have been drunk in his body, but his mind had been wonderfully perceptive all the time. From the depths of his loneliness he was trying to pass on some measure of comfort. There could be no good in denying him. "Perhaps I can explain a part of—do you have anyone you love very deeply?"

"No." He placed his hands together, resting his chin on his thumbs. He gnawed moodily at his upturned knuckles and Sally thought for a moment that he had relapsed into drunkenness. "No. I do not have any such person. Nor would I know what to do with such an individual if anyone should be so misguided. You haven't answered my question."

"I'm trying to, because I believe you are essentially a very frightened man . . . not just because of these few hours . . . I wouldn't be surprised if you had been dreaming up ogres for a long time just like I have been doing . . . and if you came to me with help, it was partly because you needed help yourself very badly."

"Suppose you were right? What about my question?"

"That's it. I excommunicated my private ogres a little while ago. I threw them out of my life. I stopped worrying about losing the things I couldn't have in the first place."

"Would the things be a man, possibly? Or am I getting too personal?"

"Yes, you are. But I don't care now. He's a wonderful, kind, clean man who has the right to know the truth about me. I am going to tell him that I am a different person than the one he thinks I am. I want him to understand that I was known all over Honolulu as the easiest lay in town. I was the visiting fireman's delight . . . two drinks and a medium-priced dinner was a guarantee of Sally McKee . . . any time, any place . . . as soon as my working hours were over. I want him to know that I've seen the inside of so many hotel rooms the cleaning maids called me by name. I want him to know that the police have my name, too—a little party in the Moana one night that was pretty dull going until everybody decided to take their clothes off and it happened that I was the only woman with four men. I want him to know that my body has been so beat, I don't think it will ever come to life again, that I was fired from three jobs because my supervisors got tired of sleeping with me. Telling you these things is easy because you are a stranger and I will never see you again, but telling him is going to be the hardest thing I've ever had to do . . . because in my heart, I will always see him. I am old. I am much older than my years should have made me. Look at my face carefully, as he will do, and you will see how very old I am. I have been saying to myself that I could begin all over again and pretend that none of those things ever happened. Until a little while ago, I believed I could escape . . . somehow I tricked myself into believing that I was still desirable, and then a little while ago, reading his last letter, I came to my senses. I looked in my mirror and I was certain of only two things. I loved this man with all the hunger of a woman who sees her last chance for love . . . and an end to her loneliness. And I was certain it could never be. Knowing what is going to happen now, has driven away my fear. My ogres are dead. I am strangely happy and I am no longer afraid of anything. Do you understand now? Does that answer your question . . . or do you just feel like a bored priest hiding behind his curtain?"

Flaherty took his hands from beneath his chin and placed them flat on his knees. He studied his hands for a moment and then turned them palms upward, in a grateful gesture. He cocked his head slightly to one side and looked at Sally McKee.

"Thank you," he said finally. "I was mistaken. You are not a fatalist. You are a very courageous young lady. Now, if you will forgive me, I intend to close my eyes and kill a few ogres of my own."

Humphrey Agnew attempted to soothe the agitation in his mind by reciting multiple groups of figures. The thought of his investments had always provided a pleasant refuge from mental distress in the past, and there was no reason why it should not give him shelter now. A thousand shares of Dole Pineapple, twenty-three shares of Matson Navigation, five hundred and twenty shares of Pacific Factors, two hundred of General Electric . . . McCormick-Deering, five hundred shares, Corning Glass, seventy-five . . . U.S. Pump and Salvage, seventy shares . . . Glycerine Associates, and Allied Chemical, one thousand each . . . Easy-Way Stores, five thousand shares—it had hurt to buy that, but now it was worth four times the price—Pneumatic Machinery, six hundred, and, of course, Agnew's Aids, which everyone agreed was nearly priceless. There were many more, cleverly diversified. All this from nothing. Fifteen years, from hawking a few bottles of Agnew's Aids to perfect security. Fifteen years of slavery, of pinching, and squirming past insults. No one looked down on Humphrey Agnew any longer. The banks said, "Good morning, Mr. Agnew," in a tone they had formerly reserved for only the Islands' rich. "Good morning, Mr. Agnew. . . ."

Everyone was disposed to greet Humphrey Agnew pleasantly these days. He was envied and frequently approached by so-called gentlemen who suggested partnership in their failing enterprises. They would never be successful. Not a penny of Agnew's hard-earned money would go to save those elegant failures. Let the weaklings crawl—as you had done for so long a time. Crawl, you slimy bastards, with your handsome looks, and your friends, and your parties which you would never open to me . . . crawl right past the man who was socially unacceptable because he was clever enough to bilk a few million Polynesians and Orientals. Crawl, and find out what it is like to be without money. Money, you would soon discover, is not an unmentionable disease. Money is the most important thing in the world.

He preened his mind with more figures and for a time became lost in the lush vision of the bank vault which contained his safety-deposit box. He could see the interior of the metal box and feel the long packets of engraved papers, wrapped in rubber bands, which made Humphrey Agnew a man of substance. It was a pity that the box could not have been made of glass and placed along the street so that the whole world could easily observe how thoroughly Humphrey Agnew had secured himself.

Then very suddenly, an ugly sight interrupted his pleasant reconnaissance of the box. Peeping beneath the securities, he saw two folded papers, as clearly as if his fingers were touching them. The two insurance policies which amounted to more than a hundred thousand dollars! And the beneficiary? Martha Agnew—wife to Humphrey Agnew! In a moment of romantic befuddlement he had changed the policies to make her the payee. Martha, the Jezebel, was going to be a rich woman if this airplane failed to make San Francisco. Rich on her late husband's money! For if the plane fell into the sea, who could say that Humphrey Agnew would be saved? The securities were not security, here. They were bits of paper in a distant box. They were lifeblood isolated from a man's body when he most needed strength! Money forced people to like Humphrey Agnew instead of hating him!

The thought assaulted his mind—tore through it on clanging wheels. Humphrey Agnew was again powerless, as poor as the miserably stupid hand-laborer who sat beside him! Now what of those fifteen years? Were they going to be lost in the next hour?

It was a scheme, the whole thing was a monstrous plot to humble Humphrey Agnew. Who would conceive of such a plot? Only Martha! Martha, using Ken Childs as a foil, had contrived to place her husband on this airplane! She wanted that insurance money! She was crazy-mad for money! Martha, the scheming whore! Your brilliant head, Humphrey, is almost severed and resting on a tray.

"She can't do it to me!" He half-rose in his seat and spoke aloud.

"Who can't do what to you?" José said. He placed a restraining hand on Agnew's arm.

"My money! My wife—"

"Why don't you forget about money? It won't do you no good up here . . . or down there, if we go in the drink."

"Easy for you to say when you have nothing to lose."

"I got plenty to lose and it ain't money."

Agnew did not hear him. For the wheels had stopped spinning across his mind and he knew exactly how he had stopped them and what he must do. Oh Martha . . . so you were sitting back there in Honolulu just hoping something would happen to this airplane? Perhaps you had even arranged for someone to fix the propeller so it would come off. Very clever of you, Martha. Keenly analytic, to conceive that if I knew about Ken Childs I would pursue him here, and then both witnesses to your disgrace would be out of the way while you collected the insurance. The idea, Martha, was not even original with you. We both read about it in the newspapers a few years ago. Wanting to get rid of his wife and his children, too, if I remember correctly, a man had arranged for them to board an airplane and mailed a bomb along for company. He was almost successful—wasn't it out of Los Angeles, Martha?

And it had almost worked in reverse for you, Martha. Understanding how I would be tormented, you knew I would be here, half-wild in my head . . . completely unable to analyze how cleverly you had tricked me. You must have been reading history, the ancient story of the unneeded mate. There were a thousand precedents, but poor Martha! What a really inept student of abnormal psychology you are! You should have more thoroughly appreciated your husband's searching mentality, the same brain which made a fortune because it was full of reading about the weaknesses of the human mind. And you should have remembered that, being a determined man, I would have a gun with me. Even if you knew all this and could foresee it, Martha, you would remain ignorant of one vitally important clause in the insurance policies. In the event of suicide, or death by the insured's own hand as it was put, the policies were null and void. They would only be pretty bits of paper, Martha, as far as you were concerned—along with the securities which were willed to no one. By the time the government and the lawyers took their share the widow Agnew could count her dollars on her pretty red-painted toes.

Fondling his pearl tiepin he turned to José. It was a pity that no one could witness now the triumph of a brilliant mind over the simple male animal. A shame that no one could observe and admire while Humphrey Agnew led this stupid workman down through the deflecting paths of doubt and temptation until, persuaded that black was white, he would return the gun. Yet the creature must be approached cautiously, stalked for a time, until his natural suspicions were completely asleep. He must never be allowed to think that Humphrey Agnew might desire anything but to regain his property. There would be something peculiarly feminine about this, Martha, a transposition, if you will, of my mind into the fragile working pattern of your own. Beast and brain, Martha. Listen, and I will intrigue even you.

"Would care for a cigarette?" he asked José.

José had been fingering a pocket rosary and his answer was preoccupied. "No thanks. I don't smoke them things."

Agnew shot his cuffs, and while he lit a cigarette for himself he controlled his voice so that its timbre was entirely different. He employed the melodious tenor well known to radio audiences in the Islands—and he recognized with satisfaction that same persuasive quality which had sold so many dollars' worth of Agnew's Aids.

"You are smart not to smoke," he went on. "It is a sign that you are a man who has his life well adjusted, and I envy you. Constant smoking, I'm afraid, has become rather a trademark of our hectic times. Believe me, it takes tremendous character to face things in a calm and collected manner these days. On myself, for example, the recent pressure has been terrific. I sometimes wonder how I've kept my sanity . . . there are even moments when I doubt that I have."

"I s'pose a guy like you does have his problems." José stopped fingering the rosary and looked at Agnew's eyes, which were now openly pleading for companionship. "I really wouldn't know much about what goes with a guy like you . . . bein' I'm just a fisherman."

Agnew brought his long tobacco-stained fingers together in a church steeple and looked toward the cabin ceiling with the air of a man transported by the beauty of his thoughts.

"A fisherman . . . ?" he said unctuously. "Ah, how fortunate you are. That is a work for a man. It explains to me your great inner peace, if you will pardon my observation. The sea, the sky . . . the uniting of yourself with the gigantic forces of nature, which is our true heritage, must bring peace to any man."

"I never looked at it like that. My family been fishermen for couple hundred years, maybe longer, I dunno . . . I never had no school so I just went along."

"Simplicity . . . the real key to happiness. You have a boat, I suppose?"

"Yeah. I got a good one. The best."

"You are proud of it and the work you do with it. I can see that."

"Well . . . yeah. I guess you could say so. But I didn't do no good trying to help them in the Islands. The fish just don't school up out there like along our coast."

"Very interesting. I wonder why . . . and I wonder, too, how it is that one person is chosen to lead such a life while another, such as myself, must strive in the jungle of modern business. Could the true wisdom you must have gained from nature possibly explain that to me, sir?"

José unhappily rubbed the fuzz on the top of his head with his three-fingered hand. Agnew's manner of speech was something he had never heard before and he was strangely restless.

"No. But there's plenty of headaches in the fish business. Take it from me."

"I don't question it . . . but the same nervous tension could not be there. You are dealing with the elementary problems of yourself, your family, and your boat . . . a provider in the historical tradition . . . whilst a man like myself . . . ? Imagine the strain of being responsible for the livelihood and the well-being of almost a thousand people. I have cause to remember very frequently that so many are directly dependent on the continued success of my business."

"I wouldn't go for it . . . even if I could."

"Again proving you are a wise man, sir. But you can understand how such responsibility could occasionally unnerve a person? There is no relief, no quiet port in which to hide on troubled days. You can understand, perhaps, how the constant pressure might warp a man's

229

thinking until there were times when he might magnify imagined grievances, and sick with fighting, give in to them? You can understand, I am certain, that at such times a man might not be himself, temporarily . . . he might do things which he would later regret most sincerely and then rush about trying to make amends?"

"I guess it gets pretty rough sometimes." José blinked his brown eyes thoughtfully. Agnew's voice was pleasantly soothing, so much so that he found it difficult to remember he was on an airplane, or that there was anything else to worry about except Agnew's problems.

"You *do* understand then! You don't hate me because I weakened a little while ago. I am ashamed when I think of it . . . thoroughly ashamed, sir. It has never happened before and I assure you it will never happen again . . . it is just that lately the strain of my business has been extraordinarily fierce. I'm badly in need of a vacation and from this moment I intend to take one. My only remaining ambition is to have people like me."

"Sure. You'll be all right. Just take it easy for a while."

"I will. But first I must regain my self-respect and that won't be easy. Do you think it would help if I apologized to Kenneth Childs?"

"Who's he?"

"The man sitting up there with the lady . . . the man I . . . threatened. . . ."

"Oh . . . well, maybe it would. He didn't do you no harm."

"I will ask him to forgive me."

"Now you're talkin' sense."

"I am normally a most sensible man. The thought of our present situation made me realize how badly I have conducted myself. If we go down, it would be all the worse for me if I thought I had failed to make amends. Believe me, I am quite normal again. I see things very clearly."

"Whyn't you say somethin' to the little girl, too? You wasn't so nice to her."

"Thank you. I will. I cannot thank you enough for being the first to make things easier." Agnew stood up, and then, as if in afterthought, he turned back to José with a half-smile.

"Oh . . . one more thing . . . and please continue your tolerance. The gun. Surely you would trust me after I had openly apologized. It's strange, but I feel that to have it back, would completely restore my confidence. It would only be a token gesture on your part and yet it would mean a great deal to me if I could shake this feeling of being watched."

José hesitated. He examined Agnew's bent figure as he might estimate an unknown species of fish. He scratched at his tuft of hair.

"Go see how you make out. I'll think about it."

Eyes shining unnaturally, Agnew's smile became full and warm. He strode resolutely up the aisle.

"Mr. Childs?" He bowed slightly to May Holst and waited in solemn humility.

"You again?"

"I've come to apologize for my incredible behavior."

"So what?" Childs watched him warily. His fists were doubled as he sat stiffly erect in his seat.

"My only excuse is the extreme pressure of my business during the past few months. It has taken a decided change for the worse, and the worry . . . I'm afraid it's just been too much for me. I hoped that a man of your experience and position might understand."

"All I know is, you tried to kill me. That's not so easy to forget."

"Please, Mr. Childs. I'm quite myself now. My apologies to the lady, too." He bowed again.

"How about your good wife?"

"I intend to phone her the moment we land in San Francisco."

"You should. And while you're about it I suggest you sweep out your mind with a clean broom. Your wife is one of the finest girls I've ever known. You are extremely lucky to have her. And in case there are any doubts lurking in that twisted conscience of yours, try believing what somebody tells you. I took your wife to a very pleasant lunch . . . twice. No one, not even you, could have found anything wrong with her words or behavior . . . during the total of perhaps three hours we were together in a public dining place. I'm explaining this for her sake, not yours, because I still don't think you deserve it. Martha will never sell you out . . . or anyone else for that matter. Now have you got that straight?"

"Yes, Mr. Childs. I have indeed. Will you accept my apology?"

Ken Childs relaxed his fists and sighed.

"Sure. Now beat it."

Turning so that José could see his face, Agnew smiled and bowed once more to May Holst. Then, penitently clasping his fingers together, he walked directly to Spalding, who sat alone behind Frank Briscoe. He maneuvered his body so that José could again watch him and began his apology. Rehearsal had improved his performance; he was like a small boy begging for acceptance. In a very few minutes he left Spalding smiling.

"Now," he said, crossing the aisle to José. "Did you see? Do you believe that I can be trusted? Haven't I proved it?"

"Yeah. . . ." There was no longer any question in José's eyes. "It always takes a lot of nerve to swallow your words."

Agnew put out his hand. "Would you . . . complete the sense of peace which has come to me now? Please. The stewardess said we haven't much time one way or the other."

"If you really think it will make you feel better . . . I guess you'll behave yourself now." José took the gun from his coat pocket and placed it in Humphrey Agnew's open hand.

"Here's your property, mister. I'd leave it at home from now on."

See, Martha? Observe the ease with which lesser beings can be persuaded to do anything—seals to balance rubber balls, bears to dance, and lions to cringe—it is all the same. It is not the meek who will inherit the earth, but the brilliant.

"Thank you, friend. Now I'll just freshen up a moment and you will see a new man."

He slipped the gun into his pocket and, still clutching it, walked almost gaily toward the men's lavatory. He passed Spalding again with a smile, and then the place

232

where the buffet had been. He paused a moment before the narrow door and then let himself in and turned the lock.

It was a small, brightly lit room and here the sound of the engines was almost inaudible. There was a chemical toilet which smelled slightly of disinfectant, a washstand with a mirror over it, and a porthole beside the mirror. He stepped before the washstand and methodically began to scrub his hands as if he were a surgeon about to perform an operation.

There is something beautifully pure about this, Martha, and the need for cleansing is more important than you would think. The Japanese, of course, appreciate this, and make quite a ceremony of it. Years of study have convinced me that those who select their own time and means of departure for immortality are scrupulously neat about it. A woman so minded, for example, will invariably bathe and perfume her body before she commits herself to knife or pills. She will, too, put on her best night gown, arrange everything about her to perfection, and assume a pose designed to remain forever in the memories of those who find her. Isn't it curious, Martha, that self-destruction is almost always accomplished as dramatically as the person involved can arrange?

I know the secret now, Martha. I have analyzed it as a natural return to the spirit of pagan sacrifice, for in ancient times only the youngest and the most beautiful were allowed to offer themselves to the gods. Now, only those superior beings who are in key with the most elemental forces of life, dare attempt these rites. You cannot stand timidly on the fringe of life and find any true beauty, Martha—you must commit yourself wholly and absolutely to the storm before you know what it is like to feel free.

He dried his hands on a paper towel and then reached mechanically into his vest pocket. He drew out a small bottle, shook a heart pill into the palm of his hand with the automatic ease of habit, and thoughtfully placed it on his tongue. He swallowed the pill and washed it down with a sip of water. He leaned forward, closer to the mirror, and examined his reflection.

See, Martha? Whore that you are, observe the change. Here is not death, but life! I have notified all concerned that I am ready to begin living and already the changes are apparent. Yes, my hair is darkening and see the flush of health about my cheeks. And my eyes, Martha . . . observe my eyes! They are young and clear and they see beyond the puny torment you have caused. People *like* me. They see that I am a young man, vigorous and brave! While the others tremble in their fear, helpless, frightened out of their wits because a mere mechanical contrivance may rob them of what they think is life—I alone am happy! *I* will decide the time of my transformation . . . the minute . . . the very second when it will be! I am a young god, Martha! Supreme!

He stood back from the mirror and took the gun out of his pocket. Whirling anxiously, he stepped to the door and flicked off the light. For a moment he stood in absolute darkness, breathing deeply. He could no longer hear the sound of the engines. Silence was all about him except for a muffled pounding which was like the reverberations of a distant drum. It was fainter each time, but it came again and again. It is my heart, Martha, my joyous heart—ecstatically pumping my new young blood!

He was raising the gun when he saw a faint luminous circle that seemed to hang in space. He moved toward it, drawn by its growing brilliance. He reached out tentatively for the circle, and found that his fingers touched the porthole. And beyond the glass, glittering with an intensity he had never seen, seeming to weep for his suffering, was a multitude of stars. His fingers clawed at the porthole, as if he could reach through the glass and gather the constellations in his hand. He wanted to shout at the stars, announce that he was about to walk upon them and kick them out of place.

Then very slowly, his hand came to his face and the coolness of it from the glass caused him to shiver. The hand which held the gun fell to his side.

"Martha!" He cried out in agony, yet he could not hear his voice. He could only hear the pounding. His thoughts spun to a stop. Jerked suddenly backward to acute perception, his brain seemed to quiver in his head like jelly. He clung to the wall and he was suddenly very cold. He was astounded to find that the stars were his only light. And this place—how had he come here?

Gradually, his thoughts stabilized. He picked them up one by one as a man might retrieve the contents of a spilled basket. What was it Ken Childs had said? "There was nothing . . . nothing between them . . . Martha would never sell out anyone?" You are lucky. She is a fine girl. No one could ever criticize her behavior . . . you are wrong, *wrong* . . . out of your head . . . a jealous fool!

The pounding. It was much nearer now. He wished the pounding would stop.

Hardly realizing that he moved, he brought the gun to his other hand. He held it a moment, moving his fingers over its smooth surface—hating it. Then his fingers stopped their exploration. There were only empty holes in the shell chamber! The fisherman, the stupid fisherman who knew far more than Humphrey Agnew, had removed every bullet!

Oh, Martha!

He threw the gun on the floor and slammed his hands against his eyes. He could not look at the stars. I will make it up to you, Martha. Give me the chance to live and I will devote my life to you, Martha!

Then emerging from his misery, he knew that the pounding came from the door. Hobie Wheeler's voice was calling sternly to him.

"Hey! You in there! Can't you hear me? Come on out, sir! We're preparing to ditch!"

17

THERE WAS NOW A GIGANTIC CLEAVAGE IN THE SKY-SPACE which held the two airplanes. The ships broke out very suddenly from the clouds' captivity, and temporarily without hindrance, they swam across an immense womb-like cavern. All about them the clouds formed high, vaporous ramparts. Straight down, the black sea served as a foundation for these walls and the only illumination came faintly from the stars.

The path of the ships across this chasm was marked only by their navigation lights. Those on Four-two-zero blinked alternately red, white, and green, in the special manner of airliners. Those on the Coast Guard plane were steady. They emerged almost simultaneously from the western embankment of cloud and continued toward the east as if supported on invisible wires.

For several minutes they moved smoothly together across this space, signaling to each other with their landing lights like fireflies parading. As the ships neared the eastern side of the opening, their minute stature in the scheme of things was emphasized by their slow approach to the clouds. In spite of the actual speed, they appeared to crawl toward the east, and when at last they were once more swallowed in cloud, their passage was ignored by the sky.

The men who controlled the limping progress of Four-two-zero were long since disenchanted with the sky. Yet the break in the cloud deck gave them a little respite, in which visually observing a like creation, they were able to believe again that their own world had not abandoned them. The actual sight of the B-17, her graceful lines barely outlined in the starlight, was of greater morale value than all of the radio conversations with impersonal voices sunk beyond the horizon. Though they were well aware that the men on the B-17 were helpless to lend immediate aid—they could not trail a tow rope and pull the lame hulk homeward—still the sense of existing at the wrong end of a telescope was gone. With this and the temporary smoothness of the air and the cessation of rain, their spirits rose until they were once more inspired to act as if they could control their futures. And so they peered out of the left window eagerly, leaning across each other and shading their eyes, staring at the B-17, absorbing the sweet fact of its presence slowly.

Sullivan broke their spellbound observation just before they plunged into the eastern wall of cloud and his voice had regained much of its authority.

"Hobie," he said firmly. "You go back now. Dan will take your place. Take the Gibson Girl along and get the passengers set for ditching. You'll have plenty of time . . . so use it. I'll turn on the seat belt sign ten minutes before we start for the water. Have everything set by then. When I turn on the no smoking sign, you and Spalding take your own brace and hang on."

"How about the rear door?" Hobie took off his earphones and hung them carefully on a hook at his side. He smoothed his hair automatically and stood up. His young face was covered with perspiration and his eyes were puffy, as if he had just awakened. He looked even younger than his twenty-two years, in the way that a young man who is really tired and suddenly dependent on bravado, can seem physically to recapture his childhood. "When shall I let the rear door go?"

"As soon as you're sure we've stopped. Don't hurry . . . remember. Get your people in the raft and wait as long as you can for us. If we can get together . . . it will be just that much better."

"Okay." He moved around the control pedestal and

237

stepped down beside Sullivan. He looked thoughtfully at Leonard and then at Dan. This was a separation, a division of effort which he obviously viewed with distaste. Now he would be forced to make innumerable decisions on his own, and however small they might be, he knew they would have to be right.

"Good luck to you guys," he said sheepishly.

He tried a smile and then walked reluctantly aft toward the passenger cabin. As he passed through the crew compartment he pulled down the Gibson Girl from the receptacle over the bunk which held it. This was a small, wonderfully compact radio transmitter, so-called because of the fashion in which its waterproof case was curved. Hobie, who was not at all sure about the derivation of the name since he could not remember ever having seen any girl named Gibson in the movies, was preoccupied with the technicalities of the machine. He mentally reviewed its remarkable operational ability and remembered that although it fitted under his arm quite easily, it had been the savior of many distressed persons. By simply turning a crank, its signaled SOS could be heard for more than a hundred miles and any surface or air ship could take a bearing on it. This was, he knew, one of the latest types and was equipped with a device for automatically tripping emergency alarm bells on ships scattered over a wide area. A kite for carrying the antenna aloft was provided if there was wind on the surface, and a hydrogen balloon was available if there was calm. It was a very wonderful little machine, capable of withstanding the most rugged treatment—yet Hobie held it tenderly against his side as he passed through the cabin door.

"All right, Dan," Sullivan said. "I'll take her now." He leaned foward and held the control wheel while Dan slipped out of the left seat. Their eyes met as they exchanged places, but they said nothing. The flight deck bounced as the ship re-entered the overcast and the rain came hissing angrily once more.

Dan did not reoccupy Hobie's seat immediately. Sullivan had put on his headphones and if any further communication was necessary during the next few minutes he could handle the message himself.

238

Dan studied the fuel gauges, forcing himself to read them pessimistically. Then he did some simple arithmetic. The total in all of the tanks was now two hundred and twenty gallons! Two hundred and twenty gallons in an airplane that was consuming very close to two hundred gallons each hour, became a very simple equation. Too simple. Something would have to give very soon.

Leonard was bent over his electric altimeter and stopwatch, unhappily seeking confirmation of the wind he already marked as a traitor. Dan stepped back until he stood beside him.

"Anything new with the wind, Lennie?"

"No."

"We're not very fat then?"

"No. I wish . . . Oh Christ, I wish we had another ten minutes of fuel! Just another ten minutes. . . ."

"You're sure that would do it, Lennie? You're *sure* now?" Dan's manner was merely curious and the tone of his questioning was as easy as it might have been on a routine flight. He could have been asking Leonard if he knew the league status of a baseball team. As he stood there, slowly passing the end of his finger down the long crease in his cheek, some of his calm was caught up by Leonard and he laughed bitterly.

"As they say in the books . . . I have now positively established our exact whereabouts. Ten more minutes of fuel would see us through this thing."

"How much would the wind have to increase in velocity to accomplish that little thing?"

"Twenty knots in the next hour."

"That's asking for a lot."

"It couldn't happen so I'm not even asking. But if it swung around a little more on our tail, and it seems to be doing that . . . well, it just could be." With a forlorn gesture Leonard placed his hands on his knees. He looked up at Dan and shook his grey head. "Ah well . . . I guess they'll pick us up before we get too damp. But it sure will worry Susie. She'll lay down the law. Probably insist I quit flying."

"Will you?"

Leonard squinted his eyes as if the question was a complete surprise to him and finding the answer brought

239

him acute pain. He took his hands from his knees to massage his belly and then returned them decisively to his knees again.

"*No,* by God!"

"In other words, you're not going to get gypped out of your pension?"

"Something like that."

"You'll get it, Lennie. I've got a feeling you'll collect."

Dan walked back to the crew compartment. It was noisier here, with the engines pounding only a few feet beyond the thin aluminum skin. But he wanted to be alone for a few minutes and have a last try at solving the problem which had troubled him ever since the first radio contact with the Coast Guard plane.

In the darkness he passed beneath the overhead ventilator. A fine stream of rain water leaked through the ventilator and splashed down his face and the back of his neck. Swearing softly, he stepped away from the ventilator and switched on the light. He yanked the black curtain across the passageway leading to the flight deck and switched on the compartment light. He leaned against the bulkhead, lit a cigarette, and thoughtfully watched the water pour down from the ventilator. Below it, there was now a large pool on the deck.

If Sullivan had his way, Dan thought, the water in this compartment would very soon be far above anyone's neck.

He drew hard at his cigarette. This was hardly the sort of thing he had expected when he asked Garfield to let him fly again. He had foreseen that uncomfortable situations of a minor nature might come to pass and had deliberately prepared himself to face such embarrassment, but this . . . ? On any flight he was likely to be the oldest crew member and as such, he had told himself, he should know enough to keep his mouth shut no matter what the temptation to draw on thirty-five years of flying experience. This was different—or was it? There were so many factors to confuse the situation. It was time, almost past time, to do some swift and very clear thinking.

Commandwise, the laws of the sky were almost exactly like the laws of the sea. The captain of an airplane was held solely responsible for the performance and safety of his ship; he automatically assumed the blame for any accident no matter whose fault it actually might be. His power, too, was absolute, and the cases of mutiny on aircraft were so rare they could not be worth considering. Once in ten thousand flights a crew member might openly question a captain's judgment, but such arguments, if the captain permitted any discussion to develop, were inevitably settled on the ground. It was not that most captains closed their minds to suggestion the moment their wives sewed four stripes on their uniform sleeves—rather that any large aircraft was a very fast-moving, highly complicated beast—and the crew members themselves were the first to realize someone aboard must be in supreme command. At two or three hundred miles-per-hour, arguments could consume priceless minutes. No captain had ever been known to try deliberate suicide and so for all practical purposes arguments just didn't happen.

And now Sullivan intended to ditch. He proposed to put his plane and all the souls on board into the wild sea at night when the safety of land was only ten minutes further. Was he doing the right thing—the *only* thing that could be done?

It was a question Dan had asked himself innumerable times during the past hour. If he could be sure that Sullivan was right, then he wouldn't care so much what happened—since Alice and Tony were killed nothing seemed to matter very much—but *was* Sullivan right? Of course he would want to ditch while he still had enough fuel to give him power of maneuver. And he was wise in flying as long as he could so that the nearly empty tanks would give the ship greater buoyancy on the water. As captain it was not his duty to gamble. Gambling was for people who could afford to lose. But there were only those ten minutes—and fuel gauges were not exact to the gallon, any more than Leonard Wilby's navigation was exact to the mile. So there *could* be a chance of making San Francisco airport, and if a part of that chance was luck, then luck must also play a part in how Sullivan managed finally to hit the water. The balance, it seemed, was almost exactly equal.

It was Sullivan's choice. Apparently he had already made his final decision, and persuading him otherwise now could be both difficult and dangerous—particularly, Dan reminded himself, when the persuader occupied a subordinate position. Much would depend on how thoroughly Sullivan had been able to retake command of himself. For a while, he had been perilously near the breaking point. The signs were unmistakable; yet now he seemed again forceful and sure of his way.

Dan tried to whistle but the tune that came to his lips was mournful and he soon stopped.

Would Sullivan listen to an old man he had every right to classify as obsolete? How secret was his pity for Dan Roman—a beat-up has-been? It was the custom these days for the younger men, highly trained in prescribed schools, to politely tolerate the old timers. They respected them, not for what they could do, because often as not they were past the keen edge of top flying, but rather the respect came from an appreciation of what they *had* done. They had built a new world, and it had passed them by very swiftly, on the very speed which gave it life. Old timers, which included any pilot who had flown before 1935 or so, were like antique furniture—admired and even loved, perhaps, but often suspected of functional instability. And in recent years, the science of aerial flight was progressing so rapidly even the younger men were having difficulty keeping pace with it. Yet dammit . . . this situation was not science. It was luck.

Dan forced himself to remember Garfield's words. "You'll find out you've had it, Dan. This is a kid's game now . . . young, bright guys with a cap full of education and minds that work like high-pressure pumps. Hang up your helmet and goggles and forget it." So?

Sullivan, except for his temporary lapse, was exactly the kind of younger man Garfield was talking about. He was even more. He already had a great deal of over-ocean experience behind him, and he would have every reason to discount the opinions of a man he knew had principally confined himself to flying smaller airplanes over dry land. And he could be right, Dan—both in his

242

refusal to accept your ideas and in the decision he had already made. You really haven't admitted that.

He held out his cigarette so that it was directly beneath the ventilator and let the dripping stream of rainwater extinguish it. He went to his briefcase, which was stowed beneath the washstand, and knelt before it. His hands went surely to the small framed picture of a smiling blond girl and a little boy. Alice and Tony. They were sitting on a plaster wall in bright sunlight and Dan remembered, as he had so many times before, that the picture was taken in front of their house in Cali—just three days before the nightmare that would never leave his mind completely at peace. How much was the memory of Alice and Tony affecting his thinking now? He asked the picture rather than himself. Am I wrong in believing that Sullivan should carry on until the tanks are dry? Am I wrong in believing that, by pressing luck, we can make it? Am I committing another crime in trying to change his decision . . . and maybe succeeding?

He rose and crossed the compartment to the bunk. Reaching over it, he pulled three life vests from their storage place. He removed the rubberized protective cover from one and, after a final glance at the picture, carefully wrapped it in the cover. He made a neat package of it, then stuffed it in his hip pocket and placed the life vest over his head. He tied the straps around his legs and chest, then he set deliberately to the task of unfastening the life raft from the heavy straps which held it over the bunk.

In its disinflated state the raft resembled an overlarge bedroll. It was very heavy and awkward to handle. Later, when the ship had come to rest on the sea, they would pull the emergency release on the astrodome and presumably have strength remaining to push the raft straight up through the small opening.

He moved the raft to the ready position by the flight-deck passageway and, picking up the two remaining vests, walked forward. He handed one of the vests to Leonard.

"The color may not become you, Lennie . . . but they're in fashion."

"Thanks for nothing." Leonard stared solemnly at the yellow vest. "I never thought I'd really have to put one of these things on."

"Better check the cartridges and make sure they're okay."

"Yeah. . . ."

As Leonard pulled the cover from his vest, Dan moved forward to Sullivan. He placed the last vest on his lap. Sullivan said thanks, but he kept his eyes on the instruments.

Dan sat down in the right seat. Taking his time, moving with elaborate slowness, he loosened his tie, buckled his safety belt, and put on his headphones. Then he leaned across the control pedestal to Sullivan.

"Our air speed looks a little better."

"A bit."

"Lennie says if we can pick up ten minutes we can make it."

"If you didn't know . . . Lennie has always been an optimist." Still Sullivan kept his eyes grimly on the instruments. The amber-red light from the panel cast deep shadows upward on his face as if a sculptor had worked at his features only from below; his strong chin and his mouth were unnaturally chiseled and his eyes appeared half-wild in their concentration.

"Lennie might be right," Dan said, without seeming to care.

"If he's wrong we've had it . . . maybe wipe out a few bridges or apartment houses. I can't risk it."

"It's going to be a risk ditching. It will be rough down there."

"I know it."

"If we hit wrong, we've had it, too."

"I know that, dammit!" A new sharpness came to Sullivan's voice.

Dan waited for his mouth to relax. "Maybe now . . . we might try easing off a little on the power?"

"A message came from Garfield while you were back there. He suggested a lower rpm."

"Why not try it?"

"I thought about it a long time ago. It won't work She's barely flying now."

"Any objection if I try?"

For the first time Sullivan looked directly at Dan. It was only for the space of a second, yet Dan saw that there was neither hostility nor friendliness in his eyes. He was dead—frozen hard in his decision.

When he looked away Dan reached for the three operating propeller controls. He gradually pulled them back until the engines were only turning over sixteen hundred revolutions per minute. The sound of the engines fell to a low murmur, almost as if they had ceased to work at all. Dan ignored the placard which boldly stated that the engines should not be operated at such a low rpm. At a time like this it was a law to be broken. He told himself that nothing would break; not for a while, anyway. He watched the air-speed. It, too, was falling off. One hundred and thirty . . . one hundred and twenty-five . . . one hundred and twenty . . . one hundred and fifteen. But the fuel flow meters also dropped. She was burning thirty pounds per hour less for each engine. Enough, *maybe* enough to make San Francisco!

Sullivan squirmed uneasily in his seat. His hands gripped the control wheel so tightly it became a rigid part of his hands and his arms.

"It won't work! She's going to stall on me!"

Dan pushed forward on the throttles until they were wide open. The combination of very low rpm and full manifold pressure, he knew, was terrifically hard on the engines. The fuel flow increased only slightly, but the air-speed returned to one hundred and twenty.

"This is no good," Sullivan said. "We'll blow a jug."

"What's the difference? We'll blow 'em all if we ditch. Hang on. We'll make it."

"You're crazy. We've tried it and it won't do. Put those props back up where they belong!" The sweat was beginning to varnish Sullivan's face again. It broke out very suddenly as if welling up from a thousand springs. Fighting for a hundred feet of altitude that he had lost, he pulled back angrily on the control column and suddenly a quiver passed through the ship—the first warning of a stall. Sullivan quickly pushed the nose down again.

"Put those goddamned props back where they were!"

245

"Nothing doin', skipper."

"That's an order!"

Dan kept his hands on his knees. Sullivan looked at him in astonished anger and then reached for the controls himself. Dan caught his arm and held it firmly.

"Hang on, chum! We'll make it this way! You can do it, man! Just hang on. Fly, and let me pray!"

"Are you tired of living? If we try an instrument approach at San Francisco we'll run out of gas right in the middle of it!"

"Maybe yes, maybe no. Nothing is for sure yet. Try it this way for thirty minutes, will you? Don't be so goddamned anxious to go for a swim!"

"It's crazy! She's starting to shake again!" The airspeed had indeed fallen off to one hundred and ten—and Sullivan had lost another valuable hundred feet of altitude.

"Let her shake! The hell with it as long as she don't fall off on a wing. Let her mush down a little if you have to. Look at our gas consumption . . . only one-fifty per hour! Hang on and *fly*, man!"

Sullivan glanced at the fuel flow meters. His eyes that had been so empty of hope now brightened a little. He pulled his hand slowly away from the propeller controls.

"If it doesn't work," Dan said, "you won't have to get me fired. I'll quit."

Sullivan took a deep breath and sighed heavily.

"If it doesn't work . . . it won't make any difference what you do."

Then, like a man preparing to jump across an abyss he knew was impossibly wide, Sullivan set himself to the intricate, nerve-scraping struggle of flying an airplane that was not really flying.

His vest unbuttoned and his belt loosened, Garfield sat on a stool at the end of the long counter in the operations office. The cigar was dead in his mouth and he had not changed its position for a long time. He stared at the clock as if he were a critic judging a painting, tilting his head occasionally to observe more exactly the precise station of the hands. A feeling of disgust had come over him. He resented this helpless waiting, sitting in a well-lit office while men to whom he was inexplicably bound in spirit fought against the night.

In a way, he mused, they were lucky. Their efforts were cut and dried; at least they could encounter a tangible part of their antagonist. For they could join the battle, lose themselves in the heat of physical exertion. Not so with the sheaf of messages by his hand. They were empty of satisfaction. The Coast Guard, Sea Frontier, CAA, Air Traffic Control, Weather—all meaningless except the terse, inescapable words from Aircraft Four-two-zero.

"PLAN DITCHING AT ZERO ONE THIRTY."

Then a change.

"ATTEMPTING LOW RPM. AIR SPEED VARIABLE ONE HUNDRED TEN TO ONE HUNDRED FIFTEEN. ALTITUDE TWENTY-THREE HUNDRED."

A request.

"ADVISE WEATHER THROUGH GOLDEN GATE ALSO LATEST SAN FRANCISCO WEATHER AND TOP OVERCAST."

All complied with instantly. Words flashed through the night sky. Words which must affect the lives of twenty-one people who only this morning awakened as other people, and looked at the sun, perhaps, without the faintest notion they might never see it again. How much difference it would have made to them if they had known! How many of them would have gone about their last living normally—keeping appointments, reading about the world's wounds in their breakfast newspaper and caring if those wounds bled, complaining of lukewarm coffee, even shaving or brushing their teeth with ordinary attention? How many of them, knowing they were condemned, would have gone to church, frantically hoping for a formal introduction to immortality and how many of them would have said the hell with it—trying perhaps for a last-minute immersion in what they considered the real way of life?

They would change, Garfield thought. Each one of them would change in his own way. Certain things that seemed important before would suddenly become value-less—because you had to stand very near to complete destruction before you could see anything clearly. Then, and only then, did the chromatic scale of values become brilliant. Red became red, and blue pure blue. Garfield knew this because in the old days of flying, before his confinement to an office, he had several times had occasion to observe the scale. If it changed me then, he thought, then it must change them now. Only if all of them were ignorant of what must happen during the next hour would there be no change—and that was un-likely. Sullivan must have prepared them for a ditch-ing. Fortunately, it was not his duty to prepare them for dying.

Yet this last message? Was Sullivan going to try to make it, after all? He couldn't. If the figures were correct the odds were a thousand to one—worse perhaps. There was one basic rule in all of flying. You could not ask time to hesitate while you found a place to hide.

For a moment Garfield visualized the fuel tanks in the wings of Four-two-zero. The liquid which furnished the power of life to the ship would be sloshing about in the tanks now—only a few inches deep. In his mind, he followed the fuel to the outlets of the tanks and saw it sucked through the blood vessel-like pipes to the carbu-retors. It was pouring through the pipes with terrifying speed, becoming vaporized, and lost forever in the hun-gry engines. Almost three gallons every minute. The life blood was ebbing from Four-two-zero. Reprieve was im-possible. Its intricate workmanship would soon be a tan-gled mess of rusting metal. It was sickening.

He glanced at the passenger list which had been placed by his hand. Flaherty, Donald . . . Rice, Howard . . . Rice, Lydia . . . McKee, Sally . . . Locota, José . . . Briscoe, Frank. . . . The names were meaningless to him. But they were people, he thought, all of them human be-ings who had begun this morning much in the manner of other humans, and now, en masse, they would end their day together. All because the molecules in a supposedly perfect metallic composition had decided to fly apart and go their separate ways. Because of a thoughtless disagree-ment among the molecules, certain children would remain unborn, others neglected in foster homes. A few widows would know the dull starvation of an always empty bed and their cheeks would sink with yearning for something more nourishing than food. Others would be much better off, and find, as the people on Four-two-zero were doubtless discovering, a different person within themselves.

The effect of the molecules' instant war was far-reaching. It could easily descend through a generation, touching the lives of people Garfield would never know. In a perverse way, it amused him to think about the molecules. It helped to pass the time.

He called across the counter to the dispatcher.

"Did you phone Sullivan's wife?"

"Yessir. She's on her way to the airport now."

"You didn't alarm her?"

"No. I just said her husband was on the way in and that you wanted to see her."

"Then she knows something is wrong."

"Probably. But her voice was quite calm."

"How about the others?"

"Wheeler lives with another pilot . . . DuPree it is. There was no answer. The same for Wilby. I called his home and no answer, then I took the liberty of calling a bar I know about. His wife had been there, but she left about an hour before."

"The stewardess?"

"Spalding's mother isn't well. She said Spalding's father was out of town on business."

"It would be easier if I could tell these people all at once. I think they might help each other."

"There's no one listed to call for Dan Roman. Do you know of any person who should know?"

"Yes. But I'm afraid you can't reach her. Dan lives alone."

Garfield looked at the clock again. How swiftly time passed when you didn't want it to pass. Forty minutes and it would all be over.

18

"I AM AMUSED," SAID GUSTAVE PARDEE. "EVEN THOUGH a human life is supposed to be the most precious commodity, we invariably behave as if it wasn't worth very much. Some sort of protective mechanism, I suppose." He was speaking to his wife Lillian and looking at her in a way he had never done before. At Hobie's bidding they had put on their life vests and now Gustave appeared more houndlike than ever with the high yellow collar of the vest encircling his neck. His drooping cigarette wiggled in his lips as he spoke and his shortness of breath was greatly emphasized by the heaving movements of the vest. With all the others he had patiently obeyed Hobie's and Spalding's instructions. He had removed his shoes, loosened his tie, fastened his safety belt, and now he sat somewhat helplessly, although his dignity remained undamaged.

"Lillian," he went on in a voice that had lost all pretension. ". . . this is rather a bad joke, you know. There was once a highly successful act in vaudeville called Wilie, West, and McGinty. It involved the construction of a brick house which eventually fell down all around the performers. So it is now, with me. For several years, more than I care to think about, I have carefully built a shelter about myself as a refuge from the likes of you. Now it has come tumbling down all around my head. If we should survive this thing, it is quite possible that after I have wiped the salt water out of my eyes, I should regard you in an entirely new light."

"Why, Gustave? What difference could it make?"

"I cannot imagine why it should make the slightest difference although I know already that it does. I have been robbed of confidence . . . I might lose you."

"You've already demonstrated that you can get along very well without me. Think of the ball you'd have."

"No . . . I was merely confident, perhaps too much so . . . that I would never lose you to another man . . . and because of that conceit I easily avoided any display of . . . nervousness, shall we say?"

"Gus!" She laughed, and there was a new sparkle in her large brown eyes. Suddenly she took up his hand and kissed it. "You *really* have had a feeling of jealousy about me? You admit it?"

"I admit nothing of the kind. However. . . ." he paused to wave a pile of cigarette ash from the heaving summit of his life vest ". . . I find the prospect of losing you under any circumstances intensely uncomfortable. It saddens me."

"Poor Gustave. So sad."

"Stop being such an accommodating bitch and listen to me. Has it occurred to you that this is an extremely difficult conversation for me to direct? I am working up to a confession."

"Watch yourself, Gustave. I wouldn't want you to say anything you'd repent once we reached solid ground."

"My thoughts tended toward a certain sentimentality."

"I'm managing not to care."

"You mean that?"

"Of course. That's the way you always wanted it."

"But you've switched! A little while ago—"

"I was, as always . . . your private door mat with a big welcome written across my face. I was Gustave Pardee's wife, a shadow seen only when it pleased you."

"But—"

"The salary was good and so was the board and room. I haven't any complaints, but I think I'll resign. I'm tired."

"You said you loved me." He glanced quickly at his watch. "Less than an hour ago!"

"Such words, dear!"

"Just what the hell has come over you?"

She spread her graceful hands and smiled.

"I'm not sure. Maybe it's this ridiculous costume. I've never modeled a life vest before and they say that apparel can change a woman's thinking quicker than anything else. If she's wearing soft, sleek pajamas she feels all sexy and impractical. If she's wearing a tweed suit she becomes the big administrator and sets out grimly to prove how smart women are. Right now, with this thing around my neck, I'm feeling pretty damn elemental. If I get out of this affair in one piece I'm going to see that our girl Lillian comes out of the shadows. It's about time she started living."

"That was quite a speech. Do you propose to include me in your new life?"

"Not on the old terms, Gustave. In your own special way, I now remember that you once put it very aptly. You said that I was more of an idea than a mere woman . . . an instrument to be played upon when your genius yearned for company. Now, very suddenly, I'm sick and tired of being an instrument or an idea. I want to be a woman before it's too late. I want to have babies to worry about like Mrs. Joseph . . . real live babies under forty. I'd like to have my husband come home a minimum of three nights a week . . . and I might even learn to cook. . . ."

"Good God!" Gustave exhaled the words in a cloud of smoke. He wiped his lips with his finger and shook his massive head.

"Why are you so astonished? Did you honestly think you could twist a woman's character around to suit the needs of your private play? I'm not a stage creation, Gustave. My matinees are every day and my night performances are every night of the week. I don't come on for a few minutes and then disappear behind a velvet drop until the house fills up again, or you just feel a rehearsal is in order. I'm *real*. This moment . . . this airplane . . . this costume which wouldn't rate a credit line in one of your programs . . . has finally given me the courage to step over the footlights." She looked down at her well-formed shoeless feet and slowly moved her toes. "I guess that about says it."

There was a long silence between them. They avoided each other's eyes and Gustave made a pretense of trying to see something out the window at his side. Finally he unfastened his safety belt and rose in his seat until he could lean over the back of it and face Mrs. Joseph.

"Mrs. Joseph," he said evenly. "Do you mind if I ask you a rather personal question?"

"Why . . . no? We all seem to be pretty well acquainted now, because of . . . ." She shrugged her shoulders hopelessly and looked to her husband for a more complete explanation.

"Ths missus is trying to say people who got nothing but trouble get to know each other sort of fast like," Ed Joseph said. He had placed a ginger lei incongruously over his life vest and the effect was that of a child uncertain of which game to play. Much of his eager enthusiasm had left him and now he held tightly to his wife's hand.

"Although this might not be the time for it, I would like to pose a riddle, Mrs. Joseph. If you had the opportunity to begin your adult life over again, what would you change? I realize this is rather a difficult question, but I hope you will try to answer it honestly. It's rather important to me just now."

"Change?" She looked quickly at her husband and seemed to move closer to him. "Why . . . I don't believe I would *change anything.*"

"You are entirely happy then? Thoroughly content? You have never felt compelled to visit a head-shrinker for psychoanalysis?"

"Mr. Pardee . . . you say the funniest things!"

"Jennifer and little Edward, I suppose, contribute greatly to your remarkable peace of mind?"

"Well, they *are* a lot of trouble sometimes . . . of course . . . but that's only natural—"

"Natural? I like that word, Mrs. Joseph. Thank you."

"I'm afraid I didn't answer your question very well."

"Yes, you did. With your eyes, Mrs. Joseph. I am deeply grateful to you."

He turned in his seat and wedged himself down again

until he could refasten his safety belt. He toyed with the buckle a moment and then examined Lillian from her nylon-clad feet to her smooth black hair.

"Now what?" she said uneasily.

"Lillian. If and when we reach terra firma . . . I would consider it quite natural if you began knitting little things."

In the seats just ahead of the Pardees, Ken Child finished helping May Holst into her life vest and made certain her safety belt was secure. Then he slipped off his shoes and put on his own vest.

"This is a stunning garment," May said, meticulously retying the ribbons on the front of her vest into more perfect bows. "Makes me feel like a catcher for the Dodgers. It's a hell of a shroud, if you ask me."

"It won't be a shroud. We'll get out of this."

"So we don't? I always dreaded the idea of becoming an old woman, anyway. I haven't been whistled at for years and the idea of growing roses for the rest of my days was beginning to haunt me. There isn't a home for ex-mistresses, you know, although there should be. We should have organized. We should have a home somewhere with no mirrors in it . . . far away some place where we would never see a young girl. Champagne should be served at all hours and music wired into every room. They have homes for unmarried mothers, but everybody forgets about the girls who never quite managed to make things legal. If there was a lawyer around now, that's what I'd do with the 'money Sterling left me. Start The May Holst Home for Broken-Down Broads. I kind of like that, don't you?"

Ken failed to answer her and she saw that his lips were working strangely as if he wanted to speak, yet could not find his voice.

"What's the matter with you?"

Again he tried to answer, but when his voice came at last it was merely incoherent and all the strength had gone from it.

"I . . . ." He looked anxiously about the darkened cabin, at the young Bucks who sat across the aisle.

tightly holding hands, and at the Rices who sat just behind them. "I . . . something's happened to me. I sat through the worst part of the blitz in London and I was pretty scared . . . but not like this."

"You've had a strenuous day . . . between one thing and another."

She planted her feet firmly against the seat ahead of her, deliberately revealing several inches of bare leg above her garters. She reached out and snapped one of the garters, which were black and embellished around their circumference with miniature roses. She laughed bitterly.

"See? No action. Not even from a man like you, who might appreciate such things. When Sterling died I swore I'd never wear another garter belt. I threw the last one away which proves you can't manufacture a lady. There's no place in this whole world for old dumb broads. When it's gone it's gone, and our brains were never built for loneliness. Nobody yet has invented successful I-don't-care pills for girls like me. So I'm licked. The only thing I don't care about is what the hell happens to this flying machine. Frig it!"

"I. . . ." Ken started to speak and then suddenly unfastened his safety belt. He lunged out of his seat and covered the few steps to the forward cabin door very quickly. He yanked it open and stumbled into the dark crew compartment. Familiar as he was with the physical layout of planes like Four-two-zero, the darkness slowed his frantic search for the crew lavatory. When he found the narrow door he went quickly inside and vomited. He fought his terror alone, in the dark, but it was a long time before he could stop the retching.

It was a long time before he could even begin to quiet the depths of his being.

They waited together in the muted light by the rear door of the passenger cabin—Spalding and Hobie Wheeler. Balancing themselves expertly against the uneven motion of the ship, their lithe young bodies swayed in a sort of hesitant dance.

"Have we forgotten anything?" Spalding asked him.

255

"I don't think so. They're as ready now as they'll ever be." He glanced down the line of seats. "Lots less trouble than I expected. You've done a good job."

"Most of them have been wonderful. I wouldn't have believed it."

"People are funny. I guess you never know."

Their nearly exact height allowed Spalding to meet his eyes directly and now she found that all of his annoying brashness was gone. There was concern about his mouth and eyes, but they were not afraid. He was somehow grown up very suddenly, she thought. I like him. I like the way he stands waiting.

"My feet are getting cold," she said.

"So are mine. When we get in we should complain about the floor heating to the company. It was never designed for ditching procedure. I'll bet no one ever thought about how cold our feet would get."

"When we get in?"

"Yeh."

"You believe we will then?"

"Eventually. Sullivan will put this thing down like a crate of eggs. And a short swim will do us good. Refreshing. Fine exercise."

"I'd rather lie on a warm beach," Spalding said slowly.

"That's all right, too. I'll ask you again. Would you go with me sometime?"

"Yes, Hobie. Now . . . I would."

A look passed between them and because it lasted overlong, they both knew it was like a formal kiss at first parting. Instinctively he reached for her hand and held it a moment, feeling its smoothness. Then as if he had suddenly remembered something, Hobie began to search the shelf above the last empty seats. He found a pillow and carefully placed it on the floor between them.

"What's that for?" she asked.

He hesitated, looking at her carefully. When he spoke at last, his voice was almost a whisper.

"Do me a favor, will you?"

"Sure, Hobie." She thought of pulling her hand away and then decided against it. His hand was warm and strong and its strength drove away the feeling of being frightened and alone. A quick review of her other young men flashed through her mind and she wondered if they would behave as Hobie under the same conditions. She decided they would probably fail.

"You've done everything so well," he said. "Can you take something else in your stride?"

"I can try."

"All right, then. Believe me, I'm not trying to scare you . . . or worry you . . . or make things any worse than they already are. It's just that I want to be sure about you.

"When I tell you, sit on the floor here, with your back to this seat. Stay there, no matter what else is going on. Don't try being the heroine because for those last few minutes there won't be anything in the world you can really do to help anybody. The favor for me . . . is the pillow. Hold it tightly over your face . . . for yourself . . . and for me. No matter what anyone tells you, there are going to be a lot of things flying around in this cabin. A moment ago I thought it best not to tell you, but I feel differently about you now . . . I've changed my mind. With the wind and the sea, neither God nor Sullivan can set this thing down tonight like an egg crate. We might just as well slam into a mountain. Dan knows it. I know it. And so . . . does Sullivan."

She took a deep breath and felt a slight increase in the pressure of his hand.

"Thanks, Hobie. I'll be ready."

"Your face would improve any landscape. I want to keep it that way. We'll lie on that beach yet."

Still holding her hand, Hobie looked the length of the cabin to see if Sullivan had turned on the seat belt sign—the ten-minute warning. It was still dark, but as his eyes roved the lines of seats a puzzled expression crossed his face. "Say, little girl," he said quietly, after he had examined the seats a second time. "Aren't we missing a passenger?"

One side of the small crew lavatory was backed by the ship's electrical panel and Ken Childs discovered that he could lean against the metal facing and obtain considerable warmth from it. Only when he pressed tightly against the panel could he stop the shivering which overwhelmed him. It was as if his arms and legs had been hoisted into a high, cold wind and forced to remain there until they were numb. And the cold was transmitted through them to the trunk of his body, congealing the blood which somehow rose upward to the base of his throat as a solid. He was choking, suffocating as he leaned against the panel in the little room, and yet he could not bring himself to leave its warmth. He knew that the muscles in his neck were swollen and rigid; he could not remember when he had last been able to swallow. This was panic and he stood as another person, regarding it with his tongue lolling against the side of his half-open mouth—watching the terrible seizures that convulsed his heavy frame. Panic. He had seen it before in other men . . . Passchendaele, with the British in 1917. But it wasn't Ken Childs then, and those poor devils at least had room to run. Panic! You of all people! Hang on, man. Wait and it will pass!

But it did not pass. The ability to stand off as a detached person and watch it progress, was the only thing that remained unchanged. Christ help me! I've never been afraid to die! How did it happen? How can I, Ken Childs, with four Canadian war decorations be the only one to get the wind up? Nobody's shooting at you now. You're still in one piece. Then stop it! Think of the others. Think of the others continuously, because they must not see you or the disease will spread everywhere through the cabin like a swift plague. It works that way! Squeeze yourself in a hard fist and hang on!

Gradually, thinking of the others, some of the torment subsided. The ache departed from his belly and he was able to close his mouth, though he could still hear his own frantic breathing. "I sound like a dog who has run a long way," he thought. "Get out of here. Get out of this warm little room before someone discovers your disgrace."

He opened the door and, by clinging to the bulkhead for support, contrived to make his way into the darkened crew compartment. His seeking hands found the black curtain in the passageway and for a time he clung to it weakly. A pale slice of light on the floor at last attracted his attention and he realized vaguely that it must come from the flight deck beyond the curtain. There was now the sound of voices, and he was drawn toward them as a drowning man might reach out hungrily for a chip of wood.

He moved cautiously around the curtain and saw Leonard bent over his navigation table. Though he was hardly more than a pace away he was so absorbed in his work he did not turn his head.

Ken stood in the shadows, watching him, foolishly intrigued with the way he constantly swept his fingers through his grey hair. Then forward of Leonard he saw Sullivan and Dan. Their voices, slightly raised against the sound of the engines, floated back to him. Sullivan's voice was high and unnatural. But it was his face, turned back toward Leonard, that shocked Ken Childs. It was like looking into his own! There was no contortion, he wasn't nearly so far gone, but behind his haggard eyes there was the same abject terror.

"Wilby! Check your final position! I'm going to take her down!"

And Ken saw Leonard reach out his hand like a prisoner begging for reprieve. He held it in the air with the tips of his fingers pointing toward Sullivan, while he kept diligently at his work.

"Wait a few more minutes, Skipper! I *think* . . . it looks like the wind—"

"Do as I say, goddammit!"

He is yelling, Ken thought. Yelling as I want to yell.
"But a few more minutes—"

"I'm not going to get caught in a trap! We've already waited too long! Hurry!"

Then Sullivan turned away and two sounds so engaged Ken's brain that he could hear nothing else—not even his labored breathing. The one was the familiar heavy thrumming which always accompanies an airplane in descent, and the other sound was Dan Roman's voice, crisp-clear, almost metallic in its hardness.

"*No!* I'll be damned if you will!"

He saw Dan rise suddenly in his seat, and his face bore the intensity of a much earlier day. The years had somehow been wiped away in the space of a second, and it was the young Dan Roman who leaned far across the separation of their seats. The palm of his hand flashed outward with incredible swiftness. There were two plainly audible smacks as his open hand struck both sides of Sullivan's face. There was no malice in either blow, but Ken did not have time or wits remaining to consider Dan's motives before he spoke again.

"Get hold of yourself, you yellow son-of-a-bitch!"

In the Coast Guard plane, hardly a mile away, Lieutenant Mowbray spoke into his microphone. He called several times without success.

"Radar reports you losing altitude, Four-two-zero. Are you going to ditch?"

Wondering at the silence. Mowbray tapped the microphone against his fist. He tried again.

"Aircraft Four-two-zero . . . this is your escorting B-17. You've lost altitude. Are you going to ditch?"

No answer.

"Aircraft Four-two-zero? You are now below the minimum instrument altitude for approaching the Coast. Time's wasting. You better climb or settle for the drink. We're right with you . . . will follow you down. Advise immediately."

Worried, Mowbray looked at Keim.

"You hear anything?" Keim shook his head and shrugged his shoulders. His fingers played experimentally along the radio switches at his side.

Then a voice came to their headsets, so strong and clear it hurt their ears.

"Roger . . . Coast Guard! We've been reading you but too busy to answer. Stand by . . . we may have a change of plans."

It was Dan Roman's voice.

Counting heads along the full length of the passenger cabin, Hobie continued his search through the forward door until he reached the crew compartment. In the darkness, he collided with Ken Childs. He seized him with both arms and held him firmly.

"What are you doing up here, sir?"

"I was . . . let me go!" Ken's voice rose hysterically. "Take your hands off me!"

"Now take it easy, sir—"

"We're all going to be killed! I heard them! They're fighting. Dan . . . old Dan! . . . he's gone crazy!" The last of his words were lost in a choking whimper and he pressed his head against Hobie's chest like a small boy begging protection from his father. "Oh help me . . . *please* . . . help me!"

And Hobie held the man who was so much older than himself, tightly, supporting his entire weight, soothing him with his hands and the power of his young voice.

"You'll be all right, sir . . . everything's going to be all right . . . just take it easy now. . . ."

He moved Ken Childs until he could brace him against the after bulkhead and, when he was able to free one arm, he switched on the light. He took out his handkerchief and wiped the residue of vomit from the older man's lips and chin and where it had soiled the front of his life vest. Then as his whimpering began to subside, Hobie pushed back his grey hair and tenderly stroked the side of his cheek. "Easy does it . . . there's nothing to get so excited about."

"I don't know what came over me." Ken shook his head hopelessly and his fingers clawed at Hobie's shirt. "I never was afraid. . . ."

"Sure. But you're all right now. Think you can stand by yourself?"

Ken tried to straighten his knees and as he did so a heavy groan escaped him. It was a despairing sound from the innermost depths of a man sick with shame, the wretched, hushed cry of a soul kicking through ashes.

"Help me!" he begged of the young man who could have been his son.

Hobie smoothed his hair again and waited until his breathing came more regularly. Then instinctively trying to match the humility in Ken's voice so that in sympathy he might regain himself, he said. "You can help us all a lot if you will go back to your seat and stay there quietly."

The older man raised his head as if in doing so he

lifted a hundred pounds. With the heel of his hand he rubbed the tear-water from his eyes.

"I'll try. Give me a minute—please."

"Take longer if you like. If anyone asks, you can say you were airsick."

"Yes . . . of course." He straightened his body and took his hands away from Hobie. "But what will I ever tell myself. . . ."

He turned toward the door slowly and Hobie saw that his shoulders were sagging, and it occurred to him that there was nothing more pitiful than a middle-aged man who moved without pride.

"Let me help you, sir," he said reaching for the door.

"No . . . please. I . . . I'd rather go back alone."

19

THE IMPACT OF DAN'S HAND AGAINST SULLIVAN'S FACE stunned him, but he recovered his physical perception almost instantly. It was the significance of the act which lingered, and it was several minutes before he fully realized that he had dropped his hands from the control wheel and that Dan was now flying the ship.

He looked at the most vital instruments. The air-speed was still on the border line between flying and not flying, but they had recovered the three hundred feet of altitude he had squandered in his determination to ditch. The altimeter read two thousand five hundred feet . . . enough to clear the coastal hills.

He looked at Dan, clearly remembering the slaps, yet unable to recall what happened immediately afterward. That short space of time was entirely blank and yet Sullivan knew he had not lost consciousness for a moment. Then how could he have relinquished his command so easily? Something had snapped. Like a rubber band stretched too far, there was no connection between now and the time before. And remarkably, the flight deck no longer seemed to be pressing inward with viselike persistence. There was the normal room to think now and the sprouting bouquets of valves and controls did not seem to be stabbing at him. Nor did the instruments appear to be telling a series of lies. They were composed, steady. Dan was doing a good job of flying—better than anyone could expect under the circumstances.

The clock told Sullivan that less than two minutes had elapsed between the slaps and this instant when everything became so clear. His fingers sought his jaw and he felt the sides of it. His skin was still warm and tingling from the blows. He felt the stubble on his chin and thought how long it had been since he had shaved. He reached in his shirt pocket for a cigarette and was surprised to notice the absolute steadiness of his hand as he lit it.

It's all over now, he thought. I am no longer secretly afraid of this or any other airplane. Holding the secret has been the whole trouble, a cancer that has been growing for months, and now that someone else knows of it and I am sure they know it . . . as long as I am no longer forced to hide my weakness, then it is cured. And the magic came from a has-been who had the nerve to name the disease out loud and call me a yellow son-of-a-bitch. The words did not sting—they healed. They shocked, as Dan Roman, who would never be a has-been, probably intended they should.

Sullivan sat very quietly in his seat, smoking his cigarette casually, each moment more aware of his reviving confidence. He thought that he could actually feel it flowing through his brain and body, and the sensation produced a vast content he had not known for a very long time. All of the anxieties, the specters which had threatened failure, were gone now that the failure had actually occurred. Every flying instinct had returned and once more he was able to weigh and balance the peculiar complications of his lifework. The enemies of his profession would not forgive his lapse, any more than he could ever forgive himself. The proof of his cure, he knew, must now depend on their complete conquest.

Acutely conscious of the penalties involved if he made the slightest mistake, Sullivan prepared to face his enemies. He must mix caution with daring and his technique must be perfect. Studying the fuel gauges he saw the course of battle clearly.

There was thirty minutes of fuel remaining in the tanks. One tank registered somewhat lower than the others. It fed the right outboard engine—number four. A simple cross feed problem then. At the first wiggle of the number-four flow meter, feed the engine from number-three tank, or number two if necessary. Dan would have to watch it and switch on the booster pump high to suck the tank completely dry. Or let the engine die and make the final approach on only two engines? That was another possibility. He had made blind approaches with two engines many times under simulated conditions during practice, but that was always with an empty airplane which was also aerodynamically clean. Here, there was an unknown. With the number-one engine hanging down and dragging, it was questionable if the ship would fly at all on only two engines. And, unlike the practice sessions, the situation would have no remedy in a handy reserve of power, waiting and available. No—forget the idea of two engines. The approach had to be made with three or the risk would exceed an immediate ditching.

Cut down on the time then? Contrive to steal even two minutes from the enemy of distance. Cheat. Throw the rule book away. Sneak past another enemy—the hills around San Francisco. The *minimum* legal altitude to approach those hills from seaward was three thousand feet. Three thousand—a sure, safe clearance laid down for normal conditions when their solidity would be enveloped in cloud. Three thousand allowed a margin for error. Tonight they would also be invisible. But there must be no error.

Sullivan remembered the actual measurement of the highest obstruction was nineteen hundred and fifty feet. So approaching the coast at twenty-two hundred would still be safe. Nerve-wracking to know the separation was only two hundred and fifty feet—but still, the hills would be cleared. All right. Leonard must stand by on his electric altimeter, calling out the readings continuously. And his readings must confirm those on the pressure altimeter in which an error of fifty feet was tolerated if not to be expected. Yet another protection?

The Coast Guard B-17. With his radar he can see

through the overcast—observe the approach of this ship to the hills. Good enough. Request that he come in as close as he dares, maintaining identical altitude precisely. He could give warning if you were too low. It was feasible. And the reward for all of this might be another two minutes of flying time because the descent to twenty-two hundred feet could begin now. With the nose tipped down even slightly, the ship would fly faster and better—make more efficient use of the fuel against distance. Start letting down very easily then, for the next twenty minutes or so, prolonging the gradual slide as long as possible—a few feet at a time. Dan must handle that.

Next? Have Dan do the flying until the last few minutes. Keep fresh for the final letdown. Meantime study the approach book as it had never been studied before. Call for the latest weather at the airport requesting advice of any change. Call Air Traffic Control to clear the area, starting right now. Make the initial approach to San Francisco range station on the direction finders and bear this wind always in mind. Scheme. Once over the station, whip her around and dump her down on the glide path. Swipe another minute there by not going all the way out the approach leg. Sharp steep turns and cowboy descents. Never mind the passengers' ears. There were many things to be done and they must be done very quickly. One of the things—

"Dan . . . ?"

"Yeah?" His face was like an ancient wind-beaten rock. He kept his eyes fixed on the instruments, sparing Sullivan only a glance.

"Thanks. . . ."

Dan raised an eyebrow. His lips became a tight thin line and he worked them thoughtfully. After a moment they formed into a pattern for whistling, but no sound came from them. "Thought I'd lost my temper long ago," he said finally. "Guess I didn't. I'm sorry."

"You should have hit harder. Thanks for knocking some sense into my head. Someday I'll explain. Right now there isn't time. We're not going to ditch. We'l make San Francisco the hard way."

Dan turned away from the instruments and his eye

266

became mere slits as he studied Sullivan's face. He whistled a few notes almost experimentally and then his mouth broke into a smile.

Sullivan turned quickly in his seat and called to Leonard.

"Any change in the wind, Lennie?"

"No, skipper . . ."

"The hell with it! Bring me the approach chart for San Francisco! Whistle me a tune, Dan! I like music while I think!"

When she first saw that his eyes were closed, Dorothy Chen reached above her head and switched out the small light. She wanted Frank Briscoe to sleep if he could because the signs of his terrible pain had become more obvious during the last hour and she could think of no way to comfort him. He had not complained, but more frequently as they talked she saw that his smile became twisted and his voice more hesitant.

He was so tired, this man; his weariness made her think of the decaying hills around her home. Like the hills, he was exhausted, yet there was still spirit in this Mr. American. He would not give in like the Korean hills near Antung had given in, or the people who lived upon them. He withstood the wind instead of bending with it—and so marked the difference between any Oriental and a Caucasian who had yet to know ten thousand years of pain.

Sitting quietly in the darkness, she once more saw the hills which now seemed so far away. Ah, so far! The house stood on one of the hills and it overlooked the yellow muddied river which even in the spring appeared to be tired. Generations of Chens had been born in that house, and the thick stone wall surrounding it had protected them for hundreds of years against everything but the exhaustion which seeped in from the countryside.

At the top of the house, there was a place just beneath the tile roof where a small girl, whose true given name was Graceful Princess, could secrete herself and look down on all the valley of the river. And from this place there were then many exciting things to be seen. The mud huts of the poor who tried to scrape an existence from the hills looked clean and warm from a distance. People appeared to move with energy through the streets of the village below, and even the few droshkies which the Russians had left behind years and years before, seemed to be vehicles of everlasting beauty. Graceful Princess, so small then, looked down from her roof and saw these things and wondered at the life which filled her valley, and told the amah about them, and accepted without question the fact that her house was the only one in the whole visible world that had a real roof. But the innocence was most temporary, as it had been for all of the Chens always, the merchants in the town, and the peasants in the hills.

For even a small girl could hear the dogs barking in the night, and then hear the first cries of rage and terror. There always followed the sound of running feet beyond the wall, then the first shots, and the barring of the gate and the main door by a father who had come to make a ritual of the act.

And so Graceful Princess grew up very quickly and became Dorothy Chen. In the short time of her life the bandits came first, ravaging the country under the leadership of one war lord after another, a ceaseless procession of them, each worse than the last. They wanted rice and women. Only money kept them from the house of Chen. Then the Japanese—small, bandy-legged soldiers who bayoneted and shot whom they pleased in the name of law and order. And now the Russians again, and who could know anything but discouragement when there had not been a single change about the valley except more exhaustion?

Mr. American Briscoe would not know about these things and so he was still capable of fighting. Mr. American Briscoe's illness was in his body, which was sad because he was a great man, but it was not in his heart, which would have been sadder. He would never know how this difference impressed a slant-eyed girl who could only be a stranger to him, or how it revived the excitement of hope. Without him so close, this life vest would have meant only one thing . . . a dream was about to be broken to pieces. It was inevitable, and to be accepted in the Oriental fashion. His tired face, even now, defied death. He had contemptuously thrown his life vest on the floor.

She saw that his eyes were open and she knew the pain had come to him again.

"I can't sleep," he said looking at her. "Must have a bad conscience. Y'know somp'n, Miss Chen? I'm hungry, too. And when a man can't sleep and he's hungry, he's in a terrible fix."

"I don't think there is anything to eat. I believe we threw everything overboard."

"Very rash of somebody. The sharks will get fat."

"Y'know somp'n?" he asked after a moment of twisting in his seat. "I hurt. All over."

"I'm very sorry, Mr. Briscoe. I wish I could help you."

"You can." He turned his head and looked at her quizzically. "Is anybody going to meet you at the airport?"

"No . . . but I have many instructions in my purse. It is with my passport and my tickets. I am to disembark from the airplane and proceed to the omnibus which awaits the passengers. I must say politely to the man who is in charge of the omnibus that I wish to arrive at the Golden Gate Hotel and pay him a fee of one and one-quarter American dollars. At the hotel there is lodging reserved for me and there I will rest until tomorrow evening when I continue to New York. It is all said very clearly in my instructions and I have read them many times."

"You will be all alone then?"

"Yes. Of course. I am quite accustomed to it. I am not so foolish to believe your streets are really full of bandits."

The beginning of a laugh made Frank Briscoe wince. He moved his hand carefully to the back of his neck.

"I know a bandit and I would like to have you meet him. His specialty is serving thick steaks at all hours. My car will be waiting for me and you would do me a great favor if you would join me at this bandit's hide-out."

"I would be embarrassed."

"Why?"

"Because I could never return such a gift."

"One of the things you are going to learn about America is that pretty girls never have to return anything. Now

269

press the button over your head. This idea is growing on me by the minute."

Spalding came quickly up the aisle. Her eyes were frightened.

"You wanted something, Mr. Briscoe?"

"Yes. Quick! A ham sandwich."

"Mr. Briscoe . . . !" The words escaped Spalding uncertainly. She shook her head as if to clear it. Her shoulders slumped and a slow smile of appreciation relaxed her mouth. "I'm sure you're the only man in the world who would think of food . . . now. Put on that life vest," she added, trying to be firm.

"Will you get me a sandwich if I do?"

"I *can't,* Mr. Briscoe. Everything went overboard with the buffet. Now, please—"

"This is great service. The stewardess throws all the food away so she won't have to serve it. Tell you what. I'm a hungry man and I got a proposition. My car will meet this plane and I think Miss Chen will let me buy her a steak in San Francisco if you come along, too. If you'll accept I'll put on the damned vest. You'll make an old man happy and the steaks are good. How about it?"

Spalding bent down and picked the life vest off the floor. She placed it very carefully around Frank Briscoe's neck, smoothing it gently around his collar. Her fingers strayed to caress the back of his neck.

"Mr. Briscoe . . . you have yourself a deal."

A surface vessel approaching a fogbound harbor may slow down, stop and wait, or even turn about if her master is inclined to prudence. An airplane cannot do any of these things. It must continue straight and true toward its destination because its functional time is limited.

The coast of California offers no easy welcome to either ships or airplanes. There is no threshold; instead the coastal mountains rise sharply out of the sea. In the vicinity of San Francisco the Golden Gate provides an entrance through this barrier for surface vessels, and the mountains, momentarily declining with the sea, are less imposing. And so the Bay of San Francisco is immediately surrounded by hills rather than true mountains. This geographical relaxation does not make the hills any softer than mountains when struck at high speed.

Guides are provided for mariners desiring to enter the narrow channel of the Golden Gate in the form of bell-buoys, lighthouses, and foghorns. Even without radar a knowing master may feel his way cautiously to the mouth of the Gate and, with a mind to the tides and swift currents, slip through the corridor of steep cliffs until his ship finally emerges into the broader expanse of the Bay itself. The master may then sigh and anchor in calm water, or proceed to one of the many docks which spike outward from the eastern fringe of the city. Under conditions of poor visibility the relatively short journey from the open sea to final safety may require two hours or even more. This leisurely way is not possible for airplanes.

Like the bellbuoys, lighthouses, and foghorns, certain aids are provided the airman to ease his San Francisco approach when bad weather moves inland from the Pacific and wraps the coastline in clouds. There is first the radio becaon on the Farallon Islands, which stand as outposts twenty-six miles off shore. It is a powerful beacon and like a magnet draws the searching needle of a direction finder surely, when the airplane is still far to westward over the ocean.

Once the Farallons have been passed, a situation made evident by a half-revolution of the direction finder needle, there are other aids which are designed to carry the airman further. They must be used in quick succession for at this point there is little time remaining.

The airport itself is south of the city. Hills almost touch its very borders to the west and the north, but to the east and south, the waters of the Bay and flat land provide a clear approach. Thus any airplane bound for San Francisco is compelled to descend from these directions if the terrain is obscured.

To accomplish this quickly and safely the commander of an airplane tuns his direction finder to the San Francisco range station. This is a primary aid and identifies itself by monotonously repeating the letters SFO every thirty seconds. The direction finder needle will swing and point directly at the station itself, which is located a very short distance from the airport. But to proceed directly in line with the needle would invite complications the instant the station was passed over. Things would happen too fast for a certain final approach. And so it is customary to initiate an approach from the Farallons in a more roundabout fashion.

The mixed signals of the San Francisco Radio range create four "legs" which spoke out from the station to the northwest, the southeast, the southwest, and the northeast. These become audible roads or channels, and on one side of any leg the signal N may be heard, while on the other side the signal A is repeated. An even mixture of these two signals creates a steady high-pitched monotone, a sound which indicates to any airman that he is flying along the center of the leg. Yet accomplished pilots avoid the center of the leg until they are almost over the station. They prefer to fly along the feather edge, hearing the monotone, yet still just able to hear the faint accompaniment of an A or an N. Thus they know exactly where they are in relation to the body of the leg. It is a difficult and delicate task if the winds aloft are strong.

As the airplane approaches the station the leg narrows, and the strength of the signal builds rapidly. Like a man feeling his way along a narrow footpath in total darkness, the skillful pilot now eases over a few degrees until he is in the center of the leg. The monotone builds to a peak and then suddenly subsides. He is passing through the cone of silence directly over the station. A small light glows on the instrument panel, the direction finder needle swings full around, and after a moment the monotone surges back again. He has reached port, but the anchor is not yet down.

Now things begin to happen very rapidly. Even under the best conditions tension on the flight deck increases because mistakes are intolerable. Of the several procedures for final approach, the quickest and most certain is the Instrument Landing System. It is also the most exacting. The airman abandons the continuous audible aids and transfers his concentration to visual signals.

There is another transmitting station situated at the very edge of San Francisco airport. Its signals create only two legs which extend over the hills to the west and the

Bay to the east. These legs are not audible, but instead cause a variety of reactions to be produced on a small round instrument located in the airplane itself—a dial approximately the size of the many other instruments. The face displays two white bars set at right angles to each other. Along the base of the instrument is a partial circle painted yellow and blue. The perpendicular bar will move into the yellow section if the pilot strays into the corresponding side of the visual leg, and it will move into the blue if he allows his plane to slip toward the other side. The leg is extremely narrow, hardly wider than the concrete runway as the airport is neared. Staying on this visual leg is a nervous business, for the slightest deviation will produce an accusing reaction on the instrument. In a strong wind the difficulties are compounded.

The companion bar is horizontal. It governs the all-important rate of descent. Forming a silent glide path, it provides an invisible bannister on which the airplane may slide over hazards and eventually contact solid ground in exactly the right place. To make a perfect approach by the Instrument Landing System is nearly impossible. The pilot is, in effect, sighting a gun, and there are too many vagaries accompanying the final descent of a big airplane to keep the bars always in proper juxtaposition. To make a good and smooth approach, using the visual system, is the mark of a professional airman. It allows him to break out through the bottom of an overcast and be directly in line with the runway under any conditions. Good pilots have been known to set their wheels on the concrete ten seconds after emerging from absolute blindness.

Now, like a mariner with his ears and eyes alert for the sound of bells or the sweep of a light, Sullivan studied the book on his lap. He reviewed once more the aerial environs of the San Francisco area, absorbing the frequencies and locations of his aids, which were all set down in the book, seeing in his mind the obstructions and the altitudes of the hills, memorizing the courses and turns to be made, methodically considering possible shortcuts to escape while there was still time. For once engaged in the final effort, he knew there would be no chance to compromise. He was about to commit himself without margin and he told himself repeatedly that every maneuver, every sequence of seconds must count.

He no longer looked across the instrument panel at the fuel gauges. The tanks read nearly empty and that was enough. From now on a completely dry tank would be firmly announced by the dying gasps of an engine. So be it.

He looked across the cockpit at Dan Roman. The man was whistling, although perhaps his lips only sought the position by habit since no actual sound came from them. He was not so at ease now and his flying was less exact. As his eyes strayed frequently from his artificial horizon to the quivering direction-finder needle, he would wander off course a few degrees. Even Dan was tiring, flying on his last reserve of calm. It was time.

Sullivan placed his hands on the control wheel.

"Take a breather, Dan."

"Okay." Sighing, he relaxed in his seat and stretched his arms. He pointed to the needle of the direction finder. It was wiggling with increasing rapidity as if anxious to make a full swing.

"The Farallons," Dan said. "Any second."

"Yeah."

Dan nodded his head at the altimeter. "We better not go any lower."

"No. I'll hold this. We'll make straight for the north-west leg of San Francisco. Start calling the tower about eight minutes from now. Oakland Control has cleared the whole area. We're practically on the ground."

"I like the way you say that." Dan leaned forward slightly in his seat and turned to look out the window. The movement was involuntary, but Sullivan understood the reason for it. There would be nothing for Dan to see except a black, dribbling space of glass. He was simply turning in the direction of the all-important engines, as a sailor might regard the masts of his ship to assure himself they were still standing.

Leonard came forward to stand silently between them. He had turned off the light over his navigation table because such work was done. Now he must wait until just before they reached the Coast to watch the green eye of his electric altimeter.

And so all of the flight deck was dark except the expanse of instrument panel. They waited in the darkness and their eyes were fascinated by two instruments—the sweep second hand of the clock and the direction finder.

They waited, trying to ignore the fuel gauges. They waited, smoking, coughing nervously sometimes, feeling the stubble on their faces, scratching at their hair and the backs of their hands, mouthing the dry foul taste on their tongues, rubbing their tired eyes—lost in their anxiety.

At last the needle quivered in a final spasm of self-importance. Then it swung slowly around and pointed toward the tail of Four-two-zero. They had passed the Farallon Islands.

In the Coast Guard B-17 Lieutenant Mowbray and Keim watched their own direction-finder needle swing around. According to Sullivan's instructions, they were flying parallel to Four-two-zero only half a mile away.

"He's made first base," Mowbray said.

"Fine, if he isn't caught stealing second."

"I'll bet they're sweating."

"Wouldn't you?"

"I'm sweating for them right now. God knows where he can put that thing down if he runs out of fuel in the next fifteen minutes."

"The middle of Market Street probably."

"Plane Commander from Radar! Four-two-zero is starting to slip down!"

"Roger. Keep me posted. How fast is his descent?"

"Looks like about fifty feet a minute."

"Roger." Mowbray moved his stabilizer wheel forward slightly, easing his ship into a very slow descent. He pinched his lips and shook his head. "Jesus . . . that guy is long on nerve!"

Now the airport at San Francisco seemed paralyzed, as if someone had suddenly choked off its breath. It spread, black and dripping, beneath the low overcast and the long runways were glistening rivers, their length and breadth strictly marked by evenly spaced blotches of light. The wind yanked a continuous curtain of mist and rain past the luminous bar of the ceiling measurement light, and at regular intervals the green flasher atop the control tower spewed an incongruous shaft of color into the atmospheric mess which enveloped everything.

There was almost no other life. The two men in the darkened control tower stood quietly. They listened to the speakers of their several radios, but no sound came from them. The accumulated glow of light reflected downward from the base of the overcast; it surrounded their tower and annoyed them because it made the far end of the instrument runway difficult to see and a morbid curiosity constantly drew their attention toward it. They waited.

Below the control tower the outbound airplanes which would normally be alive with activity and noise were nearly deserted. A few mechanics appeared occasionally from beneath the wings, but they moved like specters in their hooded rain-suits rather than human beings. Their flashlights flickered infrequently. A baggage truck, its cargo covered with wet tarpaulin, moved slowly out to one of the planes and stopped. No one moved to unload it. All planes, regardless of their destination, were being held.

At the AirInc receiving station the man named Pickering sucked on his empty pipe and listened thoughtfully to the intake of air through the bowl, because it was the only sound which interested him. The other operators were engaged with the distant traffic far over the Pacific. Pickering had only Four-two-zero to worry about. The last message was still on the typewriter roll before him.

FARALLONS ZERO TWO THREE EIGHT TWO THOUSAND FIVE HUNDRED. REQUEST TOWER STAND BY FOR EMERGENCY APPROACH. WILL ATTEMPT MAKING SFO.

Pickering looked at the clock set in his radio panel. Four minutes had passed since the message. No, four and one-half minutes now. They would still be over the sea, beyond the hills to the west. God help them. He waited.

In the airline operations office, Garfield, too, watched the clock. As if he mistrusted it, he frequently examined his wrist watch, pulling his coat sleeve back angrily. The constant *chip-chip* of the teletype machine annoyed him and he spoke sharply to the dispatcher.

"Turn that damn thing off!"

When the dispatcher had obeyed him, Garfield walked slowly to the window and pushed it open. He felt the dank night air against his face and breathed deeply of it. He listened for the sound of engines although he knew perfectly well it was too soon. "Well . . . ?" he said aloud to the night, not knowing why he said it. "Well . . . ?"

And still there was no sound of engines.

Garfield closed the window and turned back into the room. He picked up a paper clip from the dispatcher's desk and very carefully twisted it into a triangular design. He twisted longer, the wire broke, and he threw it in a wastebasket.

"I can't stand this any longer," he said to the room in general. "Going over to the terminal. If needed I'll be in the control tower."

He jammed his hat more firmly on his head and walked briskly out of the room. He descended the stairs rapidly and let himself out the front door of the building. For almost a full minute he stood beside his car, looking up at the sky and wiping the raindrops from his eyes. He could hear the radio in the guard's shack and it was a tune he had once enjoyed. But now it infuriated him because there was still no sound of engines.

20

Hobie Wheeler knew the descent had begun before he saw the flashing seat belt sign. He could feel the slight change of pressure in his ears and that was enough.

"Okay," he said to Spalding. "This is it." His voice was unnaturally solemn and he knew it. He didn't like the sound of his voice, but there was nothing he could do to make it more normal. "Ten minutes. Let's make a final check."

He looked down the length of the passenger cabin. "Switch on the dome lights. Let's cheer up this place."

In contrast to the small reading lamps, the lights in the cabin ceiling seemed overbright, and as if the passengers shared an electric connection with them, they twisted nervously in their seats and squinted at the lights. Their faces shone garishly in the new light and even Ed Joseph looked pale and sickly. His wife began to whimper and for a moment Hobie considered returning the cabin to semi-darkness. The lights also revealed pieces of new wreckage where the buffet had been, and small things like gum wrappers along the floor of the aisle became absurdly prominent. The yellow life vests were like an ugly splash of mustard; the coats and hats, the occasional flower lei and small boxes resting in the luggage racks above the seats looked like the leavings from a rummage sale. The very walls of the cabin appeared worn

278

and dirty. The portholes became two lines of black staring eyes.

Moving quickly together, Hobie and Spalding each gathered an armful of coats from the rack by the door. They went to the head of the aisle and worked along it together, passing out the coats, checking on safety belts and life vests—trying to smile.

"My coat is the white one," Nell Buck said to Hobie.

"When does it happen?" Milo asked.

"About ten minutes. You'll be all right. Take your time coming back to the door. Wait until I yell."

"I wish I was someplace else."

"So do I. Take care of your wife."

"That I will."

Spalding began on the opposite side of the aisle with Ken Childs and May Holst.

"Did you have a coat, Mr. Childs?"

"No. I'm cold inside . . . not outside."

"Inflate your life vest, please. You too, Miss Holst."

They fumbled anxiously with the cartridge cords. The vests ballooned outward and May poked at her bosom experimentally.

"Some brassiere," she said.

"Good luck. Don't smoke from now on."

"Good luck to you, girl."

Spalding moved to the next seats and handed Lillian Pardee her mink coat.

"Seat belt tight?"

"I think it's all right. This is for real, isn't it?"

"I'm afraid so. Inflate your life vests, please."

Gustave Pardee pulled gravely at his cartridge cord and when his vest filled a look of complete surprise came to his eyes.

"Well, well!" he murmured unhappily. "Even I might float."

"Thank you for being pretty wonderful," Spalding said quickly, and then moved on down the aisle.

Hobie checked the Rices, then continued on to the next seats, which held Flaherty and Sally McKee.

"Just remember your instructions and you won't have any real trouble," he said.

"Is the Coast Guard ship still with us?" Flaherty asked.

"Right off our wing. He'll stick with us. Put out your cigarettes, please."

"I really ought to take my briefcase. There might—"

"Sorry, sir. Nothing doing. Now inflate your vests."

Sally McKee shook her head hopelessly. Her hands remained motionless in her lap.

"Pull the cords like you were shown, lady."

"I . . . I can't. I'm terrified. I can't seem to move."

Hobie reached across Flaherty and pulled the cords on her vest. There was a soft hiss as the cartridges were punctured. Sally gasped and closed her eyes. Her face was dead white.

"Don't worry. Good luck."

Hobie moved on to Locota and Agnew.

"We're all set, see?" José said with a smile that made Hobie want to shake his hand. Their life vests were inflated, their collars were open, and their seat belts were tight.

"Good work. Remember. Take your time coming back to the door."

José kissed the rosary in his hand and offered it to Hobie.

"No thanks, mister. Thanks just the same."

Disappointed, José wound the rosary around his three good fingers and returned it to his lap.

"If anything happens to me, would you pass on this message someday?" Agnew said. "Tell my wife in Honolulu I loved her. The phone number is—"

"Tell her yourself, mister. You'll be all right. I'm not worrying, and I'll be the last guy off this airplane."

"Do you have to be?"

"That's what I get paid for." Hobie left them hurriedly. The telephone by the door was ringing.

When Spalding reached the Josephs her progress was slowed. Clara Joseph was very near to hysteria. She clutched Spalding's hand and held it fiercely. Her sobbing became more incoherent as her husband tried to calm her.

"I don't want to die! I don't want to die!" She repeated the words over and over again. "My babies . . . oh, please don't leave . . . Edward!" Her voice rose to a shriek and then she fell miserably against her husband. Spalding took a small bottle of Seconal pills from her blouse and handed to it Ed Joseph.

"Give her these when you can. They will help." She went on to Frank Briscoe and Dorothy Chen. There was so little time remaining.

"All set, you two?"

"We're still hungry."

"Inflate your vests now. Our steak date is postponed until tomorrow night."

"That's a promise?"

"For sure." She started away and then returned. She held out Frank Briscoe's chiming watch.

"Maybe you should keep this now. I loved thinking it was mine, even if it was only for a few hours."

"Nonsense. You can keep it as dry as I can."

"But—"

"If it's still working tomorrow night at seven, take a taxi to the Shadows Restaurant. If it isn't working, say the hell with it and come anyway. I'll be waiting for you."

She pressed his arm. "Thanks . . . sir."

"And don't call me sir. Ruins romance and my appetite."

She left him and went at once to Hobie. He was just hanging up the telephone.

"What?"

"Sullivan says to stand by for anything. He's trying to make San Francisco."

"Can we?"

"I don't see how. We're eight minutes out, he says."

"Only eight minutes!" A mixture of joy and relief came to Spalding's face, but it faded as soon as Hobie spoke again.

"Uh-huh. Technically we're out of fuel right now. If we don't make it, things will be lots worse than a ditching."

Even as he spoke the cabin swerved and they were thrown awkwardly against each other. The number-four engine, right wing counterpart of the long useless number one, backfired several times. The explosions were flat and muffled like the reports of a machine gun heard far down a valley. There were a few moments of ominous quiet. Hobie cocked his head to one side and listened intently. Then the cabin swerved back violently as the engine took life again. Yet the backfiring continued intermittently and Hobie moved his head slowly from side to side.

"Huh-uh." His voice was barely audible. "We've bought it."

After anxious experimentation, Sullivan found that by holding the ship in a five-degree bank so the right wing was down, the number-four engine would continue to run.

"The tanks are so damn near dry the cross feeds and pumps just won't feed her!" Dan yelled.

"Get on the horn! Tell them what's happening! May help some guy some day! And get our final clearance down!"

With the ship slightly off level, Sullivan's flying task became far more difficult. He was forced to trim the ship to compensate for the lowered wing and this not only subtracted from the speed, but caused the instruments and controls to appear at odd purposes. Sullivan persevered because, as he had foreseen, he now had no other choice.

The first of the hard land was beneath them in the blackness. Leonard, clasping his electric altimeter between his hands as if to squeeze the vital information from it, was calling out in a high cracked voice the constantly changing separations of Four-two-zero from instant disaster. Like a probing rod his altimeter was sounding the depths directly beneath the ship and a green eye was reporting the findings.

"Five hundred and fifty feet, Skipper!"

"Roger!"

"Four hundred! A little less!"

"Watch it!"

"Three hundred thirty . . . ! Two hundred fifty! Ground's coming up fast!"

It is the hills, Sullivan told himself—the westward hills of San Francisco. The amount of separation would decrease even more in a moment, to the point where the nerves were past caring, and then as the hills and buildings surmounting them were passed, the separation must increase again to bearable dimensions. It would be so!

"Two hundred feet! Skipper! This ain't good!"

The sweat broke out on the palms of Sullivan's hands until he found it difficult to hold the control wheel. One at a time he wiped them on his pants.

"One hundred and eighty!" Leonard's voice was a terrified cry.

Instinctively Sullivan pulled back on the control yoke. His whole being wanted to go upward and he strained at his seat belt as if he could physically lift his ship. But the air-speed fell off immediately to a hundred and five miles an hour. The ship shuddered in the beginning of a stall. Sullivan shoved the nose down again. He cursed. He must not let that happen again. He must imagine that the rain and cloud whipping at the windshield was the same as it would be at ten thousand feet. A separation, *any* separation, was safety. And yet it was so close. His bowels loosened suddenly and he had to pinch his buttocks to contain them.

"Coast Guard B-17 to Four-two-zero. Twin Peaks coming up on your left in a minute or so. Remember those radio towers!"

"Roger!" Dan Roman said into his microphone. "Thanks."

"Stay on this course. Don't descend any more and you'll be all right."

"Yeah. Thanks." Dan sat rigidly in his seat. There was nothing he could do to help Sullivan now except serve as another pair of hands. His attention was entirely on the sensitive fuel-flow meters. They would give the first sign of an engine dying of starvation. No use looking at the fuel tank gauges any longer. They all read empty.

"Just *two* hundred, Skipper!"

It would become still less, Sullivan thought, as the final hills were passed over. It was now up to the engines. If they continued to run smoothly for the next three or four minutes he could clear them. If they stopped—twenty-one people were dead.

One new development eased his strain. The sound of the San Francisco radio range had changed from the pronounced repetition of the letter *A* to a high mono-tone. Sullivan was slipping into the northwest leg sooner than he had hoped. The station itself must not be far away. When the sound of the *A* became almost entirely lost in the monotone, Sullivan turned the ship to a course of one hundred and eleven degrees. The course for the cone of silence. The course for home. Good. The direction-finder needle pointed straight ahead. It was already quivering in anticipation. Please God, a few minutes more!

Outside the windows the clouds took on a pale brassy glow. The lights of the city, feeble in the depths, were powerful enough in accumulation to illuminate the over-cast. Street lights, car lights, factory lights, the night blessing of so many people whose life span was un-predictable—all combined to wrap Four-two-zero in a soft golden halo. Here aloft, the life spans were pre-dictable. They must rejoin those below in a very few minutes, or they would end abruptly.

"Three hundred feet, Skipper! This is better!"

The hills were falling away. They were past and con-quered.

"Four hundred feet!"

Good. Now the airport would soon be beneath, then the flat land, and the Bay beyond it.

"Five hundred! We're livin'!"

Heaving a great sigh that emerged soundlessly from the foundations of his soul, Sullivan pushed forward on the control yoke. The air-speed increased to a tolerable reading and his own altimeter began to unwind. Now, no matter if the engines stopped, there was at least a slim chance. He could attempt a crash landing on the airport if it could be found in the murk after a sudden descent, or there might be the Bay, or the flat land surrounding it. All of these possibilities might only result in com-plete destruction, but they were less certain than slam-ming into a hill.

The number-four engine sputtered, ran smoothly for a moment, and then gave out a series of violent back-fires. Dan quickly changed the cross-feed valves from the number-two tank to the number three. He put the booster pump on high speed. When the engine still failed to give power he reached down and pulled the mixture control to full rich. The engine surged to life again.

"We'll have to run number four on full rich!"

"Okay! Do anything you have to! Keep the bastard running!"

"Did you hear the weather?"

"No. I'm sticking with the range."

"Tower gave us a special. Three hundred feet. One-mile visibility. Light rain. Wind west northwest twenty to twenty-five."

"It could be worse. Same altimeter setting?"

"Yeah. Twenty-nine eight-eight."

"Tell them we're coming up on the station. We'll go into an ILS approach. I want the runway lights up full blast!"

"Okay. Hang on. We'll make it, chum!"

Now the monontone in Sullivan's earphones swelled in volume rapidly until it became a high whine. The small white light glowed on the instrument panel, the direction-finder needle swung full around, and then there was peace in his earphones. Four-two-zero was passing through the cone of silence.

"This is going to be a fast one, Dan! Check me, and stand by with the flaps and gear!"

"Right with you, chum. Take it easy. We're cleared straight on down."

His eyes moving rapidly from the air-speed to the altimeter, to the yellow and blue indicator of the Instrument Landing Indicator, Sullivan put the ship into a steep left bank. The compass spun in its liquid and the gyro numbers whirled past the observation gate. Descending rapidly to fifteen hundred feet Sullivan settled momentarily on a course of due north.

"I'm not going all the way out to Belmont marker," Sullivan said almost to himself, yet loud enough for Dan to share his decision. "We haven't got time."

"Watch it then. There's a two hundred and six foot radio tower around here some place." Dan spoke from memory, for there was nothing to see outside the windows. The overcast was still heavy and a squall of rain lashed angrily at the glass.

The vertical bar of the Instrument Landing Indicator

crept slowly from the yellow section into the blue. Watching it warily, as a thief might reach out for a wallet, Sullivan began a slow turn back toward the airport. The bar suddenly moved past the center position and inclined toward the blue. Sullivan corrected instantly and settled on a westward course. His legs ached from constant pressing of the rudder pedals. The back of his neck was like stone.

"Get the inner marker, Dan!"

Dan rapidly cranked the direction finder on his side. The needle pointed straight ahead.

"*M . . . M . . . K . . .*" he repeated, listening to the signals. "Inner marker identified. But you're way below the glide path, chum."

"I know it. I don't give a damn. We're right on the leg and that tower has to be behind us!"

Sullivan pointed to the Instrument Landing bar. It stood in the center of the dial, exactly between the blue and the yellow. "There's nothing in the way from here on in. Keep your eyes out the window. Let me know when we're contact!"

Sullivan took a deep breath and grimly pushed the control yoke forward. Just as he did so the number-four engine coughed twice and instantly ceased to give power. The windmilling propeller cut greedily into the air speed.

"Feather it, Dan! Quick! No time to fool with it!"

He reached to the ceiling panel and pressed a red button. A shudder passed through the ship and the number-four tachometer fell down to zero. The ship sank rapidly.

"Give me full power on the other two!"

Dan pushed the propeller controls and then the throttles full forward. The two good engines howled under the strain. Sullivan ignored them. He was intent on the vertical bar and his altimeter which now read four hundred feet.

"See anything?"

"Not yet!" Dan reached for a valve by his feet and turned on the windshield wipers. They slapped back and forth with furious energy.

"Contact yet?"

"No."

"This is a sweat-er!"

"You're doing fine."

"When we pass the inner marker I'm shoving her on down regardless."

"Yeah."

His face close to the windshield, Dan leaned far forward in his seat searching for the first red glow of the approach lights he knew must be ahead. He thought of the black bay water beneath them and then he saw the lights.

"Approach lights dead ahead! Maybe a mile!"

"Give me the gear!"

Dan slammed down the landing gear lever. There was a muffled roar as the wheel housing doors opened and then three green lights flickered on the instrument panel.

"Three green lights and pressure!"

"Okay. Fifteen degrees of flaps!"

Dan moved down the control lever and again looked out the window. The long line of neon approach lights was clearly visible now. They were spaced like steps of a stairway and led downward to the end of the runway and final safety.

Suddenly they were sliding over the lights and at their very end, Sullivan eased back on the throttles and control yoke. There was a moment of soft floating as the runway lights swept past and rose in line to meet them. In contrast to the soft murmuring of the engines, the windshield wipers seemed much louder as they reached each extremity of sweep. There was the heavy brush of tires against the concrete—and Four-two-zero returned gracefully to earth.

21

AVOIDING THE GLARE OF THE FLOODLIGHTS, GARFIELD stood unnoticed in the shadow of the passenger ramp, his raincoat pulled up tight around his neck and his hat tilted far forward to protect his cigar. His feet were sopping wet, yet he forgot them as he became more intrigued with the spectacle before him. And the newspapers were making a spectacle of things, all right. The glistening wet fuselage of Four-two-zero reflected a barrage of flash bulb explosions. As the passengers emerged from the rear door—some still wore their life vests, Garfield noted unhappily—the reporters seized upon them and began asking questions. The constant flashing revealed their faces in brilliant relief against the night, and for a time he amused himself by trying to compare the real passengers with those he had involuntarily created in his mind.

He saw a young couple and, watching the manner in which they found the world separately rather than together, was certain they were recently married. The girl's hair was blond and wet and now it hung down about her frightened face in unbecoming strings. They were both ill at ease and the reporters allowed them to go after a very brief questioning. They ran down the ramp into the arms of several elderly people who embraced them anxiously. The armor of youth is extremely thick, Gar field thought. You can dent it, but penetration is difficult. In a year, two years, perhaps, those two will have forgotten about their flight. Since everything for them is exciting, nothing is exciting; and so in a way, the young are the most sophisticated of all people.

"You're Gustave Pardee, aren't you?" Garfield heard a reporter ask.

"I was. I'm not so sure now. Please let us alone. We are very tired." That you are, Garfield thought. But you were tired before you ever boarded my plane. And now having seen at least a portion of the chromatic scale, you are astonished that there is always a thing so real and near as death. It is, as you have possibly observed, Mr. Pardee, a clever device for the measurement of all men. You appear to have faced it admirably as witness your haste to flee from the mention of it. I congratulate you.

"Give us a few words about the flight, Mr. Pardee!"

"I could not tell you in a million words."

"When is your next production, Mr. Pardee?"

"It will take longer than usual. Next year, I hope. Now . . please!" Taking the woman who was obviously in love with him by the arm, he used his bulk to ease her through the crowd.

Garfield did not look after them for his attention was drawn by a blond woman who stood irresolutely in the doorway. She drew back from the flashing photographers; only Spalding's comforting hand kept her from full retreat. For a moment Garfield believed her fear was the lingering kind. He considered leaving the shadows and going for the doctor, the smell of death had deranged this woman, and then he realized that whatever had devoured her courage was not connected with the plane.

A strong voice in the crowd called out the name Sally. There was a commotion beyond the gate and a large man pushed his way to the ramp. He ran up the ramp, hatless in the rain, and after a moment he came again to the door of the plane. He was holding the woman's arm. They passed very close to Garfield and a bulb flashed just as their heads reached the level of his eyes. Her face was etched clean against the black sky and Garfield thought that he must be mistaken in the image which remained for a moment, as if a negative had been exposed on his brain. The woman was smiling! She was, if anything, nearly hysterical with joy and nowhere in her eyes was there the slightest hint of her ordeal.

Puzzled, Garfield watched them make their way arm in arm through the crowd.

Then it was possible to entertain the idea of disaster and be entirely untouched by it? No. That woman had merely been for an airplane ride. Her death appeared when she came to the door—for some reason she could not face it. Everything that had gone before, she must have compared with this moment, and found it tolerable.

Garfield shrugged his shoulders. The measuring devices which before this night he had found reliable were obviously subject to error. I am, he thought, too prone to place all things, including death, in scales and measures which I can easily comprehend. Because aviation is exact and must be, I think all else must be exact. And so now I am fooled because there is no set way of measuring emotion. Emotion, the twisting of a human heart which has nothing to do with blood flow, can make the possibility of disaster a very relative quantity.

A man and a woman came down the ramp and their behavior eased his troubled mind. Garfield felt that he could readily understand them. They looked like people should who had come from a vacation and had almost crashed in the Pacific Ocean. They still wore their life vests and they carried several bedraggled leis. They gave their name to the reporters as Mr. and Mrs. Joseph. They looked sick and tired and confused. They almost ran down the ramp. Garfield thought it was highly probable that, when they had had time for reflection, they might try to sue the company. It would depend on how many hundred times they related their story, and if in their audiences, there chanced to be a lawyer.

Then a small thin man appeared. He faced the flash-bulbs defiantly, ignored the calling reporters, and made his way down the ramp as quickly as he could. At the base of the ramp he asked the airline agent for the location of the nearest telephone. Garfield heard him say that he must call his wife immediately. It was of the utmost importance.

An instant return, Garfield mused. For this man with

the pearl stickpin, the ties with earth had never been broken and never would be. Escape was a telephone, a convenient electric net in which to toss his immediate feelings. Here he had just passed successfully through what must have been a tremendous experience, yet Garfield was willing to bet he would not mention it on the telephone. No, he would be talking not to his wife, but to himself. He was a bound captive, so enmeshed in his earthly cares the miracle of his escape was already forgotten. He was a blind man and Garfield was sorry for him.

Ken Childs appeared in the doorway and Garfield recognized him at once. He was about to leave the shadows and greet him—a stockholder who had been through such a flight would want to yell at someone in authority—and then he changed his mind. He was not sure now that he did recognize Ken Childs, the gay bullyboy who had walked roughshod to a fortune in a business where there were not supposed to be any fortunes. His face was the same, but he was visibly shaken—deep down, Garfield believed, so deep he would never be the same man again. His every gesture as he patted Spalding on the arm and began to descend the ramp, was humble. And a humble Kenneth Childs was such an absorbing sight, Garfield found he was unable to move. We have here, he thought, the carcass of a man who has already died. May he rest in peace. I will call his hotel tomorrow and buy him a drink because now he might be worth knowing.

A woman followed closely behind Childs. Garfield saw that she was fat, in a buxom late-fortyish way, and she laughed as she waved at the photographers. Watching her, he began to feel better about his measurements and values. Hello, honey. There will always be one of you around to make things agreeable. You are the real brave, I guess. A day which ends with the taste of mush is the only thing you fear—you don't care how the flavor gets there as long as it's there.

He was rather surprised to observe that Ken Childs waited patiently for the woman at the foot of the ramp, and when the reporters reluctantly released her, they went away together. I will call him in the morning,

Garfield said to himself. Drinks for three will be even better.

A small man, with a hat set exactly level on his head, bowed to Spalding and trotted down the ramp waving his arms at a noisy group who pressed hard against the passenger gate.

"José! . . Papa! . . José!" they shouted.

An enormous woman with a mustache waved a knit bag. Garfield counted the children surrounding her. Eight. If each of these had but one child, then sixteen souls would have been touched if this little man had gone down into the sea. Sixteen who were not even present. Here, dazed by the commotion, was the small and willing hero who was the focus of their lives. He crossed himself quickly before he kissed the woman with the mustache and embraced the children. He bred them and he fed them and that was such a busy burden for any man, he, of necessity, left everything else to God.

He was nearly consumed in the maw of his family when a mechanic touched Garfield's arm. The mechanic wiped a dribble of rain from the end of his nose and placed a greasy thumb near the very end of a white stick.

"Thirty gallons, Mr. Garfield. That's all there was left in all the tanks. Too damn little to really measure."

Garfield grunted. "So?"

"You want I should leave the ship here . . . or tow her to the hangar."

"The hangar. When this mess of crowd clears out."

Thirty gallons? Four, perhaps five minutes and Sullivan might have been both executioner and executed. Sullivan had been a fool to risk it. Anger flashed through Garfield and he bit hard on his cigar. Ground him forever! See that his license was taken away if the fight took years. He had won on sheer luck but these people passing down the ramp were not pawns in a game. Sullivan was a fool . . . but wait! Who are you, standing with your feet firmly planted on the ground, to say exactly what a man should do when everything is against him? Were you there when the propeller left the ship? Did you see the fire? Were you above the ocean in the night watching the fuel disappear, sweating, near-frantic with concern because circumstance

292

gave you the power, made you the high and the mighty, for so many lives?

The anger left Garfield very suddenly and he was glad that he had remained in the shadows rather than rushing to the flight deck as he had first intended. No, there were times when it took a fool to win, even in a thing so cursed with black and white decisions as aviation. There would be no charges placed against Sullivan. Rather, he deserved a commendation.

Now a tall man accompanied a very small woman down the ramp. Still thinking of Sullivan, Garfield could not help imagining how differently they would have looked clinging to a raft. Her mink coat would not be draped so carelessly about her shoulders and her husband would not look as if he had stepped from a Brooks Brothers window. Could they see themselves clawing at the raft, half-drowned, and terrified as wave after wave swept over them? No, because it was obvious their lives had never been geared to contemplate such a thing. And so they were merely completing a flight that had proved to be inconvenient. They were already complaining to the airline agent about a missed connection.

Garfield heard the small woman say, "Howard. Tell this man we *must* have reservations for New York tomorrow. We'll miss Elvira's party! It's important to you."

"But what have the Cooleys got to do with sled dogs?"

"*Really,* darling. Don't be tiresome. You might as well play safe until you're sure how things are going to work out."

"All right," the man sighed. "I suppose we shouldn't miss the party. All right. All right. . . ."

No change here. Back on familiar ground, these two immediately resumed their search for the familiar. The agent had been instructed to offer them a suite at the Fairmont Hotel—compliments of the airline. Garfield was not surprised when they visibly relaxed and accepted the offer.

The man behind them blinked unhappily at the flashbulbs. Garfield was momentarily puzzled. Why should such a distinguished-looking person appear so bewildered? He was halfway down the ramp when he returned to the plane and disappeared for a moment. Then he came back apologetically, carrying a briefcase. He is still in the sky, Garfield thought. He is unwilling or unable to leave it because he has not yet been able to place his experience in a pigeonhole. The analysis of same will probably provide him with a wonderful excuse to get drunk for a long time.

An Oriental girl appeared—she would be the Chen on the passenger manifest, Garfield remembered. She backed out of the door and he saw that with Spalding's help she was supporting a short, stocky man who moved down the ramp with the greatest difficulty. Near the bottom a uniformed chauffeur made his way through the crowd and took Spalding's place. A flashbulb caught Spalding in the act of kissing the man on the cheek.

"Meet us out in front. We'll drive you home," the man said.

"Ten minutes, Mr. Briscoe, and I'll be there . . . for sure," Spalding said.

The crowd began to disperse and the photographers put away their equipment as they cursed the rain. Garfield crossed the nearly deserted ramp and waited beneath the shelter of Four-two-zero's wing.

He was looking up at the number-one engine when he became aware that four men had come to join him. Without taking his eyes from the partially exposed guts of the engine, he knew who the men would be. Sullivan, Dan Roman, Wilby, and Hobie Wheeler.

"Hi," Garfield said.

"Hi. . . ."

They stepped ahead of the wing and stood looking at it solemnly while the mechanics hitched a tractor to the nose wheel of Four-two-zero. They were silent because the soft murmur of the rain drumming on the metal wing was the only bearable sound.

At last, when the tractor growled and the turning wing swept slowly over their heads, Garfield broke their reverie. He spoke to Sullivan and his voice was strangely without strength.

"I think your wife is waiting for you," he said.

"Yeah. I don't want to keep her standing too long. We're expecting."

"Call me when you're rested. We'll have a talk."

"Yeah . . . sure."

Sullivan picked up his briefcase. He said good night to the others and their answers were preoccupied monotones. Then he walked away. As if his departure had left them without anchor, the others said their good nights quietly.

"Souvenir?" Garfield said, looking down at Leonard's hardwood tray.

"Yeah. I guess the rain won't hurt it . . . but I better get it home."

"Good night."

"Good night, Dan. We'll get together soon."

"Sure, chum."

Garfield pressed the collar of his coat tighter around his throat. Now he realized that he was chilled and his feet were very wet. Yet he lingered uncertainly, looking after Dan Roman, who was already a hazy figure through the rain. Seen from a distance, his slight limp appeared more pronounced as he carefully avoided the glistening puddles on the concrete. "So long . . . so long," he said half aloud. "So long . . . you ancient pelican. . . ."

Then as he turned for a last look at the sky, he heard the distant sound of a man whistling. He found it very satisfying.

ABOUT THE AUTHOR

ERNEST KELLOGG GANN was born in Lincoln, Nebraska, in 1910. He was graduated from Yale University, School of Fine Arts. Author of eleven novels and numerous short stories, he served as Captain of Air Transport Command AUS from 1942 to 1946 and was decorated with a distinguished flying award. Mr. Gann now lives in Sausalito, California, with his wife and three children.